Also by Milly Adams

Above Us the Sky
Sisters at War
At Long Last Love

The Waterway Girls Series
The Waterway Girls

Why YOU love Milly Adams ...

'As usual I have thoroughly enjoyed this author's book – it was absorbing and full of suspense ... The historical information was interesting too and showed a forgotten side of the war led by women.'

'I really enjoyed this ... the characters and the way of life are all so very real feeling, and I am really pleased to see that there is a second book about these characters; so pleased, in fact, that I have already pre-ordered it :)'

'Excellent book – what went on then was totally different. They contributed so much to the war effort. Very interesting, can't wait for the next'

'I loved this book, really good story, was sad when it ended'

'I enjoyed this and will look forward to the next. Fans of Nadine Dorries and Donna Douglas will find this worth a look'

'A good story about believable people, combined with fascinating history, and brilliantly accurate descriptions of life on board a narrow boat'

Love on the Waterways

Milly Adams

arrow books

1 3 5 7 9 10 8 6 4 2

Arrow Books
20 Vauxhall Bridge Road
London SW1V 2SA

Arrow Books is part of the Penguin Random House group
of companies whose addresses can be found
at global.penguinrandomhouse.com.

Copyright © Milly Adams 2018

First published in Great Britain by Arrow Books in 2018

www.penguin.co.uk

A CIP catalogue record for this book is available
from the British Library.

ISBN 9781784756925

Typeset in 11.5/14.5 pt Palatino
by Integra Software Services Pvt. Ltd, Pondicherry

Printed and bound in Great Britain by Clays Ltd, St Ives Plc

Penguin Random House is committed to a
sustainable future for our business, our readers
and our planet. This book is made from Forest
Stewardship Council® certified paper.

Acknowledgments

Many thanks to all those people and memoirs that helped with *The Waterway Girls*, Book 1, and in addition, to the Aylesbury Arm of the Grand Union Canal, which inspired me to think of it as a place of healing, which was essential to the novel. It really is a lovely six miles; tranquil and unspoilt.

I must also thank Mr Pendse, an amazing orthopaedic surgeon who put together my shoulder after I was remiss enough to trip on the handles of my bag (why was I such an idiot?), and to Graham, my High Wycombe Hospital physiotherapist who beat and thrashed me (not really) to a stage where I could type and not hold up the writing of this novel.

Mr Pendse also said, after digging, delving, plating and screwing, that I had the bones of a thirty-year-old woman, which has earned him my undying devotion. The same cannot be said of Him Indoors, who was heard to mutter, 'Shame about the rest.' Well really!

To my newest 'grand': delicious little
Miss Delilah Dore

And my latest godchildren, equally delicious:
Catherine, Sophia and Luke
With love, of course

Map of the London to Birmingham Grand Union Canal

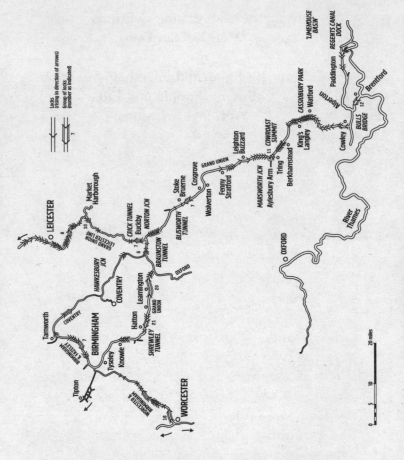

Broaden your waterways vocabulary ...

Basin – a partly enclosed area of water at the end of or alongside a canal, housing wharves and moorings

Bilges – the bottom of the boat

Butty – engineless boat towed by the motorboat

Canal frontage – land abutting the canal

Counter – deck

Cut – canal

Gunwale – inner ledge around boat

Hold – where the cargo is carried; both motors and butties have holds

Lock – the main means of raising or lowering a boat between changes in water levels on a canal

Long pound – a long length of impounded water between two locks

Moor – to secure a boat against the bank

Motorboat – the narrowboat with an engine

Prow or fore-end – front

Short pound – a short length of impounded water between two locks

Slide hatch – sliding 'lid' above cabin doors to keep out the rain

Snubber – long strong rope for towing a butty along a long pound

Stern – rear

Straps – mooring and lashing ropes

Wharf – structure built for cargo loading or discharge

Windlass – L-shaped handle for operating lock paddles

Bull's Bridge, Southall, is the location of Grand Union Canal Carrying Company's (GUCCC) depot

Limehouse Basin, also known as Regent's Canal Dock

Grand Union Canal **Paddington Arm** runs into Regent's Canal, leading to Limehouse/Regent's Canal Dock

Tyseley Wharf, Birmingham

Chapter 1

Monday 27 March 1944 – the Waterway Girls heading from Limehouse Basin to Alperton

Polly Holmes steered the narrowboat *Marigold* along the centre of the canal while Verity Clement made a cuppa in the cabin. Though it was early afternoon, it was still so cold that frost glistened on the roof and coated the sixty-foot tarpaulin covering the cargo.

Polly dug her chin deeper into her muffler and rested her elbow on the tiller, hearing the slap of water and ice against the hull of not only *Marigold*, but their motor-less butty, *Horizon*, on tow behind. Sylvia Simpson, the newest crew member, was at *Horizon*'s helm. Polly hooted the horn to her and listened, but whispered, 'No doubt there'll be no reply.'

She was right and waited ten seconds before trying again. She sighed with relief as she heard a short toot. Clearly Sylvia was thawing a little, though there was a way to go until she stopped being angry at catching Verity's cold.

There wasn't much traffic on the Paddington Arm of the Grand Union Canal so far and it meant that

Polly could relax as she steered past bomb-damaged factories, terraces and warehouses. She felt she'd been travelling at three miles an hour for the whole of her life, not just six months. Mark you, she laughed to herself, they roared along at the heady speed of four miles an hour when unloaded. Crikey, how could she stand the excitement?

Ahead loomed a bridge over which red London buses toiled, followed by a lengthy convoy of canvas-sided military lorries. Polly yanked her woollen hat with its oversized bobble low over her ears, her hands numb with cold. She pulled her gloves from her trouser pockets. Why on earth hadn't she put them on earlier? She knew why; she was too busy thinking of her future with Saul, a boater, and that was not what she wanted to be doing, so instead she concentrated on the cold.

'Damn you, weather,' Polly groaned. 'We're supposed to be heading for the joys of spring, not suffering your temper tantrum. What on earth is all this snow and ice about? Don't you know there's a war on – and something's brewing, to judge from the flurry of army transport all over the place. Are you the enemy, too, to cause us this much trouble?'

'First sign of madness, ducky, talking to yourself,' Verity called up from the cabin.

'Madness helps,' snorted Polly, sick to death of the ice that had clung, jagged and thick, around the hull and along the bank of the canal – which those on the boats called 'the cut' – for the last four days.

She also loathed the swirling snow showers and the freezing mist, but which was worse? Oh, shut up, she told herself; look on the bright side, for heaven's sake. So instead she thought of the cabin range belting out heat, drying their clothes and keeping them warm overnight. Life came down to the basics, she mused, but then she shook her head. She mustn't muse, because it would lead her back to Saul.

She opened the cabin's double doors, shoved back the slide hatch and stepped onto the shelter of the cabin's top step, hearing a wail from Verity. 'Hey, now I'm in a draught.'

Polly laughed. 'Stop fussing, you're a Waterway Girl now, and having a lord for a father cuts no mustard here, so just grin and bear it, like a trooper. You need a change of air anyway. And where's my tea?'

She grinned to herself, knowing she could tease her friend about her high-flown roots, but only so long as no boater heard. It had been struggle enough for the girls to be accepted on the canal, or cut, without having a 'ladyship' as a crew member.

The sun emerged from between the cloud, just for a moment, as it had at Limehouse Basin yesterday, when the pallets of aluminium were being unloaded from the rusty merchant ships moored at the wharf, to be swung immediately by cranes into the queue of narrowboat holds.

Polly wondered now, as she had when they secured their tarpaulins, if the aluminium would be used for fighters or bombers, once they delivered it to Tyseley Wharf in Birmingham? Who knew, but it would be something connected with the war effort. Her grin faded.

No, not the war, because it reminded her that Saul might be trying …

She forced herself to remain in the present, peering behind at the butty and giving another short hoot on the horn. Sylvia replied immediately, this time with a toot-toot-toot. Good. Anyway, Sylvia wasn't the only one with a cold. Polly coughed, her throat sore, her nose running. She wiped it on her sweater sleeve. Her mum would be shocked – or would she? Probably not. Her mum was used to the state of her by now.

Verity tapped Polly's leg, squinting up at her from the depths of the tiny cabin, her blonde hair escaping from her woollen hat. 'I've made cocoa instead. I'll bring it up.' Before she did, though, Verity called back, 'Dog, don't come up; stay curled on Mistress Polly's bed in the warmth. And, Mistress Polly, this cocoa will put hairs on your chest and clear that cold.'

Polly sniffed, grimaced and eased the tiller slightly. 'Not sure that I find the thought of hairs on my chest has much to recommend it.'

Verity laughed and put three steaming mugs on the cabin roof. One was covered with a side-plate and wrapped in a mitten. She shook her head at Polly. 'You are remiss, my girl. You should have trained that dog to keep the fire going.'

4

As she said this, she propped herself up against the cabin, wearing a blanket over her shoulders, held together with the Inland Waterway badge they'd all been awarded after completing their Ministry of War Transport training. It was a training that had enabled them to manage cargo-carrying canal boats and replace the boaters who had gone off to war, before the Reserved Occupation order had come in for twenty-five-year-old boaters and over. It was an age-limit that proved discretionary, because the younger men had almost immediately been encompassed by the RO, too, for a while – a decision that had just been reinstated, thank heavens, thought Polly.

She watched the wind whip away the steam from the mugs and wished that her fear could be as easily dispersed. Saul, at twenty a year older than she was, had been denied permission to sign up in 1943. He should therefore have been tied to the cut, but to her horror he had tried to break through the RO in the New Year and sign up for the army, but had hurt his leg in a lock fall and it was for that reason he had been refused.

She looked up now, as starlings swirled above the canal – swirling, swirling, just like her mind, because at Limehouse they'd heard that Steerer Mercy's son-in-law had just enlisted, despite the RO. How? – that's what Polly wanted to know. And how dare he, because it would encourage Saul; and he'd probably die, like her twin, Will. She made herself concentrate on the tiller beneath her elbow, the mug in her other hand. She sipped, swallowed, breathed deeply and dragged up the words of Bet, their instructor: 'You've passed, but it's the cut that will really teach you how to be strong women, no matter how scared you are.'

She straightened; of course, that's right, she was strong and formidable, even if she was damned frightened. She sipped again, really tasting the thick, soothing drink, and finally registered that Verity was still leaning against the cabin, staring at her, muttering, 'Polly, my girl, you look as though you're going into bat against those sprouting chest hairs – all fierce and then worried. What's up?'

Polly laughed. 'Trying to work out how to train Dog to keep the fire going.' She saw a narrowboat pair approaching; they were unloaded and therefore high in the water, on the way to pick up cargo from Limehouse Basin. She steered off-centre into shallower water to allow clear passage. Steerer Simms tipped his hat and called, ''Ow do.'

'How do,' the girls called back.

Verity watched the boats pass, and to Polly it looked as though a cloud had passed over her friend's face and had left her miserable. Polly guessed why and her heart sank. What a pair they were, although Verity's problem was far more pressing than her own.

She nudged her friend with her boot. 'Anyway, to get back to my chest, Miss Verity Clement, no hair would dare to sprout beneath my two vests and three sweaters; or if the thought ever crossed its mind, it would have a monumental struggle to survive.'

She must keep up Verity's spirits until the poor girl met her estranged boyfriend, Tom, at the Alperton pub this evening. How would it go, after so long? She didn't dare think. Verity forced a laugh, a cocoa moustache running along her top lip. Polly sipped, and dug for a handkerchief, coughing and blowing her nose.

She realised then that Verity was pointing to the third of the mugs. 'I know Sylvia can make her own in the butty cabin, but it's my apology to her, for spreading my wretched germs. Please say you'll take it. She still gets me so on edge, and I haven't the patience for that today.'

Polly gulped her own cocoa. 'Right you are. After all, you need to conserve your energy for the almost impossible task of making yourself beautiful for this evening.'

Verity laughed, long and loud.

Polly grinned back, relieved, and asked, 'What time did Tom say?' Tension immediately swept across Verity's face and her blue eyes darkened, and Polly could have kicked herself. They were close to another bridge, and Polly didn't give Verity a moment to brood, but nudged her again. 'Keep an eye on the parapet, Verity.'

They both peered ahead, ready to sidestep any children intent on hurling debris at the boater 'scum'.

There was no one on this bridge, just as there had been no one at the others; the children were fair-weather bullies, it seemed.

Polly slowed and hooted, to warn any approaching boats that they were entering the narrow bridge-hole and that they should give way. She called for Dog, who hurtled from the cabin, wagging her tail. 'Good girl, Dog, you might as well come with me and stretch your legs. Take the tiller, Verity, and pull her in really tight to the bank, so I can get off.'

Verity laughed again. 'Pull in tight, indeed. Teaching your grandmother to suck eggs, Captain Holmes?'

'That's enough cheek, Grandma. There's another bridge in a hundred yards, so pull in tight again and I'll jump back then.'

Verity pulled a face at her, taking over the tiller, and Polly muttered, 'I'll present your cocoa with fulsome apologies for the cold you gave Sylvia, but I confess to you now that I've made it worse, by calling Sylvia "Rudolf the red-nosed reindeer" first thing this morning.'

Verity pretended to be shocked, but then almost wept with laughter. 'Well, her nose *is* alarmingly red at the moment, and life would be so much easier if she found at least one or two things amusing.' She suddenly grew serious. 'But do your best, Polly. I don't want Sylvia being sniffy – literally and meta-phorically – when we arrive at the pub, and if she's rude to Tom … He's got to love me again, you see, he really has.'

Polly shook her head, reaching out and holding Verity's hand. 'He already does, or why would he be coming?'

Verity's grin didn't reach her eyes. She pointed to the towpath. 'I've pulled in, Polly, so stop rabbiting on, and just deliver the drink.'

Polly gave her hand one last squeeze, grabbed the mug of cocoa, left the plate and half jumped off onto the towpath, calling back quietly so that Sylvia couldn't hear, 'Didn't spill a drop, and don't worry about Sylvia being difficult this evening. I'll sweep her down the other end of the pub to sing a duet with my lovely Saul. Come on, Dog.'

Dog followed, running backwards and forwards, sniffing, while Polly waited for the butty to reach her. When it did she stepped on board the prow deck – or 'counter', as it was called on the narrow-boats – again with no spillage, while Dog stayed ferreting about on the bank. She walked rather than ran along the slippery, frosted top planks laid over the cargo, checking the tarpaulin as she went, reaching the cabin roof and finally easing herself onto the counter, holding out the cocoa. 'Cargo's all tickety-boo. And cocoa for you, courtesy of Verity. That's one of Mum's knitted mittens it's sitting in.'

Sylvia nodded, sniffed and took the mug in fingerless-gloved hands, her nose a close match to her red hair, which curled around her green woollen hat.

Polly kept her mouth shut.

Sylvia, one hand on the tiller, muttered, 'Nonetheless, Verity should have coughed into a handkerchief. It's not fair to give us her cold. Colds are the last thing we need, on top of this horrid weather. If you live in a community, you learn not to—' She stopped and gulped her cocoa.

Polly gazed ahead as they were towed by *Marigold* from the bridge-hole, trying to be patient, and replied, 'We're hardly a community, Sylvia.' Then she paused, for perhaps they were – a boaters' community; anyway, what gave her, Miss Polly Holmes, the right to be so snotty? She began again. 'I've never thought of us like that before, but even so, Sylvia, if one person in a team, or a community, gets a cold, we all get it. We share everything else, after all.'

Sylvia was groping for a handkerchief, dragging it out of her trouser pocket and sneezing into it. She gave a cough for good measure, then said, 'There's no need to be sarcastic, Polly.'

Polly thought for a moment and suspected that Sylvia was right. 'Sorry, my mouth runs away with me sometimes. You'll be coming to the pub with us, won't you, so that I can buy you a medicinal drink as my mea culpa? And maybe there'll be a chance to sing with Saul. It's special because Verity is meeting up with Tom at last and—'

'I know,' Sylvia snapped. 'I'm not senile. You've told me that already. And don't mock the Holy Mass – mea culpa, indeed.'

Dog, her shaggy white-and-grey coat spattered with dirty snow, barked as she loped along the towpath towards the next bridge-hole, her tongue hanging out in sheer joy. The *Marigold* hooted a warning to any approaching pairs, then entered the darkness beneath the upcoming bridge.

Polly drew in a deep breath, her hands clenched in her pockets, as she realised that she had upset Sylvia yet again; but it had been like walking on eggshells ever since she had joined them as their third crew member. 'I really wasn't mocking. I just didn't think, so I'm sorry. And I know you barely drink, beyond a sweet sherry, but a cold requires a large dose of alcohol, so I insist that I treat you this evening. Take it as an apology. Anyway, our trainer Bet – the oracle – used to swear by a brandy. Now, I must get back.'

Polly waved, walked warily along the top planks and then leapt off the prow onto the bank, running, jumping onto *Marigold*'s stern counter just as she left the bridge. Dog followed and slipped into the cabin, to bask once more in the heat of the range. The cold seemed to bring an early dusk with it, but perhaps it was only a thickening of the cloud base. Polly sat on the cabin roof, leaving Verity to steer, and said, 'Surely there's not going to be another snow shower? That will just pile on the misery.'

'Oh Lord, what if it holds up Tom? We can't wait, Pol, not even for such an important personal thing. We must keep up with the schedule.' Polly started to reply, but Verity overrode her. 'I know – if he can't get through, because the snow's so heavy, I'll leave a note—'

Polly interrupted, wanting to take Verity in her arms. 'Hey, it's not going to happen. Tom's a soldier and was your family's chauffeur, and he will know exactly how to get where he's heading.' But it was no good; she could see Verity's nervousness and pain and couldn't bear it. They continued, passing unloaded boats high in the water, heading towards the east and Limehouse. Polly changed places with Verity at the tiller, repeating, 'It will be all right, I know it will.' She knew no such thing, but damn it – it had to be.

They travelled on, *Marigold* nudging aside the drifting ice, while the barrage balloons glinted over the warehouses, houses and trains of London, straining at their tethers. The afternoon drew on and the wind got up. Polly shivered in the cold, her fingers and toes numb, until she finally pointed at Verity. 'I insist you go into the cabin, there's no point in both of us freezing.'

Verity shook her head and peered ahead. Polly wondered, for the hundredth time, if Tom really would be there? He could hardly be blamed if he wasn't, because how could he trust anything Verity or her family said, after the lies that had led to their bitter break-up? Nonetheless, if he didn't come, Polly would damn well want to ... She steered, resting her elbow on the tiller and peering through the drab light. Well, what would she want to do? Pull Tom's hair out, slap him perhaps; but the person she really wanted to do that to was Verity's mother, Lady Pamela Clement, who had caused all this heartache.

As though Verity had read her mind, the girl lowered herself from the cabin roof to the counter and came to stand beside Polly, her fury almost staining the cold air. 'Oh Lord, how tricky it must have been for my parents, to have a daughter who fell in love with the chauffeur – and he with her. Heavens above, what on earth would they tell the neighbours?'

'Oh, don't do this to yourself,' Polly murmured.

Verity took no notice, but just powered on. 'Well, they didn't have to tell anyone anything, did they? Mother saw to that. And I'd never have known the truth, if Tom hadn't seen me from the bridge when his army lorry broke down, and you heard him yell, "Why did you make your mother pay me to leave you alone?" That's why Tom left me; not because he wanted to go, as Mother had told me, but because she told Tom I wanted him gone. Such lies, to hurt us both.'

She was pacing the tiny deck, slapping one hand in the other.

Polly reached out and held Verity's hands still. 'It doesn't help to go over and over it, and you are nearly at the finishing gate. Think of this evening instead.'

Verity took no notice, her cheeks wet. 'But how could Tom believe Mother's lies, after all we'd been to one another? Why on earth did he think I would offer money to get rid of him? And why would I believe Tom would ask for money to walk away? How could we so easily believe the worst of one another?' She was sobbing. Every time she revisited the situation, she wept. And every time there was nothing Polly could do to make it any better, except whisper stupid platitudes, which did nothing to ease the hurt and regret.

She had another go, however, steering ahead into the freezing wind. 'Hush now, it will all be sorted out this evening. Hush, little Verity, you've done all you can. You wrote all those letters trying to find Tom, after he saw you on the cut, until finally one letter did. And it was *his* suggestion to meet. Why would he want to see you, if not to love you again?'

Verity said nothing, but just stood, lifting her face into the icy blast, dragging her arm across her eyes. Polly waited, knowing how lucky it was that Saul loved her, and she him; at least that much in their lives was certain. Together the two girls stood silently, the tiller between them, the ice clunking on the hull. Somewhere a duck quacked, and along the towpath an old man walked a dog, his cap pulled down hard. Finally Verity half laughed. 'Lord, I'm such an idiot. It's amazing I don't have icicles hanging from my eyes. So sorry, Polly Pocket. Must stop being a fool.'

She hauled herself back onto the roof, her shoulders hunched, and pretended to read *The Times*. At last, quite calmly, she said, 'I wonder if the Allies will get past Monte Cassino soon?'

Relieved, Polly took up the running. 'I hope so. At least the Russians are making progress on the Eastern Front. Soon the Allies must surely invade France?' Were they on safer ground now?

Verity was folding the newspaper; and the answer was no, because she said, 'I wonder if Tom is about to leave the country to go into action? All he wrote was that he was glad to read my side; nothing about love. Nothing about my mother – only that he'd moved on.'

She looked so sad, and Polly didn't know what more she could do, or say, except the same old thing. 'Come on, Verity. Tom's coming, that's what's important and, let's face it, there's a great deal to be explained, and a lot of trust to be rebuilt, on both sides – *both* sides, do you hear, not just his.'

Polly had lost count of how many times they'd been through this, but nonetheless she ticked things off on her fingers.

'It was meant to work out for you both, otherwise why would the Fates make Tom's truck break down on that bridge? Why would I have heard him, as I headed off on the bike to the lock?' She knew it was flimsy, but what else could she say?

Polly steered *Marigold* away from the centre as another narrowboat pair approached, passing left side to left side, as the temperature seemed to drop even further. Verity said nothing, just chewed her lip.

Polly raised her hand to the passing butty. 'How do, Mrs Mercy.'

''Ow do, you lasses.' Ma Mercy worked on her crochet, her breath puffing like a dragon's while her small granddaughter sat on the roof. What did Ma Mercy feel when her son-in-law, Ted, wangled his way into the army, despite the RO? He'd handed back his boat and butty to the Grand Union Canal Carrying Company, of course, so at least she now had her daughter as an extra hand.

Polly felt her agitation begin to rise to match Verity's and slapped it down, but all she could think of were the envy and shame in Saul's eyes when they heard the news of Ted's departure and Saul said, 'It not be fair, sweet Polly, for 'im to go and do 'is bit, but they said no to me.'

Verity said, 'What will I do if Tom doesn't come?'

Polly had run out of reassurances and said nothing, as she realised the snow was falling heavily now. Oh no, please no. She waited, and sure enough Verity tapped her with her booted foot. 'Reassure me, Miss Polly Holmes. Say he'll force his way through snowdrifts ten feet high.'

Polly smiled and came up with yet another different take on her answer. 'Don't be daft. This is London, not the north of Scotland, so the snow won't be deep. Besides, remember that Tom said he had moved on? Well, so have you. After all, you're not the same spoilt, flouncy Lady Verity Clement you were when I first met you, so why shouldn't it work out well?'

Verity stared at her, then burst out laughing. 'And talking of moving on: you're not the prissy, uncertain girl I first knew.' They grinned at one another.

Verity picked up the newspaper, drawing out a pencil from her trouser pocket and starting on the crossword. She'd leave some gaps for Saul to attempt, when she passed it on to him. Saul had learned to read, with their encouragement, just as they had taught his nephew Joe and a few other children.

Joe, who was now staying with Polly's mum so that he could go to school, had said that reading had made him know so much more. It was what Saul said, too; but perhaps if he hadn't learned, he wouldn't want to go to war, because he wouldn't know what was really happening? Polly knew where this was taking her, so she lifted her face to the snow. It was falling in large flakes, and through them flew a skein of geese with a great swishing of their wings – heading for where? The Serpentine? St James's Park? Who knew? Who knew anything any more?

She must have spoken aloud, because Verity leaned forward. 'Dearest Polly, what the hell are you talking about?'

Polly smiled, patting her friend's leg. 'I wish I knew. What *is* certain is that we're nearly at Alperton. Sid will have the fire crackling in the pub, and the beer will be weak but warm; Saul will catch us up, having been loaded quickly at Limehouse; I'll buy

Sylvia a large sweet sherry as an apology for I'm-not-quite-sure-what; and Tom will come on the Piccadilly Line, as arranged, or we'll wring his neck, because I can't go through your second-guessing for much longer. Look, the snow is lighter already.'

Verity slipped down and hugged her. 'Oh, Polly, I'm such a frightful bore, aren't I? But I'll listen to you, if you're ever grizzling on and on, I promise.'

'I bet you don't. You'll just give me a sharp smack and tell me to stop my hysterics.'

'How did you guess?'

The two of them stood firm, their heads up into the wind, on either side of the tiller. The storm was over – for now.

Chapter 2

**Monday 27 March – *Marigold* and *Horizon*
moored up for the evening at Alperton**

Verity sat on her double cross-bed at the rear of
Marigold's typical seven-foot by nine-foot cabin, her
magnifying mirror in her hand. She looked into it,
then groaned, noticing Polly grinning from her perch
on the narrow side-bed opposite the range.

'What's so funny, Polly Holmes?'

'Nothing. I'm just pleased we're moored up in
plenty of time and supper is finished – all right, it
was rabbit again, but it's ...' Polly conducted with
both hands. Verity grinned and joined in,
'Off-ration.'

'Exactly,' said her friend. 'Now I'm off to the
counter for a cigarette, but shall I roll you one while
you put on some slap and make the best of a bad
job?'

Laughter burst from Verity. What would she do
without Polly in her life, and how many times a day
had she thought that recently?

She tossed the mirror down onto the bed. 'My
heart's beating too fast, darling. I don't think I've

ever been so nervous in my life. And why on earth did I ever buy a magnifying mirror? My pores are like grubby craters, and my skin's so dreadfully chapped and weather-worn, it's depressing. Best not to have a fag, thanks. No time.' She knew she was wailing and didn't give a monkey's. 'It's already twenty to eight and I have much work to do, if I'm to make any sort of a silk purse out of this sow's ear. Thank you for washing my hair. Look, it's almost dry.' She ran her fingers through it, then pinned it up so that it fell in loose curls. 'How's this?'

Polly nodded. 'Most certainly the start of a silk purse. Now, I'm off. Use my non-magnifying mirror.' She dug it out of her bag at the end of her bed and tossed it towards Verity. 'It will show you as you are: just gorgeous. Much like me, in fact. Just think: two silk purses; but let's be fair and make it three. I must make more of an effort to include Sylvia.'

Verity thought deeply then said, 'It's as though she really does prefer her own company. Perhaps we are a pain – have you thought of that?' She heard Polly's cough as she gathered up the makings of her cigarette.

'Never let it be said,' Polly muttered, before coughing again.

Verity reached out and pulled down the painted cupboard front on her right, to make a table, dabbed on just a little of what was left of her face powder, then clicked shut her compact; its mirror had been broken years ago, so she was well clear of the seven-years-bad-luck phase. She smoothed on the remains of her rouge to highlight her cheekbones. 'What do you think?' she called, as Polly disappeared up the steps, shoving open the doors, her tobacco pouch and cigarette papers in her hand.

Polly bent and peered back. 'Perfect.' She disappeared, shutting the doors behind her.

Verity double-checked in Polly's mirror. The oil lamp didn't give the best light, but that was a blessing, and the pub's was dim too; so yes, all would be well. She applied what was left of her lippy. It was called 'Passion Pink'. What she really needed was something called 'Courage' that would sink into her and give her just that. What would Tom think of the stuck-up Lady Verity Clement living in a space far smaller than his rooms above the garages of her family home, Howard House? She looked around the cabin. Who on earth would have thought, a year ago, that she could think of this as home?

The range was crackling. Dog was lying on Polly's side-bed. Verity eyed her tobacco pouch. But no, there was time enough for that. Instead she sat quietly, trying to compose herself. The two letters Tom had written were in her make-up bag, well thumbed. She latched up the cupboard front and stood, smoothing her trousers. Should she have worn a skirt? No, it was time Tom met her as she now was.

She sniffed her armpits, but while they weren't exactly sweet violets, they were pretty neutral; she had, after all, strip-washed, so that all body odour would be muted. Usually they just moored up, crammed some food into themselves, wiped down the boats, flicked a bit of water around the gills and then dashed for a drink, a game of darts and a meet-up with Granfer Hopkins and Saul.

Sometimes, when they'd run out of things to wear, they'd wash clothes in their boiler on the bank, but although cleanliness might be next to godliness in the real world, it was not on the canal, or not for these particular 'Idle Women', as they were called – with fingers pointing to their Inland Waterway badges. Things weren't helped by the absence of a bathroom on the boats, with just a bucket for the necessaries, unless they used the pub's toilets. Her parents would faint, but she didn't see them any more, so why would they know, or care?

She heard Polly calling from the counter, 'Come on, Verity, we should be getting there, in case Tom's early. Did you mention in your letter never to use your title?'

Verity scrabbled in her make-up for her precious perfume and dabbed a little of Jean Patou's 'Joy' behind her ears. 'I'm not sure, Polly.'

The cabin doors opened. Polly peered in. 'Righto, I'm going to top up the firebox; don't you dare touch it or you'll have to start washing all over again.' Polly almost leapt down the steps, and used tongs to build up the fire.

Last thing this evening, Verity reminded herself, they must bank it with ash as well as coal, to stop it dying before morning. Where would Tom sleep? Did Sid do rooms? She hadn't thought of that. Or would he just appear, say what he had to say and leave? Verity's mind was racing along with her heartbeat, but then she stopped. What was she thinking? Tom might not come at all. Her hands were sweating with panic. She said, 'I hope he doesn't come. It's all too difficult. Really it is.'

Polly straightened, dusting her hands free of coal and then wiping them down her trousers, leaving smudges. 'Don't be ridiculous. He'll come, or *I'll* want to know the reason why. It's been a ruddy circus round here lately, and I'm almost ready to throw myself off a bridge.'

Verity burst out laughing, but it verged on the hysterical. Again she thought: thank heavens for Polly. But staring at her friend's smudges on her trousers, she wondered what on earth the immaculate Tom would think of them all; he who used to clean his nails religiously, and scrub the oil from his fingers, and press his trousers when he'd finished tinkering with her father's cars. But would he care? What did 'move on' mean? Move on in general, or to someone in particular?

Polly was washing her hands with carbolic soap and called over her shoulder, 'Did you get your nails clean?'

Verity shook her head. 'Don't be daft, Polly, do we ever?'

Polly sniffed her armpits. 'I can't smell myself any more, unless I'm away and amongst the "great washed". Will I let you down? Perhaps I should wash and change, too?'

Before Verity could shriek that there wasn't time, her friend was yanking her sweaters over her head, throwing them on her side-bed and stepping out of her trousers. She poured cold water from the jug into the bowl and sluiced what parts of herself she could reach, then scrabbled in the locker beneath her bed, dragging out stained but washed trousers and several tops. These she flung on, the sweaters dragging the hairgrips from her chestnut waves. 'Bugger,' Polly breathed, picking up the grips from the floor.

'Indeed,' agreed Verity, snatching up her hairbrush from her make-up bag and pinning up her friend's hair in a frenzied rush. 'As though you could ever let me down, you silly goose. You look wonderful. Will's old sweater is just the right colour to set off your hair. Now can we please go?'

They all wore Polly's brother Will's cast-off sailing jumpers, which were ideal as they kept the wind and rain almost at bay. Mrs Holmes, who had donated them when her grief over Will's death had subsided, had knitted more sweaters for the girls, buying old tattered ones at jumble sales and pulling out the wool. It led to strange multicoloured garments, not to mention the proffered hats and gloves, but who cared, because they became grimy within days anyway.

Verity hesitated suddenly. Tom had said he'd been given leave, which is why he could meet her. What if he didn't come, but was actually somewhere else, dead or hurt, and she didn't know? No, he couldn't be; not when she loved him so much, missed him every second of the day. No, she wouldn't have it.

She felt the tears threaten, and as she watched Polly stroke Dog, she swallowed and made herself stop, right this minute, saying firmly, 'Come on, Polly, we're really going to be late, if we don't go now.' Verity paused, reached across and dabbed Polly behind the ears with the stopper of 'Joy', throwing the perfume back in her make-up bag. 'There now, we're both utterly delightful, so you lead the charge.'

The *Marigold* and *Horizon* were moored up abreast, lashed alongside one another, rather than one behind the other, and Verity felt the slight movement as Sylvia stepped from the butty onto their counter. There was a knock and Sylvia called out, 'I'm ready, as ordered, and it's freezing out here. Let's get into the warmth of the pub, because if we're late, your friend will probably leave, Verity, and all the fuss you've put us through will have been for nothing. But at least then we'll have some peace.'

Dog barked. Verity sighed. Polly dragged her out of the cabin and onto the counter. She shut the double cabin doors and slid closed the hatch.

Once outside, the air was so cold it took their breath away; and, worse, heavy snow was falling again, cloaking everything in sight, including Sylvia, who was already on the bank. She had brushed her red hair, but had not changed. Verity tensed. Please, please don't let her notice that Polly has, or she'll nip off to do the same, and it will end up like some ridiculous music-hall skit.

But Sylvia was now walking along the towpath, her arms crossed, her shoulders hunched against the cold. Verity felt Polly slip her arm through hers, her voice muffled by the scarf she had drawn up and over her nose. 'Courage, Verity. Let's get a drink and bask in the warmth of the pub fire. Besides, I want to see my lovely, adorable Saul. Chop-chop.'

They stepped from *Marigold* onto the towpath. Along the bank, at the side, in front and behind them, they heard the wives of the boaters chatting as they stirred the clothes boiling in pans on grills over fires. 'They're so hardy,' Verity murmured. 'It never occurred to me to do the washing on a day like this. Well, it seldom does occur to me, and for once I feel ashamed.'

Beside her, Polly nodded, pulling down her muffler for a moment. 'Perhaps they'll come in for a glass of stout later.'

Verity was looking ahead. 'Saul's just turned off along the path to the pub.' They passed an older woman, stirring the pan, her shawl crossed and tucked into her broad belt, her long skirt stained and worn at the hem.

'How do, Mrs Porter. How's Jimmy?' Polly called.

'Fair to middlin'. Got this cold you 'ad, Miss Verity, so 'e's tucked oop in bed. I 'ears yer meeting up with yer young man. If'n he comes, that is. Never can tell, these days, can yer? Strange goings-on, ain't there?'

Verity sighed. She had long suspected that news was carried on the wind along the waterway; either that, or Sylvia had been blabbing. 'Sorry about giving Jimmy the cold, Mrs Porter, and I suppose one can't tell with men, these days. They're strange, as you say. Not sure I'm any great shakes, come to think of it.'

Mrs Porter stopped in her stirring and stared at Verity. 'I meant the trains, lass. Never can tell, so yer bear that in mind if'n he don't come. Similar, a cold don't do no 'arm to man nor beast, and I reckon our Jimmy likes to be at ease in his side-bed on a day like this, reading his books, thanks to yer two teachin' 'im. Opened 'is world, even though he only be just six.'

Verity felt Polly pulling her along and heard her calling, 'We've got to go. If Verity's lad comes, we need to be there, Mrs Porter.'

Mrs Porter resumed her stirring. 'Right yer are. Pong nice anyway, yer do. Bit of smellies behind yer ears, eh?'

The women along the bank had heard, and laughter followed them as they turned off the

27

towpath onto the pub path, seeing Sylvia entering its lobby with Saul and Granfer.

It made them hurry.

They entered the pub's outer door, closing it carefully to avoid light spilling out and breaking the blackout, before pushing open the lobby door into the smoke-filled room in which the men milled. A few women sat at tables, and an accordion player was giving 'It Had to Be You' some welly at the far end. The table by the fire was available for them, as usual, as all the fireside tables were along the cut. It had become a fixture, after they had saved young Jimmy Porter from drowning when they were still trainees.

Verity frantically searched the room. There was no sign of Tom. She bit her lip, then dragged off her scarf. It was pink and grey cashmere, bought by Tom, though it was so stained and dirty that the colours were almost non-existent. She looked at the large station clock on the wall, one that Sid had bought in an auction sale, but then felt her whole body relax; it was only five to eight.

She had written to explain that the pub fronted the canal, but that there was a pub sign on the road frontage. Perhaps she should go and wait beneath it? She watched as Polly made her way to the bar where Saul waited, looking over his shoulder as she came towards him, reaching out and drawing Polly to him. She watched as Polly nestled against him, as though she fitted.

Envy and regret vied in Verity. This could have been her and Tom, if they'd both believed in one another, and not in her mother's lies. She turned for the door. Yes, she'd wait outside; but then Thomo, a boater, called from the dartboard. 'Yer giving us a game, Verity? Reckon we'll be t'winners, so best bet against yourselves, eh?'

'Maybe,' she called.

'Ah, that's what we 'eard. Maybe 'e'll play with yer?'

She nodded. 'If he can make it. The trains ... the snow ... the war – you know.'

'Aye, that'd be right.'

It seemed the clientele of the whole pub were listening and nodding, but now they turned back to their bitter and resumed their murmured conversations. Verity changed her mind and made for the table. Polly had been right; Tom was a soldier and could find his own way to the door. She sat, watching as Saul kissed the top of Polly's head and nuzzled her ear, making her laugh. He would never believe such a story as her mother had spun, nor would Polly. Nor would Verity now, because they'd all grown tall in their own belief while working on the canal. She watched Sylvia making her way over to their table, carrying a glass of water. She invariably tried to get to the bar, sort herself out a drink and get settled, so that she didn't have to pay for a round.

The bar door opened and Verity swung round, but it was Steerer Wise, off *July* and *Midsummer*, bringing in snow on his hat. At a shout from Sid, the hat was snatched off and slapped against his leg. Over by the dartboard Thomo grinned at her. She tried to grin back, but knew it was only a weak effort. 'We best be on for that darts match later,' he called. 'Remember, bet against yourselves, eh? Ain't that right, Saul?'

Saul was approaching, carrying a couple of tankards of mild. Polly was chatting to Granfer, who carried a tray with tankards of bitter, and a sweet sherry for Sylvia. She remembered that Polly had promised the girl a drink. Saul said, 'Don't yer be too sure, our Thomo; them girls know their bullseyes from their near-misses, as yer damned well know.'

Sylvia looked suitably surprised when the sherry was placed in front of her. Granfer grinned. 'From our Polly, says 'tis for yer cold, and no arguments.' He then winked at Verity. 'Come on, lass, cheer oop, bear with 'im, wi' this snow – and he be barely late, yet.'

By nine o'clock Verity was on her second pint of mild, and beyond bearing with anyone. Tom wasn't coming. She sat staring into the remains of her drink. Sylvia had returned to the butty, complaining that she was too tired to be hanging about, and needed some sleep to get over her cold. Saul was poring over *The Times*, which Verity had slipped out earlier to collect from *Marigold*, taking time to walk to the road and wait for a while.

Polly leaned forward, chatting to Granfer, who sat next to Verity and was sucking on his empty pipe. 'So is your runabout, young Harry, doing a good job, Granfer, while Joe's with my mum?'

'Oh aye, opens the locks for us, quick as a wink. Right little demon, 'e be, our 'Arry. Rush-rush, but likes his painting, like Saul and our Joe. 'E just painted Steerer Bent's water can. 'E be my cousin's grandson, 'e be.'

At the sound of the door opening, the murmur of voices dropped a gear, as Verity and everyone else turned to look, but it was their ex-trainer, Bet Burrows, and even through her desperation, Verity felt a shaft of sheer joy. She nudged Polly, 'Do look.'

The two girls rushed over, talking over one another as the woman they adored opened her arms, laughing and coughing. 'My girls, my lovely girls.' She enfolded them and they clung to her, almost as though she were a mother hen.

Verity heard the wheezing of Bet's chest and pulled away, her hands on her hips. 'Just why are you here? I can hear the rattle, hear the cough, and you said you wouldn't be back until you were quite better.'

Polly chimed in, 'What on earth does Fran say about it?'

Bet, her face thinner than it had been in October when they started as trainees, but fuller than in the darkest throes of pneumonia, which she had developed a month or so later, shooed her two new trainees before her to the bar, with Verity and Polly following. Verity got there before Bet, barring her way. She called, 'Sid, don't you dare serve this woman until we hear that she has the go-ahead from her "nurse" to be back on the cut.'

It was Bet's turn to stand with her hands on her hips. 'The Ministry of War Transport, in the form of Potty Thompson, needs me back, to try and train more women and release a few more men. The doc has passed me fit, except for my flat feet. What's more, Fran has stood down for now. She's busy anyway, teaching at the village school. I didn't send a note because I knew you'd both nag.'

Granfer called from their table by the fire, 'Not just the lasses; us'll all be at it, if'n you're not right. I got yer a chair, and yer trainees can take a seat near as dammit.' He pointed to the chairs that he'd gathered around their table.

Thomo called from the end of the bar, 'Good to see yer back, Bet, and yer can be the girls' third for the darts.'

Bet laughed and reached forward, gripping Verity's and Polly's hands. 'It's good to be back, and the moment the snow gets into my tubes, I'll call it a day. Does that sound fair to you?'

One of Bet's trainees came up with a tankard of stout. 'The publican said to get that down you. Do you the world of good, so he says. I think my mother said it's good for breastfeeding women as well.' Verity felt Polly nudge her, as Bet's mouth dropped open. The girl said, 'I don't know why I said that. How embarrassing. I think it's tiredness.'

They all laughed, and Verity felt a great weight fall from her. She was here, amongst friends, and if Tom didn't come, she would just have to get on with it. She wouldn't be the first to cope with a broken heart and she certainly wouldn't be the last. She snatched a look at the clock, but ... but there was still time.

She gripped Bet's arm. 'You're going to take your place on our darts team again – no excuses allowed.' Anything to take her mind off Tom.

Bet looked from her to Polly, then at her trainees. 'Girls, off you go and sit with Granfer; we have some brothers to beat. Make sure you place your bets, gentlemen and ladies, because the girls are back and are about to teach these boys from *Venus* a lesson or two. Get your money on with Sid.'

The match was tense, and close, but the women won, promising Thomo, Timmo and Peter a return match at the next pub. Polly collected their winnings from Sid, after he'd divided it up on the counter: £2 for *Marigold*'s darts kitty and £1 for Bet. Then Polly leaned forward, asking Sid something. When she heard the answer she beckoned Verity across.

'What's up?' Verity called, standing up.

'Just come over.'

Verity reached Polly, who called to Sid, 'Tell her what you told me.'

'Give up a minute. High finance going on 'ere.' He'd moved to the other end of the bar and divvied up Saul and Granfer's winnings, and then the next steerers', ticking off their names on a scrap of paper. Polly was tapping the bar and called again. Sid nodded, tucked the stub of pencil behind his ear and came over. 'Good deal, that was, girls. No one knew who would win, for the teams were so close to one another, so I did all right. Now, what was it you wanted?'

Polly sighed. 'Stop teasing, you know very well.'

Sid, his shirt collar open, and his black apron darkened with beer splashes, put his hands on the bar. 'Ah yes, young Verity. Your Polly asked if we'd had any telephone calls. The missus took a few, which she reckons was either from ruddy kids messing about in a phone box or some poor bugger who tried pushing Button A, only for it not to work. Polly's right – could be yer lad, I reckon. Never gave it a moment's thought until she asked. Course, it might not be.' He snatched a cloth from his apron pocket and wiped the beer spills on the counter, then went over to Steerer Ambrose from *Sunburst* for his order.

Verity closed her eyes for a moment. Could it be? She gripped Polly's hand, saying, 'But even if it was Tom, surely he could find another telephone box that worked? They're so close together in London.' She didn't know whether to hope or not.

'Come and sit down, and let's think about it,' Polly said.

'In a minute. I need another drink.' With another tankard of mild in her hand, she followed Polly to their table, but, really, there was nothing more to be said. If it was Tom, he'd given up too easily. If it wasn't, he still wasn't here, so she didn't listen to any of their ramblings. At ten o'clock Verity knew it was all over and just drank steadily, replenishing her tankard and snapping at Polly, who wanted her to come back to the boat at a quarter to eleven.

'You go. I want to be alone for a bit,' she said, her lips almost numb with drink. She could hear the slurring of her words. They left her – not just Polly, but Bet and the trainees, and Saul and Granfer, too. She was alone and she felt lost. She drank on; after all, why not?

At eleven fifteen, Polly and Saul returned and sat with her, not drinking, just waiting. At twelve, Sid called time on the lock-in, and Verity, her eyes half shut against the world, couldn't work her legs; how strange – only it wasn't. She used to drink like this when Tom left her; it had made everything, including her heart, numb. She felt Saul haul her upright, putting his arm around her. She wished she was Polly: so safe, and loved. She couldn't get her legs to work on the path, but Saul half carried her. The cold hurt her face, her neck. She had left her scarf on the back of her chair, but couldn't find the words to tell them; her friends, the ones who had found love.

Her world lurched and then they were on *Marigold*'s counter. Sylvia must have heard their boots, or felt the shift of the boat, because she slid back *Horizon*'s hatch, opened her doors, looked out and tutted. Verity heard Polly say, 'Not one word, Sylvia. Really, not even one more tut. Summon some compassion, please.'

The butty's doors shut with a bang, followed by the hatch. Saul murmured, 'That be tellin' her, though she be another lass with a 'eap of misery stuffed inside her.' Verity heard the doors of *Marigold* open and Dog's bark. She was almost home, almost warm. She heard Saul say, 'Yer not to give up hope, our Verity. Coulda been 'im on the telephone, and not another anywhere nearby; or if there was, it were broke, too. I'll take yer down into the cabin.' He shifted his arm slightly.

Verity opened her eyes wide. The snow was still falling, the wind across the counter was freezing. She formed a reply, carefully and only slightly slurred. 'He must have lost the use of his legs, then. There are many, many other telephone boxes, our Saul. Thank you for your help. I can get into the cabin.' She shook him off, but the next moment she felt the whack of the counter as she fell face-down onto it. It was cool, and wet with freezing snow. Perhaps she would drown? She hoped so.

She felt Saul lift her in his strong arms. And although she should be strong, as Bet said the women on the canals were, Verity couldn't hold back the tears at the thought of the endlessness of her life without the man she loved.

Chapter 3

The next morning Tom leaned back against the side-wall of the pub at Alperton. His fractured shin ached even more in this bitter cold and itched beneath the plaster. His toes stuck out from the cast and, even though they were covered in a couple of army socks, were freezing cold. Yesterday the nurse had wrapped round some waterproof gear to keep the foot dry, which was a blessing. She was a good 'un, and was engaged to a matelot. Tom hoped he survived.

The hospital had been reluctant to discharge him, after just three days. He'd lied, explaining that he had to see off a relative who was embarking for who-knew-where. They had checked with his CO, who explained that Tom's leave had been changed to sick leave, and if the doc thought he was able, then they should let him go.

The doc had finally signed the form, and the sister had given Tom a couple of sticks because he didn't want the crutches, knowing he'd only get tangled up, getting on and off trains. He'd hitched his grip over his shoulder, wincing because it was still bruised from the crash between their jeep and the idiot on the motorbike; and had lurched off to the station yesterday afternoon. He'd continued sitting in the train when it jerked to a stop because of some signalling problem, but by the evening they'd all been turfed out, until the lines were sorted. He'd tried phoning the pub more than once from outside that station, but the damned Button A wouldn't work, so he'd spent the night sitting huddled on the platform until the trains were up and running again this morning.

He straightened, took a walking stick in each hand and limped round to the pub's entrance, which indeed faced the canal, as Verity had written. The snow – deep, crisp and even, as the carol said – hadn't yet been cleared. Perhaps it was just as well, as ice tended to be more lethal than snow, and he didn't fancy going over and doing even more damage to himself. He had to get fit, and quick.

He stared across the garden at the canal frontage, feeling nervous, excited ... and what? But his thoughts were disturbed as he realised there were no boats moored up. Surely Verity had waited, after all this time – perhaps the boats were further along the bank?

He limped along the path towards the waterway, though it was more treacherous than it looked, because the ice beneath the snow had been scuffed into ridges. He made it to the bank unscathed and stared into the still water, where the ice lay in chunks. Presumably the boaters had bashed their way free. He checked both ways; not a sausage. He stared up at the stone-grey sky, which looked as cold as his bloody foot. His mouth was dry with despair. She'd gone. He looked both ways again, blinking. They weren't tears, it was just the wind.

He swallowed and dragged out his handkerchief, wiping his face, blowing his nose and shoving the handkerchief back in his pocket. He straightened. God, he was a fool. He'd believed Verity's words, but how stupid was that; he was only a damned chauffeur, like her mother had said, when she told him it had just been a game to Verity. She had insisted Verity wanted Tom to leave her alone so much that her mother was to pay him off, to make sure he did.

He rested on his walking sticks, more defeated than he'd ever felt in action. Was she bored, and thought she'd get back to playing her old game, when she knew he'd seen her from the bridge? Well, he thought, with rising pain and anger as he limped back down the path, that was the end of it; and what a fool he'd been to think otherwise.

He felt sick, and his head had begun to ache from tiredness and pain. He'd slog back into London proper and try and find somewhere to doss down for the rest of his sick leave. What then? Well, there'd be all the faffing about at the barracks; and when he was fit, there'd be training exercises, because – judging from the build-up of military transport

– something would kick off soon. The big push? Well, he bloody hoped so. There was a war to win, and perhaps he'd get his head blown off, and who the hell would care? He certainly wouldn't.

He dragged out his handkerchief and wiped his face again, slipped, then righted himself. 'Bloody women,' he muttered, just as he heard the bolts on the pub door being slid back.

The green front door opened, and an overweight middle-aged bloke stood there, with a black apron tied round his middle, smoking. There was a pencil behind his ear. 'You looking for someone, lad?'

'Not any more, I'm not. You're Sid, are you?' Their breath puffed out and merged. Tom rested on his sticks, easing his leg.

'Yes, lad. That's me – Sid, the publican. And you, my fine feller, 'll be the missing love of 'er life. You tried phoning, did yer?'

Tom stared at him. 'You know Lady Verity then?'

Sid stared back. 'I knows Verity, right enough. Don't know about any "Lady Verity", and best yer don't splash that around, cos she don't, and the boaters might think it highfalutin.' Sid tossed his cigarette into the snow. It hissed and died.

Tom said, 'Lady or not, she didn't have the decency to wait until I arrived. So that's it then, I'm not playing her bloody silly games any more.'

The words hung between them, like their breath. Sid looked past him to the canal, digging his hands into his trouser pockets. 'Them lasses have a schedule to keep, carrying war supplies, and no young pup should stand there on his one good leg and gainsay that. How'd you feel, back in the field, cos I can tell from the khaki greatcoat you're wearin' you're likely to be there anytime soon. So, I say again, how'd yer feel if yer didn't have no gun, cos the boaters had stopped off to wait for some tit-headed idiot who didn't arrive when he said? Some khaki lad who couldn't even totter with his sticks to the next phone box and try again. Cos it was yer, weren't it, ringing and ringing?'

Tom rubbed his forehead, knocking his beret to one side, his bloody headache worse now. Sid was still looking at him, and Tom knew he had to say something, so although he still ached with anger he said, 'I put my hand up – duff Button A.'

Sid had his papers and baccy out now and was rolling one. He raised an eyebrow and tipped the tobacco tin towards Tom, who shook his head.

'I have my own, but haven't a hand to dig 'em out while juggling these sticks.'

Sid turned and headed into the lobby. He stopped and looked back. 'Come on, then; that were a hint, if ever I 'eard one. The missus will have a pot of tea on the go, so we'll wrap ourselves round a cuppa. You can get yer smokes out while you think whether to turn tail or get a bit of backbone and go after the lass. She was saying early on in the evening that she'd leave a note for you, but she got a bit ... well, you know, miserable; and had a pint or several too many.'

Tom looked back at the canal, then up at the sky. There was more snow to come. The wind lifted his beret, then it settled. His toes beneath the socks were numb. He could do with a cuppa to give him a bit of puff to get into London.

'Just for a minute, then, Sid. Thanks.' He limped into the lobby. Sid held open the door into the bar and jerked his head. 'Hurry it up, then, we don't want the wind takin' the 'eat out of the place.'

Tom entered the darkness of the Public Bar, which was rich with the smell of beer, woodsmoke and last night's tobacco. There was dead ash in the grate, and a scarf on the back of a chair at the table by the fireside. Surely it was ...? He limped across the flagstones and reached out, fingering it. Yes, though the cashmere scarf was stained with oil and dirt, there was still the vestige of colour – and scent, Verity's scent. Sid waited, holding up the hinged bar flap. 'Yes, that's yer lass's. She forgot it, but someone will catch 'er up somewhere with it. That's how dirty them girls get on the job.'

Tom dropped the scarf, letting it swing. He turned and saw the dartboard. He was flooded with memories: standing behind Verity, placing a dart into her smooth white hand. Verity leaning against him, the smell of her perfume. What had she called it? Was it 'Happy'? No, no, that wasn't it. 'Joy', that's what it was. He looked again at the scarf. That was the smell. She had sat there in the warmth of the fire all evening, and then slept in the warmth of her *Marigold* overnight, unlike him. Had she been waiting to laugh at him? His head was beating a tattoo.

Sid called, 'Cuppa or not? Make up your bleedin' mind, cos I'm not standing 'ere all day, holding up the counter for the good of me 'ealth.'

Tom followed him into the kitchen, where a plump woman in an apron was up to her elbows in the sink. She looked over her shoulder. 'Thought I 'eard you chatting, Sid. That's Verity's bloke, is it? Tea in the pot, then bugger off into the bar, I'm busy here. Don't be long; you need to sort out the cellar and lay the fire, once you've sent 'im on whichever way he chooses. Shame she didn't leave a note, but she was – let's say – right conflummoxed, that she was, and who's to blame 'er.'

Sid nodded and poured the tea. 'Bit weak,' he said to Tom. 'Rationing, you know 'ow it is. We'll take it out the sergeant-major's way, cos she bites.'

Sid carried the two enamel mugs into the bar and led him to the fireside table.

'All the pubs along the Grand Union Canal keep the fireside table for Polly and Verity, and if they don't come, then it'll be kept for their old instructor, Bet, now she's back training on the cut.' He gestured to the chair with Verity's scarf. 'Take the weight off your pins. Drop yer grip on the floor. Your leg?'

Tom sat, resting his walking sticks against the table, and letting his grip slide from his shoulder to the flagstones. 'Bit of a road prang, busted my leg.

So I'm on sick leave, and then I want to get back quick as I can, because—' He stopped.

Sid nodded. 'Yes, looks like a second front's on the cards, so good luck to yer, lad.'

Tom sipped his tea, and it seemed to ease his head, just a fraction. He took out his roll-ups. He had a couple made up. 'Have one, as thanks for the warmth, and the wet.'

Sid took one, and a light too, sucking in the nicotine and then exhaling up into the air. 'Your Verity and her pal, Polly, play darts along the cut and bet on themselves. They keep the money in a kitty jar. When Joe, a youngster, got into trouble, they used the kitty money to help pay for a solicitor. Though the legal beak did it free in t'end, so that dosh is back in the jar, being added to for an emergency. They're well liked, and 'ighly thought of, lad.'

What the hell did Tom care how highly thought of her high-and-mighty ladyship was? He drew on his roll-up and, as he sat back, the smell of Verity's scarf seemed to waft ever more intensely: 'Joy' and dirt. He supposed, now that Verity had no staff, she didn't turn her hand to washing. He drained his mug, waiting for Sid to do the same. They stubbed out their cigarettes in the ashtray, where there were other stubs stained with lipstick; it was Verity's colour. So she could still afford lipstick in these days of rationing? Of course her sort always could.

Tom wanted to shred it, grind it into the ground, but he also wanted to put it in his pocket to keep it close. Oh God, his head was aching fit to burst, and it felt as though his heart was, too; and he couldn't damn well think.

'Well,' he said finally, gathering his sticks together. 'Best be off.'

He rose. Sid, too. The publican walked him to the bar door. 'You didn't ask me why the fireside table is always kept free for 'em, lad.' He seemed to be barring the door.

Tom muttered, 'No, I didn't, cos it doesn't interest me any more.'

Sid gripped his arm. 'Then you're a right bloody fool – just like I'd be, if I hadn't chased after my missus. The least you could do is to catch 'er up and have a talk. You get her to tell you why they 'ave a reserved seat, just so's you can see the sort of lass you'd be chucking away. What's more, you should bloody believe her when she tells you the truth about the past, and the ruddy mess her mother made of the girl's life, and yers too, no doubt. Believe 'er, not the mother – that's what we think, them of us on the cut.'

Tom looked down at Sid's hand, gripping him tightly enough to bruise. If he hadn't a broken leg, he could down the bloke in a second.

Sid looked from his hand to Tom's face. 'D'you want to give it a try, lad? If so, be warned: I've chucked out better than you, with one 'and behind me back. You need to get yer 'ead in order, that you do. I sees it all the time – blokes looking into pint glasses, the pity for themselves dripping from 'em, their thoughts all in a tangle. If you'd been a man, you'd 'ave tapped your way to another phone box, course you would; and sorted this bloody mess, cos you ain't lost the use of your legs. Not like some poor buggers. Yer just behaving like a bloody kid. Go after her and get the truth through yer noddle, for Gawd's sake. Can't 'ave the lass drinking herself stupid every night.'

Tom shook himself free and walked through into the lobby and out into daylight. It was snowing again, and the scuffed ridges on the path were almost completely hidden. He set off for the station, his head lowered as the snow grew heavier and seemed to deaden all sound. But he couldn't get the remembered thud-thud of Verity's darts out of his bursting head. And with the sound came the sight of her as they used to play in the Red Bull, the pub in a village near Sherborne; and Verity's delight when she and he won.

He almost felt her throwing her arms around him. He heard her chatter as they walked back to Howard House, arm-in-arm, pledging their love. He felt he was breathing in the scent of her, and saw the plans of his garage that they drew in the air. A garage where he would mend cars, and she would keep the books, when this war was over. She'd take a class in bookkeeping, she'd said, and she'd learn how to type up invoices. Had it really been a game? Had it?

He paused. He had Verity's recent letters in the pocket of his uniform, and they didn't read like those of a girl in the middle of a game. Or did they? That was the trouble: how could he know? The day was so grey with cold that no bird sang and there was no one walking except for him, his sticks digging into the snow, his boot squeaking faintly as he peg-legged until he reached the station. He stopped, staring at the entrance, where sandbags were stacked. He could get on a train, find a room and leave Verity and her bloody letters and games for good and all, and then it would be over.

People were entering. The men had snow on their hats, the women snow on their umbrellas. But if he went without seeing her, he would never ever know the truth. One middle-aged ARP warden stopped and touched his arm. 'You all right, sonny? Them toes must be ruddy freezing. Need an 'and?'

Tom shook his head. 'Thanks, just taking a breather.'

'You could take it in the dry?' The warden's eyes were kind.

Tom said, 'You get on. I have to take a moment to sort me head out.'

The warden just nodded and walked on, before turning back, pulling the scarf around his mouth. Had Verity worn her scarf like that, around her face, her mouth – those lips that were still 'Passion Pink'? He tried to feel nothing or, if not nothing, then anger, but all he could do was remember the scent of her;

someone who was known only by her name, not her title.

The ARP warden said, 'Easier sometimes to put yer thoughts into words, if yer talking to a stranger.'

Tom looked at the bloke. He found himself speaking, all in a rush. 'I loved this Lady Verity, when I was her chauffeur. She said she loved me. We were going to work together, setting up a garage. Her mother came and said Verity was just bored, playing a game, and had asked her to give me money to bugger off and leave her alone. Or words to that effect. She then told Verity some cock-and-bull story about me wanting to leave, but demanding money to go. I believed it. She believed it. But we almost met, not long ago, and she wrote and said her mother had lied to us both. We agreed to meet. The train broke down – the lines, or something – and the phone box wouldn't work, and she didn't wait.'

The bloke just stood there. 'So you haven't seen her?'

'No.'

'So you'll never know the truth of it.'

Tom shook his head. 'Not that I care any more.' His head was really bursting now, and he inched towards the station.

But the ARP warden came with him and said, 'Fine kettle of fish, I reckon. Yer should chase it down, lad. Could be yer've both grown up a bit since then, and wouldn't be so ready to believe what someone else tells yer.'

49

Tom shook his head, and snow fell from his beret. He took one more step towards the station, then stopped again. He knew he could have walked to the next telephone box last night; he could even see the ruddy thing. But now he faced the truth – he'd wanted to test Verity, see if she'd wait, because that would prove she loved him. Did he also want to hurt her, worry her, as the Clement family had hurt him? He didn't know, and didn't want to think about the whole bloody mess any more. It was all such a damned muddle.

The ARP warden took another step with him. 'I often wish I could talk things through with my missus, but she copped a bomb in the Blitz. Too late now ever to share a word with 'er – even a cross one, and we 'ad a few of them. That's a heartbreak, lad, but yer can do summat about yours. But only you – if yer get me meaning.'

He walked on, leaving Tom motionless. He tried to follow, but the scent of Verity wouldn't leave him, and neither would Sid's words, or the ARP's, or his memories, which were more vibrant and clear with every moment, and at last he nodded to himself. Oh, what the hell harm could it do, to take a canal girl her scarf? It wasn't as though he had to be anywhere else.

He slipped and slid back to the pub. His headache was marginally easier by the time he rapped on the door. He shrugged when Sid opened it. 'I thought Verity would need her scarf, so I might as well take it.'

Sid just nodded. 'Reckon that's as good an excuse as any. Follow me in, but stamp your boots – well, boot – free of snow before you do.'

The two men sat at the fireside table while Sid mused on the best way of catching up with *Marigold*. Within minutes they were joined by the missus, which was all the name Tom was given. It was she who said, slapping the table, 'For heaven's sake, yer pair o' slowcoaches. Use the cut, and flag down the next pair as comes along. Yer can send a message by them flyboats to tell 'em to wait at Cowley lock fer this package.' She pointed at Tom.

Before he could draw breath, Tom was back out in the snow, with Sid in a mackintosh, holding an umbrella and standing on the bank. 'We'll flag 'em down with me brolly. The traffic's been pretty steady, so someone'll take you on to Cowley, cos yer'll be too late for Bull's Bridge. I'll hail a flyboat to get a message to the girls to wait, though the boys won't stop to take yer.'

'Why not?'

'Ah, the name tells you; they're young lads carrying beer, or some such, and they just keeps goin', night and day. They can't keep it up for too many years, but they make a packet while they do.'

They stood staring towards the east, and within ten minutes a pair, roped abreast, hove into sight. Sid nodded. 'It's Steerer Mercy on the *Lincoln* and

Ma on the butty *York*. You'll see the boats are red, white and blue, means them are Grand Union Canal Carrying Company's boats, like most of 'em are, including your lass's. Not many independents on the cut any more. Mercy's 'ave had a right quick turnaround at Limehouse Basin, I reckon.'

He waved his open umbrella up and down and received an answering hoot. 'They'll pull in, cos if it's deep enough to moor up overnight, it's deep enough to pull in. Some edges aren't. They'll expect you to jump aboard, but when they see the sticks, they'll hold 'ard and give yer time.'

'I suppose "the cut" is the canal?'

'Yer gettin' the idea.'

Within another ten minutes Steerer Mercy brought the breasted pair into the frontage, throwing the engine into reverse. The propeller churned the water as Sid pushed and Steerer Mercy pulled Tom on board *Lincoln*. Ma Mercy called from the butty's stern counter where she stood, with the tiller beneath her elbow, 'Who be this, Sid?'

''E's that bit of unfinished business of our Verity's. He didn't limp on to the next phone box when he couldn't get Button A to work, so the least he can do is take the scarf she left on the back of her chair. Or so he reckons. I'll get the flyboats to take on a message for the *Marigold* pair to wait at Cowley.'

Steerer Mercy barked a laugh. 'Best drag that plastered leg on over to the butty with Ma, young 'un. She'll stuff yer in the cabin, so you can take that scarf off from round yer neck. Pink don't suit a bloke, not even if 'tis so darned grubby it's almost black.'

Tom snatched off the scarf and tried to keep out of the way of the tiller. He called to Sid, who was closing his umbrella. 'Thanks, mate. Really, thanks. I owe you a drink.'

Sid's bellow reached Tom as he stepped crabwise across to the butty. 'More'n one drink, laddie, and a couple each for these good people, too. You treat Verity right, now. She's a keeper, if ever I saw one. Well, her and Polly are, but not sure about that Sylvia. Something going on with 'er; summat deep that makes her right prickly, and I don't envy them two girls, copin' with her.'

Tom waved one of his walking sticks towards Sid. 'Thanks to the missus, too.'

Ma Mercy opened the cabin doors, sliding back the roof hatch. 'Down you go, laddie. You've got it to yerself, because our Sheila's in the motor cabin with the child. She'll be lock-wheeling – yer know, walking or biking ahead to get the lock ready, less yer want to do it?' Her laugh was loud and long. 'What yer think, me old chap?' she called to Steerer Mercy, who tipped his finger to his hat, his clay pipe clamped between his teeth. Ma half pushed Tom onto the top step leading to the cabin. 'Bend yerself and in yer go. Warm yourself, why don't yer? Sit on the side-bed opposite the range. There's tea in the pot, mugs in the painted cupboard.'

He ducked down the steps, marvelling that Ma Mercy wore only a long skirt and a jumper, with a shawl that was draped around her shoulders and tucked crossways into her wide belt, while he wore his greatcoat and had been freezing. The warmth greeted him, but he could barely stand upright in the smallest room he had ever seen; it could only be nine feet by seven at the most. An oil lamp hung on a peg on one of the walls, which sloped slightly inwards, and on which also hung pierced plates and horse brasses.

Ma Mercy called down, 'Afore yer settle, lad, toss oop me crochet, if you will, and then pass me a couple o' teas.'

He found a sort of tangle of wool on the side-bench that she pointed to and handed it up to her, then filled three enamel mugs, added milk and hobbled up the first step with two of them, holding them out to her.

'Ta,' she said. 'When we're breasted together like this, 'tis easy to pass it to me chap. When we's on a tow, we has to run along top planks. Your girls go abreast sometimes, like we all do, though it took 'em a while to get the 'ang of it. Go and rest yersel'. We're pullin' in at the Grand Union depot at Bull's Bridge, but someone'll take yer on to Cowley lock, never fear.'

Tom sat down on the side-bench and stared at the range's firebox, sipping his tea. He felt exhausted, his leg hurt and itched beneath the plaster, and he thought he was getting chilblains on his thawing toes. He tried to stretch out, but the aisle was only eighteen inches wide. He looked at the pierced plates, and at the cupboard to the side of what looked like a wide bench at the end of the cabin – or was it a bed? They must eat and sleep here, if it was, and he couldn't quite believe it. A curtain was hooked up at the side, which could be dropped to close it off. He finished his tea and needed a pee.

Ma Mercy laughed. 'Use the cut, or there's a bucket in the end store afore the hold, fer yer doings.'

Tom changed his mind and sat back, slipping from his coat and dozing, his mind full of Verity living day after day on a boat like this. Verity, of the soft hands and the life of a lady. He held her scarf. No wonder it was dirty, but now, in the soft light from the oil lamp, he saw that much of it was oil stain, so how would you get that out anyway?

After a few hours he woke again, this time to the sound of the *Lincoln*'s hooter. Ma Mercy called to him, 'We're backing into Bull's Bridge lay-by. It be the depot for the Grand Union Canal Carrying Company. Right mouthful, eh, but me old chap's spied Steerer Porter taking off and shouted a word. He's going to take yer on, so 'e is. So oop yer come, and get ready to step across to his boat, *Oxford*.'

Tom shrugged into his greatcoat, slung his grip over his shoulder and mounted the steps, dragging his leg behind him. Ma Mercy supported him as he stepped across to the Porters' motor *Oxford*, which lay alongside.

Steerer Porter gripped his arm, a pipe between his teeth, too, and his hat pulled down. 'Right, lad, got ya; we'll be taking yer on, to make things oop with your lass, or not.'

From the tiny deck, Tom looked about him at what seemed to be hundreds of narrowboats with their butties, moored at a frontage about a quarter of a mile long. Washing hung motionless, as though frozen, from lines strung behind the cabins. Some women were washing over fires on the bank. Everyone seemed so busy, and from the yard that he could see at the end of the frontage came the sound of sawing, banging and the drumming of machinery from the machine shops, and smoke from the chimneys. There were houses set back in the distance on the opposite side and a church spire.

'What yer lookin' at?' A boy of six sat on the *Oxford*'s cabin roof and stared at Tom, tracing the words of his book with his finger.

How can he sit there, Tom thought, in all this cold? He felt the vibration of the motor's idling engine. 'Just getting my bearings,' he replied, impatient for Steerer Porter to pull away.

The snow was thawing on the roof and from the top of what looked like a brightly painted kettle, next to the boy. But that could be because of the heat of the black chimney, from which smoke curled and to which, Tom now realised with a shock, the boy was chained – like an animal.

Steerer Porter called across to his butty, *Cambridge*. 'Ready, Missus? There bain't be room for abreast, going through the locks. Won't get 'em gates hard back against the lock walls, for the ice.'

'Aye, let's be off.' Mrs Porter was standing at the tiller, her shawl wrapped around her and tucked crossways into her belt, just as Ma Mercy had worn hers.

Tom felt awkward, standing about like a spare part on the motor's deck. He edged up hard against the cabin, trying to keep out of the way, but Steerer Porter said, 'Yer need to be on the butty, lad. 'Op on now, while we're alongside.'

Tom half laughed. 'Hop's a bit far-fetched – I'll have to drag this damned leg.' He struggled over onto the butty, and immediately Steerer Porter untied the ropes lashing the butty and motor together and set off, slowly. A boy of about eleven emerged from the butty cabin and, to Tom's amazement, leapt onto the cabin roof and almost danced along the planks that lay over the top of the tarpaulin-covered cargo, jumping down out of sight at the front end.

Ma Porter said, 'My chap'll throw the tow-rope to 'im as he eases out from t'lay-by, and the lad'll put it over the stud on our prow counter and my chap'll tow us. The counter's what a landsman would call a deck.'

Tom felt the butty *Cambridge* jerk as *Oxford* took up the tow. The lad ran back along the planks and jumped down onto the deck – no, not deck, what did she call it? ah yes, the counter – and disappeared into the cabin, slamming the door behind him. Tom looked ahead as Steerer Porter towed them past the depot yard, and he studied the small boy chained up, who was coughing. Mrs Porter touched Tom's arm.

'It's what we do to stop 'em falling into the cut. Though I s'pose you'd call it the canal. Jimmy has a cold, but wants to be out in the air. Soon 'e'll be able to help with the locks, but for now we 'as my brother's lad, Bobs, who be our runabout. He'll do what Sheila did on t'Mercys' boat yer've just left, and what yer lass'll be taking 'er turn doing – lock-wheeling or, to you, opening and closing them locks. Lots of locks there are too, my lad.'

Tom steadied himself on his sticks as *Oxford* and *Cambridge* set off along the cut, passing the moored narrowboats and then the yard. Mrs Porter nodded. 'You get yourself in t'cabin with Bobs, why don't yer? You been in the wars, I reckon – the real wars – but if yer can get from one boat to another, yer can find another telephone box.'

Tom shook his head, angry at the nagging that all these people were doing. He was here, wasn't he, trying to catch Verity up? He struggled to keep his voice level, but failed, his headache roaring again. 'Nothing so brave. I was tipped out of a jeep in an accident and have two weeks' sick leave, then I'll be back, in the office if I have to, until I can get this plaster off.'

Mrs Porter nodded, raising an eyebrow at his tone, and he felt embarrassed, but still angry, because what the hell was he doing, rushing about the canal and getting a load of grief for not finding another telephone, when Verity ...? Oh, but it wasn't canal, was it; it was the bloody cut.

Mrs Porter urged him, 'Get yourself down them steps then. Our Bobs'll be back doing his lessons on the cross-bed, so you take the side-bed.' She watched as a boat rushed past, fully laden.

Tom asked, 'Is that a flyboat?'

Ma Porter nodded. ''Spect they're carrying a message to your lass.'

'She's not—' He stopped. Just shut up, Tom Brown.

Again Tom found himself negotiating steps down into the warmth. He hoped the flyboat did carry a message for Verity, because now he really needed to see her, to stop all this 'big bad wolf' gossip, and then he could bugger off. He was tired, cold, his leg ached, his toes were frozen what's more, and he hadn't eaten since yesterday and was starving, and he'd damn well had enough. He saw, suddenly, the ARP warden's face, the loss that had drained the light from his eyes when he mentioned his dead wife, and he sank back against the cabin wall. What if Verity ...? He couldn't bear the thought. In fact it was all such a muddle that he couldn't bear to think about anything any more.

Bobs was sitting on the wide bed at the end of the cabin, and the range was belting out warmth. Tom sat on the side-bed opposite the range, wriggling out of his coat, removing his cap and dropping his grip onto the floor. 'Hello,' he said to Bobs.

The boy just grunted, then muttered, 'Got me readin' to do, before I sees Verity and Polly at Tyseley Wharf. They'll have more lessons for me. Verity, she does reading; Polly, she do numbers this time, but they change turn and turn about.'

Tom stared at the boy. 'Verity does?'

Bobs looked up. He sucked his pencil and then bent down, writing some words in a little notebook. 'Course she do – she's right clever, they both is. I writes what I don't understand, then they tells me what it means.'

Tom reached into the pocket of his coat and touched her scarf. Who the hell are you, Verity Clement?

After a moment Bobs said, 'You all right, Mister?'

'Course I am, Bobs, but I didn't know she ...'

Ma Mercy called down. 'Bobs, yer give that Tom some bread, and there's pheasant left from last night. Reckon he needs feeding, cos there were a bit of a snarl bursting out from 'im a minute ago, so 'spect 'e's got an empty belly, and no one can sort 'emselves out on a parcel of air where food should be.'

'Pheasant?' Tom was amazed, although he seemed to be feeling that rather a lot recently.

Bobs was busying himself at a small table he'd made by pulling down a cupboard front, to the right of where he was sitting. 'Saul, one o' the boaters, snared it as 'e went along t'cut; or were it Thomo, Ma?'

Ma Porter called down. 'Saul it were, yer lass's friend's chap, young Tom. Now, get some food in yer, and yer'll feel a bit more straight in yerself, I reckon. 'Spect yer 'ead fair beating, too. This'll sort it.'

Bobs handed him a thick-cut sandwich, and Tom crammed in a mouthful, then gulped down the tea that Bobs also gave him, thinking he'd never felt so hungry in his life. He took another mouthful of sandwich and then a gulp of tea, and again, and again, until both were finished. Bobs was back at his books, but came and took the plate and mug. 'Yer feeling less snarly, is yer?'

Tom had to laugh. 'Yes, much less snarly. I'm sorry,' he called to Ma Porter.

'Ah well, can't do enough for our lasses.'

Bobs said, 'They saved our Jimmy when 'e fell in the cut, yer see; they jumped in, got themselves perishing, unhooking him from the propeller deep down. They pumped his chest, they did, to get t'water out. And your lass paid, so she did, for Jimmy in hospital, but she ain't got money now. 'Er ma put a stop to it when they 'ad a barney about something 'er mum said to some young bloke that were a lie, or so the cut talk says. 'Spect that was yer, cos yer a young bloke and we're right miffed with you for not seein' 'er when yer said yer would.' He sucked his pencil, looked at his exercise book, then up at Tom. 'She and Polly wanted Saul's lad, Joe, to read, yer see, and Jimmy too, so they does me as well. Gives us opterns, or some such.'

Tom's mind was clearer now, his head more settled and the snarly was on its way out, he thought, as he tried to concentrate on what Bobs had said. And as he slowly disentangled the words, he found that his heart was full.

Bobs repeated to himself, frowning, 'Gives us opterns? Opsins?'

Tom thought a moment, then said, 'Gives you options, I reckon you mean.'

Bobs looked up and grinned. 'That's the one. I knows what it means, but can't rightly remember 'ow it goes. Anyway, them lasses said just t'other day that they 'ad wanted our Jimmy to like books, and to read, cos they'd saved 'is life, so they must take some share of respo ...' The boy stopped, and tried again. 'Responil ...'

Tom swallowed – 'responsibility', yes, that was the word. He didn't speak because he wasn't sure his voice would work, knowing now that Verity was a girl who had become a woman, one who deserved to be loved; and it must be by him, because his love for her was roaring again. What's more, it was more than time he behaved like a man, not the boy who'd believe her mother, when he should have known his Verity.

Bobs asked, 'What d'ya reckon the word is?'

Tom stared at him, brought back to the cabin. 'I reckon it's "responsibility". It means to take care of, to have a duty towards.'

Bobs looked at him and then at his notepad. 'Yes, "responsibility" sounds right fer what they did fer Jimmy; they saved 'im, so 'ad responsibility to do their best for 'im. All right, Mister, yer does know yer words, so yer can 'elp. Be less for 'em to do.'

Tom checked his watch, seething not with pain or anger, or self-pity, but with regret and impatience. 'Will we catch them up, d'you reckon?'

Bobs shrugged, handing him the notepad. 'We will or we won't. All I know is I'll be out o' the warmth afore we reach the lock, pedalling me legs off along the towpath to get there t'open oop the gates, so me uncle doesn't have to wait. Have a look at these words. I ticked the ones I knows and left t'others.'

Tom looked at the words. 'Jasmine' was unticked. He only knew the plant because it had climbed the wall in Verity's walled garden at Howard House. He could see it now, white stars on the fresh green leaves, and he remembered its glorious scent. The terraced house he had come from didn't have a garden, just a yard, and there was only an outside privy. He and his mum had shared it with his grandparents and an auntie, all of whom made sure he did his lessons and used the library, and pronounced his words properly. All the time they were saving money to give him an apprenticeship in the garage so that he could make something of himself. They were all dead now. Bombed to smithereens, like the ARP's wife.

He stared at the list of words, now out of focus, as he realised the courage Verity had shown to cast her lot in with a common chauffeur and look forward to a life over their own garage. How could they have doubted one another? How could he have carried his doubt for so much longer than her?

Bobs said, 'Would yer like to listen to me read, Mister?'

Tom nodded. 'That I would, lad, very much.' But what he really thought was that Verity had to be at Cowley, she had to have received the message and she must forgive him, though he wasn't sure if he could forgive himself.

Chapter 4

Tuesday 28 March – just before midday at Cowley lock

Verity pulled down Mrs Holmes's gift of a pink, blue, green and black striped woollen hat, knitted out of odds and ends. Once it covered her ears, she tugged the grey blanket she'd whipped off her cross-bed more tightly around her as she sat alongside Polly on the cabin roof. They had moored up south of Cowley lock. 'Did you ask Sylvia to join us?'

Polly shook her head solemnly, her arms crossed. 'Oh no, I sat here with you, staring across at the beech trees, deliberately ignoring her.'

She leaned into Verity, who was forced to laugh, before elbowing her away, muttering, 'Get off me, you lump.'

Polly sighed, pulling her hat well down, too. 'Of course I asked Sylvia, you daft thing, and because we're strapped abreast, she could easily hop, skip and jump over to us, but she's reading something and said she was quite happy. I have to say, though, she did add that she wished Sid had been more explicit in his message, so that we knew what package we had to hang about for.'

Verity laughed again. 'Did she really say "happy"? Our Sylvia? Oh, if only she was. We're failing her somehow.' She felt herself struggling for the words, which Polly supplied.

'I know. Sylvia seems almost tormented and, if not that, then preoccupied and quite beyond our reach. Is there any more we can do to get close and be a real threesome, or will we go on being rebuffed, losing our temper and making everything worse?'

Verity shrugged, then winced, as a wave of nausea overcame her. Why had she drunk so much last night? Well, she knew why, but talking about Sylvia stopped the ridiculous thoughts of the non-existent Tom – because that was what he must be, now. A great big nothing. She replied, knowing that dearest Polly was diverting her from that great big nothing, so she would play the game, 'Polly, lovely girl, we've tried everything, and apart from changing ourselves completely, I don't know what we can do. I think we just need to try and be more patient, until what-ever is churning inside Sylvia settles. Unless, my fine friend, we are simply not her cup of tea at all; deeply unlikable, in fact? Well, we can't please everyone, can we?'

Polly leaned into her again. 'We most certainly can't. The fact is that sometimes people just have to make up their own mind about others.'

The two girls looked across the wide stretch of water that lay at the foot of the lock. Verity always felt there was a tranquillity to this particular stretch of the cut, lined as it was with tall beech trees, shrouded now in a freezing mist. In the autumn the leaves shivered on gracious branches, before falling and lying like a cloak on the water. Soon it would be spring, and presumably the fresh green young-sters would shiver, in just the same way. She didn't know – none of them did – as they had only joined the scheme in the early autumn of 1943.

A sudden gust made Verity shiver too, but if the breeze got up, it would lift the mist. She dragged her blanket more tightly around her shoulders. At least the snow had stopped. 'Oh, come on, Sid, get yourself in gear; chop-chop, as Bet would say.' She muttered, 'Bet's miles ahead – everyone is – while we're here, sitting like a couple of grannies chewing the fat. I hope the blasted water isn't icing up around us, and I hope even more, Polly Holmes, that this little nudge about people making up their minds isn't some sort of homily about the vagaries of Tom Brown and the need to accept his obvious decision; which I do, really I do. I just wish I hadn't drunk so much. This hangover is making me want to head down the river to my doom, like the Lady of Shalott.'

Polly was dragging on her gloves, but her fore-finger emerged through one of the many snagged holes. 'Damn. I'll have to darn it.' She hunched into her blanket. 'You, my girl, wouldn't look anything like as gracious as that rather tiresome Shalott lady who was so bothered by curses; and neither do we have a punt that you can lie in, looking elegant in your death-throes.'

Verity raised an eyebrow. 'If you've quite finished …' She picked up *The Times*, looked at the crossword and then gave up.

Polly said, 'Sid wouldn't be sending your scarf, would he? That's absurd; anyway the flyboat boys said it was something essential.'

Verity leaned forward to check on Sylvia, who had jumped from the roof of the butty onto its counter. The boats nudged one another. Dog barked from the motor cabin, then settled again. Verity called, 'You all right, Sylvia?'

'No, because this is quite ridiculous, and I'm going into the warmth of the cabin. Why on earth you two always leave something wherever we go, I do not know. If it's not your scarf, it's your hat, or your newspaper. Sid must have had enough, and thought to teach you a lesson. There's a war on, you know. People are relying on us, but what do you care, scattering yourself all over the place.' She slammed the cabin doors behind her.

Verity sat back. 'Crikey, that's the last time I stick my head above the parapet for a while. But she's got a point. How's your cold, by the way, Polly? Sylvia's seems better; she's not sniffing so much and I gather, from the shouting, that her throat's no longer sore.'

Polly laughed and checked her watch. 'Mine's on the wane, too, and I haven't a clue as to how long we should wait. It's midday now, and we want to get through the Berkhamsted-to-Tring locks, and even try to make it as far as Fenny Stratford by dusk. Should we give it another half hour?'

Verity thought of Sid, and his kindness to them, and despite her hammering head she felt a qualm. 'But if we let him down, I'd feel bad. Perhaps he owes someone a few bottles in return for a favour or two, and they've called it in.'

Polly waved to a pair of passing narrowboats heading for the opened lock and called, as their wash rocked them slightly, 'How do, Steerer Wilkins.'

The steerer waved back. Verity said to Polly, trying to make herself more comfortable on the roof, 'On the other hand, if we don't go soon, you'll not catch up with Saul, or will he wait at Fenny?'

She knew the answer before Polly spoke. 'Granfer and Saul will try and keep to the schedule, come what may, or they'll feel they're letting down the war effort. We'll catch up with them south of the Braunston Tunnel if we rattle on. So what shall we do – wait an hour?'

While she was speaking, Sylvia had clambered out of the butty cabin and stood glowering, arms crossed, shivering. 'I've banked up my firebox, wiped the pots and I think we should only give Sid's package another few minutes. Why on earth did he insist on us waiting at Cowley, when whoever is bringing it could have caught us up anywhere?'

Verity and Polly looked at one another. Verity's hangover was banging and she couldn't think straight. Polly said nothing for several moments, but then it was as though a thought had occurred to her. She started to speak, but then stopped. She began again, sounding preoccupied. 'But ... but ... Oh, I don't know, Sid might need us to take the parcel somewhere just past Cowley? If it *is* a parcel, that is.'

Sylvia tapped her foot, dragging her blanket ever tighter, and puffing out breath so full of irritation that it positively billowed into the ether, slapping her hand on the cabin roof in time with every word. 'Don't be silly – what else can it be? An essential package, the flyboys said. Why on earth can't the steerer bringing it take it on? The whole thing is absurd, and I insist we should leave within ten minutes.' The girl stopped. Verity promised herself she'd never let even a smidgeon of mild pass her lips ever again, but then Sylvia yelled once more, 'The flyboat boys probably got the message wrong. Package, indeed.'

Verity winced. And Polly's shouted reply to Sylvia didn't help. 'We will stay as long as it takes, Sylvia. We owe Sid; he took Bet to the hospital when she had pneumonia, which was before your time. So is that quite clear? We wait, because it's what Sid wants.'

Verity pulled at Polly's arm. 'Calm down. Sylvia's right, and will you both stop making so much noise?'

Polly turned on her. 'You can shut up, too. Are you deaf as well as hungover? I've just said: we owe Sid and therefore we wait. Go inside your cabin, Sylvia, and keep warm. You, too, Verity, if you're going to grizzle.'

Verity felt quite sick with shock as Polly slipped from the roof and stood by the tiller, staring down the cut, trying to see through the deepening mist. Verity muttered, 'Well, someone got out of bed the wrong side this morning, if I'm not very much mistaken.' For some reason she wanted to cry, which was ridiculous. She'd cried all the tears she was going to shed – ever – last night. But Polly was her loving friend, one who hardly ever turned on her. 'Polly, I'm sorry,' she murmured, joining her at the stern of the counter, but Polly hushed her, holding up her hand for silence.

Together they looked down the cut, the trees motionless in the bitter mist, snow still on the hedge-rows, and somewhere there was the cry of a fox. They heard a motor, but realised it was approaching downhill, from the north. It was Steerer North. Once through the lock, he tipped his hat at the girls. 'How do. 'Aving a breather, is yer?'

'Something like that,' Polly yelled.

Verity wished with all her heart she'd whisper. Ma North waved from the butty, *Burton*. As the pair passed, the smell of rabbit stew wafted from the butty's cabin, and Verity knew that she would have to eat soon or her head would burst. Ma North called while doing her mending, the tiller under her elbow, 'You still waiting fer Sid's package then, as we heard yer was?'

Sylvia barked, 'Yes, and it's wasting time.'

Polly smoothed the moment. 'Still waiting, thanks, Mrs North, but we'll have to move on soon.' She and Verity had become used to the boaters knowing all the news almost before it had been created.

The boats pat-pattered past. Their kettle, and the dipper which collected the water from the cut for washing, both of which were kept on the roof, had probably been painted by Saul, and sure enough there was his special red flower, and the tiny blue bird. 'He's such a good artist,' Verity said.

Polly nodded. 'He is indeed.'

Verity murmured, 'Tom carved wood, you know. He had a passion for it, said that each piece of wood grain is different. I wonder if he still carves? Not that it's any of my business.' Yes – that's what she must remind herself.

Her thoughts were brought to an abrupt end by Sylvia, who almost shouted, 'For heaven's sake, you two, we must get on. And just look at you, Verity, all pale and sweating, and I expect you stink of stale beer. If last night has taught you anything, it is surely that it's time to stop turning to drink when something goes wrong. And think of your lungs, not to mention your poor wretched livers – and I mean you, too, Polly. They must be in a frightful state, with your smoking, and your pint of mild. And what about your souls?'

Verity and Polly spun round. 'Souls?' Polly queried.

Sylvia flushed, her hand up. 'It's just a saying one of my teachers used to trot out. Forget I said it.'

At that moment Verity heard a motor approaching from the south. 'Hush, is this it?'

Sylvia and Polly peered down the cut, too. Dog barked from the cabin. 'Quiet, Dog,' called Polly.

They watched the pair emerge from the mist, the smoke from the chimneys of the motor and the butty hanging in the air. Verity couldn't make out which boats they were, and there was no sign of them slowing. 'All right,' she called to Sylvia. 'We'll go, if this isn't the delivery.'

Sylvia said, 'But we'll miss the lock if we let them through first.'

Polly was adamant. 'We're not scrabbling to get in front of them; it's rude, and that's an end to it. We'll wait until they stop or not. If it's "not", we'll set off up north in their wake.'

She dragged out her cigarettes as Sylvia said, 'But—'

Polly snapped, 'Oh, do shut up, Sylvia, just for once in your life.'

Verity lit their cigarettes. Sylvia was taking up position at the butty tiller, her face down towards her knees. 'Will we go on up north on short tow or abreast?'

Verity could now make out Steerer Porter approaching on *Oxford*, with Mrs Porter on short tow behind. 'Let's do the same as the Porters; the damned ice has built up between the wall and the gates, and they didn't open properly for the Norths.' She raised her voice. 'Sylvia, perhaps you'd get us set up for towing, please.'

Steerer Porter, Jimmy's dad, was slowing. They heard, 'Toot-toot.' Then again, 'Toot-toot.'

Polly stepped forward, replying with three toots, peering even more intently through the mist, and sounding relieved and excited. 'At last.'

The *Oxford* came alongside, and Steerer Porter pointed to the bank. Polly nodded. *Oxford* and *Cambridge* steered in. Mrs Porter called as she passed. ''Ow do – we got Sid's bit of doings.'

Verity yelled, once the Porters had stopped, tight against the bank, 'I'll go. I could do with some exercise.' She hopped onto the bank and trotted forward, along the length of the *Marigold*, keeping to the grass at the edge of the towpath, where there was less hidden ice beneath the snow. She waved as she ran past Mrs Porter on the butty counter. Mrs Porter called something, but Verity carried on, barely able to see Steerer Porter on the *Oxford* through the thickening mist. Her head was protesting, but Steerer Porter would want to get away before someone else pinched his place in the lock.

She reached the *Oxford*. Jimmy must have been on the roof, because his book lay next to the empty chain. He was probably hunkering in the warmth of the cabin. Steerer Porter was laughing as he jerked

74

his head back to the *Cambridge*. 'Ma's got t'package, di'n't you 'ear her call?'

'Oh, sorry,' Verity said. She turned, cupped her hands round her mouth and shouted, 'Mrs Porter, ask your runabout, young Bobs, to put the parcel on the towpath, and I'll pick it up, so you can get straight off. Sid's addressed it, I hope?' She was trotting back as Bobs flew along the top planks of the butty and leapt off the prow counter onto the bank, heading for the lock. 'Hey, where's the parcel?' she yelled.

'See for yerself,' he shouted over his shoulder. 'Back yonder.'

Verity ran on as *Oxford* and *Cambridge* pulled away, seeing through the mist an old man emerging on two sticks in a long coat. But there was a bag or grip, or something like that, on the bank. So that was what all the fuss was about. She trotted on, keeping to the verge. She heard a shout, looked over her shoulder, but it was all right – Bobs was on the top of the rise, shouting to Steerer Porter to budge up in the lock, as he shut the gates behind the pair.

She swung round and almost collided with the old boy. She swerved, skidded on the icy path, almost fell, but was caught by a pair of strong arms. All she heard was the clatter of his walking sticks as they rattled to the ground, but then his shout, 'Bloody hell.' They skidded, arms flailing, and finally fell together in a tangle of limbs.

For a moment the breath was whacked from Verity's body, and as she struggled to rise, something heavy and unyielding weighted her left leg. Beside her the old boy levered himself up on his elbow and groaned, 'This isn't how I thought it would go, Verity.'

She fell back and stared up at his face – *his* face. She shrieked, 'Tom?'

'The very same,' he said quietly. 'I tried to telephone, but I couldn't get Button A to work.'

His eyes were the same, those brown eyes. His face was thinner, his hair short now and free of the infantry beret, which had fallen onto her chest. 'There are other telephone boxes,' she said, sounding calm, though she could barely breathe with confusion, joy and, finally, hope.

'I know, and you're right, I could have walked on to another telephone box, but I'm a fool. However, there was no need to barge me, Your Ladyship. It's not as though we're playing rugby.' He was laughing at her. Laughing, after all this time, all this agony. Your Ladyship? Was Tom sneering? Is this why he'd come?

She shoved him away, kicking her legs free of the weight, whatever it was, and scrambled to her feet. 'It's not funny – none of it is,' she yelled down at him, seeing him pale visibly and his lips become thin. 'You, Tom Brown, left me waiting for you, breaking my heart all over again. And how dare you call me "Your Ladyship"? I've never been like that with you. Never. And what's more, I've whacked my bum, and my head. And I have a hangover. In fact everything about you and me hurts, so why don't you just bugger off.'

She didn't know where the words were coming from, but they were loud and strong, until suddenly her voice broke. She'd hurt him, and he'd hurt her, and here Tom was, lying on the ground, and how could he laugh as though it was a game? Well, it damn well wasn't, any more than it had been a game to love him. He was as bad as her mother. And why the hell had Sid said it was a package, instead of a damned great lump of a soldier who couldn't be bothered to walk to a phone box and just thought it was funny?

It was then that she realised sweat was beading Tom's forehead and he was groaning. He was also half lying on the walking sticks. Walking sticks? Why? He rolled slowly onto his back. Then she saw the cast on his lower leg.

'Give me a chance, Verity. I'm sorry, but after all this time, we crash and bring one another down, and it's just so typical of the whole bloody mess. But look, I'm not laughing now, and especially not in my heart.'

Verity stared from him to the *Marigold* and *Horizon* as she tried to sort out – what?

She said, 'Why are you here? Did you come just to take the mickey? You have to tell me why you didn't walk to the next phone box. It's only one leg you've hurt, after all.'

Tom eased himself up onto his elbow. 'Oh, Verity, you're right, but I'm a fool and I think I wanted to hurt you. I don't want to do that any more. I've got things clear in my head, at last.'

'Well, good for you. That just leaves me then, doesn't it, and nothing's clear for me.' Part of her wanted to hold him, kiss him, but Tom had wanted to hurt her last night, so why had that changed today?

He looked up at her. 'I'm sorry, dearest Verity, really I am. I missed you so, and when I thought you didn't love me, it broke my heart and I was just so angry, upset and stupid. Yes, utterly stupid. But you didn't wait, either, though I—'

'Tom Brown, I can't wait – not doing this job,' she interrupted him, sinking onto her knees next to him, pain and anger tearing at her love; because yes, love was there as well. 'I have work to do, but you *could* have limped along to the next phone. But you say you wanted to hurt me, and those feelings don't change overni—'

It was his turn to interrupt. 'I know, and I am so sorry. Apart from anything else, I couldn't think straight when I arrived because I had the headache from hell, and felt – as one of the boaters said – all snarly, until Ma Porter fed me. It was then that I started—'

She stared at his beautiful face: a headache? Was that all: a headache, for heaven's sake? 'Well, I've got a headache too,' she interrupted.

He grinned. 'Mine was because I hadn't eaten for so long, but yours was because you drank too many beers. It was because of me, and I was trying to say, as well, that I realised—'

Verity drew back her arm to slap him. 'The arrogance, the bloody cheek, how dare—'

Polly grabbed her. 'Hey, hey, what's happening? Is this who I guessed the package would be? Why's Tom down there on the ground? Why on earth were you trying to slap him?'

Tom lay there, shivering and as white as a sheet. He tried to rise up from his elbow, but instead fell back on the ground, his head resting on the snow and ice. Sylvia loomed over them now.

'What's Tom said? Why are you hitting him?'

Verity shouted, snatching her arm from Polly, 'No one's hitting anyone.'

Tom groaned and half laughed. 'Oh Lord, I was just being bloody stupid, trying to say Verity mustn't drink because of me, and I tried to say that I have heard what your life is like, so I knew why you couldn't wait, and how I ... It just came out all wrong.' He closed his eyes, shook his head and moaned. 'Oh God, what a fool.'

Sylvia said, 'He must be drunk to be lying there – no wonder he and Verity get on well. Let's get him upright and get him to the lock-keeper, who can deal with him. Look, there's a pair coming through from the north, now the Porters have gone on. We can grab the lock when they're through.'

It was bedlam and Verity shook her head, yelling, 'Will you all shut up. Yes, this is Tom – the package – and he's on the ground because we bumped into one another and slipped, then crashed. If I'd known it was him, I'd have barged him into the cut.'

'Why's he laughing then?' Sylvia shouted back. Sure enough, Tom was.

'Because he's Tom, that's why. And it isn't funny at all.' Verity's head was pounding, but she wasn't going to say that or she'd get another lecture about drinking from Sylvia, and probably from Tom as well.

'I don't know why I'm laughing, when it's all gone so wrong and I just keep spouting nonsense. And I can't even stand up without help, so if you just left me here I wouldn't blame you.'

Polly was on her knees now, on the other side of Tom, feeling his forehead. 'He's clammy. He might be laughing because he's in shock from the fall, and he might be talking rubbish for the same reason. Does your leg hurt, Tom?' She was bending over him, speaking slowly.

He raised himself slightly, made a grab for Verity's hand and looked at her fiercely. 'I should bloody say so, but no more than it hurt before; and no more than my heart, if she won't hear me out. I've been an utter bloody fool for months, and again just now, but I can't grab my thoughts because I feel really odd.' He struggled to sit and, when he did, he turned to Polly and Sylvia. 'I reckon she took me down to keep me with her – or so I hope.' He was shivering, sweating and his breathing was shallow and fast.

Sylvia frowned and looked at Polly. 'Shouldn't we get the lock-keeper to call an ambulance? If he's not drunk, he's delirious.'

Verity felt his forehead, wanting to hold Tom to her, but she didn't know what he was really thinking, so she wouldn't; it was too late. Tom tightened his grip on her hand. 'Verity, and you girls, I'm not delirious, or drunk. I've never been more clear-headed in my life, when I think of how much I love this woman. I'll be all right, if I can just stop lying about on this bloody freezing towpath, saying such bloody silly things, and get into a cabin where it's warm. In addition, ladies, if the facilities are a bucket, please help me to my feet and I will find a bush, because I need to pee. Sorry, so sorry, but I really do. Then I'm not leaving her, not my Verity, until I've had my say; and then you can throw me out with the scraps, if that's what she decides.' He lay back suddenly, paler still, if that was possible, trying to catch his breath.

Polly raised an eyebrow at Verity, who was running Tom's words through her mind, feeling the strength of his hand and hoping – oh, how she hoped – that he meant every word he said. But how could she know? Finally Polly said, 'Oh, for goodness' sake, we can't leave him here, it makes the place look untidy. Tom's coming with us. And shut up, Verity, before you even start. We've got to get under way.'

Verity made herself nod and say, 'All right, let's get him to a bush, then on board. You can come through the lock with us, Tom, and we can leave you near a station. Can't have you going AWOL.' She felt angry, confused and unwilling to let love draw her back into misery. 'Sorry to be frank, but that's the situation. There's a war on and I, well, I don't know … I just don't know.'

Tom tried to lever himself up. 'The whole of the cut has been telling me I've been a fool. And now I've made it worse, but I mean it when I say I love you, Verity, from the bottom of my heart.' He sank back down.

Sylvia came round to the back of him and grasped Tom under the armpits. 'Come on, let's get him up, for goodness' sake.'

Polly and Verity hauled him to his feet. For a moment Verity thought he was going to pass out, and she wanted to hold him close and cover his face with kisses.

He hung his head, panting. 'My sticks, if you wouldn't mind.'

Sylvia gathered them up and placed them in his hands. 'You need gloves,' she said. 'Polly's mum knits them, and we have lots. Incidentally, since no one else has done it, let me tell you that the dark-haired one is Polly; I'm Sylvia, the newest on the boat; and you know Verity. Well, of course you do.'

Tom straightened, blowing out his breath. Starlings flew overhead. The girls walked him through the frost-spiked grass as far as some bushes a yard or so from the towpath. They walked away and, when he was done, led the way to the boat, walking on the safer verge; and somehow they levered him on board and into the motor cabin. Dog set up a great deal of barking, the hair rising along her back, but within seconds she seemed to come to a decision and her tail was wagging as Tom sat on the side-bed. The girls crowded the eighteen-inch aisle, until Verity reluctantly sat next to Tom, to make more room.

'Is there water in that bowl?' he whispered, nodding towards the painted bowl on the range rest. 'And may I have just a sip of water?'

Sylvia looked relieved. 'Oh yes, to both. Always as well to wash hands after ... well, after the ...'

Verity and Polly sighed and looked at one another. Sylvia ground to a halt. Polly filled a mug from the jug and handed it to Tom, as Sylvia turned, reached forward, slipped soap into the water and placed the bowl, like a benediction, on Tom's lap. He drank, washed and dried his hands as Sylvia stood over him and then she whipped the bowl up onto the counter, slamming the cabin doors behind her.

As one, they listened to the splash and then the scrape of the kettle on the roof of the cabin. Within minutes Sylvia reappeared, bringing the cold in with her, and replaced the refilled bowl on the range rest.

'Thanks, Sylvia,' Tom said.

Verity watched his strong hands, which had held the mug. Hands that she had loved. Did she still?

Polly said, 'Are you going to explain about the ins and outs of the bucket, Sylvia, or shall we leave that to Verity?' Sylvia looked appalled. Polly said, 'We'll designate that to Verity then, but should we get on, girls? The lock awaits. Tom, you must wear gloves if you come up top. Verity can see to that, though perhaps take 'em off before the sergeant sees them, especially if she can only find the pink ones; and, looking at her thunderous face, she might just hunt for those especially.'

Verity forced a smile and muttered, 'I'll go further, and find the striped ones.'

Tom laughed tentatively, searching Verity's face. After a moment she smiled, longing to reach out and run her finger down his cheek, but she couldn't. How much did he really care? Dog had rested her head on his lap and Tom was stroking her, as some colour returned to his face. Verity had forgotten how gentle he was. Polly and Sylvia both hesitated.

Tom, looking exhausted, murmured, 'I will wait until Verity feels like talking, but until then I'm staying on board. Sorry, all of you.' He leaned forward on his walking sticks, looking pale, sweaty and drawn, the muscles working in his jaw. 'And thank you.' He looked at each of them in turn, and they nodded. His gaze returned to Verity. 'I've missed you so much and thought so many things, and when I saw you from the bridge I thought it was a mirage. I carry your letters.' He patted his greatcoat. 'Always. I just didn't know how I really felt, and what I believed, until now. I had a talk with an ARP war—'

Sylvia interrupted. 'We need to catch the lock.'

Polly echoed, 'We really do. So, Verity, I'll start up the engine and then go on to manage the lock; you steer, and you can talk to Tom from the counter. He really should stay in the warmth of the cabin.'

Verity headed for the counter, but Tom reached out and held her back, just for a moment. 'I'm not going out with the scraps until we're done.' He paused and went on, 'We were like a couple of children, that we so easily believed the worst of one another. I know, from all the things I've heard over the last few hours, that I'll be lucky if you feel we could go forward. You are so special and I love you so much. I should have come through wind, snow and fire yesterday evening, and from now on, I will.'

He dug his hands in his greatcoat pockets and a look of surprise crossed his face. He said, 'I forgot – I have your scarf. It smells of dirt, and "Joy". It should be bottled, because it's intoxicating.' He held it up.

Verity said, 'Ah, so that's real reason you came, just to keep Sid's bar tidy?' She found herself smiling, but it was superficial.

He laughed. 'Yes, all this way, just to return your scarf.' This is how they had always been, she thought; joking, laughing, but that had been out of love. Had she been too fragile on the bank, too heartbroken, too scared, too angry, to recognise his love? He handed the scarf to her, their hands touched and she could have wept, but was it out of love, or the loss of love?

She climbed out of the cabin onto the counter. The engine was ticking over. She put it into gear, and *Marigold* jerked as it took up the butty weight and they glided slowly towards the open lock. It was then that Verity realised Tom was standing on the bottom step, climbing up crabwise, dragging his plastered leg behind him.

'May I?' he said.

She nodded. 'You may, but you'd be better in the warm.'

'No, because then I am further from you.'

She ignored that. 'Just perch on the roof, if you can lever yourself up.' He tried unsuccessfully, so she got her shoulder behind and beneath, shoving him up.

Tom said, 'What happens now?'

She deliberately misunderstood him. 'I'm going to edge *Marigold* through the open lower gates of the lock, right up to the sill, having slipped the tow-rope off this stud, just before we enter.' She pointed to the stud behind her. 'Sylvia will then glide the butty alongside us, into the lock, using the momentum that has been built up.' She pointed ahead. Tom eased himself off the roof, and she snapped, 'Just stay in one place, Tom, you need to rest.'

He ignored her and, leaning on one of his sticks, stood over the stud. 'I want to help you, so please let me, Verity. Tell me when to throw off the tow.'

He was standing close. Their eyes locked and she saw the pain, and the longing. She dragged herself back to the job in hand. 'Now, if you would.'

They entered the lock and the butty came alongside. Verity cut the engine and they glided ahead until they nudged the sill. The frost-slimed walls loomed on either side, though somehow the mist hadn't found its way down here. Polly and Jack, the lock-keeper, closed the gates behind them; gates that had a bank of broken ice holding them away from the walls.

Polly then dashed to the top gates. Tom stood beside Verity, with the tiller between them. Verity said, 'Polly is using her windlass to wind open the paddles, or sluices, you might call them. See the water gushing in? It is lifting us to the higher level of the cut. Bit like a staircase, I suppose, each step taking us all the way up the rising ground – or down.'

'Remarkable,' Tom muttered as the boats rose.

'Yes,' Verity agreed. 'She will then cycle on to the next lock.'

Once they reached the top level, Jack the lock-keeper notated the docket Polly held out, then pushed it back into her pocket. Verity heard him call to Polly, 'Got an 'itch-'iker, I see.'

Polly laughed. 'We have indeed, but we'll drop him overboard if he doesn't behave.'

Jack said, 'I 'eard he didn't walk to the next phone box? But reckon 'im and 'is leg slipping about in the snow would make it difficult. Difficult, but not impossible.'

Tom grimaced at Verity, who shook her head, surprised that she found herself wanting to defend him. She said quietly, 'The cut is like a tannoy; everyone hears about everything, but they don't discuss it until they know and trust you.' At that moment Dog leapt up the cabin steps and onto the roof. 'Go on, Tom, she said, 'join your new friend. You need that rest.'

Tom managed on his own as Polly and Jack opened the lock gates and Verity started up the *Marigold*, easing out onto the cut, attaching the butty's tow-rope over the stud, and feeling the jerk as *Horizon* fell in behind them.

'You girls are like a well-oiled machine, but I knew that, because I learned a lot on Ma Porter's butty. That's what helped to change my thinking. And yes, it was as quick as that,' Tom murmured, and Verity saw him looking at her, not just with love, but also respect.

Chapter 5

Tuesday 28 March – early afternoon, leaving Cowley lock

Verity steered the *Marigold* while Polly cycled along the towpath, lock-wheeling as they steadily climbed towards Watford. Verity had tried to make Tom return to the warmth of the cabin, but he had refused. 'I need to be here – freezing with you – because at some stage we, or rather you, will find the words, and I don't want to miss the moment.'

She realised, as the miles passed, that Tom was more his own man now, someone who would never work for people like the Clements again. Even as she thought this and they passed other pairs heading south, dog-walkers on the towpath, a few fishermen freezing in this weather and the backs of terraced houses, warehouses and factories, she said nothing. She simply steered, or watched the geese flying over, or studied the bridges for children, although it was still too cold for them to come out to gob them. The mist was still thickening.

Why had her father not stopped her mother's interference? Verity wondered. Why had he said, last time she went home with Polly, to force the truth from her mother, 'Don't give up on us, darling'? But then he had done nothing to make her want to be with them.

As they drew alongside Watford, Verity slipped into the cabin to plate up the rabbit and bacon stew, which should keep them all going. There was enough for Tom, especially as she had baked potatoes on the top shelf; potatoes bought off one of the allotment sales tables set up along the cut. In the next lock she handed a plate to Sylvia, who waited on the butty alongside, and Polly jumped down from the lock edge, shoved Tom up and ate her stew on the roof with him, while Verity forked hers, standing by the tiller.

No one spoke, just as she and Tom had not really yet spoken. Verity made herself concentrate on the bits of bacon, not the rabbit, because she was as sick of rabbit as Polly. Would Saul or Thomo have managed to trap pheasants on this trip, as well as the rabbits? Oh, she did hope so, although she knew that she shouldn't complain about her long-eared friends, as it kept the girls' meagre rations ticking over. Aloud, she wondered if the mist would ever lift, or would it still be here in the summer?

Sylvia called across from the butty, 'Don't be absurd – it's only the last of the winter.'

Tom scraped clean his enamel plate. 'Ah, but like an Indian summer, a late winter can be harder than at any time in the preceding months, and sometimes snow even falls in April.'

By the time Verity finished her stew, the lock was up to the level of the top cut. Time to open the gates. 'I'll do it,' she declared.

Tom shook his head. 'Please don't. Polly, would you do a few more locks? It's time Verity tried to talk, and me, too – it really is.'

Polly nodded and handed her empty plate to Verity, but said to Tom, 'I won't have Verity hurt again. No one on this cut will. What happened isn't your fault – far from it, apart from letting her down at the all-important meeting at Sid's – but it isn't her fault, either, and you should know that. You have both been manoeuvred by the Clements, but you are adults, so sort it out. I will be watching, and into the cut you will go, Tom Brown, if you so much as say one word out of turn.'

Sylvia said, 'Quite right, Polly. We won't have her hurt, but neither will we have you hurt, Tom.'

Polly and Verity looked at one another and smiled. Were they becoming a real team of three, after all?

Once free of the lock, they headed along the cut towards yet another lock, but Verity said, 'Unlike you, Tom, I'm not ready to talk, or listen. Not quite.' He just nodded as they continued to climb the multitude of locks alongside Cassiobury Park and eased himself from the roof, collecting the plates and opening the cabin doors.

'I'll wash these, and make a cuppa for us all. Sylvia and Polly can have theirs in the next lock. I'm getting the hang of it all now. But why do you spend so much time looking at the bridges we come to? Do you think you'll see another convoy of soldier boys?'

'You might well find out why, young Tom; and no, it's not to see soldiers, though it's hard to miss them. Something is building, we think.'

Tom crabbed down the steps, washed the plates and cutlery and then made tea. He carried two mugs in each hand, and placed Polly's and Sylvia's on the cabin roof as the boats exited a lock and set out for the next. 'I'll give them a call once we're in the next lock, but for now I have things to say, even if you haven't. How about it?'

Verity nodded, though she was scared. She pressed her elbow against the tiller, feeling the engine's vibration as usual. Yes, as usual. She sipped her tea, and that tasted weak, as usual. She prepared herself to listen.

'I have loved you since the day I arrived at Howard House, Verity.' Tom was leaning against the cabin, looking at her intently. 'It wasn't my place to feel that way, but neither was it yours to love a chauffeur. But somehow we came together, and I never once felt that you thought you were superior.'

Verity shook her head. 'Of course I didn't.'

He held up his hand. 'Let me make an idiot of myself once more, and then you can tell me to go to hell.'

She nodded.

Tom continued, 'There's no "of course" about it. And your mother was right, you know; it *was*, or is, inappropriate.'

Verity knew he was speaking the truth. Her friends, if they were ever such, had thought so, as had everyone else, because where would they 'fit', and what would they do, out of their 'places'? In her heart she had felt it too, sometimes, but when she was with Tom she always knew they'd find a way. The only ones who seemed to understand were Rogers, the butler, and Mrs B, the cook; though understanding wasn't agreeing, and they often looked as though worry consumed them.

She inched the tiller over, as a pair passed on the way south with a full load. Coal from the Coventry coalfields for a factory? Or wood for Aylesbury, perhaps? Who knew.

Tom went on, 'You wouldn't listen to your mother's concerns, and I didn't encourage you to do so. I think your mother felt she had to do something to end it, foreseeing disaster – for everyone's sake, and not just hers.' He examined his hands in their striped gloves, as though looking for inspiration. He continued, 'But, dearest Verity, if your mother hadn't lied to you, and to me, by cooking up a slightly different story for each of us, I don't know what would have happened. Would we have petered out, or simply continued in an impossible situation? The results of your mother's behaviour changed me for the better. I am more of a man now, more able to see clearly, to understand others. What's more, I can see why your mother did what she did.'

Verity was listening so carefully that she forgot to breathe.

Tom continued, 'It's given us a fresh start, if we want one, because we've moved on in our separate ways and grown up, but I truly don't believe we've grown apart. I've made mistakes. I've been idiotic and miserable, blaming others. I've been cruel, childish. Yes, of course I should have crawled to that telephone box, and I knew that then and know it now. But please know that I love you, beyond all doubt. I love you more than anything else in my life – in my world – and always will; and I like and admire you, too. You are here, in my heart, if you want me, and even if you don't. You are lodged there, and no matter where the army takes me, there you will remain. We're two adults, two independent beings, free to decide who we love. And I have decided.' He stopped, then spread his hands. 'That's all I have to say.'

Verity felt it was as though he was describing her 'path' as well as his own and, thinking of her mother, she imagined a daughter that she herself might have one day: wouldn't she want what she thought was best for her daughter? Yes, probably; but she knew that whatever Tom said, she, Verity Clement, would never be as cruel to her own child as her mother had been to her, with her sharp tongue and her lies, which had left her heartbroken. There had to have been another way.

Tom was leaning against the cabin, looking at her. Verity said nothing as she sorted out her thoughts.

Finally she held up her hands. 'This is who I am now – dirty, calloused, tough. My friends are these people.' She waved ahead and behind. 'My absolute friend is Polly, whose twin brother, Will, died in a tank in North Africa. She loves a boater, Saul, and will marry him, God willing. Bet was our trainer; she fell ill with pneumonia and took a long leave, but she is back now. She is my absolute friend, too. Both of them – and the cut – turned me from a spoilt, miserable, resentful brat into someone of use.'

Tom said nothing, just listened. The engine ticked over, pat-patter; the wind was in her hair, so the mist would lift; Dog was asleep, and birds flew overhead. Yes, this was her home; this was the world that had made her. 'But it is not just the day-to-day life on the cut that's changed me, Tom. Joe, Saul's nephew, lives with Polly's mum and dad for now, as his mother has gone missing. We fear that Leon, her husband, might have killed her, but all on the cut go on looking for her, just in case. Perhaps she'll float to the surface; perhaps she'll appear on the bank one day, ready to look after Joe. We taught him to read, and he is going to school in Woking and is safe from his father now. Saul and his grandfather have also learned to read. This is the world that has also made me.'

Tom, sitting now on the cabin roof, was listening so hard that she thought he'd fall forward, but he said nothing.

'These are my people: the lock-keepers, the boaters, the wharfmen; and heaven help them when the war is over, because who knows if canal transport will continue? Heaven help us all when the war ends, because where will any of us be? What's more, being here and listening to you makes me realise a great many things about myself. I do think I have more understanding. I do know – and this knowledge has never wavered – that I love you, and every day without you has been full of heartache. I do know that if we end the war and we are together, we will carve out a good life.'

There were no locks for the moment as they approached Kings Langley. Both stayed utterly silent, until Tom eased himself down and held Verity so close that she could hardly breathe. He said, 'I have ten days to two weeks' sick leave. If you can't come away with me, can I stay here with you and make myself useful? I want to know all about you, the real you, but I don't want to rush you. I want to get to know your friends – all of them, the whole bloody cut – if you, and they, will let me.'

Verity had no answer for him.

He understood and said, 'When you know, just tell me.'

As clouds threatened, they reached Marsworth Junction, having climbed the Tring locks to the summit. The cold shrouded them, the wind had died and the mist returned. They started the descent while there was still some light, one lock after the other, and this time Sylvia took over the lock-wheeling, on the condition that it was Verity's turn tomorrow. Tom managed on his leg all day, but looked drawn and pale.

'Don't you ever stop?' he muttered as he cleaned the outside of the cabin, having already done the inside; polishing the range brass rail and wiping the pierced plates hanging on the wall.

Verity felt as though she was a block of ice melded to the tiller. 'Do you ever stop advancing on the enemy? Don't worry, we'll get as far as Leighton Buzzard and moor up near the pub. You can buy us all a drink, and who knows – Saul might be there, or, if they've gone on, he could well have left a pheasant or two for us.'

Tom dipped his cloth over the side into the cut, wringing it out, then attacking the roof. 'There's ice forming.'

'Then wipe more quickly.'

'Oh, don't. This is supposed to be sick leave.' There were birds swooping over the cut and dogs barking. 'So, may I stay on?

Verity had decided the moment he asked, but had waited to see if second thoughts drenched her with doubt. They hadn't. 'Yes, I'd like that so much. I will ask the others, because it depends on them, too. We're a team, or trying to be. Polly will be all right, but Sylvia might object. It will mean someone sharing her cross-bed with her in the butty cabin, you see, and the third person taking the side-bed. You and Dog can settle down together in the motor cabin, which Polly and I usually share.'

He looked at her while he wrung out the freezing cloth. 'One day we'll be able to share the same room, if you ever feel able to marry me. Would you, do you think – marry me, I mean?'

'Do you think you'd ask me?'

They left it there.

Chapter 6

**Tuesday 28 March – after dusk, moored up at
Leighton Buzzard**

Once they had moored, Verity turned the tiller
around to give more room on the counter. There
were several pairs tied up ahead of them, their crews
probably all tucking into a meal, because there was
no one boiling up clothes on the bank, or children
playing. Or perhaps the men would be in the nearby
pub and the women with them? Or the women were
crocheting as the children slept?

Sleep? Verity thought she could do with some of
that, but so could they all. It was a good tiredness
she felt, though, one filled with triumph, because
they had made up time. It had helped having Tom
taking over the tiller later in the afternoon, so that
she and Polly could share much of the lock-wheeling,
keeping up a better pace.

Behind her, Tom caught the tow-rope thrown by
Sylvia, as the momentum carried the butty prow
forward. He handed it immediately to Verity who,
as arranged, leapt onto the roof and ran down the
top planks of the motor, keeping pace with the butty.

She secured the short tow on the fore-end stud, and together she and Sylvia lashed the butty tight abreast, while Polly and Tom secured the stern.

Verity and Sylvia ran back along their respective planks, before easing themselves down to their counters. Tom had disappeared into the motor cabin to beat up the eggs for a rosemary omelette, and to cut up the remaining baked potatoes and leeks from lunch.

He had promised them a feast, though Polly and Verity had laughed. He had looked suitably wounded, so they'd all laughed even more, including Sylvia. Beside Verity on the counter, Polly dusted off her hands, her voice drenched in tiredness. 'Not just a quick learner on a narrowboat, but a cook supreme? Herb omelette, indeed.' In the dim light Verity saw that freezing droplets festooned her friend's hat, and her huge bobble looked bedraggled.

'I didn't know that, either, but there are so many things I didn't – and don't – know about him, or had forgotten,' Verity murmured, knowing that she had to ask them to let Tom stay for the length of his leave. Polly was probably all right, but what about Sylvia?

Polly put an arm around her and hugged her close. 'So, you said you wanted to talk to the two of us?'

Sylvia was still standing on the counter of the butty in her three sweaters and nodded, her arms crossed. 'You did, so do get on with it. I'm freezing.'

Verity looked from one to the other. 'Yes, Pols, I did want to talk. May we come aboard, Sylvia?'

She felt Polly tense, because she didn't often call her 'Pols'. Sylvia snapped, 'Hurry up, and why are you making such a meal about it?'

But Polly said, 'You're leaving the cut, aren't you?' Her voice was level and without emotion, but in the gloom her face told a different story.

Verity swung round, one foot already on the butty. 'Of course not, you daft thing. Come on, I can't talk astride the gap.'

Sylvia tutted and opened the door to her butty cabin, then disappeared into it. The signs weren't good, and Verity wondered where Tom could sleep if, or when, Sylvia refused. She followed Sylvia down the steps, with Polly on her heels. The butty cabin was immaculately tidy; on the shelf that the GUCCC had put up for the women on the scheme the books were in alphabetical order, and the brass of the range gleamed. It had previously been Bet's cabin, and she had reclaimed her horse brasses and the pierced plates. Nothing had replaced them. Verity looked around curiously, because they seldom crossed the threshold. In fact she couldn't remember the last time.

There were no photographs, no strewn clothes or bookmarked novels scattered on the bed; it was almost like a cell, and it made Verity realise how the motor cabin, with its personal memorabilia and clutter, really must offend Sylvia. No wonder she almost fainted when she had to step over Dog cluttering up the aisle or, even worse, sit with Dog on the side-bed when she came to eat.

Sylvia waited on the double-width cross-bed at the rear of the cabin, with its crocheted curtain hooked back. She gestured them to the side-bed. They sat, but on the edge, neither of them daring to lean against the plumped-up plum-coloured cushions.

Polly nudged Verity. 'Come on, then. Supper will be ready any minute, and we mustn't upset the chef. Besides, Saul and Granfer were parked up ahead of us along the cut, and we can introduce Tom to them. When's he going?'

Verity drew in a deep breath. 'Well, that's what I need to talk to you about.'

Sylvia said, 'He can catch a train from Leighton Buzzard, I'm sure.'

Verity caught her own warped reflection in the gleaming copper kettle. If she and Polly sat quite still, perhaps Sylvia would buff them up, too.

Polly leaned forward, turning to look at her, her elbows on her knees. 'Come on, out with it.'

Verity puffed out a breath. 'I suppose a cigarette is out of the question?'

Sylvia sat bolt upright, shaking her head. 'You suppose right.' Her eyes narrowed. 'I know what all this is about. You want him to stay on, don't you?'

Polly grabbed Verity's knee. 'Really?' She shook Verity's leg. 'You really have made it up then, sorted it out? We thought as much, didn't we, Sylvia?'

Verity said, 'We haven't made it up completely, but we're working towards it, and we need a bit of time.'

Sylvia said nothing, just sat looking at Verity. Then she clenched her hands together. 'Of course I'm pleased for you, but staying for how long?'

Verity swallowed, her shoulders dropping slightly; it wasn't a flat 'No' anyway, but she hadn't broached the matter of the cabins yet. 'Until we return to Bull's Bridge, so about ten days. Tom's on sick leave, you see; and yes, we realise we've both changed, and that we should have challenged my mother and not accepted her word. We think we've both grown up – a bit, anyway – and perhaps we even understand some of her reasoning.'

Polly was grinning and hugged Verity. 'Wonderful, wonderful news. I like him, and you can tell Tom loves you, can't you, Sylvia?'

'Where will he sleep?' Sylvia responded.

Here they were: at *that* moment. Verity sank back against the cushion, then remembered where she was and shot up, but too late – Sylvia was frowning. Verity ploughed on, 'Yes, well, there are three of us, and one of him, and Dog.'

Sylvia crossed her arms. 'We can't have loose morals, and that's that. There will be no sharing.'

Polly was sitting quite still, but then she started to shake. A bleat of laughter left her, to be covered by a cough. 'So sorry, still the vestiges of this cold you gave us. Where should Tom sleep, then?'

There was a heavy silence, broken only by the fall of a lump of coal perched on a pyramid of other lumps. It sank into the firebox bed of red-hot ash.

At last Verity said, 'Well, Sylvia is quite right, so we'll have to split up, won't we? Tom can't sleep on the counter in this weather, so he and Dog will have to share one of the cabins. Within each cabin there is the cross-bed and the side-bed. The cross-bed will take two, the side-bed one. I'm asking you, Sylvia, on my knees, if we three can share your cabin. I promise we will be neat and tidy.'

Sylvia was aghast. Polly began shaking again. Verity dug her in the ribs, hard.

Sylvia muttered, 'I can't possibly have a dog in here; it's not a kennel.'

'Good decision, Sylvia,' Polly almost shouted. 'Dog can keep Tom company in the *Marigold*. We will only be a nuisance at night, because we can use our own cabin in the day. Where would you like us: cross-bed together, or one of us in it with you?'

Sylvia's expression said that she wouldn't *like* them anywhere, actually.

Verity said, 'I can't thank you enough. Do let us know where we should sleep, to be of least trouble to you.'

Sylvia actually shuddered. 'Verity, I don't actually remember agreeing, but Polly seems to have decided, and it would be churlish to spoil this chance for you. You and Polly will have the cross-bed. Bring your bedding every evening and remove it in the morning; wash in your own cabin. I will take the side-bed.' She paused to draw breath, then looked at them doubtfully. 'I think it's fair for me to ask that there will be no smoking in here?'

It really was a question. Her expression was confused, as though she couldn't quite work out how they'd arrived at this point.

'Very fair, we'll smoke up on the counter if we feel the urge, won't we, Polly?' Verity was surprised and grateful, and stood as though to kiss Sylvia, who leaned back. Verity sat down again. 'Thank you, really.'

Polly smiled at Sylvia. 'You must come to the pub this evening, because we'll be introducing Tom to everyone, and it wouldn't be the same without you. Bet and her trainees are moored here too, so she'll be there.'

Verity said, 'Yes, do, but you can meet Tom properly over his evening delectation, heaven help us.'

By nine they were fed and watered, and they set out into the freezing mist for the pub, which was just along from the mooring spot. Tom and Verity walked behind Polly and Sylvia. Tom whispered, 'I should buy them a drink, for all the cabin upheaval.'

'Great idea.' Verity still felt astonished to be breathing the same air as him, and to have spent hour after hour with him, as equals – he not a chauffeur, and she not Her Ladyship.

Tom slipped his arm around her. 'I can't believe I'm here with you, sweet Verity. I thought this was gone forever, and now I feel I can begin to live again.'

In step, they walked along the road, just for a few hundred yards, and then into the pub, and the noise, and a mixture of cigarette, pipe and wood smoke.

Saul was at the bar, but his 'Polly' antenna was working well and he spun round, the love streaming from him. He came across immediately, shook Sylvia's hand and kissed Polly on the lips. 'I 'as the drinks ordered. The table's free; Bet's trainees 'as the one behind, and Granfer is telling 'em whoppers. Yer must be Tom. Yer got 'ere then, finally?'

Tom nodded. 'I did, and I'm going to be asked this a lot tonight, aren't I? But it's no more than I deserve.' He shook Saul's hand. 'I'll buy the drinks – least I can do, after fouling up. I owe Sylvia, Verity and Polly anyway, for budging up in the butty cabin, leaving Dog and me to spread ourselves in the motor.'

Saul grimaced. 'Ah, so yer've been recruited, 'ave yer? They'll work yer t'bone. I'll help yer carry.'

The two headed to the bar without a backward glance. Polly and Verity looked at one another, shrugged and linked arms with Sylvia, heading for the free table by the fireside. Bet, Granfer and the trainees joined them, moving their table to line up with *Marigold*'s and adding a couple of chairs for Tom and Saul.

Verity sat by the fire. Sparks burst and flames licked around the logs, which were more like great tree trunks. For so long Tom hadn't been here, for so long life had been empty. She watched him at the bar: the way he moved, the turn of his head, his khaki trousers, one leg cut perpendicularly to above his knee, so that it flapped on either side of his plastered leg when he walked. She heard his laugh as Steerer Mercy, who had caught them up, teased him about the telephone boxes along the route of the canal. Then he – her Tom, her man – was coming; limping, bringing the tankards of mild, and a sweet sherry for Sylvia.

It was this she would remember when he had gone away to war. It was tonight she would hang on to, if anything happened to him: his smile, his easy acceptance of the boaters who were calling out, 'Ring-ring.' And from Thomo, 'Press Button A.' She'd remember Tom's laugh, which she'd all but forgotten in the anguish of his loss, ringing out loud and true. She drank in the look he gave her as he reached them and handed out the drinks, first to Bet and her two trainees, Merle and Sandy; the little bow he gave to Sylvia, and the thanks he gave for making room for his girl and Polly in her cabin; the sigh as he sat down next to her and gripped her hand. 'I thank God I'm here with you.'

She studied him. 'God? You were the most godless of individuals.'

'Ah, but I've seen things that I hope you will never see, and witnessed courage beyond belief. It changes us, one way or another.'

She sipped her mild and saw that Sylvia was leaning forward, watching Tom as though she was running his words round inside her head. Verity lifted her glass to Sylvia. 'Thank you, Sylvia, for letting us share.'

Sylvia looked at her as though she was preoccupied with other things. After a moment she murmured, 'Verity, we're a team, like you say, so it's what we do – share – just as we share one another's colds.' They all laughed at her joke, and Sylvia blushed, surprised. 'Oh,' she said, 'I've been funny. It feels nice.'

Chapter 7

Tuesday 28 March – midnight: Saul and Granfer in their butty, *Swansong*

Saul stirred the tea leaves in the brown teapot. They'd been used twice already today, but there was a bit of colour, so the cuppa would still taste. He reckoned cocoa would be better for Granfer, but this is what the old chap liked at the end of the day.

'Give it another stir, lad. You warmed t'pot?'

Saul laughed, 'Yer know I did, Granfer. Yer watched me do it.'

'Aye, maybe, but I might have closed me eyes for a second, yer know. One too many beers this night, but good to see Verity's lad's got 'is head straight.'

Granfer was sitting on his cross-bed, which he'd left made up when they went out to the pub. His grey blankets were pulled tight, without a crease in sight. He always said he'd learned to be neat and clean in the first war. 'Neat and clean, once yer got out t'mud of them trenches. Get's to be a habit, our Saul. Can't abide rucked beds, that I can't; reckon I'm like that princess who weren't partial to the pea that were where it shouldn't 'ave been.'

'Yer being a princess is something I'd like ter see.' Saul poured the tea and placed Granfer's on the cupboard-front table.

'Ta, lad.' Granfer looked up with a smile. 'It'll settle us fer t'night. 'Ow's our young runabout doing, d'yer reckon?'

As the wick of the oil lamp flickered, Saul sat on the side-bed, cupping the mug and staring at the fire. 'Our Harry were asleep on the motor side-bed, snug as a bug in a rug, when I looked in. He's a good 'un. Not sure 'ow long we can keep 'im, though. His da'll need 'im back. On t'other hand, not sure about a lot o' things right now.'

Outside an owl hooted, then another. A fox called. The coal in the firebox was burning red. Saul would bank it in a minute, but now he had words that must be said, and he didn't know how, that was the bugger of it. He sighed. There were other words to her – that 'someone else' who made his world turn – that had to be said an' all, but not yet, not until … He couldn't find words for any of it, even in his mind, let alone words that'd come out of his mouth. Cos once said, they'd couldn't be taken back, so he had to be certain of his path.

Granfer took up his pipe and chewed on it. 'Saw yer talking deep with that young spark o' Verity's. Reckon I knows what about, an' all. Saw yer talking to Steerer Mercy, too, cos it be his Sheila's Ted who be gone to war. Yer Polly saw yer busy with 'em, too.' Granfer took the clay pipe out of his breast pocket and chewed on it. 'Time yer spat it out, lad.'

Saul swirled round the dregs of his tea. He wished he could predict his future from the leaves. 'Yer knows I read the papers and the things in 'em about the war, and 'ere I am, reserved for the carrying of cargo, when blokes like Verity's Tom are up and at it, and blokes like Mercy's daughter's husband 'ave broken away from t'cut to do his bit. I needs to go, if I can, Granfer. Me leg's better and it's shame I feels. Afore I could read, I just didn't know so much that was happening.' He couldn't find any other words, because when he thought about what others were doing he just wanted to punch the wall.

Granfer nodded. 'Course I knows that, lad. Course I do. It's why I went t'other war. But what'd Mercy and that young spark, Tom, say?'

Saul reached over for Granfer's empty mug, washed both and put them away in the cupboard. The oil lamp was spluttering now, casting leaping shadows on the walls; walls hung with plates that his grandma, and her ma before her, had washed and loved; brasses they'd all polished. He had to fight to save all this.

He hunkered down and used the shovel to dig out coal from the coal box under the bottom step, building up the fire good and proper. Then he sat back on the side-bed, trying to gather the information he'd picked up into something that made sense. Granfer waited until at last he was ready.

'That Tom, he said some bloke in a bed next to 'im in 'ospital had been muttering about some sort of floatin' 'arbour being built that'll 'elp with the war when it comes to taking it to the enemy. He said it were an 'arbour to land trucks and suchlike when they went over the Channel. That Tom, 'e said the lad were all muddled in 'is pain, but it sounded as though it were carried out under the lot who run t'girls' canal training scheme, cos it's War Transport. The real 'arbours is under the Nazis so them can't land there.'

Granfer had taken out his pipe and was turning it over and over. 'Ah, so yer reckon if yer's already on the waterway, they could swap yer over?'

'Don't know, but worth a try. He said to find someone with learning, like a solicitor, who knew 'ow to break the Reserved Occupation thing, and who'd help me write a letter to them War Transport lot, to get taken on for the war. Steerer Mercy came oop to us then and 'e said 'is Shelia's Ted had paid some bloke to write 'is letter, but 'e didn't know who.'

Granfer nodded. 'So, there's nought to stop yer tryin', now yer know t'road, or is there?'

'Lots to stop me, Granfer, as yer know, and I'm looking at one of the buggers, right now.' The two men laughed quietly.

Then Granfer sighed and reached out, touching the hooked-back crocheted curtain. 'Yer grandma made this, but 'tis old now, ragged and won't do fer much longer – bit like me – so don't let me stop yer. I reckon, yer see, it be time to move on t'bank. There's yer Auntie Lettie at Buckby, where all the old boaters go when they pull up their tillers. She says the local 'andyman has popped his clogs, so there'd be a bit o' work for me. I'm tired, lad, working all the hours God sends, at seventy-eight—'

Saul interrupted, 'Yer seventy-nine, Granfer.'

'Aye, maybe I am, and the cold gets into me bones, yer know. And now our Joe's with Polly's people on the bank, I doubt he'll want to come back onto the cut when the war is finished. Will there even be a cut left, with all them trains and lorries? So if yer go, we'll hand back t'boats to the Grand Union, and I reckon I'll take me knick-knacks and head to Buckby.'

Saul felt his shoulders relax. He'd been thinking for a while that Granfer was tired, his chest was bad, and Auntie Lettie had written a note to Saul, sending it to the Bull's Bridge depot, saying it were time the old chap put his feet up. Besides, she needed company. So she must 'ave written to Granfer, too.

Granfer pushed the cupboard door shut and leaned forward, resting his elbows on his knees. 'Don't get me wrong, lad. It'll mither me summat rotten to have you at war, but I knows you got to do it, for your soul. But do Joe come t'Buckby, or do he stay with Mr and Mrs Holmes?'

The fire was crackling. Saul lifted his hand, as though stopping Granfer's words. 'But what if I don't get taken for the fighting, Granfer?'

'Then I'll see the war oot, o' course I will, but I can't move to another boat without yer, and nor can I work the pair with just two runabouts. But look, lad, we *must* talk o' Joe.'

Saul knew that, but how could he tell his granfer that he was too old to be having Joe; it weren't fair on the lad or on the old chap? He said carefully, 'What d'yer think is the best for 'im? Really, from yer 'eart?'

The old chap still sat, his elbows on his knees, his pipe in the corner of his mouth, his hands entwined, his thumbs tapping out something only he could hear. 'What's best for our lad is summat he can't be having: his ma; cos we don't know where she be, or even if that bugger Leon left her living on God's green earth.'

Saul stared. It was the first time Granfer had ever echoed what he himself often thought. That Joe's dad, Leon Arnson, had killed his wife – Saul's sister, Maudie. Leon was a basher, and Joe had told them that, after a right royal ding-dong, Maudie wasn't there any more; and then Leon had locked Joe in his motor cabin, after beating him, too. This was when Saul and Granfer had rescued him, while the beggar Leon was in the pub.

'So what's second best, Granfer? Cos for now Leon's in custody, after egging on that escaped German POW to fire Polly's cargo of wood, and stabbing Dog, so at least the lad's safe from him.'

Granfer filled his cheeks and blew. 'Yer won't like it, but 'tis fer the boy to stay on the bank with Mr and Mrs Holmes. 'E's 'appy, they's 'appy and he's doing his learning at school.'

Saul smiled inwardly with relief, but all he said was, 'That's right good thinkin', but now I needs to work 'ow it's all to happen. But 'ush-'ush, cos no one might want me, or them up at the top might not let me go, and I won't be upsetting my Polly by tellin' 'er, cos it might not happen, so 'tis a waste of her pain.' He rubbed his face. 'They should take me, though, Granfer, don't yer think, with them women trainees coming along to fill the gaps of us blokes?'

'Not sure there's enough coming along, though, lad. But yer go on wi' yer plans; it's worth a try and will settle yer, one way or t'other.' Granfer tapped his watch. 'Now, I needs me kip, cos we've got to push on and get through Stoke Bruerne tomorrer and Blisworth Tunnel, to make up fer the time we spent waiting for yer lass. So off to yer pit, and I'll to mine, there's a lad.'

In his cabin, with Harry sleeping on the side-bed, like the youngster he was, Saul lay on the cross-bed wishing that Polly was with him, to talk it all out, but he didn't want to tell her till he was sure. Steerer Mercy pushed him along that way too, cos his daughter's chap hadn't said nought till it were all signed and sealed, to save his Sheila's heart.

He tossed and turned. Trouble was, it felt like he was lying to his Polly, but each time he had thought to say what was in his head, the sight of her precious face, the touch of her hand in his, made the words dry in his throat.

'Yer all right, Uncle Saul?' Harry called from the side-bed, his voice heavy with sleep.

'Yer get back to sleep, our young 'un. There're the Fenny Stratford locks fer yer to wheel tomorrow, and right good of you and your da to give us a lendin' of yer.'

There was no reply, just the slow, heavy breathing of a sleeping lad. Saul remembered the days when he was thirteen and on the boats with Ma, Da and Maudie, in convoy with Granfer and Grandma, who had a runabout in their pair. There seemed nothing to worry about then, no choices to make. Again he sighed. Was it better not to know yer letters? Not to know more than travelling the cut, and where the kingfisher might swoop and the otters would breed?

Would Joe ever come back to the boats? Saul felt he wouldn't, except for a holiday. Could he stay with Mr and Mrs Holmes while Saul was gone, and until he was finished at school? Well, the only thing was to write, and that he'd do tomorrow, and by then he might have thought of someone who could write that letter to the war people, so that this load of shame could slide from his back.

Before they left the pub the girls had used its facilities, and on the walk back Sylvia murmured, 'I have to admit there are some very good points about spending a couple of hours in a pub – namely the toilets.'

The others laughed and Sylvia looked taken aback. 'That's a good joke,' said Polly.

Sylvia smiled and half laughed. 'Oh, I see.'

On their return, Verity and Polly took turns at a stand-up wash in the motor cabin, while Tom was banished to the counter.

Polly called to him, 'Hey, you on the counter, I do hope you used the facilities at the pub, or you'll regret it, young man.'

Tom replied, 'Ah, I'm not a soldier for nothing, Polly Holmes. First you work out the lie of the land, find out what will make your life easier. And what's more I have a torch, should I need to totter to the bucket along the gunwale – that's what you call the strip running either side of the cabin and hold, isn't it?'

Verity and Polly were sniggering as they dragged on their boots and pyjamas. 'It is indeed, but do not – and I repeat, do not – go that way, for heaven's sake,' laughed Verity. 'Go over the roof and onto the engine cabin, then drop down to the store. Otherwise Polly will get drenched when you slip off the gunwale and she has to dive in to get you out.'

'Oi,' shouted Polly, 'it won't be me, I'll have you know. It'll be little Miss Verity, and she'll take so long putting on slap, to look good for you, that you'll drown.'

They put the darts kitty into the cupboard, having won again. Verity looked at Polly. 'Right, we have a blanket each. You can have the outside, so you don't have to clamber over me if you need to go to the bucket. How's that for fair?'

'Sounds good to me, but please, please don't snore. Sylvia's being really good to let us do this.'

Verity shook out her blanket and wrapped it around herself. 'I don't snore.'

'What rubbish, you're like a roaring train.' Polly was clambering up the steps, calling back. 'You've banked the firebox for Tom?'

'Of course, bossy. And we've got to hurry. Sylvia wants to get to sleep, and I don't blame her.'

On the counter Tom was smoking as a light smattering of snow fell, looking as though it was falling upwards. Some trick of the wind? Verity wondered. Polly stepped across to the breasted butty, calling softly, 'We'll be up at five-thirty, Tom, trying to make it through Blisworth by the end of the day. It's a mile-long tunnel, so sometimes you get an echo that you can wish on.'

Verity stood by Tom, who said softly, 'Goodnight, Polly, and thanks. Dog's just on the bank, so I'll wait until she's ready.' All the time he was pulling Verity closer. She heard the butty cabin door open and close, as Polly disappeared inside. Dog bounded onto the deck. Tom kissed Verity, his hand in her freshly brushed blonde hair. 'I love you so much, Verity Clement.'

He said it against her mouth, and she replied, 'And I love you, and have since the day I first saw you.' Her mouth was on his. Dog yelped at their side, pawing Verity's pyjamas.

Verity pulled back, laughing. 'Time for bed, I believe, and you're shivering.'

He pulled her to him once more, kissed her and, as he let her go, he whispered, 'I will have the kettle on at five-thirty. I have a sort of alarm clock in my head. Tea for four persons, madam.'

Verity stepped onto the butty counter, then opened the door into a dark cabin, illuminated only by the light from the firebox. She could see Polly sitting on the edge of the cross-bed, and tiptoed down the aisle.

'You sleep well. Five-thirty start, remember,' Sylvia muttered, turning over on the side-bed to face the wall.

Verity whispered, 'Thank you for this, Sylvia; really, really thank you. Tom will have the kettle on, he said, when we wake, so we will nip up and out of your way. Make sure you come for toast and a cuppa when you're dressed.'

Sylvia sat up and pulled out earplugs. 'What was that? I use these because I can hear you snoring when you've had too much to drink. Not that you have tonight, but who knows what Tom's nocturnal habits are.' Verity flushed. Sylvia tapped her arm. 'I failed to hear what you said. Tell me again; and hurry, I'm tired and need to sleep.'

Polly repeated, 'Tom will have the kettle on, and you're to remember to come for toast and a cuppa. Now do come on, Verity; you're on the inside, so I can't settle until you're in place.' She inched out of the way, and Verity shoved over against the back wall and dragged the blanket over her and Polly. 'Throw yours over, too, and we'll keep warm.' Polly groaned. 'Your feet are freezing. Put them somewhere else.'

'Do stop moaning,' Verity grunted, poking Polly, who shrieked.

Sylvia called, 'I've dropped an earplug. Settle down or Sister will—' She stopped abruptly. 'Oh, never mind.'

Verity and Polly lay quietly. Polly whispered, 'Who is Sister?'

Verity stared up at the ceiling. 'I have no idea, but who knows, one day Sylvia might tell us.' Tonight she felt different, full of caring, full not just of happiness but of completeness. Tom was back, and they were making their way towards one another. In the motor cabin they heard Dog bark, once.

Polly whispered, 'She just wants us to know she's all right.'

Verity gripped her hand. 'We know she is, because she's with Tom, and one day I will be where she is.'

Sylvia said, 'I hope not. She's on the floor, isn't she?'

Verity gripped Polly's hand even tighter, and then they both burst out laughing, Verity managing to say eventually, 'Oh, well done, Sylvia. That really was a good one.'

'Goodnight,' Sylvia said. 'Earplug has been found and is going in, right now.'

The other two said goodnight, whether or not Sylvia could hear. 'And thank you.'

Chapter 8

Wednesday 29 March – *Marigold* and *Horizon* continue north

Verity and Polly arrived in the motor cabin at five-thirty in their pyjamas, boots and each with a blanket wrapped around them against the cold. Tom had been true to his word, and the kettle rattled as it simmered on the range. He was fully dressed, and they turned him onto the counter while they dragged on their clothes. They were quick, because their vests and three sweaters went on as one, and their socks, pants and trousers took mere seconds. Face and teeth were washed, the water in the bowl was chucked over the side, toast was spread with a dab of margarine, and a knife showed the toast a whisper of Polly's mother's marmalade. All within ten minutes.

Sylvia joined them, sitting on a towel on the icy roof with Polly, while Verity and Tom clustered around the tiller. Verity had half feared that Tom would have limped off, with his grip over his shoulder. He was staring up at the sky, his tea forgotten. 'Would you look at that.'

Above them Hurricanes and Spitfires were milling about, then roaring higher and higher until they disappeared. 'Probably from Leighton Buzzard. Everywhere seems so busy these days,' Verity muttered, shading her eyes against the cold wind.

Polly swung round, ignoring the aeroplanes and concentrating on the boats that were still moored up. Verity followed her line of sight and saw that Saul and Granfer Hopkins had already left, and Polly's shoulders slumped. Tom said, as though he could read Polly's mind, 'I saw Saul heading for the postbox by the pub, and then they took off.'

'Probably writing to his nephew, Joe,' replied Polly, the disappointment heavy in her voice.

Verity sighed. It wasn't easy loving someone these days, but perhaps it never had been? Beside her, Tom touched her arm, taking her empty mug. 'What's the plan for today?'

Verity looked from Polly to Sylvia, both of whom pointed at her. She laughed and pulled a face. 'Seems that I am to lock-wheel this morning, while you, sir, lounge in the heat of the cabin, or do some housework chores for the two bullies. They will steer.'

Sylvia slid from the roof. 'It's too cold up here, and time to get on.'

They each took a boat shaft and stabbed at the ice around the hull, sweating and swearing. Tom took the stern counter, for he was too much of a liability to stand on the roof and jab. Finally they were free, and Polly shouted, 'Come on, Verity, let's get this wretched engine sparked up and moving. Tom, into the cabin with you. There's yesterday's *Times* on the bookshelf. Take Dog with you, if you please.'

They trod carefully as they crossed the roof and went down into the engine room, fiddling about and talking nicely to 'the beast', as they called it. Polly heaved the flywheel, and the engine coughed and caught first time. She dusted off her hands and grinned at Verity. 'This will be a good day.'

As they emerged, the engine's idling pat-pattering was music to their ears. Verity muttered, 'I felt sure the beggar would mess us about in this cold.'

Polly had heaved herself back onto the roof, avoiding the bike they kept for cycling ahead to the locks. 'Who do you mean: the engine or Tom?'

Verity laughed, following her friend as they eased themselves down from the slippery roof. 'You, Miss Holmes, are not funny.'

'Course I am,' Polly replied as she took up her position at the slide hatch, her elbow resting on the tiller. She engaged the engine and they were off. She steered out towards the centre of the cut, avoiding Steerer Mercy's pair, moored just along from them. Steerer and Ma were preparing to leave.

'How do,' Verity called as they passed.

Ma, on the butty, nodded, and Steerer tipped his hat, his empty pipe clenched between his teeth.

Very soon they approached a bridge and looked up; the parapet was clear of children, but not of transport; a military convoy was revving itself up and over the cut. Some soldiers waved from the back. Verity wished Tom's injury was more severe; but fractures healed, and soldiers became well enough to fight.

She shut her eyes against the thought, and as they heard someone hooting on the other side of the bridge, Verity said to Polly as they slowed, 'You keep your Saul here, on the cut, where he belongs, Polly Holmes, or I'll want to know the reason why.'

Steerer Stanley came through from the bridge-hole. ''Ow do.'

The girls replied, then Polly muttered as she put the *Marigold* into gear, 'I'll try to keep Saul here, but something is on his mind ... I'm not imagining it, am I?' She didn't wait for a reply as she steered through. 'Sometimes he's somewhere else. It might just be ... well, I don't know.'

Verity muttered, 'It could be Granfer. His chest isn't good, so don't imagine things until you know. After all, Saul's been refused for military service, on the basis of the Discretionary Reserve, and not a lot's changed.' The trouble was, Verity wasn't sure what Saul was thinking and why he'd talked so much to Steerer Mercy and Tom in the pub.

Polly pulled towards the edge. She snatched a look at Verity. 'Go on, grab your bike and take off, little speedy lock-wheel girl.'

Verity hauled the bike off the roof, telling Tom, 'Stay in the warm, and do what Auntie Polly says.'

She heard his laugh as she set off along the towpath, looking over her shoulder and calling, 'We might catch up with Bet and the girls at the lock. They left really early, but will be slower than us; or so Bet said last night, with that voice she uses when things aren't going well.'

Polly's answer followed her along the towpath. 'Well, you should know, after her experiences with you.'

Verity grinned as she cycled in and out of the icy ruts, especially when she heard Tom call, so that Verity could hear, 'Tell me more, Polly.'

She pedalled, head down, watching the snow and ice, and steering for the grass where there was more grip. The wind was unforgiving, but it would be, at this hour of the morning. The damned mist still clung to her, and the hedgerows and the trees. The birds still sang, though, and so did her heart as she caught sight of a pair approaching, heading south. She braked, stood with her legs on either side of the bike and waved her hat. 'How do, is the lock ready?'

''Ow do. So far 'tis, but there's a pair before you – Bet's, it is.'

'Right you are, thanks.'

She pedalled on as the sun came fully up, and everything seemed to brighten. Even the snow trapped amongst the tussocks in the fields glinted. She sped on, because it would be good to see Bet putting the girls through their paces, but when she reached the lock, she saw they were only just about to enter it. That really was slow; even slower than Verity and Polly had been, surely? But then she hesitated – no, probably not, as she remembered some of their mistakes and cringed. There was that time they had been stuck across the width of the cut ... Poor Bet.

She cycled up the slope and let the bike fall onto the grass, close to Bet's trainee, Sandy, who was a nice girl, with her hair pulled back in a French pleat and a friendly smile. She was closing the gates behind the butty. Well, that was all right, she thought, waving at Bet, who called, 'Nice to see you, Verity. Help my lock-wheeler if she needs it, would you?'

'Of course.' Verity checked back down the cut and there was *Marigold* coming into view. Well, they'd wait, without hooting and panicking the trainees.

She prepared to help close the lower gates, but Sandy had already done it and was running towards the top gates, her wellingtons slapping against her trousers. She'd be better wearing short boots, as she, Polly and Sylvia did, but probably the trainees weren't prepared to invest in some, until they knew if they had passed their training. As she stood on the kerb above the lock, Verity closed her eyes, straining to remember the girl's real name. She'd been told last night. Ah, that was it: 'Sandy' was a shortening of 'Alexandra'. She called, as the girl started raising a paddle on the far gate with her windlass, to let the water in, 'Need a hand, Sandy?'

'Oh, if you don't mind. I'm rather slow.'

'We all are, at the beginning.' Verity crossed the narrow platform that ran along the top, feeling her feet slide on the ice. She dragged her windlass from the back of her belt and wound the paddle.

'Gosh, you're so fast,' Sandy said, her hand slipping as she lost purchase on the spindle.

Verity looked down as the water gushed through her own paddle. 'Take a deep breath and attach it again, then wind steadily.'

Sandy did so.

'Steady, steady,' Verity soothed her. 'It's not a race.'

Sandy didn't look up, but said, 'The trouble is, it *is* a race. We all have to get there as fast as we can, and not hold others up.'

Verity itched to take over, but that was no way to help. She returned to the bank and, once there, she looked down. The paddle on Sandy's side was lifting, and water was gushing into the lock. 'Good,' she called. 'Keep going, nearly open.'

Sandy wound and wound.

'Your hands will be sore, but keep going – go on, go on,' Verity shouted. 'All right, it's wide open, come to the kerb, and I expect that there's a brew being made in Bet's cabin. As the water rises, nip down those lock steps rather than jumping down onto the boats today, as the roofs and counters are really icy.' Sandy came to stand beside her, watching the water rising, as though mesmerised, while Verity called down, 'You all right, Bet? Is a cuppa on the cards for your worker?'

Bet gave the thumbs up as the boats began to lift. Verity looked back along the cut. *Marigold* and

Horizon were both waiting patiently. Polly obviously realised it could be some while, because she was mooring up and, before Verity could count to fifty, Tom, Sylvia and Polly were alongside, looking down at Bet, who pointed to Tom. 'So, your apprentice is getting stuck in. Doing the housework, is he? Nice to see you, Tom. Got a nice pinny, have you?'

Tom called, 'A white one with frills. I've wiped down the ceiling, the floor, taken some ash from the firebox, refilled the coal box ... Need I go on?'

On the other side of the lock, the lock-keeper was standing at the door to his office. Sometimes he had eggs for sale and, as he kept pigs, occasionally a few slices of bacon were available. Verity was just about to call and ask when Polly yelled, 'No, don't jump, Sandy – use the steps.'

Too late, for Sandy had jumped down onto the motor-cabin roof while Verity sighed in exasperation.

'Why didn't you listen to us?' she yelled, then realised she sounded just like Bet. The four of them held their breath as they peered down. Verity clutched Sylvia's hand, but Sandy seemed to have made it safely.

'Lucky girl,' whispered Sylvia.

At that moment Sandy's feet went from under her and she slid sideways, shrieking in terror, before crashing into the gap between the motor and the lock wall, sinking beneath the surface.

Bet, who had tried to reach her as she slid, crouched on the counter and leaned along, managing to grab Sandy's jacket. She started to haul her towards the stern counter and out of the freezing water, but slipped herself, falling backwards. Sandy sank down again, as the butty nudged the motor into the wall.

Sandy's shrieking became a scream as she was crushed, a scream which chilled the blood. Verity snatched a look at the paddles, at the same time as Polly said, 'Should we shut off the water? The boat'll be grinding her.'

Verity tried to clear her mind. Should they? 'No, we just have to keep the boats off her. The sooner we get her to the top, the sooner we can get her to hospital. Sylvia, get the lock-keeper to call an ambulance.' They set off for the lock steps. The screaming they heard now was of sheer agony.

Bet was yelling to her other trainee, as she reached for Sandy again. 'Get over here, Merle; don't stay on the damned butty like a stuffed dummy. Shaft the motor off the wall. Girls, get down here and help her.'

The screams were endless, but now at last Merle was shafting the boat away.

Verity and Polly were already on the steps and had reached the motor, inching along the gunwale, not the roof, followed by Sylvia.

Tom yelled, 'Sylvia's right: she's of more use with you. The lock-keeper is getting the ambulance.'

Verity had reached Bet, who was face-down on the counter now, her hands white as she clutched the shoulders of Sandy's jacket; the girl's hair was soaked, but her screams had stopped, her head had slumped sideways and blood swirled in the rising water. Verity grabbed a motor shaft from the roof and helped Merle on the counter, and together they pushed against the weight of two laden boats. Polly rushed to the butty and returned with another shaft, and this time, stood on the cabin roof, close to the chimney whose heat had thawed an area, she shoved, too. Bet yelled, 'Hurry, I've still got hold of her.'

Sylvia had joined Polly and they all worked to Verity's shouts: 'One, two. Come on. One, two. Don't get tired, just count.'

They shoved, easing the motor from the wall. Bet, kneeling now, dragged Sandy up, up, but the shafts slipped on the icy wall and the butty swung back, smashing against Sandy's legs. The girl's screams cut through them all.

Polly yelled, 'Come on, come on – shove, shove, get it off her.'

The two boats moved away, bit by bit. Bet was coughing, hanging onto Sandy's jacket and trying to pull her up as a gap was created, but Sandy was no longer responding. 'She's a dead weight, and she's stuck. Her boots have snagged on something, or are full of water. She's unconscious or ...' Bet paused. 'Oh dear God, she can't last in this water, it's too cold. I'm going in. Verity, get down and hang on to her.'

Bet wasn't waiting to unlace her leather boots, but hauled off two of her sweaters. Verity and Polly shouted as one, 'You're not going into that water – it'll kill you.' They exchanged a look.

Polly nodded and Verity shouted, 'Sylvia, Merle and Polly, keep shafting, and don't let the gap close, whatever you do. Bet, keep a hold from the counter, and do as you're bloody well told.'

Before she had time to think, Verity plunged down the gap into the water. The cold took her breath away and the shock paralysed her. But what about Sandy? Was she even alive? Panic urged her forward, and somehow she kicked and dragged herself along between the motor and the wall, her hands slipping on the icy hull, catching on the fenders. The motor surged towards the wall, the fenders slamming her into it. She bit down on her scream.

She heard Polly roar, 'One, two.' A space was created again.

Verity hauled herself towards Sandy, as Bet clung to the girl's jacket. Polly shouted to Verity, between pants, 'Be careful, idiot girl, for heaven's sake.'

From the lock kerb she head Tom shouting, 'For God's sake, get a move on or you'll freeze up and go under. Polly, keep shoving.'

Somewhere she could hear sirens. 'Idiot, yourself,' she called to Polly, and found that speaking made her breathe. She made a huge effort to kick forward and lunged at the girl, grabbing her hair, holding up her head and shouting, as Bet was doing, 'Sandy? Sandy? I think she's still breathing, but it's hard to tell.'

'Bugger that – get her free,' Polly screamed. The boats were grinding together, as a shaft slipped and screeched against the wall.

Verity drew in some sort of a breath. 'Sandy's stuck, she's not moving.' She breathed in deeply and forced herself right down into the water – deep, deep, as they had done with Jimmy. Yes, she could do this; she had done it before. She opened her eyes, but the lock water was cloudy. She felt down the girl's legs and found her waterlogged wellingtons, caught on a fender that had broken free.

She pulled down on the right boot, but her hands were numb now and slipped. She tried again, but her hands slipped once more. Her chest was bursting. Sandy wasn't moving, but the hull lurched against her, then away. She reached up and hooked the fingers of one hand over the top of one of the boots, then squeezed the foot between her body and her hand, sinking deeper into the water, pulling, pulling, until finally the boot was off. She reached for the other, but had no breath left. She rose, gulped in air, water that tasted of dirt and blood. Bet was still hanging on, her face as white as frost. Polly was shafting, the sweat running down her face.

Tom yelled, 'I'm coming. I can't stand this.'

Verity gulped in air and down she went again, but she couldn't think, she felt so cold. What should she be doing? She couldn't remember. Sandy? Her leg. Yes, that's right. The boots. One leg didn't have one. She felt along and there the other one was – a boot on a motionless leg. She worked her useless hands up the boot. *Work, damn you*, she ordered her fingers.

Her left hand helped her right-hand fingers. She hugged the boot to her and used the weight of her body again, then sank as her fingers pulled on the boot. It hadn't been so cold with Jimmy. Down she went, down; it was such a heavy weight. She sank suddenly, holding the boot. It was off, empty. No, not empty – full of water. She let it go, then kicked her legs. Were they kicking? She couldn't feel them. Something nudged her. It was the hull. She'd be crushed between the hull, or between the fenders and the wall. She clawed her way up the slimy lockside, kick-kick, her chest hurting. She must breathe. She felt hands in her hair, pulling. She broke the surface.

Bet was heaving Sandy up, and now she saw that the lock-keeper was on the counter, too, pulling with Bet. They got Sandy on board. Her hair, Verity saw, was no longer in a French pleat, but instead was falling like a curtain, and dripping. Still the boat was rising. She heard Polly shrieking, 'Get Verity out. Quick, quick. We're shafting, but we're getting too tired.'

Hands had stopped pulling her hair and had seized her under the arms, and they were already pulling her up and Tom was shouting, 'Come on, lass. Come on, darling. Up you come.' He was lying, heaving her upwards and across. She was coming, higher and higher, and now he was rolling onto his side, still heaving. Her body caught on the fender – the water wanted to pull her back down, but Tom wanted her more, she knew that. He wanted her, with him; she knew he did. He pulled, and there was the lock-keeper and she could see them, but couldn't help them. Nothing would work, nothing would feel. Finally she came up with a whoosh, like a cork out of a bottle, into Tom's arms.

He fell back, and Verity lay on top. He held her tight. 'We've got to stop doing this. First the towpath and now the counter. And, by the way, I'm holding you to keep you warm; it isn't because I love you so much I could die, do you hear me? Say you hear me.'

They lay there while someone threw a blanket over them both, saying, 'You're an idiot, a daft – and wonderful idiot, Verity.' Ah, Polly. Ah, Tom and Polly. Everything was all right. She felt sick, her head was hurting inside, and outside there was nothing but Tom shouting. She opened her eyes.

He was looking at the cabin. 'Tie both legs off. The cold's reduced the flow of blood, thank God. Use anything to tie her off below the knees. The heat could start any damaged arteries pumping.'

Verity lifted her head and saw they had risen on a level with the lock kerb. She struggled free of Tom, lying on her side, looking at the ambulance and the men. They had a stretcher lying on the icy ground between them, waiting. The lock-keeper was standing by the tiller, his sleeves soaking, and he was shivering. 'Warm him,' she whispered.

She watched Tom somehow scramble free of her, replace her blanket and help Sylvia and Polly carry Sandy to the kerb, where the ambulance men took over. Verity tried to shout, 'The lock-keeper must be in the warm. He must.' No one heard her, but she couldn't hear herself, either. Were her lips even moving? Was her heart beating? Were her lungs breathing? 'Bet – look after Bet.' Still no one heard her.

But perhaps they had, because the lock-keeper was being helped to the kerb and into the ambulance. She heard him shout, 'Get yer bleedin' 'ands off me. All I needs is me coal fire; yer look after the girls, for Gawd's sake.' He was out of the ambulance again, like the jack-in-a-box she'd had as a child. He walked off, across the top-gate gallery. Verity watched. He seemed miles away, miles and miles. Someone should take the boats out of the lock to let others through. And where was Bet?

Ah, nearer, much nearer. Bet was wrapped in a blanket, sitting on the butty counter by the tiller, with Merle at her side. Verity heard Polly say, 'Bet, you need to go too, to be checked over, with Verity. You're both too cold.'

Verity could see blood was dripping onto the kerb – or was it pumping? – from Sandy's legs; she couldn't tell. Someone was hooting, impatient for the lock. Couldn't they see the ambulance? Polly was up on the kerb now, shouting at the pair waiting to go south, 'We have injured people. Stop your hooting or I'll shove your horn where the sun doesn't shine.'

Verity heard Tom's laugh, and inside she laughed herself, because Polly was shouting and being rude, so everything was all right. She lay on the counter, under the weight of the blankets, laughing and laughing, but she couldn't hear her own laugh. Everyone was so far away and she was so tired. But then Tom was hauling her to her feet, Sylvia was on the other side and they helped her to step onto the kerb. 'Come on, into the ambulance.'

She refused. Tom shook her. 'Listen to me.' But what was the point of shaking her, for she was shaking anyway.

She looked at him, and held the blanket tightly, though she couldn't feel it. 'I won't go. I just need to get warm,' she said, her words falling at his feet in little bits because she was shivering so badly.

Tom called to Polly, who came over to Verity and wrapped her in her arms, rocking her. 'I think you should go; but if you won't, you will go with Tom to the cabin and stay there with him, and he will hold you, all night, until you are warmed right through. That's what the ambulance blokes say. It's what I say, and it's what Tom will say – or I will swing for him.'

Verity nodded. When Polly used that voice, everyone agreed. Besides, she couldn't really think; all she knew was that she wasn't leaving *Marigold*, *Horizon* and her friends. 'Sandy?' she asked.

Polly shook her head, 'I don't know.'

Sylvia had heard and came across from the ambulance. 'We're going to moor up overnight on the other side of the lock, with Bet's other trainee, Merle, and we will find out about Sandy tomorrow. Then we can make our plans.'

Heavens, thought Verity, as Tom put his arm around her, Sylvia's as bossy as Polly. Sylvia helped as together they half carried her back down the slope of the lock to their boats, and all the time Sylvia was talking, telling them that Polly was going to take Bet's pair out of the lock, with Merle, and moor up the other side. 'As we've heard, there's a pair waiting to come south. The lock will be ready for them, then Polly'll come back and we'll take our boats through, because the lock will be ready for us. Tom, you'll have to steer the butty while I fiddle about with the tow-rope.'

Verity couldn't keep her eyes open, but it didn't matter, as someone was leading her; no, she was wrong, some-two were leading her. She laughed, but it just gurgled in her head. The feel of the ground changed and moved beneath her, just a fraction. She was on *Marigold*. 'I'm home,' she said. 'I will be fine now, but is Sandy? Is Bet?'

138

'I can't understand what she's saying.' It was Tom, wonderful Tom. She tried to open her eyes.

Sylvia said, 'Tom, it doesn't matter. You are to take Verity into *Marigold*'s cabin and strip off her clothes. I trust you to close your eyes. Then wrap her in a blanket and she will lie on the cross-bed. You will take off your own wet clothes and wrap yourself in a blanket. Then put your greatcoat or another blanket over both of you. You will hold Verity and let your body warmth work its magic. I will hang your clothes and Verity's in the engine room and they'll be dry very soon, and then I will come and cover you both with as many blankets as we can find. But now I am needed. Either I or Polly will return and make sure the fire is still built up.' Then she left them to it.

Tom opened the cabin doors, limped down before Verity, then half pulled her, half supported her into the warmth and into his arms. He said into her hair, 'I am going to do as Matron says and close my eyes, and undress you and help to keep you safe.'

Verity stood there like a child, hearing his words, although they wouldn't stay and just slipped from her head. She felt her sweaters, trousers and everything else being pulled over her head or feet. A cloth and warm water wiped her down, and a blanket was wrapped around her. Ah, bedtime.

Tom led her to the cross-bed. 'Lie down,' he murmured. She did. 'Move across,' he said quietly. She did, but couldn't feel the bed, couldn't feel anything because she was so cold, and her breathing was difficult and she just couldn't open her eyes, however much she tried. But she kept forgetting to try. She heard him, so close, whispering into her hair, 'I am here, lying with you, holding you, giving my warmth to you, as sailors do. Did you know that they do that when one of them falls in?'

Sailors, she thought. Will, Polly's twin, had sailed in his dinghy and then sailed on a troop ship to war, to Africa, North Africa, and been killed in his tank. They wore his sweaters and she, Verity, was scared how Polly would feel, if Saul ever left for the war, too. You shouldn't lose two people; it was too harsh. Tom could die, too. Saul could. Sandy could. Polly had sailed on the cut to be near, in a way, to Will. Lovely Polly, her friend, her very best friend. And Sylvia, who could be her best friend, too. Verity forced her lips to move. 'Yes, I think I knew that about sailors,' she said, her lips feeling strange and stiff.

Tom replied, 'I don't quite understand you, but I am going to keep talking to you. You must answer, on and off, throughout the night. You must stay with me, do you understand *me*?' She understood, but was too tired to reply. She felt him shaking her. 'Nod if you understand, dearest Verity.'

Instead she forced her lips to work. 'Yes,' she said. 'I understand, but let me sleep.'

'Clever girl, that was better, and you can sleep, for a little while,' he agreed. 'But remember that you

140

are wrapped in a blanket, and I am going to rub-a-dub you. It will help warm you and keep your body working. Say you understand. Come on, open your eyes and say you understand.'

'Yes, I do,' she said, and felt as though she was jolting. She felt something else, heard something else. Pat-patter, pat-patter. She smiled. '*Marigold*. We won't be late. We're carrying aluminium. We can't be late. I'm cold, we won't be late. But Sandy?'

She felt Tom's arms around her, holding her tightly. He said into her hair, 'No, my darling girl, we won't be late, we will deliver your cargo. Trust us, we will deliver it. Won't we, Sylvia?'

Verity heard Sylvia say, 'We will catch up, don't you worry. Now I've put two more blankets on you both, over your greatcoat, and another is on the side-bed, with my coat and Polly's, if extra are needed. Dog will stay here, and Tom can call her onto the bed. It's another body – unhygienic though the thought is. I've got your clothes and, when we turn off the engine, I will then bring them from the engine room to here, where the range will finish drying them. Polly or I will make a cup of tea soon, with lots of honey from Bet's hives; and you, Tom, will sit Verity up and make her drink. Warm her up from the inside. This is what we will take turns to do all through the night, until we are happy that she is all right.'

Verity heard the words, then said, 'But you are not happy, Sylvia. We know, but we can't reach you.'

There was silence. Tom smoothed her hair. 'Hush,' he said. 'Just breathe, and I will rub-a-dub you again.'

For such a long time he lay with her, and Verity could hear him, feel him; and Dog was on her feet, but she was still so cold. Tom made her talk, made her drink, then Sylvia made them both drink, and then Polly did too, and slowly Verity thawed. And at last they let her sleep, with Tom's arms still around her. She woke into the darkness and he was still there, still holding her, and Dog was still lying on her feet. Tom said, 'I never want to let you go. I want to stay with you forever and a day, so will you marry me?'

She played the words in her mind. Had she heard them or just thought them? She didn't know. She turned, opened her eyes, lifted herself on her elbow, warm now, but still shivering. Dog yelped in her sleep and rolled on her back, her paws in the air. The oil light was casting its golden light, the fire in the firebox had been replenished. Who had done that? She must have asked.

'First Sylvia, and then Polly,' Tom murmured, tiredness drawing his face into deep lines. 'I couldn't leave you for a moment, for we had to keep you warm. We all had to do that. Sylvia will replenish the firebox again soon. She brought in our clothes. They steamed, but are dry now.' He pulled her down. 'Sleep again.'

She stared into his eyes. 'I have no money, except my pay.'

He shook his head and grinned. 'That's not true.'

She felt disappointment drag at her. Tom wanted marriage, but thought she had money. She said, feeling cold again, 'It is true.'

He continued to grin. 'I saw you win at darts. You have the kitty.'

She rested her forehead on his, smiling. 'I had forgotten how rich I am.'

He was laughing softly. 'You are. You have your girls. You have Dog and the cut. You have me, if you'll have me, although I haven't got even a kitty. Verity, we can make our own way when this war is over. Don't decide now, think about it.'

She tried to, but instead she slept.

When dawn broke, Tom dressed, slid back the hatch, crabbed his way up the steps, opened the doors onto the counter and topped up the kettle from the water can. It was warmer, more like the coming of spring at last, with barely any sign of frost or ice. He returned to the cabin, shutting the doors and slide hatch, and set the kettle on the range. Verity was still sleeping. Should he wake her? Perhaps for tea in a moment? He heard movement on the counter, then a light knock.

It was Polly. 'May I come in?' She opened the doors, slid back the hatch and dodged down the steps, shutting the doors behind her, but leaving the hatch half open. 'Let's have some air in for a moment. How's she doing?'

'Pretty good, I think. Her temperature is stable. She's just tired. What news of everyone else? Then I need a pee.'

Polly sat on the side-bed. 'Bet's back – coughing, but back.'

There was another knock. 'May I enter?' It was Sylvia.

Polly called, 'Come on, Tom's brewing, but crossing his legs, too.'

As Sylvia came down the steps, Verity stirred and sat up, her blanket wrapped round her. 'Is it party time?'

Her voice was hoarse, and Tom said, 'For heaven's sake, keep warm.'

'We're about to be a man short, because Bet and Merle will need help,' Polly said, accepting a mug from Tom.

There was a pause. Sylvia said with a sigh, 'It had better be me. I'm still the new girl on *Marigold*, so I might pick up some tips anyway.'

Tom was sitting next to Polly, as Verity shook her head. 'What are you talking about, Sylvia? We're a team – we'll take it in turns, doing a day at a time. What do you think, Polly?' She said the words, but knew she had no strength, not quite yet. But soon she would.

Polly was sipping her tea. 'Absolutely. I'll take today, Sylvia tomorrow and Verity the next day, if she's up to it, which I doubt. That should bring us to Tyseley Wharf. All agreed?'

Tom had distributed tea to everyone, including himself. The tea leaves were left over from yesterday. Polly pulled a face. 'Tom, we start with fresh ones each morning. This is disgusting.'

'Quite,' said Verity.

Sylvia agreed. Dog yelped as though in agreement, wagged her tail and slept again, at the bottom of the cross-bed.

Tom muttered, 'What am I, a mind-reader? Who's to take Verity's place today? While you think about it, I'm going to see a man about a dog and will be back shortly.' He crabbed his way up the steps and limped to the bank.

Polly frowned, deep in thought. 'Well, how about us going along abreast, which means we can just about manage with someone on *Marigold*'s tiller, steering for both. Then we can keep Verity in the cabin for a while longer while one of us lock-wheels for us, and also for Bet's boat.'

Tom reappeared and climbed back down the steps, grabbing his tea and sitting on the edge of the cross-bed. 'What have I missed?'

Polly said, 'We've just been sorting out your duties. Of course there's no pay, Tom Brown, and you need to be good at obeying orders, but we think you can steer the boats if we lash 'em abreast, with Verity's guiding eye on you.' Tom laughed. She continued, 'Is that all right with everyone?'

They all nodded. But who would dare not to? thought Tom.

'Verity might feel up to brewing the odd mug of tea – proper tea.' Polly arched an eyebrow at Tom. 'And even sorting out some food, but let's see how it goes.'

Verity eased herself to the edge of the cross-bed, wrapped in the blanket, leaning on Tom. 'I'll dress – I'd prefer it. And let's get going or we'll lose even more time. I'll also make another pot of tea; a proper one, as the Mistress ordered.'

Tom looked from her to the other two, shaking his head, musing that he had thought his army mates tough, but he hadn't reckoned on these waterway girls. He carried his weak tea out onto the counter. 'It's hot and wet, and I'm not fussy,' he laughed.

'Shut the door – were you born in a barn?' they yelled in unison.

From the counter he looked along at Bet's pair of boats and saw Bet busying herself on her motor counter and pointing towards the north, as Merle nodded, and Tom knew that there was no way the cargoes were going to be held up.

He lit a cigarette, placed his mug of tea on the roof, smelt toast and heard Sylvia slowly climb the stairs, followed by Polly. Polly took off, towards Bet's boats, while Sylvia placed some toast on the cabin top for him. 'Verity'll decide when she's up to doing more. She knows not to overdo it, because she doesn't want to be laid off.'

Dog leapt for the bank and did what was needed, then sniffed to her heart's content, paying particular attention to the hedgerows, while Sylvia sorted out the lashing of the boats as Verity joined Tom on the counter, a blanket around her. He protested. 'Back into the warmth.'

'In a minute, but thank you,' she said, kissing his cheek. 'For looking after me all last night. I sensed you were there and then, as morning came closer, I really knew you were there and I've never felt so safe.' She took Tom's cigarette from his mouth, inhaled, coughed and replaced it between his lips. He felt the moisture of her. She exhaled.

He said, 'I love you so much. I never realised how much anyone could love anyone else until last night. And I admire you – all.'

She shook her head. 'We're only doing our jobs, sweet boy.' She leaned into him. 'Sweet, sweet boy.'

He felt her trembling. 'Come on, be sensible – back downstairs for now.'

Verity nodded and returned to the cabin without complaint, as pale as a sheet.

Bet was talking to the lock-keeper. Sylvia called from the prow, 'Any news of Sandy, Bet?'

Bet called back. 'She'll keep her legs because, as your Tom said, the cold stopped her bleeding to death, as did his tourniquets – and Verity's spectacular grubbing about, whipping off Sandy's wellies. But of course Verity will owe her a pair of wellies, so tell her that, Tom.' Tom heard Verity laugh in the cabin, then cough. Bet continued, 'Naturally it's second nature, after she and Polly unhooked

Jimmy from the propellers a while ago. If you save a third, we'll have to give her our sugar ration. Drinks on me, when we reach wherever we get to. Come on now, chop-chop, we need to get going.'

Tom was astonished that there had been no thank-you. He opened the cabin doors and said as much. Verity, lying on the cross bed beneath the blankets, said, 'We're boaters, we don't; we just oblige in return at some stage. What more do we want? We have our table by the fireside, by virtue of helping Jimmy – little though it was, and something anyone would do.'

'We boaters' resonated with Tom. Well, there were worse people to be. He insisted, 'Now sleep. Get your strength back. I've always wanted to be the captain of a ship.'

Verity started to laugh, but it turned into a coughing fit.

'Sleep,' Tom insisted.

Chapter 9

Saturday 1 April – at the home of Polly's parents: Jotom, 12 Pinewood Avenue, Woking

It was the start of the school holidays, and Mrs Holmes, Polly's mother, had promised her husband Thomas that she and Joe would do some weeding at his allotment and would be home in time to put lunch on the table. The weather had warmed magically, although perhaps that was too strong a word. 'Better to say it's not so cold, so the soil *could* be loose,' she said in the hallway of Jotom, tightening Joe's scarf and pulling his woollen hat down over his ears.

Joe wriggled free and jerked his hat back up. 'I didn't say nothing about the earth being cold, Auntie Joyce.'

She laughed. 'I started by thinking about the freeze, and then that the soil would be looser around the roots, and out it came – just like it does when you're doing homework and something's in your head. If the ground's still too hard, we'll tidy up the runner-bean poles and pick some sprouts.'

She clambered to her feet, thinking of the letter she had collected after the post arrived when breakfast was finished, and, more importantly, after she had unpicked the massive bobble from Joe's new hat. She hid a grin as she pointed to his wellington boots, lined up with Thomas's and hers, on newspaper beneath the hall window. They had been Will's boots when he was ten.

Joe yanked on the boots, then looked at her. 'You caught me good and proper about the bobble of me new hat – it was so huge, like Polly's, and pink, Auntie Joyce, and so awful, but I didn't know what to say. I didn't know about the jokes people played on April the first, yer see. I'll get you next year, so I will. But though it were a joke, I want yer to know I didn't want to sound mean about it.'

Mrs Holmes laughed. 'You weren't mean, and I should have understood you wouldn't know about April Fool's Day. You must go on keeping me on the straight and narrow while you're here, Joe.' She tightened her own scarf, told him to do up his mac and they set off down the cul-de-sac. As they walked, Joe chatted about Easter Sunday in just over a week, and the egg hunt she'd promised him after church, and Joyce felt her heart sinking. Saul's letter was in her pocket; she had recognised his writing, but could not yet bring herself to read it. In fact she never wanted to do so, because it must be that Saul and Granfer wanted Joe back.

They turned right out of Pinewood Avenue and she half listened to Joe's chatter as they rattled along. The gardens of some of the houses looked unkempt, but it wasn't surprising. So many men were away at war, and families had been evacuated or were perhaps even dead.

Joe pulled at her sleeve, and she smiled down at him. 'Auntie Joyce, did you hear me? Miss Fletcher, my teacher, was telling us that Simnel cake has been made for hundreds of years for Easter, and the eleven marzipan balls on the top are to remind us that there were eleven good apostles, and the twelfth – the missing one – was bad. He was called Judas. It must be sad to be bad, mustn't it, Auntie Joyce, and not be part of your gang any more?'

Mrs Holmes slowed. Joe sometimes asked questions like this, and she waited, knowing what would come next. Sure enough, as they entered the lane to the allotment, Joe said, 'D'you think my dad is sad to have been so bad, and not part of the cut any more?'

She never quite knew what it was best to say. She had discussed it with Mr Burton, the solicitor that Polly had worked for, before she left to become a canal trainee. He was also her husband Thomas's ARP colleague. Mr Burton had been kind and had helped obtain Joe's release from custody, after the police thought he had fired the cargo of wood carried by Polly's butty.

'What do you think, Auntie Joyce?'

Mrs Holmes realised they were at the allotment gate and she must produce an answer, and she repeated pretty much verbatim what she and Mr Burton had cobbled together. 'I expect he is sad, but if you do something really bad, like your father did, by telling that POW to set the cargo alight and selling black-market whisky to the club owner in London, there are consequences. You do understand consequences, don't you, we talked about them a few weeks ago?'

Joe was pushing the gate open. 'Oh yes,' he said. 'If I fall, it'll hurt.'

They were walking along the grass path towards Thomas's plot. Mrs Holmes nodded, forcing down a laugh. If Polly was here, they'd have exchanged a look and would have enjoyed the accuracy and simplicity of children. Dear Polly. She stopped dead. Saul's letter. Perhaps it wasn't about Joe. Perhaps there was something wrong? She shook her head. No, no, Saul or Verity would have telephoned.

Joe had found a discarded pea stick and was whipping the tussocks as they walked. What had they been talking about? Ah yes, consequences.

'The thing is, your dad knew there could be consequences, but he did it anyway. So yes, he might be sad because he is on remand, waiting for the trial. At the trial there will probably be more consequences. But that's the way it is. I suppose the answer is to think hard, if you're tempted.'

Joyce felt helpless. Mr Burton had made it sound so much more sensible, while she feared she just sounded weak. But now Joe was running ahead, calling, 'Last one there's a cissy, Auntie Joyce. And yes, I does see. It was his decision, and he'll learn not to do it again.

Anyway I'm glad he'll be locked away, then he can't hurt us, and maybe Mum will come back.'

Joyce ran after him, her wellington boots slapping against her calves. She didn't want to think of Maudie returning, or of Joe going back to the cut. Not until it happened anyway, and then she would find a way to bear it. After all, she had recovered from Will dying.

They reached the allotment. Joe had the key and unlocked the shed. 'Oh, come on, Auntie Joyce, 'urry up, we have lots to do.'

Inside the shed she watched as Joe rooted around in the toolbox until he found a hand-fork for her, and then grabbed the hoe from the rack for himself. Thomas was so neat; she supposed it came from being a storeman and needing to know where everything was. On the shelf beside the box of packets of seeds was a photo of Will and Polly. They weren't identical twins, but as near as possible.

Joe led the way outside and while he hoed the spring cabbage, clinking against stones and scraping up young weeds, she dug out dandelions near the second planting of broad beans. The roots of the wretched things went so deep that they were a complete pain to get out, and the ground really was too cold, but it was good to be out here, at one with nature.

To get a better grip she stuffed her gloves in her pocket, and the envelope rustled. She would open it when she was home, having a cuppa, and Joe was out playing with Bernard from Roxburgh Avenue, who was bound to come knocking. How would Joe feel, leaving Bernard and school behind, to return to the cut? She levered up the dandelion root, snapping it. 'Oh, damn.'

Joe looked up from clinking the hoe around the cabbage. 'If that was me or Polly, you'd say, "Language", Auntie Joyce.'

Joyce looked up, saw him trying not to laugh, although it burst from him, and she joined in. 'How right you are, but dandelion roots are enough to try the patience of a saint, and I'm definitely not one of those.'

With the sound of Joe's laughter drowning out the noise of the birds in the hawthorn hedges, she returned to ferreting out the remains of the root.

Later that day, having baked a few hot-cross buns with very little sugar while Joe and Bernard played football in the garden, she sat down at the back-room table where she and Joe had eaten their lunch of egg and chips – his favourite – though she had insisted that he had also finished his cabbage. She poured herself a cup of tea and drew out the letter from the envelope. It was nothing short of a miracle that Saul could write at all, having only started to learn a few months previously. She laid the letter on the table, smoothing out the folds. It was written in pencil and the letters were not joined up, but one day she thought they would be. She stared out of the window again, hearing Joe's shouts and Bernard's replies.

She had been appalled at Polly originally, when her precious daughter, in whom she had invested such hopes, had fallen in love with a boater. It made her blush to remember how snobbishly she had behaved. This shame came to her especially in church, where somehow giving in to the sin of pride seemed even more crass and cruel.

Thomas had also had concerns about Saul, because he worried about how his daughter would live when the war was over. Would Polly go on having to use a bucket for years to come? And what about children? Then they had taken on Joe, while the crimes against his father were dealt with; and Thomas had said one evening, while looking at a photograph of Will, that it was Polly and Saul's life, so the youngsters should bloody well grab whatever happiness they damn well could, because who the hell knew what lay around the corner. Thomas had sworn more, after Will died; but perhaps, in her own mind, she did, too. He had turned to Joyce, his arms crossed and with that fierce look on his face, which told everyone he meant business.

She opened the letter:

Dear Mr and Mrs Holmes

I does hope you is well. We is too, me and Polly and Granfer. Verity's Tom has come back to her and they is happy as can be on the boat. I am writing because I have been full of shame, and vexation, because I reads in the paper that the war is bigger than when I couldn't read, somehow, if you understand me. So in my heart, I have decided that if I am to be any sort of a man I must try to leave this Reserved job on the canal, as theys call it, and fight like Verity's Tom, and all them others, and your Will, who died. I should at least be out there for them, you see, for men like Will. I can't lift me head much, and walk proud no more. And Leon is locked up, so no danger no more to them girls, or to Joe, or to you. My leg is better too, so that should count. Does you knows what I mean? I's not good with words yet.

Thing is I'm right troubled because I don't know how to break out of the cut, and Verity's bloke, Tom, and Steerer Mercy says I needs to go to someone important who can tell me how. Mr Burton is the only important person I sort of knows. Tom said too that there must be someone who leads the transport of the war, and they might be the ones for me, or know who is, cos I might know things they need. I wonders if Mr Burton knows about all of that?

I have thoughts that you does know how I can write to Mr Burton because yer know him well. So praps you'd tell me where to write to?

But course I need to ask you other things too. You are kind to Joe, and looking after him for now.

The letter stopped and continued on a second page. Joyce Holmes put the letter down, unable to read on, trying to absorb all that Saul had written thus far. He wanted to leave to go to war, because of the shame he felt. She had realised, a month or two after meeting Saul, that he was an exceptional young man, who had made her daughter happy in a way that she had feared Polly would never be. She saw that he was even more exceptional now. Yes, she did understand his shame. It was what she felt when she thought of how she had disapproved at first of his relationship with Polly.

Joyce looked out of the French windows at the two boys kicking the ball back and forth, but with a purpose, because Bernard was trying to hit the goal marked in chalk on the back of the garden shed, and Joe was trying to stop him. She sighed; it was a bit like war really.

She stared down at the letter. She must go on, and face whatever it was that Saul wanted, if he was to leave, which was probably that Joe was to return to help Granfer on the boats. She placed the top sheet next to her tea, which she had neglected to drink, and read on:

But if I gets to go, and leave the cut, Granfer will live on the bank with Auntie Lettie, and the boats will go back to the company. I been thinkin' our Joe won't want to be with old people like Auntie Lettie and Granfer in Buckby, and I thinks that you took in our Joe instead of letting the police stuff him in the home when they thought he were guilty, with Mr Burton standing guarantor then. So if I gets to go would you keep our lad fer us til I gets home. I knows it's a damn great ask, but ask it I do, and will not go if it is a no, since that boy is the sun and moon to me, like your Polly be too. I will have to think hard about what happens if I don't get back. Just for now I can't think of more than praps going.

From the garden she heard a massive cheer from Joe. Joyce swung round with the letter in her hand. He had scored a goal and was leaping up and down while Bernard just laughed, stuck his tongue out and ran to pick up the football from the flower bed. For two pins, she would have cheered along. Of course – of course they'd have Joe. She drank her tea, cold by now, but tasting like ambrosia, then sat back in her chair, feeling that she could have turned cartwheels.

There was more in the letter and, as she read it, Joyce thought of her conversation about conse-quences with Joe at the allotment:

And now, to my lovely Polly. I haven't told her of my thoughts, because I doesn't want her heart to hurt while I waits to see if I am to go. So I would ask you to cross yer own heart and tell her nothing of my plans yet awhile, cos I will tell her when I hears from that place that sorts the war transport.

I knows I can trust you and I knows you know she is the breath in my body but that sometimes we just have to leave and breathe on our own to do our duty.

I write this with gratitude and wait for a reply to Bull's Bridge depot. If I get taken, I will talk to our Polly, and I will come down to see Joe, and you, cos you are Polly's Ma and Da, and so we is family.

Saul Hopkins (Mr)

Chapter 10

Saturday 1 April – early morning, south of a bridge just north of Cosgrove

Tom stood at the tiller of *Marigold*, heading slowly towards a bridge north of Cosgrove on what he called a soft morning: warm sun, non-existent wind. But then he heard a repeated hooting from inside the bridge-hole, and Verity, now mostly recovered from her dip, stepped away from his side. She said, 'That's Bet's hunting horn, and no sign of her. Lord above, are they stuck? It's been the foulest journey for them.'

Verity was slower than usual getting onto the roof, but that was the only way anyone would know that she'd been knocked for six so recently. And what's more, Tom thought, she'd never said another word about it. His love and admiration overwhelmed him as he watched her shading her eyes, as though she could see into the darkness beneath the bridge. He asked, 'Hunting horn, my lovely girl?'

Verity murmured, 'Her father's, my lovely boy.' They laughed quietly, but then she continued, 'I'll tell you more later. But she gave us one, and kept one. Listen, there it goes again – that's every three seconds. Something really is wrong. Oh, I do hope it's just the engine, and not Bet's chest.'

They heard Polly hoot from *Horizon*, on tow behind.

Verity hesitated. 'Moor up, Tom, quickly. It's deep enough here; see the mooring studs set in the bank. It could be that either Bet's ill, or that ruddy *Hillview*'s broken down again. If it's Bet, we can nip down and start the pair up, and take it through to get help. If it's broken down, we'll have to set to.' She cupped her hands around her mouth. 'Pols, we're mooring up.'

Polly's reply came. 'To see what's what?'

'Yep, bring rope.'

Tom slowed, steering into the bank.

Verity tied up, calling out, 'Neat bit of driving. You should have been a chauffeur.' She grinned, though the humour didn't reach her eyes.

He knew better than to try to cut through the façade and said, 'I seem to remember chauffeuring for a spoilt little princess. You—'

His words were brought to a halt as she leapt onto the counter and kissed his mouth. 'Enough.' She stood back, her grin fading. 'Oh Lord, this trip has been a nightmare.'

He raised his eyebrows.

She said, 'All right, I know the only way to sort it out is to go.'

'Quite.'

She grabbed the bike from the roof, and a coil of rope from behind the chimney. There was a shout from the towpath and Polly was there, her legs on the ground on either side of her bike, rope coiled over her shoulder, too.

They were gone, and Tom stayed, cursing his leg, but then realising he wouldn't be here, on sick leave, if he hadn't broken his shin. 'So stop with the grumbling, for heaven's sake,' he told himself.

Verity was right; it had indeed been a tricky journey, and the girls had not only taken turns on Bet's pair, *Hillview* and *Sky*, but stayed close by every foot of the way, partly because of the stuttering engine, and partly because of Bet's awful cough. It's what a team should do, he thought, lighting up a cigarette, although they should also listen to advice. Bet should have let him tinker with the engine when it gave up the ghost yesterday afternoon, instead of working on it into the night. Now one or other of them had broken down.

He kept an eye on the traffic coming up behind and pulling in, smoke rising straight up from the boats' chimneys in the windless air. Nothing, of course, was coming through from the north. On the parapet of the bridge, children were jeering. He called to them, 'Are boats banking up much on the other side?'

'Too bloody right. I reckon it's a boat broke in there, cos you boater scum can't even bloody keep an engine working.' The lad threw a stone. It plopped into the cut yards short of him. Tom understood Verity's and Polly's need to chase up the bank after them, and even Sylvia was tempted, she'd told him, when they moored up while Bet worked on the engine yesterday. Sylvia was a funny one; not so much sad, but it was as though she lived in a world that wasn't quite everyone else's. He wondered how she had got on, working Bet's boats with her today.

For a while Saul had stayed back with their convoy, but they couldn't all be slow. Tom eased himself onto the bank, letting Dog sniff and potter; but maybe he should train Dog to advance with stealth, then grab one of the children by the scruff and bring them down to the boat, where they could give the little devil a cloth and set him, or her, to cleaning the boat. The thought made him laugh aloud, and he nearly jumped out of his skin when, from behind, he heard, "Ow do.'

He spun round. It was Steerer Norton. 'How do,' Tom replied. They stood together in silence as sparrows chattered in the towpath hedgerow, setting Dog barking and chasing towards the bridge. 'Dog, get back here.'

Dog stopped, turned, but didn't rush back; instead she sniffed and scurried to left and right.

'*Hillview* be stuck, be it? Engine needs a good and proper over'aul. Bet could call in at Mikey's just up Buckby turn-off. 'Tis Saul's mate, and it be quicker than the maintenance yard. Or p'raps it's Bet and 'er chest? Ah well, best 'ave a look-see.' Steerer

Norton's hands were in his pockets and his yellow kerchief at his neck fluttered in the breeze, his leather coat undone.

Tom shrugged. 'Polly and Verity have just gone. The damned engine has been making Bet's life a misery, and it's probably decided to break down at a chokepoint, which is anyone's worst nightmare. Perhaps she'll let me work on it under the bridge, but it'll take time.'

Steerer Norton tipped back his hat. 'No need fer that, they'll 'aul it out and you can sort it 'ere.'

'Haul?'

'Look yonder.' Steerer Norton started to walk towards the bridge-hole, and now Tom saw Polly, Sylvia and Verity, their ropes tied around their shoulders and waists, hauling on tow-ropes. What the hell? Tom started forward, but what could he do? He was sick to death of being so useless, and hurled one of his walking sticks onto the counter. Dog bounded after it, bringing it back, tail wagging. Tom grabbed it and limped after Steerer Norton, but heard someone else approaching from behind. It was Steerer Mercy, who only seemed to be strolling, but was covering ground like a greyhound. ''Ow do,' he said as he scorched past. The two steerers passed the girls, too, and disappeared into the bridge-hole, with their heads down.

Tom met the girls, who were trying to dodge the stones and mud being thrown from the parapet as they hauled *Sky*, the butty, from the bridge-hole. The girls, heads also down, mud-spattered and with sweat beading their foreheads, didn't acknowledge him, but just continued hauling. He'd wondered at the callouses on Verity's shoulders, when he had wrapped her in the life-saving blanket, and now he understood.

He slotted in behind Sylvia, feeling stones hit his shoulder, not to mention the woollen hat that Verity had insisted he wear instead of his beret. He threw one of his sticks aside, knowing Dog would collect it, and dragged her tow-rope over his shoulder, stomping along, using just one stick for balance. 'One of the girls at last,' he grunted.

They laughed, but didn't stop. Sylvia called over her shoulder, 'Once we get them going, it's not so bad, and we'll be out of range of the children soon. They have pathetic throwing arms.'

Verity panted, 'They should try getting on the tow-rope – that would improve their throwing action.'

Tom felt the rope-burns on his hand, and the rope digging into and rubbing his shoulder, even through his greatcoat. 'The men are heading for the motor?'

No one answered such an obvious question. So he ignored the ache in his leg and matched their steps. He heard a voice from the rear call, 'Pull back on the rope. Pull back – stop the bugger, she's clear of the bridge. The blokes are about to haul out *Hillview*, God bless 'em.' It was Bet, coughing, as she hurried to catch them up.

Tom heard Verity mutter, 'Poor Bet, she must wonder why she ever returned to the training scheme.'

Ahead of Tom the three girls were all leaning back, straining to halt the drift of the butty, but the weight of the load was taking them forward. Tom yelled, 'Dig your heels in.'

Sylvia shot back, 'What the hell do you think we're doing?'

Verity laughed, 'Language, Sylvia.'

'Oh, shut up,' Polly and Sylvia shouted, but they too were laughing as they leaned right back like a tug-of-war team at a village fete. Tom knew that if he did the same with his plastered leg, he'd not stay upright, so he clung to the rope like some maiden aunt, doing his best, with his walking stick hooked over his arm, feeling a perfect fool. *Sky* stopped at last, just short of *Marigold*.

He bent over, hands on his knees, panting. Bet ran back, still coughing, to help the men and Merle, who were still in the bridge-hole with the motor, *Hillview*. The girls coiled all the ropes, as the children started throwing more stones. Straightening, he saw Polly dodge forward, grab the walking stick that Dog had returned, and run towards the bridge, throwing it up and over the parapet, calling to Dog, 'Fetch.' The children screamed and disappeared from the parapet as Dog tore up the slope, barking. Tom heard the shout, 'Quick, the bloody dog'll eat us.'

Polly called Dog back. She came, with Tom's walking stick in her mouth, and Tom could have sworn she was laughing. Polly certainly was.

'Good throwing action,' he shouted.

'My brother taught me.'

He knew his place, so while the others were sorting out the mooring, he made tea, carting the mugs to the towpath. As the girls drank it down, *Hillview* was hauled out by Merle, Bet and the two steerers. Tom said, 'What I can do is get that damned engine fixed enough to get it to Mikey. You girls must convince Bet, or God knows what's to be done.'

Sylvia nodded and murmured, 'Of course *He'll* know.'

Tom was confused and said, 'The trouble is, I'm not sure *she* will, so Verity ...' But he saw that Verity was already running towards Bet and talking earnestly, even wagging her finger. Finally they approached Tom together and stopped by the *Marigold*. Bet sighed and smiled at Tom. 'I refused your offer yesterday, but I'd kiss your feet if you would have a go at the damned thing. Just do enough to get it to Mikey's yard, if you would.'

'If you leave my feet alone, I'll sort your engine,' Tom said. 'You've some tools, I expect.'

He followed Bet along the towpath, calling back to Verity, 'I bet you're glad you don't have to haul like that every day – or every week, come to that.'

Verity shouted, 'Just every two weeks.'

Again he thought he'd misheard, and hurried on with Bet.

Once they were through Stoke Bruerne, Polly lifted the bicycle onto the roof, took up *Horizon*'s tiller, and Verity re-joined Tom on *Marigold* while Sylvia continued on *Hillview*. Within the flick of an eye it seemed they were going through the long Blisworth Tunnel, following Bet, whose engine, Tom had declared, was tweaked enough to reach Mikey's. Verity pointed above them to the arched bricks, worn where the boaters would lie on the cabin roofs and walk their boats through, while the runabout took the horse over the top. Tom murmured, 'I never realised how hard any of it was. And I mean *any* of it.'

Verity said, 'If you get an echo, you can make a wish.'

He called, 'I love this woman.' As his words echoed, he said, 'I'm not telling you my wish, though you can guess, perhaps.'

She replied, 'Perhaps.' They headed on, in the darkness, her hand in his, the only things visible the glowing ends of their cigarettes.

He murmured, 'So, no more locks now until Birmingham.'

Her laughter echoed. 'If only that were true. No, this is when I sort out lunch and leave it to cook in the range. And there are more locks as we approach Norton Junction. We're still climbing after all.'

She prepared bacon-and-vegetable stew, but dreamed instead of halibut, or steak. Yes, that would be good, but she was also thinking of Tom's wish and hoping it was for marriage.

On they travelled, out into the daylight, and their journey was easier now, but then they climbed the Norton locks, and it was magical that such cold and harsh weather had given way to this 'soft' day, as Tom called it.

At the last lock Sylvia left Bet's *Hillview* and joined Polly on *Horizon*, and Verity felt immediately better because the team was together again. As she transferred to *Marigold* to join Tom, she absorbed the thought and said, 'Well, I never.'

Tom looked at her. 'Well, "you never" what?'

'I must have been missing Sylvia. Until now we've always felt relieved at her absence.'

Tom slipped his arm around her. 'She mucked in well, when Sandy fell in. Perhaps she felt part of it and liked that? Be interesting to see if she keeps in the team, as it were. She's a private one, for whatever reason. We have had one or two blokes like that. Sometimes they meld, sometimes they don't. I suppose you just have to hope for the best and, as long as they do their jobs, that's good enough.'

'I suppose so, but I want Sylvia really to be one of us.'

'Whether she wants to be or not?' He was laughing softly.

'Oh, all right. I'll write to you and let you know, shall I? You'll have nothing better to do than think of the cut, will you?' She was laughing, too, but she felt that at any minute she'd grip Tom to her and beg him not to leave.

Within minutes, it seemed, Bet was hooting as she turned right for Buckby for a proper engine overhaul, while Tom hooted the electronic horn in reply, knowing better than to use the hunting horn, which seemed reserved for special occasions. *Marigold* would carry the message of Bet's delay to the office at Tyseley Wharf, Birmingham. Tom asked, as they carried on through the darkness of the Braunston Tunnel, 'So, what's the story about the hooter?'

Verity explained about Bet's father, who had hunted and owned a couple of hunting horns. Bet had brought them onto the canal and left one with *Marigold*, keeping the other.

'She must be fond of him,' he said.

Verity waited for a moment as the light at the end of the tunnel grew. 'I'm not sure. He killed her mother, some sort of breakdown, and is still in one of those hospitals.'

Tom said nothing, but gripped her hand. 'Poor woman. Poor man. Poor Bet.'

They wheeled their way downhill through the locks after they exited the tunnel, and the stretch past Leamington brought them to late afternoon. They kept going for a while, but there was no way either Polly or Verity was ready to climb Hatton locks in the half-light, so they moored up along the bank, which they knew had enough depth. There was no pub, so after a meal they set up the brick fireplace on the bank and got the boiler going. It wasn't too dark, so even if an ARP warden was powering along on his bicycle, he'd hardly whistle and shout, 'Lights.'

They washed some of their dirty clothes, taking it in turns to stir the boiler, warming themselves beside it. Tom joined the three of them. 'You look like a coven of witches,' he laughed.

Sylvia stared at him. 'There are no such things as witches, and they shouldn't be mentioned – the very words are an offence.' She stormed off, back to the butty. 'I'm going to bed, so come in quietly.' She slammed the cabin doors behind her.

Tom looked after her, and then at the girls. 'I'm sorry, I didn't mean anything by it.'

Verity sighed in disappointment. 'It's not your fault. Sometimes we just touch a nerve, and who knows why.' She and Polly rinsed and wrung out the clothes, then strung them on a line behind the cabin to drip. They'd dry the next day. They changed into pyjamas in *Marigold*'s cabin, wrapped them-selves in blankets and tiptoed across to the butty, leaving Tom and Dog to the seclusion of the motor cabin. Verity felt like throwing herself in the cut again, so that she could be held all night by Tom.

Polly nudged her. 'Don't you dare,' she whispered as they paused outside the butty-cabin doors.

'How did you know?' whispered Verity.

Polly grinned as the sky danced with searchlights. 'It's what I'd want.'

They tiptoed into the butty cabin in their boots, carrying socks, because Verity wasn't having Polly's cold feet on her – a feeling reciprocated by Polly. The light from the range fire, banked up with coal and ash, lit a path for them. They crept along and onto the cross-bed, pulling up the blanket. Sylvia said quietly, 'Sleep well, both of you.'

Verity smiled. 'Sleep well, Sylvia.'

It was an unexpected rapprochement. Polly whispered, 'I hope Saul's held up at Tyseley Wharf and I can have a bit of time with him. He's seemed more perky, don't you think, since Tom's been here? Perhaps he feels as though he's got a new friend.'

Verity whispered back, 'I've been too busy looking into my own bloke's eyes to bother with yours.' They laughed quietly, but Verity stared at the ceiling, wishing she could tell Polly that in the pub that first night Tom and Steerer Mercy had talked to Saul about possible ways of enlisting, and that could be the reason he seemed happier. She turned on her side, wishing she didn't know, because she felt as though she was lying to her friend. Well, she almost was, but as Saul had said to Tom, why upset Polly unnecessarily? And he was right. But it still took her several hours to get to sleep.

Chapter 11

Sunday 2 April – the *Marigold's* arrival at Tyseley Wharf

The Hatton locks, in spite of being much closer to Birmingham, had become Polly's least-favourite flight, but it was mainly because she was always exhausted after the long slog. It was also something to do with the rushes, which looked so dark and sinister. But it was Verity's turn to lock-wheel and she thanked her lucky stars that she was just steering.

Polly changed with Verity to handle the Knowle flight of locks, the last before Birmingham, and as she cycled past *Marigold* she envied Verity and Tom their time together, but knew it was short. Dodging a puddle, she wondered about Saul again, hoping he'd forgotten about enlisting; but would the longing start again, once his new friend Tom left for war?

She cycled past allotments, waving at those who were hoeing and planting. Was her dad doing so yet? Were her mum and Joe helping? She remembered how she and Will would be drafted in to weed, and to pick the sprouts. She liked the picking, but not the weeding, because the soil seemed to clutch at the roots. Was she clutching at Saul? She must not, for the boaters needed their freedom. She cycled on.

A flyboat passed on its way to London. She waved, and the young men called "Ow do.' She looked behind as Tom steered away from the centre, giving them space. She could see Verity cleaning the outside of the cabin. Behind, on the butty, Sylvia was doing the same. She smiled to herself and cycled off again; there were locks to open and close, miles to travel, cargoes to deliver, with the team.

She whizzed beneath a bridge. Ahead an elderly couple were walking their equally elderly Labrador. She slowed. 'Good morning.' It seemed rude to use her bell. She swerved onto the grass verge, and the man called in his Birmingham accent, which underlay the boaters' dialect, "Ow do.'

She lock-wheeled until they were past Knowle. Next stop, Brum, as the boaters called it. The bridges were more frequent and warehouses lined the cut, shutting out the spring sun. Barrage balloons tugged at their moorings. Factories belched smoke from their soot-stained chimneys. Soon, very soon, at the end of the week, it would be Easter. It meant little to Polly, because they had a cargo to deliver.

The traffic became more congested as they had to wait for oncoming pairs to come through bridge-holes. She kept on cycling under the overhanging trees rather than return to the boats, reluctant to invade Verity and Tom's privacy, or that of Sylvia, who seemed preoccupied and distant once more.

She skirted a wide part of the cut, with some dead leaves still on the surface, even after the long winter. They were half an hour away from Tyseley now, and from the public baths and a bed at Mrs Green's boarding house. She flashed a look behind her. Would Tom come to the baths? She heard *Marigold*'s hooter signalling that they would pull in under the next bridge for her. Soon they'd be amongst the noise of the wharf, the warehouses and the cranes, breathing in the smell of soot and industry.

'But please, please don't unload us too quickly. Please be busy. Please let us have a hot bath, and a bed on land,' she said aloud as she finally clambered onto the butty, in order to leave the lovebirds on the *Marigold* in peace for a little longer, and slung the bike on the roof.

Sylvia said, 'I can't wait for a bath either. I do so hope the wharf is busy, and I'm sorry Saul won't be there this time. We were so wretchedly slow that he and Granfer must be at least a couple of days ahead.'

Polly smiled. Sylvia's remoteness came and went, and it had gone again. Did Tom make the difference, or was it, as Tom had suggested, the teamwork she experienced when Sandy fell in?

Within twenty minutes they were at the wharf, the kerb of which was almost on a level with the boats, unlike Limehouse Basin, which always loomed above them. Pairs queued ahead, still unloaded, and even as they moored, they heard other boats approaching from the south and Polly's heart lifted.

She said to Sylvia, 'Maybe we'll get that bath and bed.'

Sylvia grinned. The foreman trotted across to Verity, moored just in front on *Marigold*. "Ow do – be tomorrer, t'will. Break yer 'earts, no doubt, to be nipping off and 'aving a shop, or whatever it is yer do with yerselves, though I sees yer have an 'itch-'iker. Been in the wars, lad? Ah well, bit of a cruise does yer good.'

Polly heard Tom's strong laugh. She smiled at Sylvia. 'Let's clean up the old dear and then head for the trams, eh, Sylvia?'

As they began, Tom and Verity went to fetch the letters. On their return, Verity pointed towards the head of the queue of boats and shouted, 'Isn't that *Seagull* and *Swansong*? They should have been loaded a few days ago, surely.'

Polly nipped onto the kerb and saw that Verity was right. She broke into a smile, jogging along the wharf and weaving past men who were arguing about who should do what, as a lorry revved up behind them. The driver wound down his window and leaned out, a cigarette in his mouth. 'Make up your bloody minds; this lot ain't going to unload itself.'

She ran around crates, keeping her eyes on Saul and Granfer, and on Harry, the runabout, as they clambered onto the kerb of the wharf. 'Saul, oh, Saul,' she called out. He looked round and she ran into his open arms and felt his strength enfold her.

'Did you break down? Why are you so late? Oh, Saul, I miss you so much, all the time.'

He tightened his hold. 'And me too, lass.'

She breathed in the scent of him, but then drew back. It was different – clean. She looked up at him. 'Have you had a bath?' His gaze slid from her, and she reached up, holding his face so that he had to look at her. 'Saul, where have you been?'

Granfer cut in. 'Ah, lass, we been to Buckby to see me sister Lettie. She writes to me now I can read and said to come fer our lunch and a bit of a natter.' He coughed, and Polly heard the rattle of his chest. Granfer continued, patting her shoulder, 'Yer lad 'ad an bath, I 'ad me chest wrapped in goose grease and brown paper. He stinks clean, I stink o' goose, but Lettie reckons it'll do the trick. She always were the bossy one. Gettin' on a bit now, she is, and her Arthur 'as gone to dust, so she's a mite lonely, or so I reckon.'

She looked from one to the other. 'I'm so pleased, partly because it held you up, but it must have been lovely to see Lettie, Granfer. Perhaps one day I can meet her, too, when we've time to stop. We can call in on Fran, Bet's friend, too, and pick up some honey from their hives. Not sure how close their house is to Lettie's?'

Harry was pulling at Granfer's sleeve, asking him something in a low voice. Granfer smiled and answered, 'Course yer can, lad. I saw yer da's boat up ahead, too, and they're loading his cargo, so he'll be away soon, and he'll 'spect yer to say 'ow do.'

Harry started to run off and then spun on his heel, tipping his hat at Polly and shouting out, "E don't 'alf smell sweet, yer Saul, don't 'e, Polly? But 'e's been right rude about us who pong. Yer just watch yerself, or yer'll be catchin' an earful an all.'

Polly laughed and turned back to Saul, who was calling after the lad, 'Yer just wait, Harry. I'll roast yer, so I will.'

She said, 'Leave the lad, you great brute, and just think about how I'll smell like sweet violets by the time we girls have been to the public baths. So why not meet us again at the Bull and Bush pub at the end of Mrs Green's boarding house street. Then Granfer will be the only one ponging.' She hoped her voice sounded light and carefree, when really she wanted to beg Saul to come. He mustn't feel tethered, though.

Saul laughed loud and long. 'I'll be doing that, don't yer fret, my lovely lass, and I'll bring Verity's Tom, too, but we have things to do before then. Now, off yer go. Verity's talking pretty straight to the foreman, and it'll be chop-chop to the baths, I reckon.'

She shook her head. 'No, it won't. It's chop-chop to clean up the boats, and only then to the baths. She'll be telling him Bet's stuck at Mikey's with a beggar of an engine. Tom got her that far by stripping a fuel line or something, but that was only a temporary measure.'

Verity came to stand with them. 'Put Saul down, you bad girl, we need you to clean up. Tom's walking

Dog, then says he and Saul are off to do boys' things and, if we're nice, they'll buy us a present. If not, they won't; anyway, they'll meet us later. He says we're to book a room for him at Mrs Green's, after he's had a bath, but I dare say Saul will want to come back to the wharf to be with Granfer?' She turned and walked back to *Marigold*.

Polly kissed Saul hard on the lips. 'Let me know about the room, and come to the Bull and Bush if you can.'

He pulled her to him, kissed her, his eyes closed, and whispered, 'I'll need to stay with *Seagull* for the night. Granfer worries me, so he does, with his chest an' all.' She understood and couldn't have left the old man, either.

'But you'll be at the pub?' she persisted.

'Try and keep me away,' Saul said, kissing her hand as she turned, then pulling her back once more and hugging her. 'We'll look after Dog an' all, whiles you're sleeping in a proper bed.'

She ran back to the *Marigold*. In the cabin Verity waved a letter at her. 'From your mum, and one for me. I sent some sums for Joe, but I expect he does them with one hand tied behind his back by now. I asked him to tell me if they were too hard for Jimmy Porter, who should be letting us have his lessons, but they've gone on. Harry's da thinks they'll be at Bull's Bridge on our return.'

Polly sat on the roof and read her mum's letter, which mentioned weeding at the allotment and her evening games of Snakes and Ladders with Joe, and dwelt on his progress at school, and how pleased she was that Tom was with them. Polly smiled, and read Joe's note at the bottom, about looking forward to the Easter school holidays and the Easter-egg hunt that Auntie Joyce had promised him; she smiled again. It's what her mum had done for her and Will, even if it was only a painted hard-boiled egg. She folded the letter and put it in her pocket.

'Mum's pleased Tom's back with you.'

Verity was washing the walls. 'Oh, you told her.'

Polly picked up the mop and bucket and carried it to the steps, then stopped. 'No, you must have done.'

There was a pause as Verity reached for the ceiling above Polly, working around her and saying finally, 'Oh, you know me. I can't remember from one day to the next, but I'm pleased she's pleased, if you follow me.'

Polly lugged the bucket up onto the counter. 'Mum just wants us both to be happy. Not sure what she really feels about Saul, though. I reckon they think I'll outgrow him, but on the other hand, perhaps they really do like him? They certainly love Joe.'

Over on the butty Sylvia was on her hands and knees, scrubbing the counter. Polly looked at her mop and bucket and sighed. She nipped along to the stores shed and gathered up the scrubbing brush, then returned, hearing the hoot of a lorry, and curses. Ahead of *Marigold* a crane was swinging a load of pallets from a lorry onto a narrowboat.

Someone was yelling. Well, someone was always yelling.

She scrubbed the counter, her knees becoming wet. Suddenly she was sick to death of being wet and filthy, and even more fed up with the endless cleaning. She kept going, her hands red and sore now, but when weren't they? Finally she slung the brush into the bucket, dipped the mop in the cut, wrung it out and rinsed the counter.

It was the turn of the cabin roof next, and automatically she set about it while the gulls called, cranes clanked, men shouted, machinery from the workshops screamed, an external telephone bell sounded and a tannoy crackled. Then it was the turn of the cabin sides. She was in a rhythm. Inside, Verity would be polishing. It would have been the maid's job in Howard House. She grinned to herself and called out, 'You should wear a little black uniform, a bonnet and pinny, Verity.'

'You should be quiet,' Verity yelled, but then laughed. 'Anyway, I'm going to offer to help Sylvia, now this is done. We have been sleeping there, after all.'

She emerged onto the deck, her hair awry. Polly said, 'You look like the woman with snakes in her hair.'

Sylvia called from the butty roof, 'Medusa, you mean. And yes, she does. And I've cleaned inside and out, but thank you anyway. I have made spam sandwiches for the three of us, and then I want a bath; and I don't want to wait too long, and that's jolly well that, so there.'

When Polly and Verity emerged from the cabin, Sylvia was on the quay, slapping her arms around her in the cool wind, her grip at her side. They heard Dog barking, and Tom came across the yard, dodging the lorries and workers. He was using just one stick now, and the other was Dog's plaything.

Verity handed him the keys. 'You know where the baths are. I wrote it down, remember?'

His salute was a good deal smarter than theirs would have been. The three girls ran across the yard, aching to be free of the cut and its environs and longing to soak in the deep, hot water, which had become a tradition inherited from Bet. They gobbled down the sandwiches on the tram, then sat back as it rumbled towards the baths, jumping off when the soot-streaked building was in sight, running to it and into the lobby. Panting, they paid their ninepence each from the housekeeping kitty.

The lady behind the counter slammed her hand on the counter bell and, like the good fairy, Mrs Green – plump, grey-haired and rosy-cheeked – appeared through the door on the right, in her starched white uniform. She opened her arms, then dropped them again. 'No,' she said, 'not till yous clean, not after last time.'

They all laughed, even Sylvia, who at the time had been mortified at the smudges they had left on the pristine Mrs Green. Sylvia said now, 'I still don't know how you stay so starched in all this steam.'

They followed Mrs Green into a cavernous white-tiled room, which was divided into cubicles. 'Same cubicles as always,' she said. She pointed to Number Two. 'That's yous, Blondie. Polly, yous is next; and little Miss Sylvia is the next, and nice and spotless she leaves it, too. Cleanliness is next to godliness, our parish priest says. He'd like yous, lass, but he'd know when 'e was beaten with t'other two.'

She winked at the three of them.

'Yer can go up to the top line marked on t'side of the bath, sluice it, then fill it once more. Towels on the back of the doors – two each. I've left soda and a scrubbin' brush for each o' yous at the end. See if yous, Blondie, and yous, Polly, can change the 'abits of a lifetime and leave it so it sparkles. Needs some elbow-grease, so it do.'

'Thank you, Mrs Green, I think,' grinned Verity. 'By the way, Bet will be in sometime with her lot. I think they're sending her a new trainee to make up the crew. They'll meet at Braunston.'

Sylvia was letting herself into Number Four. They heard her bolt the door. Mrs Green nodded. 'I 'eard. Nothing much happens that my Alf don't 'ear about, swinging around in his great big crane. Staying tonight, is yous?'

'If you have rooms, Mrs Green. But we need an extra, for Tom Brown.' Verity sounded tentative all of a sudden.

'Yes, I 'eard about 'im an' all. Didn't turn up when he should 'ave, but managed to swing it anyway, so he must have something, if you've forgiven him. In yous go, Blondie; it's three-thirty now, and I dare say you needs to be at Bull and Bush fer yous tea, and darts.'

Verity entered her cubicle and bolted the door. Polly heard her murmur, 'Oh, bliss.' The sound of the tap running covered anything else.

Polly waited while Mrs Green opened the door to Number Three. 'There you go, Miss Polly Pocket, and I 'ear yous and yous Saul are still sticking it out. Warms me 'eart. He's a good 'un, a keeper. You just remember that, that's what I says. In yous go.'

Polly entered. The white tiles gleamed. She stood on the doormat, bolted the door behind her, dropped her grip, removed her boots and socks and turned on the tap. Did Mr P. O. Thompson at the Ministry of War Transport tell the trainees about the filth? Well, Potty, as they called him, hadn't told her, not in any detail. Neither had he told her about the public baths that saved the sanity of many a girl, or woman, who joined up. But Bet did, and to heaven she would go.

The steam was billowing as Polly ran hot water into the bath almost up to the 8-inch line. She ran in some cold, tested it, ripped off the rest of her clothes, putting them into the dirty half of a sheet they each carried, and stepped in. As she lowered herself she heard Verity singing softly, 'I'm in the mood for love.' Sylvia joined in, with her marvellous soprano, 'Simply because you're near me.' Polly eased herself down, letting the warmth wash over her, listening to the other two and catching up in the second verse. 'Oh, is it any wonder.' And all three of them chimed in with: 'I'm in the mood for love.'

Then there was silence, until Verity said, as though half asleep, 'Never ever wake me. I am in heaven right now, and I don't think I can live any longer without running hot water.'

Polly smiled, almost floating herself. But then Sylvia said, 'One day the war will end, and we'll look back on this as a time of immense freedom and purpose. It's not real life, you know. It's just a pause.'

Verity pulled out her plug, the water glugged as it drained, and Polly knew she would be spooning the gunge from the bottom of the bath, then spraying the tub with the hand-shower as she shouted above the noise. 'Well, it's a pause that would be greatly improved by hot running water, so there. And now I'm going to wash my hair, have another soak, and only then am I going to scrub-a-dub-dub the bath. We will then toddle to the Bull and Bush and hope that, just for once, Gladys can serve our fish or sausage tea without a fag in her mouth, and her ash dropping onto the chips.'

Polly knew, at that moment, that Sylvia was right. This was just a pause, but one filled with friendship, shared hardship and love. She sat up, hauled herself out of the bath and rubbed herself dry. Where had Saul and Tom been off to so secretly? She feared it was to sign up, but Saul had just been turned down. She ran another bath, soaked, washed her hair, counting the tiles on the wall, not thinking of the war, or of Saul, or Ted – Steerer Mercy's son-in-law, who had beaten the Reserved Occupation order.

She let out the water once more, then scrubbed furiously at the bath, as the soda fumes stung her eyes. She dressed, putting on her boots, and sat down on the painted wooden chair, listening to the rustling, the whistling of Verity, the humming of 'Begin the Beguine'. She joined in.

Yes, Sylvia was right. This was a pause in the whole of their lives. She clung to the word. A pause, and who knew how long that meant. It could even be forever, but in the meantime she would write it on her mind, and live in the present. She heard Verity drawing the bolt and joined her in the white-tiled corridor, and Sylvia, too. Polly said, 'Those were wise words.'

'Which ones?' Sylvia asked, hitching her grip onto her shoulder. Her hair was still wet and smelt of shampoo.

'That life on the cut is a pause.'

Sylvia nodded, looking down. 'They are wise, aren't they, but they're not mine.'

Verity turned. 'Whose then – your mother's?'

Sylvia shook her head and said nothing more, just walked along and out into the foyer, thanking Mrs

Green, who waited for them by the counter. Mrs Green put her head on one side. 'They is wise words, whoever said them, lass. I'll think of 'em when me sons come to mind, out there on them seas, protecting the convoys. We got to live, girls. Live in the pause, and not be frightened. Fear is a right nuisance, and it be just thoughts.' Mrs Green held open the door to the outside. The noise of traffic hit them.

'We'll go straight to the pub for our tea, and then on to you in the evening. Should we know what numbers our rooms are?' Verity huddled behind her scarf.

Mrs Green smiled. 'Four, Five and Six; and yous young bloke, Tom, is on the floor below. Can't be having any 'anky-panky, even if it is wartime; that's what I say.' As they left, she kissed them, one by one.

She always smells of washing soda, thought Polly. As they walked down the steps Verity said, 'Let's make a pact, the three of us. Let's try not to think of what might happen in the future. And if it comes into our heads, we'll say to ourselves, or to one another: It's just a pause.'

Sylvia said, 'But what happens after the pause?'

Polly slipped her arm through Sylvia's. 'We go on, with whatever our lives become. It's all we can do.'

Verity muttered, 'Fine words butter no parsnips.'

'Ah, but at least they're fine, and we must either believe, or pretend to believe, in them.'

*

They stood at the side of the road, waiting for a break in the traffic. A lorry from the wharf stopped, hooted and gestured them across. They waved and began to cross. He hooted as they passed in front. They jumped, he laughed and they did, too.

Polly said, to no one in particular, as they were caught in a stream of pedestrians heading the same way, 'Who'll bet me it's Verity who gets Gladys's fag ash, when she brings us the Bull and Bush food? Any takers?'

'Don't you dare break your ethics and bet, Sylvia. Because this dreadful girl will jog our Gladys to make absolutely sure it drops over my plate.'

They were laughing as they hurried along in the glum light. Clouds had gathered and seemed to bounce back the light from the searchlights. Polly realised how the accoutrements of war had become part of everyone's lives. But since the Blitz had finished, there was no cause for alarm; after all, the Luftwaffe was busy in the east, fighting the Russians, and the Allies ... Stop thinking, Polly insisted to herself. She finally said, 'Never mind the bet then, we'll just thrash the locals at darts.'

They had almost reached the now-familiar Bull and Bush, the door of which opened onto the corner. Once upon a time, pre-war, light would have fallen out onto the pavement, along with the drunks, but the blackout was still in existence, and the beer wasn't plentiful or strong enough for too many drunks. Their boots seemed to crash against the pavement as they hurried along, weaving round a pile of discarded rubbish and past the bombed-out buildings they had come to know so well. Sometimes a charred beam would crash; the last time an Edwardian iron fireplace, which had hung like a piece of strange art on a bedroom wall, had creaked and fallen, only to be caught on some sort of cord. It still dangled there. Rosebay willowherb would probably grow over all the damage when the weather grew warmer, just as it grew over the ruins everywhere else, come summer.

The girls heard laughter from the pub and smiled at one another. They crossed the road and went into the lobby, closing the door behind them, and only then did they draw aside the heavy curtain and enter the fug of cigarette and pipe smoke. Sylvia snapped at Polly, 'I hate this. We wash, get clean, come here and leave, stinking of stale smoke. I wish I'd gone straight to the boarding house.'

Polly and Verity didn't look at one another, but Polly said quietly, 'Mrs Green won't be back yet, but you can wait on her steps. She'll be there soon, but what will you eat?'

Sylvia tutted. Verity grimaced, 'Stay with us and have a generous helping of ash.'

Sylvia said too loudly, 'Like I said, I don't know why we come.'

Polly felt anger stirring, at the insult to the regulars. She muttered into Sylvia's ear, 'Why do you fight the inevitable. You know full well this is our world, and that it's the same every trip. If you don't want to come, go back to *Horizon*. For heaven's sake, we're in a pause, aren't we? It is what it is, and it's not forever; and it's safe, and think of those fighting. That isn't safe. And what's more, these people live here, and like it.'

Sylvia crossed her arms and stomped to a spare table right in the corner of the room, beneath a tatty print of seventeenth-century Birmingham.

Verity raised an eyebrow at Polly. 'Oh dear, cross-patch,' Verity said. 'Feel better now?'

'Oh, shut up,' Polly murmured, turning back to the bar.

Verity leaned on it with her. 'I say even more firmly: Oh dear. Let's buy Sylvia a large sherry, if Boris has one under the bar. Sweet, very sweet, because ...' The girls exchanged a grin.

Polly shook her head. 'It's my fault. I'm just not in the mood for one of her moods, so I'll pay.'

Verity nodded. 'That you will. A large sweet sherry, if you would, Boris; and a pint of mild for you, my girl, and the same for me. Polly, Sylvia really is getting much better, and I hope it means she's happier.'

The menu was the same as always, chalked on the board behind the bar. Polly called to Sylvia over the hubbub, 'Fish and chips or sausage and mash?'

A group of men playing dominoes, with mufflers at their necks, nodded at Polly. One called, 'Game of darts soon, Missus?'

Verity called, 'Dig deep into those pockets, boys. The Waterway Girls are here.'

A group of three women who were drinking stout cackled. 'Yous tell 'em, lass.'

Sylvia looked up from playing with a beer mat. 'Fish and chips, please. And thank you, Polly.'

Polly smiled with relief as Verity picked up the tray of drinks. Boris was wiping the counter, then flung the cloth down, took out his ordering pad, licked his finger to flick over the page and fumbled above his ear for his stub of pencil. 'Right yous are, Polly, what's it to be? Her over there wants fish and chips, right, but the sausages is off.'

Polly raised her eyebrows. 'It'll be so difficult to choose then, won't it, Boris? I know, let's have the fish.'

Boris could hardly write for chuckling. 'Yous girls just tickle me up, yous do.'

They drank at their table, sitting back to watch the life of the pub. Polly thought it probably hadn't changed much for decades, except that there were no young men. Pause, she thought; breathe.

She felt a nudge against her boot. 'Here's our food,' said Verity brightly. They all tensed and watched Gladys approach, carrying a tray that held three fish and chips plated up, with bread and margarine. The cigarette was in the corner of Gladys's mouth, her grey hair stained yellow where the smoke rose.

Sylvia groaned quietly, then whispered, 'All right, you win. To make it bearable, I bet a sixpence that it falls on Verity's.'

'You beast,' hissed Verity, as Polly laughed.

Gladys lowered the tray onto the table. 'Fish an' chips, with mushy peas,' she said. The cigarette wobbled up and down as she spoke. The inch-long ash shuddered and fell. The girls traced its descent. It landed between the plates. Verity nudged Sylvia and held out her hand, palm up.

'Later,' Sylvia muttered. 'I might want double or quits on your two boys.' She was looking behind Polly. 'Who have just come in to land.'

Verity and Polly spun round, and Polly's throat thickened and tears threatened. What on earth was the matter with her? They waved frantically, while those at the dominoes table watched with interest, nudging one another. The ladies across the room – one of them wearing a hairnet, Polly now realised – went into a huddle as Tom limped his way across in his khaki greatcoat, using his one stick, while Saul ordered at the bar.

Tom pulled a chair across from the dominoes table. 'All right, is it mates?' he asked.

'Yous welcome to it, and tek this other fer yous mate, an' all.' One of the old boys shoved another chair across. 'Sausages is off, so 'tis to be fish, chips, peas and ash.'

They all laughed, but quietly, because Gladys was old and though everyone wished she'd stop smoking for the good of her health, and the food, they didn't want to upset her.

Tom sat down. He seemed to have brought the cool with him. Droplets of rain stained his greatcoat and beret. He gripped Verity's hand. 'All clean and bathed then?'

'Oh, indeed we are,' she said, raising his hand and kissing it. 'You smell clean, too.'

'I met your Mrs Green, when Saul and I went into the Men Only side. Very firm, she was, as she led us to Harry Harris, who took over. Saul didn't bother, just read the paper, as he'd had a soak at his auntie's. Our Harry Harris isn't much of a one for smiling, is he? And I gather from Mrs Green that I have a room on the floor below you girls, and there's to be no 'anky-panky.'

The domino players burst into guffaws. 'Aye, right enough. That sounds like our Alice Green. Them players from t'theatre 'as the smiles wiped orf their faces good and proper, but who's to know what happens after lights oot.'

The women across the other side of the fireplace called over, 'Don't you believe it. Our Alice has the ears of a bat, and 'as chucked out them tiptoein' where they didn't oughta be.'

Tom winked at Polly, Verity and finally Sylvia, who flushed and stolidly ate her chips. He said, 'It seems to me that's one battle too far, so I'll keep my powder dry and wait until she's me missus, shall I?'

The men nudged one another again, while the women huddled together, whispering.

Polly looked from Verity to Tom. 'Missus? Something you haven't told your team, Verity?'

Verity ignored her, but asked Tom, 'Missus?'

'Well, not sure what we'd call you, but I reckon it's just plain Missus, or would it be Missus Lady Verity?'

Verity put her finger to her mouth, 'Hush.' She looked around, but no one had taken him seriously.

Sylvia laid down her knife and fork as Saul approached the table with a tankard in each hand. 'If you haven't asked Verity yet, Tom, you've just assumed, and that's patronising,' she said, shaking the salt over the chips. 'And rather rude.'

Saul placed the tankards on the table. Polly pointed to the chair next to her. Saul said, 'Not yet, cos I'm going ter feel a right fool, but I got ter do it – and so's yer, Tom. Yer said yer was goin' to, and our Sylvia's got it right.'

Sylvia stared at Saul, as Frankie, one of the domino players, said, 'This be better 'n a show, it be. I reckon I knows what's to 'appen. Anyone taking a shilling on it?'

One said, ''E never would, not in 'ere. Don't be bloody daft.'

Old Cedric, who was playing darts, and was one of the many who had wanted Polly's hat with the large bobble for a tea-cosy for his missus, yelled, 'Get on wi' it, lad, for the love of old Reilly.'

Tom said, 'I can't get down like Saul, cos of me leg, but I would if I could.'

Saul had sunk onto one knee. 'We've been buying rings, but we needs summat to put them on. So's I want to put mine on your finger, Miss Polly Holmes, if yer'll say yes to marrying me, when this war is done. I'll ask yer mum and dad later, but no point, if yer says no. No point in tellin', ever, till things is sorted, is there?' He sounded so anxious, and his eyes were so intense, that Polly felt she'd never loved him so much.

The pub had fallen silent, waiting for her answer; and for Verity's, because Tom was standing now, an anxious look on his face, too, as he held out a ring. Tom said, 'They're not new rings, cos there aren't any, but we found this little shop—'

Sylvia, who was eating, interrupted him, putting down her knife and fork again and dabbing at her lips. 'Please stop, Tom, or you'll end up telling Verity how much you spent. And, girls, do answer, or the drinkers will have a heart attack, because everyone is holding their breath. Remember that to accept the path you are to tread is a sacred oath.'

Polly barely heard the words, because she was bending to kiss Saul on the forehead and pull him to his feet. 'Of course I will.' As she spoke these words, Verity was saying the same thing.

The rings were too big, but the girls would wear them around their necks until they reached Bull's Bridge or perhaps they'd stop off at Alperton, from where they would be able to get into London to have them altered. The regulars were clapping now, and calling out that the drinks were on Saul and Tom, who bowed and promised they would see to it, once they'd eaten.

At that moment Gladys bore down on them with two more plated fish dinners, and her cigarette where it always was. There was no ash, so it must already have fallen. The boys searched the plates when she had gone, and yet again Gladys had missed. Saul winked at Polly. ''Tis a sign of good luck, my Polly.'

The girls won at darts, the boys bought drinks for everyone, but Boris cut the bill in half because it was good news, for a change. It was then that Polly saw the black armband on Frankie's sleeve as he put on his coat and tucked his domino box into his pocket.

At ten o'clock it was time to leave for Mrs Green's, so Saul turned back to catch the tram, waving and calling that he would keep an eye on Dog; and if they were late, he and Granfer would start the unloading for them.

Polly watched him go, then followed the others up the steps to the boarding house, past Mrs Green, who admired their rings and scooted them up the stairs. 'Yous know the way, girls, and I'll show yous young man the way to yous room. I have good 'earing. So don't even try.'

Tom promised.

Polly lay in her bed – so soft, so wide, so dry, so clean – watching the fire flickering and feeling the steadiness, the landlubber feel that always took her by surprise. She drank in the quietness; there was no lapping of water, no calling of owls, no shouts from other boaters who had not yet retired for the night and no sound of the wind. She played with the precious ring, hoping that she who had worn it before had imbued it with happiness. Well, if not, she would change all that.

'Darling Saul, the love of my life, the man I will love forever.' Is that what Sylvia, who had such a strange way of putting things, had meant by 'a sacred oath'? Polly didn't know, but wondered how often she and Saul would pass one another on the cut, unable to stop, unless they happened to coincide overnight. But they would wave, their eyes would meet and they would know that they belonged to one another and were so lucky to be away from the front line of the war. She sighed with relief. That's what Saul's preoccupation, and then his brightness, had been all about – the ring.

She smiled into the dark. She, Polly Holmes, was an idiot.

Chapter 12

Monday 3 April – *Marigold* and *Horizon* unload before heading for Coventry

Verity and Tom met for breakfast in the dining room at six-thirty the next morning, along with the other two girls. Tom pulled out Verity's chair, she sat and felt his lips as he kissed the top of her head, and the pressure of his hand on her shoulder. She knew that her unhappiness was over; her pain over her mother's actions was healed because she and Tom had found one another again. And even if the worst happened, she would know that he had not betrayed her.

She looked around this room that had become a sanctuary for the three girls. The same autographed sepia photographs of repertory actors hung on the walls. On one of the bookshelves near the fireplace were photographs of Mr and Mrs Green's two boys, in Royal Naval uniform. Verity wore her ring, but it kept slipping down her finger as she spread margarine on her toast, so she tucked it in her purse, which she rammed deep into her trouser pocket. She'd find string to hang it round her neck later today. Tom gripped her hand whenever it was free. There were two other guests, elderly businessmen at separate tables, breakfasting behind yesterday's newspapers.

Verity checked her watch. 'Come on, hurry up, everyone. They might be ready at the wharf and we can't be late yet again. Shove that toast in, Polly Pocket; you're too old for soldiers, for heaven's sake, especially when there's no egg to dip them into.'

Polly said, as she stuffed a whole soldier into her mouth, 'Mind your own business, Bossy Boots. Did you sleep, Tom?'

Sylvia pointed at the pristine white tablecloth. 'You spat crumbs, Polly – that's disgusting. Don't talk with your mouth full.'

Verity nudged Polly, saying, 'Sylvia is right. You're a disgrace, isn't she, Tom?'

Tom was drinking his tea and grinned, but said nothing. Verity repeated the question. He replaced his cup. 'I heard, but I wouldn't dare bring down the wrath of you paragons of virtue until I had swallowed.'

They were all laughing, including Sylvia. Verity snatched another look at her watch. 'No, really, enough of this – chop-chop. It'll be seven-thirty before we get there.'

Polly nodded and called over her shoulder to Mrs Green, who was opening the door to let the two men out, newspapers folded neatly beneath their arms, 'I expect Alfred's up and at it at the wharf, isn't he, Mrs Green?'

She bustled up in her apron. 'My Alfred said yous'll be unloaded sooner rather than later, so yes, crack on, girls; and yous too, Tom. Good luck, lad, when you're back with the unit. Keep yous 'ead down, and a clean white handkerchief ready at all times.'

They were all laughing when they rose, with Polly muttering, 'Just like Mum. All is well with the world if we have a clean hanky, not to mention spotless fingernails and well-shined shoes. But we fail on the latter, too.'

Mrs Green patted Tom on the shoulder. 'Me boy says every soldier should 'ave an 'anky for surrendering, but keep it in yous pocket, else they'll see it in the dark and shoot yous instead.'

They were still laughing as they hugged Mrs Green and trooped down the steps into a cool, damp wind.

They hopped off the tram at the wharf and Verity held back to pick up a newspaper from the kiosk. Tom raised an eyebrow. 'Have you time?'

Verity nodded. 'Saul and I share the crossword, and I've also got time to ask you about Saul. I could tell Polly was worried when you two went off together, and her relief when it was to ask us both if we would marry you.' She drew Tom to a stop. 'But now I need to ask if there's more news, because Mrs Holmes mentioned in a letter to Polly that you were here, with me. Polly thought I'd told her mother, but I haven't, so it must have been Saul. Polly's my friend, and I need to know why Saul wrote to her mum.'

Tom wouldn't meet her eyes. She shook him and he said, 'Look, he'll tell Polly when he's ready, and I think he's right not to worry her until things are certain.'

Verity stared at him. 'What things? How far has it gone?'

The muscles in Tom's jaw were working. She knew that look, and it meant he wouldn't be budged. 'You know he talked to me in the pub, and I replied, as did Steerer Mercy. So what Saul's done since is between him and his conscience, at the moment anyway. But you have to know he loves Polly more than himself – more than anyone, I think. And anyway, we're needed now.' He pointed to the tannoy, from which was coming the call, 'Crane B to the *Marigold* pair. Crane B.'

'Oh, quick,' Sylvia called from across the yard. 'Come on, Verity, we need to get the covers off.'

Verity hesitated and Tom shook his head. 'Verity, Saul has the right. Just be there for Polly, as she will always be for you.'

Sylvia called again, 'Come on, Verity.'

Verity whispered, 'He'd better bloody well tell her what's going on, once he's got himself sorted out, that's all I can say, because I feel as though I'm lying to her already.' She dashed after the other girls, leaving Tom to limp behind. She snatched a look over her shoulder and called back, 'Catch us up, but stay out of the way. You could get hurt.'

Polly and Sylvia were well ahead. Verity dropped her paper and ran back for it. Tom yelled, 'You go on, I've got it covered.' She rushed ahead again, wanting to shout and scream at him, but why? He was right in a way; it wasn't her business.

To either side factory chimneys were doing their usual job of belching out dark, acrid smoke, and men were criss-crossing their path. One called, 'Get a move on, Crane B's nearly there. I don't know – you trainees, just a bunch of Idle Women.'

Verity shouted without slowing, 'Idiot. We're not trainees any more.'

Another bloke in overalls laughed. 'You think we don't know that, but you're still Idle Women.'

'And you're still an idiot,' she shouted, taking out her fury on him, and followed the girls to where *Marigold* was docked. She saw them leap on board, and when she arrived Saul and Granfer, true to their word, were on the gunwales, having taken the top planks down. They were now undoing the tie-strings of the tarpaulin.

Granfer took a moment to point to *Horizon*. 'Yer do the butty, girls, we'll get this lot sorted.'

Verity glanced over her shoulder. Tom had almost reached them. It began to rain. 'Well, of course it damn well has,' she muttered. 'Get into the cabin, Tom,' she snapped.

He shook his head. 'No, I'll help.'

Polly yelled at Tom as she hurried to the butty, 'She's not thinking of you, but of the ruddy newspaper. Take it under cover into the motor cabin, then you can get the fire going in both, please. If you try and do more, you'll pitch into the cut and she'll have to dive in after you, because you'll sink like stone with your plaster.'

Everyone laughed, except for Verity, who was suddenly swept by a vivid picture of Tom going in, the plaster dragging him down. Here on the kerb she could almost feel the cold water, and as she headed to *Horizon* she was swept by nausea and dizziness and suddenly the world went dark, and all she could feel was that water. Freezing water. All she could taste was blood in the water. All she could see was mashed legs, and the sound of Sandy's screams coming out of nowhere and going on and on.

She heard, as though from a distance, Polly call, 'Verity, come on. Verity, what ...?'

Verity bent over, trying to breathe, but she couldn't. She sank to her knees on the concrete and the only thing she could hear were Sandy's screams, which were growing louder. Her nausea deepened.

'Verity!' It was Polly screaming her name. No, not more screams. Verity bent over, her head touching the ground, but Polly was there beside her, her arms around her, calling frantically, 'Tom, Tom.'

Verity could barely hear them over the screams, and she needed them to hush. She told Sandy, 'No, no, be quiet. I'm trying. You're stuck.' She was under the water, pulling off those boots. Pull, pull.

Sylvia was calling too. 'What can you hear, Verity? Who's stuck? Let us help.'

Tom's voice came, loud and clear, and cut through everything. 'You girls get back to the butty, you need to get that tarpaulin off. Verity Clement, listen to me. It's a flashback, a sort of panic thing; it will pass. I was expecting it – better out than in, as the vicar didn't say to the tart.'

Suddenly, at the sound of his voice, it was going: the noise, the taste, was fading. Verity sat back on her heels and she was laughing, but it sounded high-pitched, strange, and she couldn't stop.

Tom pulled Verity to her feet. He gripped her shoulders and shook her slightly. 'It's hysteria, darling girl, but you're safe; you are here with your friends. You are safe. Sandy is going to be all right. As I said, it's called a flashback. It's over. It might come again, but probably not. Perhaps a few dreams, but it's not real. Nothing else is real but you and me – here, safe. There is nothing else we can do anything about; nothing, do you understand? You can't take on the problems of the world.'

He had pulled Verity to him and had drawn out his white handkerchief. It was as though he was warming her, as he had in the cabin overnight, and was wiping her face as he had done gently, so very gently. And he was right: her heart wasn't beating like an express train, but slowing; her mind wasn't whizzing so fast, but slowing, and now she could breathe, pause, breathe.

He wiped Verity's face again and, as he did so, she remembered that someone else had washed her gently, when she was a small child. And someone else had been rough and had pulled her, smacked her. She leaned against Tom, but she couldn't remember who it was who had been gentle, like Tom. Who? Who? She smelled something; it was getting stronger. What was it? She buried her face in Tom's uniform, and then she recognised the scent: camellias. There, it was stronger now, here on the kerb, in Tom's arms.

He whispered, 'It's not real. It's over – you saved her. You saved her. Be proud.'

Verity pressed deeper into him, thinking she'd make him wet and cold, but no, that was then, when Sandy fell in; but Tom was correct: Sandy was all right, would be all right; and yes, she remembered now that Polly had a bit of do, after they saved Jimmy. She had said then that there was a terrible feeling of panic and sickness, but it hadn't happened to her again, not really. It hadn't happened to Verity back then, but instead it had waited until her Tom was here, God bless it. She relaxed.

But the smell of camellias, when she was small ...

Tom's words played in her mind. She whispered, 'Oh my, Sylvia won't like the vicar and the tart.'

Tom was laughing now. 'Hush, Granfer and Saul have taken over the butty tarpaulin, so the girls are coming back, looking worried to death.'

Tarpaulin? Verity thought. Oh, crikey, the tarpaulin. She wrenched free of him, feeling shaky. 'Tom make up the fire, we'll need tea soon.' The words were calming, normal, and Sandy would get better. Polly and Sylvia were with her now, gripping her arms, telling Verity that she had to stop worrying them to death or they'd have to strangle her. They were all laughing, but it wasn't a real laugh, from anyone.

Polly whispered, 'Do you remember when it happened to me? It's horrid, but it passes.'

Tom led Verity to the butty cabin. She sat with him, while the girls went back to helping Saul and Granfer. The boat rocked as the aluminium was taken from the hold. Tom made tea and carried mugs to everyone, but Verity sat, trying to remember the screams. She couldn't. The smell of camellias lingered, though. How strange.

She heard the tannoy call Polly to the office to receive their onward orders. Then Sylvia came into the cabin, saying, 'Please, please let it be a clean and easy load from here, not coal from Coventry and the Bottom Road.'

Polly came back, waving the docket glumly. 'Coal from Coventry, so we go along the Brum Bum.'

They groaned and, with the unloading finished, all three of them cleaned the hold, sweeping up the debris of broken wood and general muck, while Tom went to telephone the barracks with an update, as he had been told to do. The girls beavered on, and the light rain settled the dust, which was a blessing.

Two of the wooden boards at the bottom of the *Marigold*'s hold were broken, and they cursed because the coal would go through to the bilges, and cleaning up after they'd offloaded it would not be fun.

Polly stood on the stern of the butty when they'd finished, and waved to Saul, who was taking on a butty load. 'We'll be off, but I hope we catch up sometime – perhaps this evening, perhaps tomorrow, perhaps at Bull's Bridge.'

Saul ran and jumped onto the counter and kissed her. 'Haul well, all o' yer. Might catch up along the way, as we may be picking up coal, like you, in the motor's hold.'

'What does he mean: haul well?' queried Tom.

'You'll see,' Verity replied, grinning, although she still felt shaky.

Sylvia and Polly on *Horizon* were towed on a long snubber, as Verity and Tom set off on *Marigold*, pat-pattering past warehouses, machine shops, the backs of factories and endless chimneys belching endless smoke. A walker waved and his dog barked. Dog barked back. A cyclist, perhaps late for work, rushed along. The water became increasingly dark and dank, the factories shutting out what light there was.

Tom made yet another pot of tea. He called from the cabin as Verity steered, 'Shall I make some for the butty, too?'

'Polly will make theirs. Incidentally, you, your leg and Sylvia are to take *Marigold* through the locks.

We'll catch you once the locks are done, and then we'll all have a rest.'

Tom was leaning against the cabin now, sipping his tea. 'What do you mean – we'll take the *Marigold*? Where will you be?' He shuddered, looking to either side. 'It's grim here.'

Verity shook her head. 'Not yet, it isn't. And wait and see where Polly and I will be.'

They continued between high smut-stained factories, the noise of machinery reverberating around them. They were still in shadow all the way, although the sun had struggled out. 'It's like being in a massive long dugout,' Tom muttered. She wished he hadn't, because she didn't want to think of the war, or of London, where he'd leave her; he'd had confirmation when he telephoned from Tyseley that at Alperton he could get on the Tube and return to the hospital for sign-off.

They motored under a bridge on which lorries and buses passed in a continuous stream. There were no children gobbing or throwing, but a young boy leaned from a window at the back of a row of terraced houses. 'Boater scum,' he called out.

'Ignore them,' she instructed, as Tom spun round. 'Don't feed their insults.'

Verity always felt as though they were ploughing through sludge along this canal. As usual, discarded old tyres bumped and banged against them. A dead dog and half a bike passed them, or did they pass it? Someone cycled along the towpath, and the dust that floated in his wake wasn't earth but a mixture of coal dust and claggy soot. They passed under more bridges and dodged the children's gobs of phlegm, and once a bucket of manure. By this time Tom had stopped yelling, 'You little beggars.' He just dodged everything as best he could, cleaning up the mess once out of sight of the little wretches.

He commented, more than once, 'The smell of the cut here.'

And Verity said, more than once, 'Yes.'

He said, 'I can see why you call it a bum.'

'Not yet, you can't.' She shook her head as girls hung out of the window of a factory and waved.

Before Tom could question her, the girls called out, 'Wotcha, ladies. Ohh, you've got a soldier boy.'

Verity hooted Bet's horn, and Polly hooted the butty's. Verity and Tom laughed.

The conditions grew worse, and Verity muttered, 'Please, please don't let anything tangle in the gear, you lovely sweet-natured motor. Come on, keep going.'

Tom grimaced. 'Lord, would we have to go in and untangle it?'

'For "we", read "I". The answer is yes, if we can't poke and cut it free from here, but we'll try as hard as we can to do just that.' As always, Verity thought instead of the fields they travelled through in other places; of the kingfishers, even the otters, and the sheep that grazed, the allotments that produced food, the wheat that grew, the aeroplanes that flew. She grinned at herself. She was a poet and didn't know it. Then, suddenly, she remembered Sylvia's words. Even the Brum Bum was just a pause. Soon they *would* be in fresh fields.

On they pat-pattered, and Tom made more tea and spam sandwiches as they approached a lock and Verity steered into the bank, just as Polly did with the butty.

Sylvia came along the towpath and leapt aboard. Verity kissed Tom. 'I'm going onto the butty with Polly, but you will not be alone, so don't fret. You just have to steer your way through the locks that Sylvia operates.' Tom looked from Sylvia to Verity. Sylvia was uncoupling the tow-rope.

'Hang on,' Tom called to Verity. 'What's happening?'

'You're about to find out why we call it the Brum Bum.'

'Though I don't,' Sylvia said, looking prim.

Tom stared from one to the other, confused. Verity said, waving to Polly, 'Be there any second. Tom, remember us hauling out Bet's boat from the bridge-hole? This part of the canal is more fragile, the locks too, so we have to take the boat and butty singly. We are the horses, or the engine, whichever sounds best.' She grimaced, then kissed his cheek as he stood, appalled. 'See you soon. Bon voyage.' She jumped for the bank.

Tom watched as Polly yelled, 'You haul, then I'll take over, Verity.'

Verity hitched the tow-rope around her shoulders and waist. She saw Tom look back as he manoeuvred *Marigold* forward, the engine pat-pattering. Then she started to drag the butty after the motor, as the rope dug in. She thought of Tom with each dust-choked step and each rub of the rope; she thought of the panic, but it was gone. She felt the shakiness, but it was diminishing. She thought of the need to wait until she was twenty-one to marry, because she wouldn't ask her parents' permission, or allow Tom to approach them.

They reached the first lock and dragged the butty in, shut the gates and opened the paddles; the lock filled, she opened the exit gates and out they went, hating the effort required to get the butty started again. As they slogged on Verity's memories ran through her head, keeping in time with her footsteps.

She used to think of Star, her mare, in the early days; but when her beloved horse fell, after being ridden to hounds by her mother, and had been put down, she thought of the cut and its people. Now, as she dragged the butty alongside a machine shop, she pondered on the darts match played with Polly, when for the first time Sylvia had smiled. She thought then of their teamwork, of their increasing friendship, of the good things – anything to stop thinking of the filth, the rawness and the smell.

On and on they went, changing places with one another. Rain started falling again, but at least it wasn't snow, though it was almost as cold. Blisters developed where the rope rubbed, and they couldn't understand why their skin wasn't hardy enough by now; they had callouses, for heaven's sake. They met a horse-drawn pair, heading towards Tyseley. Why did they come this way? The girls didn't know.

It was along here that Saul's brother-in-law, Leon, had made the sign of a gun at them, because Saul had rescued his nephew, Joe, from him. Well, that wasn't the only reason. It was also because Polly had beaten off Leon and his men, with a chair outside a pub, when they attacked Saul, much like a lion tamer. That had taught the bugger.

Verity called to Polly, who was steering *Horizon*, 'Where do you think Maudie is? How can a mother just leave that bugger without taking Joe?'

Polly yelled, 'Same answer as always, Verity. No one knows, and anyway wouldn't Saul have heard something from Maudie, if she was alive? If she is dead, where is she? I can't bear to think she's under water like this.'

'Then we mustn't think it.'

They fell silent. It was the same conversation as always, so why the hell did they go over and over it? It was something to do with the misery of the Brum Bum, Verity decided, dragging out the last spam sandwich from her pocket. She opened the greaseproof-paper wrapping with one hand and her teeth, chewing filthy grit along with the spam. She rammed the wrapping back in her pocket when she had finished, unwilling to add to the debris in the canal – hauling, always hauling, but on this trip it was towards Tom. She smiled to herself.

Chapter 13

Monday 3 April – arrival at Coventry to take on coal

Tom steered through the locks and the stretches of water in between, called 'pounds' apparently, feeling like a shirker, because he should be taking his turn handling the locks for Sylvia, or hauling the damned butty for the girls. When he said as much, Sylvia just shook her head. 'It's our job, we can manage, but thank you. If you fell, we'd feel bad.'

The rain began again and kept falling heavily, then fading, but always falling. His greatcoat was soaked, the rain ran off his beret into his eyes, but he stood as the other boaters would be doing; and in the oven a pheasant stew was simmering. Pheasant from Saul's nocturnal activities. That bloke should be in the Special Forces, because he must be able to move silently through the dark and could probably live off the land, just as they had to; and Tom expected that Saul could kill, if necessary. Tom hesitated. Could Saul really, though? There was something essentially gentle about the bloke. How would Saul fare in the army, if his plan worked out? Had he found his 'important person' to try and sort it?

The tiller was slippery under his hand, and a second horse-drawn pair passed them, heading for Birmingham. A child steered the butty, standing on a box, while a couple of slightly older lads hauled it.

The steerer of the main boat called, "Ow do' and tipped his hat, looking curiously at Tom, but saying nothing. On the bridges over the grimy cut he saw soldiers breaking stride to cross, as dictated by the manuals, because the resonance of the men's marching could shake a bridge or pontoon down, but surely not old Victorian ones like these? The factories looked dreary, and the sky even worse. He didn't light up a cigarette because it would fall to bits in the rain.

He muttered, 'I thought it was all beer and skittles. You know, gliding along in the sunshine. I have blisters on the palms of my hands from the tiller, so what on earth are yours like, Sylvia?'

She was sitting on the roof of the cabin, beneath a large black umbrella more suited to a businessman, and the sound of the rain falling on it was drowning out the pat-patter. Though Tom had seen no other boaters using them, he couldn't help wishing he had one, too. She balanced the umbrella and held out her hands. He saw the callouses, the grimy split nails. Sylvia said, 'Polly and Verity will be getting blisters over their shoulders and round their waists from the tow-rope. We do it every couple of weeks, so you'd think the skin would toughen. One of life's many mysteries.'

Tom nodded. 'It's a hard life, far more so than I ever imagined. It's the day-after-day bit, whatever the conditions, that must wear you down, not to mention the children gobbing, and the filth.'

'But we're safe, when you won't be, when you're back with the army. And although you won't have children spitting, you'll have guns firing, and death will always be a possibility.'

Well, thank you for reminding me, he thought, knowing why Verity and Polly found Sylvia difficult; and then, within minutes, why they felt guilty for feeling annoyed, as Sylvia continued, 'I think you're all very brave, because it's not something you'll like – killing someone, I mean.'

He studied her as she sat beneath the umbrella, her expression preoccupied as though wondering if she could kill. He said, 'Being killed is not something I'd like, either.'

A lock was looming now, as rain sheeted down ever more heavily. Tom mentioned it.

Sylvia nodded. 'I know – don't worry. I'll rattle along, and we'll be through before you can say boo to a goose. Just another thirty seconds and I'll be off.'

He could think of nothing to say, as she looked over her shoulder, judging the distance to the lock. She nodded, closed up her umbrella, laid it carefully next to the kettle, jumped onto the bank and ran along the sludge-drenched path. The lock was ready, because the horse-drawn pair had been through. Within the lock the smell of the cut was even worse, but he barely noticed it now, as Sylvia wound the paddles. As he watched he realised that Sylvia reminded him of a spring that was wound tightly – too tightly to do anything other than hold itself in that tension; a spring that mustn't relax or it would uncoil and fall apart.

When she returned and they were on their way again, and Sylvia was sitting on the roof beneath her umbrella, he said, 'Where do your parents live? Are they in the Midlands?'

She looked at the warehouse they were passing. A boat was moored at its unloading wharf. She pointed. 'There, can you see the flyboat? It'll be picking up beer, or something that needs to go somewhere in a rush. Those young men don't stop for anything. I think they must just take shifts to sleep.'

He nodded. 'Perhaps they do.' Sylvia was not about to relax the coil even one iota.

Quite suddenly the rain ceased as they pattered along the short pound, and he snatched out his cigarettes and offered one to her, knowing she'd refuse. She closed her umbrella and laid it precisely against the kettle. He lit up, dragged on it, chilled to the bone, wondering how Verity and Polly were doing, so glad that Verity had Polly's friendship, and Sylvia's too, though it was at a different level.

And what of Bet? How was her engine getting on? The damned thing was almost done for, he was pretty sure.

Sylvia said quietly, 'I have no parents. I grew up in an orphanage, north of London.'

'I see.' He thought that in fact he did, at last. 'I'm sorry, that must have been hard.'

She shook her head. 'The nuns were kind. We were a family, or perhaps a community. We children quarrelled, of course we did, but within the community, and soon the new ones settled in. Life was ruled by bells, by order, by tradition, by faith. That's why I'm not scared of death, just of dying. As long, of course, as I do as I should, as God ... Well, we should do what is right, for then there is no regret.'

He said again, 'I see.' He did. Yes, perhaps it was a bit like the army – another world. But he was a man. Sylvia had been a child. He lit another cigarette from the stub of the first, which was burning down too quickly in the wind. It was stronger now, and looked as though it was shoving more black clouds in their direction.

Another pair was coming towards them. Good, it meant the lock would be ready for Verity and Polly.

He said, 'Were you very young when you entered the orphanage?'

'I can't remember. I only remember the community.'

He nodded. 'I expect you miss it?'

She looked at him, searching his face, his eyes, then said, 'I used to wonder why boats came towards Birmingham on this Bottom Road, but I think it must be that they are carrying coal from Coventry to Birmingham. You can see they are loaded. We never *come* this way, and I keep forgetting to ask why.'

They continued down the locks and Tom thought of the ARP warden who had let him talk because, as he said, it was easier to talk to a stranger. But one day this girl must talk to her friends. He stared ahead as a wider stretch of water hove into sight. Sylvia lowered herself from the roof, pulling at her sweaters, which had rucked up, and instructing Tom to stop and they'd moor up. He slowed the *Marigold* and drew in. Sylvia nipped into the cabin and came out with a trip card, shoving it in her pocket.

'I'm taking this to the lock-keeper's office. The butty will be through soon, but not too soon. Why not stoke the range, make some tea and try and dry off; perhaps wash your hands and make some spam sandwiches. I've taken some money from the kitty for eggs. Sometimes the lock-keeper, Mr Edwards, has some – and vegetables. Perhaps he'll have some winter or even spring cabbage?' She stepped onto the bank and tied up *Marigold*. Dog stirred in the cabin and barked.

Tom opened the doors. 'Come on out, girl. Stretch your legs.'

Dog bounded onto the towpath. Sylvia put up her hand. 'No, Dog, don't follow. Mr Edwards isn't keen on dogs, you know that.' She set off up the slope to the office, then stopped and called back, 'It's just hard to leave.'

'The orphanage?' Tom called, and into the silence that resulted he answered himself, 'Yes, it's always hard to strike out on your chosen path, but we all have to grow up and do just that.'

He thought he heard her say, as she scrambled up to the top of the slope, 'That's the choice I need to make, you see.'

He shrugged. It was the choice they all had to make. He heard the butty's hunting horn, far distant, but it meant the girls were on their way. He clambered crabwise down the cabin steps to stoke the fire, wash his hands and make tea and sandwiches, longing for the plaster to be off his leg, but not wanting it to be, either, because with the plaster on, he had a few more days with Verity.

That thought reminded him to phone the army depot from Coventry. The sergeant he had phoned from Tyseley had said there was a bit of a sweat on and so to touch base, if Tom didn't mind very much, from Coventry. The sarcasm had been unmissable. He closed his eyes. Well, he did mind, very much.

He spread margarine on the bread and cut spam into slices, then slapped them into sandwiches. He thought they'd all start looking like lumps of spam any day now, and certainly if they were to be cut open, they'd be pink inside. He checked the kettle, wanting to distract himself from the thought of anyone being cut open. He was here, and soon he would see Verity again. Every minute without her hurt.

The butty was hauled from the opened lock gates, and Tom brought the sandwiches and tea on board it as they took turns to scrub their hands, avoiding the blisters on either side of their callouses. Tom watched as the oily soot remained embedded in them, whilst his hands were still relatively virginal. In recompense, he attached the short tow as Sylvia returned, bearing eggs and cabbage. They moored as darkness settled. He slept alone in the cabin; well, not quite alone, he muttered to Dog.

At the crack of dawn they were off again. The rain of yesterday had left Tom stiff and aching, but hadn't set back his leg function, which was improving daily, although if the doc thought it was because he'd been lying on a couch, eating peeled grapes, he'd be told loudly how wrong he was. The image made him laugh aloud. They were on the flat, with no more locks for a while, and fields on either side. He was sure he spotted a raptor, but didn't pay much attention, because Sylvia had moved to the butty and Verity had now joined him on the motor. They stood on either side of the tiller, close together. Occasionally they spoke, often they kissed; invariably his arm was around her, with the tiller captured between them.

The wind gusted across the fields and, just past a ruin of a farm at the side of the cut, Verity took the shaft from the roof and ran along the top planks, calling back, 'We're liable to ground on the silt along here. The bottom is too close to the top, as the boaters would say.'

They grounded more than once, and each time she shafted them off, digging deep, the water running down her arms and soaking the sleeves of her sweaters. She called out, 'Steer more towards the centre. We've discovered the other side is deeper, so we feel entitled to stray.'

'While we're talking about deep water,' Tom said, steering as she had directed, 'you might feel I'm up to my neck in it, because I must call the barracks from Coventry, in case there's a sweat on. I just didn't know how to tell you back at Tyseley, when you were so agitated about Saul's intentions, whatever they might be – if you understand what I mean? I was frightened it might spoil the days we've had.'

Verity stared ahead as he straightened up the motor and said nothing.

He pulled her to him as she returned and kissed her dirty old woollen hat, loving every stitch of it because it was hers. 'Talk to me,' he muttered.

'Of course you must. There's a war on,' she said, making it easy for him. 'After all, you've been in the lap of luxury with three lovely nurses obeying your every whim, and that can't go on.'

He kissed her, hard.

She said against his mouth, 'I've had you for a time, and of course you must go when you are told, but I think I understand why you didn't tell me.'

Her courage made Tom love her more than ever, and together they travelled on and he realised how used to this life he had become, as Verity washed some clothes on the range and strung them up behind the bucket cabin.

'It's the bucket I won't miss. In fact I'm pretty sure I'll have nightmares about it all my life, or panic attacks.'

She leapt off the roof and slapped him. 'Don't mock my affliction.'

They laughed together, because she mocked the panic attack herself, and it had not happened again; even if it did, she knew what it was, and would ride it out.

They pat-pattered towards a bridge over which a squad broke step. One of the squaddies looked across and yelled, 'AWOL, are you, lad?'

'I wish,' Tom replied, waving his stick. 'Broken leg, but no sick leave for me. Instead I'm here steering a ruddy boat.'

The sergeant bawled to his troops, 'Get yourselves over this bloody bridge, because this isn't a bloody picnic – it's a bloody war.' He leaned on the parapet. 'They'll want you back pretty damn quick, lad. There's no time to waste.' The troops hurried on to the roadway. Tom smiled as he heard, 'By the left. "Left," I said, laddie; that's yer bloody right, for Pete's bloody sake.'

Verity looked at him. 'Seriously, Tom, I know you'll go from either Coventry or Alperton, and it's all right. We're the same as thousands of others, and we've had these days, and you've not complained of the pain once. I love you, Private Brown.'

He pulled her to him and kissed her hard. 'It doesn't hurt when I'm with you.' It was a lie, but soldiers learned to ignore pain.

They travelled on, alongside ploughed fields, which Verity said they had watched turning from wheat to ploughed land, and which were now showing traces of green again. While he steered, Verity washed down the cabin, inside and out. He laughed. 'When did you ever do dusting at home?'

She flicked him with water. 'This is home – here on the boat, with my friends and you.'

It made him sad. 'Sometimes things aren't as simple as they seem. You need to talk to Rogers and Mrs B about your mother. So go home and talk; there's some sort of an undercurrent, or so I think.'

She wrung out the mop over the side. 'Why do you think that?'

Tom shrugged. 'I'm not sure, I can't get out of my mind Rogers' mention of things not being as simple as they seem at Howard House. Perhaps there *is* something going on that makes, or has made, your mother's life difficult? She can be very kind.'

They were approaching another bridge. This time POWs were being marched across. It was these men who gobbed them this time, and Verity lunged at the hooter, blowing the hunting horn again and again, making them jump. But not just them; Tom, too, and his laughter as they went beneath the bridge echoed back.

The bridges became more frequent. Verity said as she sat on the roof, 'I'll think about going to Howard House, but for now, lovely boy, Coventry isn't far. You can always tell if civilisation is close, from the frequency of the bridges.'

Buses, cars and pedestrians crossed the cut over narrow or wide, old or new bridges. *Marigold* and *Horizon* pat-pattered past a coal mine. Tom watched miners coming off-shift, their faces black, their shoulders hunched. Polly and Verity had looked similar at the end of their hauling activities, though not quite as black, not as hunched, but probably just as exhausted. Now he saw that there were lumps of coal on the towpath, as well as deeper coal dust, filth and litter. He noticed that lumps of coal also floated on the cut. While he continued steering, Verity fished them out with a net on the end of a pole.

She saw him looking. 'We created these coal nets ourselves. We can't have rationed goods going to waste, and the coal soon dries out.' She stored it in the bucket cabin.

They kept going and slagheaps now reared up on either side, and before long they were at Coventry's loading yards. He saw Polly alongside, cycling furiously, overtaking the *Marigold*. Verity said, 'She's going ahead to queue for our orders.'

They passed many pairs moored up alongside the bank, some loaded, others not. Verity waved at one. 'How do, Steerer Porter. Has Jimmy finished his homework?'

Steerer Porter tipped his hat. 'We're just off, but 'tis left at the office. They'll give it to whoever goes in for yer orders.'

Tom hugged Verity close. 'You are an extraordinary woman. It's so important for children to read.'

She shook her head. 'But is it? Saul wouldn't be so restless if he didn't read the newspaper. He'd just accept his lot, and not fiddle about with enlistment plans behind Polly's back, because that's what he's doing, isn't it …?' She petered out. 'Well, what's the point of me saying anything.'

'There isn't any.'

They both watched as Polly reached the Orders Office, and Tom steered, wanting to put his arm around Verity, but she was double-checking the traffic in and out of the loading arm of the cut. 'Let me take over, Tom. I need to get the boats in position. And I don't want to talk about this again, because it's just making me angry, and you fed up. And we'll end up rowing about some silly bugger wanting to rush off to war, and I can't bear to spoil what we have.'

He moved from the tiller, sitting on the roof and saying, 'We can be cross with one another and still be in love, idiot.'

'Idiot, yourself. And you didn't deny that was Saul's plan, so now I know definitely.'

Tom sighed, groaning, 'Enough. Look, Verity, promise me,' he went on as she checked for other traffic. 'Promise you'll stay schtum.'

She said nothing, just sorted out the butty and motor. As she finally moored *Marigold* she called, 'I promise.'

As she did so, Polly cycled towards them, a huge grin on her face, waving not just the loading order, but what looked like a letter. When she arrived she shouted, 'A note from Bet. We're invited, after loading up, to a pre-Easter meal with her and Fran. She's cleared it with Bull's Bridge, because her engine refit won't be finished until Saturday. Merle's gone onto another boat, so Bet's waiting for two new trainees to arrive. She's also left a note for Saul and Granfer, because she's fixed it for them, too.' She skidded to a halt. 'Tom, there's a message for you as well. Chop-chop. You'll have to queue, but you're to make a phone call. Sydney has the number. Verity, I've Jimmy's homework for you.'

Tom's heart sank. It must be urgent for them to call *him*? Was he to report back now? He limped off down the cut, as trucks of coal arrived on what looked like a mining railway line.

He queued outside the Orders Office, amongst boaters who tipped their hats at him and stood quietly, their windlasses tucked into the backs of their wide belts. Tom leaned on his stick, his leg aching from the standing he'd been doing. What would the medics think of his plaster, which was almost black, as was his uniform? For a moment he worried, but then he thought, What the hell does it matter, against the backdrop of all of this.

In the background lorries revved, narrowboat engines throbbed, hooters sounded from both the boats and the mines, the tannoy bellowed and men shouted. His Verity was in this world, day after day, and thought nothing of it; or if she did, she bit down on her complaints. Would she keep her promise? She must, but he should never have let out as much as he had, so who was he to make a fuss?

He eased along with the queue, wondering how she would really manage as the wife of a chauffeur – though after the war would that role exist any more? Would they ever make enough money for him to run his own car-repair garage? Could she bear it? It wouldn't be wartime and temporary; it would be forever, and if she married against her parents' wishes, Verity would be an outcast from her real world. He looked around, watching the bustle of the cut and hearing the laughter as the men jostled one another, intent on some task or other.

But was Howard House her real world any more? Somehow Verity really was more alive, more in tune with herself, here, working and earning her space in life. Or was that just wishful thinking?

He shuffled along, as orders were handed out in the office and steerers left with their dockets in their hands. Pre-Easter at Bet's? She seemed so important to Verity and Polly, like a mother hen. As for Sylvia?

Well, nowt so queer as folk, his mum used to say, but if you've been brought up in a Catholic orphanage, of course you would think of heaven, hell and all points in between; and how extraordinary to be able to accept death. He laughed to himself.

The steerer in front turned. 'Yer goin' to share yer joke?'

Tom shook his head. 'Just thinking, mate. Women, you know.'

The steerer, an old boy, about a decade younger than Granfer – although burned dark as a nut by the wind, rain and sun, just as Granfer was – nodded. 'Aye, women, eh. Who knows what they's thinkin', 'cept yer done it wrong.'

All the men laughed. Tom grinned, but he was thinking of these men's wives, who steered, made lunch, lock-wheeled and then boiled up clothes on the bank while their blokes were in the pub. But the blokes were here, getting the orders, and somehow keeping food on the table, living in a tiny room cos they couldn't afford to live on the bank. What a team these couples made. He reached forward and lightly punched the old boy. 'Wouldn't be without them, eh?'

'Right enough. Reckon yer made things oop wi' yer Verity then? But telephones foller yer around. Got to make a call, ain't yer? What to do? Is yer goin' back to yer sergeant, to 'ave him beat yer balls, or not?'

Tom laughed again. 'I reckon my business gets carried on the wind, and while I'm chewing coal dust, you're all chewing on my doings.' The whole queue laughed then, as they continued shuffling forward. The old boy gave him a roll-up he'd just made, and set to with another for himself.

Tom struck a match, then lit both. They inhaled. Above them pigeons flew their clumsy way towards distant woods, and high above them planes flew as well, in some sort of exercise.

Tom said, 'I'll be going on duty now, or maybe when we reach London.'

The steerer a couple of places in front of Tom turned. 'London be better. More time wi' yer Verity, and lunch with Bet. Us didn't take kindly to them women comin' on the cut, but they been good, most o' them. Them that ain't go on 'ome, cos they can't be cluttering oop the cut. We've cargoes to shift for yer lads in uniform.'

Before Tom could answer, the queue suddenly got a move on and the steerer disappeared into the office. Tom stared after him, his worries over Verity, her present and her future settling, because she would never clutter up whatever place she chose in this world. Not now, not ever, whatever might come, or whoever she might lose. The same went for Polly, and it was as though a great weight was lifted from his shoulders, because yes, he had helped out Saul just a bit; but if Saul was lost, Polly would manage.

At last he was in the office. He could have skirted past the steerers, of course, but they wouldn't have liked it, and he valued his nose and didn't want it broken. He grinned at the thought, knowing it wouldn't have come to that, but a few words would have been said and perhaps a foot stuck out. Then the other leg would be in plaster.

Sydney, the old boy behind the counter, whacked down a piece of paper. 'Yer the squaddie, ain't yer? Phone them 'ere and get yer orders, though you'd best be scrubbing that uniform, and how about that plaster? A bit of blanco, I reckon.'

Tom picked up the phone number and headed for the telephone at the end of the counter. He knew there was no point in keeping his voice low, because whatever he did, the gossip would travel. It was Sergeant-Major Morris this time, who barked, 'Coventry, yer said. What I want to know is why ain't you on a deckchair with knots in your handkerchief, sucking a bleedin' lolly?'

'One word, Sergeant-Major. A woman.'

'That's two, Soldier. Best you get to Alperton, as we thought. We're all right till then, but the medics'll need to see you up here, before we can 'ave you back, so don't go to the 'ospital. There was a bit of a panic, but it's gone over. You can put your knotted 'anky on your head at Bet Burrows's; can't 'ave you missin' your Easter egg. You got to be back by the eleventh, if yer please. Can't say fairer than that.'

'Thanks, Sergeant-Major.' But Tom was talking to himself, because he heard the click as Morris slammed down the receiver. Morris was one of the good ones. The powers-that-be wanted him to take a commission, but he wouldn't. He preferred to be hands-on with the blokes, to keep them alive, as he said one night over too many beers. And besides, why waste his time worrying about which knife to use in the Officers' Mess, or any of that bollocks.

He dug out money for the call, but Sydney shook his head and muttered, 'I were in the last lot, so keep yer head down and come back and make an hash of yer life, like the rest of us.'

The boaters laughed and tipped their hats as Tom made for the door. The office smelled like Verity: of coal, dirt and sweat; and like Polly and Sylvia, too, and probably himself. He grinned to himself as he limped back to the loading platform. How on earth did Morris know about Bet? He stopped. The old boy behind the counter, that's how. He laughed.

Coal dust was everywhere. A child ran past him carrying orders in his mouth, and hooking up his trousers. Tom heard a hoot, and saw the *Seagull* heading down the loading cut. Polly would be pleased. He hurried. He had five days: four of them with the girls, and the fifth for travel; because he realised that come one, come all three. They were a family, but did they actually realise it?

Trucks of coal were trundling along beside him, heading for the loading platform or wharf, he supposed. Men sat on top of the loads, smoking. Tom expected the coal dust to ignite at any moment. Others were already loading *Marigold* and *Horizon*, and coal gushed down chutes into the holds, as men guided it with the backs of spades. Black dust billowed.

He heard a bellow, 'Where's that tea then, lass?'

He saw Verity, standing on *Marigold*'s roof with her hands on her hips, her head thrown back, her woollen hat with its small bobble wobbling, laughing as Polly stabbed her finger at the bloke.

'What do you want, jam on it? I said it'd be ready any minute now.' Polly's massive bobble was waving from side to side and would make a weapon in itself, Tom thought, as he heard Verity's and Polly's combined laughter soaring over all the noise of coal, men and chaos. He would remember the sound till his dying day.

Suddenly he realised that enlisting was Saul's way of fighting for the girl he loved, just as he, Private Brown, would do.

Chapter 14

Wednesday 5 April – pre-Easter celebration at Buckby

The *Marigold* turned off towards Buckby under the command of Verity, who had already checked Jimmy Porter's homework. Polly, on the butty with Sylvia on tow behind, had some easy reading books on the shelf, and had chosen several to pass on when they arrived at Bull's Bridge. It was hopeless to expect his parents to pick up his mistakes, but it gave Jimmy huge pleasure to read to them, and they to listen. It was opening their minds, Mrs Porter had said.

Sylvia steered as Polly stood on the counter, chewing the end of her pencil, wondering about the wisdom of opening minds, for were they disturbing the traditions of the cut? Sylvia interrupted her train of thought. 'Are you sure the invitation includes me? I'm not their friend, in the same way you two are?'

'Of course, it's for all five of us.'

'Five?' Sylvia looked confused.

Polly tucked her pencil in her pocket. 'Dog, of course. Fran now accepts him under sufferance, but any nonsense and Dog's out on the porch again. But that applies to all of us. One wrong step and out we go.'

Sylvia was looking at her. 'Ho-ho, a likely story.'

Polly said, 'Just you wait and see. I'm always surprised that Fran hasn't a ruler to smack our hands.'

Sylvia sniffed and adjusted the tiller slightly. 'Now I know you're being silly.'

Polly was still smiling as Verity slowed the motor. 'We'll be mooring up here, just before Crick Tunnel, Sylvia. Fran might come and meet us with her tricycle and awful cart, but now that we know the way, no doubt we'll be trusted to find Spring Cottage ourselves. We can't all fit into the cart anyway, thank heavens.'

'What about Saul, Granfer and Harry? How will they find the cottage?'

Verity was pulling into the bank. Polly readied herself to moor up the butty. 'Granfer and Saul visited an aunt here recently, so I expect they'll know. Buckby's where a lot of the boaters retire, but there must be youngsters hereabout too, because Fran teaches at a school.'

Verity shoved the boat into reverse, the water churned and *Marigold* stopped. *Horizon* slid into the stern hull with a slight jerk, but Verity was already ashore, shouting to Tom, 'Heave her back, Tom, and tie her up on the mooring ring.' The rings were placed at regular intervals along the bank.

Polly collected the brace of pheasant hanging on the back of the store cabin, dropping them into a hessian bag and slinging them over her shoulder. Fran liked the idea of Saul nicking pheasants from the woods, and she and Sylvia would have to argue the toss about that, as the third member of the *Marigold* crew thought it immoral to add to the ration when others couldn't. As Polly carried the pheasants along the gunwhale she heard Fran's yell, 'Ah, pheasant. The password for entry into the cottage. Not sure we've any Easter eggs, though.'

Bet and Fran were standing on the bank, Bet with her hands deep in her pockets, her short dark hair lifting in the wind. Fran stood beside her, wearing similar trousers and sweaters and the same boater tan. Well, she would have one, having lived with Bet on a narrowboat for several years. What's more, it was anchored just along the cut, and Polly was sure they were just waiting until the end of the war to head off in it again.

Fran was beckoning them with a broad grin, 'Come along, chop-chop, it's nearly midday but not too late for coffee. Real coffee. I ground up the beans myself.'

Verity had already launched herself on Bet and Fran, hugging them and introducing Tom to Fran, who said, 'Have the girls been beating you up already and breaking bones, Tom? Naughty-naughty, you're no good to man or beast like that. Bit grubby, too, so I'm not signing the plaster and writing kind words, no matter what you promise me.'

Sylvia was hanging back on the butty counter, waiting nervously. Polly dashed into the cabin, banked up the fire with coal and ash, then snatched up the book she was going to pass on to Jimmy Porter, for Fran's opinion. She bounded onto the counter. Sylvia nagged them, 'We should lock.'

Verity snapped from the bank, 'No need, with Leon in custody.'

Polly took hold of Sylvia's arm. 'If a boater sees you, they'll be offended that you even dreamed they would steal. And don't be nervous of Bet and Fran. Believe it or not, Fran doesn't bite, or not often. Dog, get onto the bank.' Dog had been sitting on the top of the cabin, her tongue lolling out, and with one bound she was onto the towpath and snuffling into Bet's hand.

Verity shook her head and Polly heard her say, 'The rule is no feeding, but I'm talking to myself, Bet, aren't I?'

Polly shut the cabin doors, while Sylvia shifted her weight from foot to foot. Polly sighed and locked the doors, but saw Fran shrugging impatiently.

When Polly finally reached the towpath she was scooped into Bet's arms, while Fran stopped stroking Dog long enough to pat her on the back. 'Nice to see you, Polly.' Then she muttered, 'So Leon still hasn't been tried. It could mean they haven't found any evidence, other than the German's confession, and the club manager's. Always a bit worrying, in case the witnesses change their stories.'

Sylvia held out her hand to Bet, who wasn't having any of that nonsense and gave her a hug instead. But Sylvia wrestled herself free and gripped Fran's arm, saying, her voice high-pitched and cross, 'But they can't let him out. He might have killed his wife as well. She still hasn't turned up, you know, and Saul watches the water all the time in case she's there.'

Fran merely said, squatting to look into Dog's eyes, 'That's enough of that, young Sylvia. It doesn't do to worry about things until they happen. I would think you should have learned that, after even a few months on the cut. A bit more of a stiff upper lip needed, if I might say so.'

Verity and Polly snatched a look at one another, slipped their arms through Sylvia's and walked her along. Polly almost sang, 'No, you may not say so, Fran. And stop being so bossy, or no pheasant for you.' Anything to avoid an issue with Sylvia, because a day with Bet and Fran in the warmth and cosiness of their cottage was a treasure not be spoiled.

Bet echoed them. 'Indeed, Fran is bossy, and grumpy. It's because she knows there's coffee, but has had to stare at it all morning waiting for you. We'll throw her a lump of raw meat while we're waiting for the kettle to rev up, and she can gnaw on that.'

Behind them Tom limped along the lane beside Bet and Fran, trying to avoid the farmer's tractor ruts and potholes, his stick clicking on the stones.

Polly called back, 'Are you all right to walk, Tom? It's almost a mile, if not more. We can always send Grumpy to Spring Cottage for the wooden cart that she tows with her trike.'

There was silence for a moment, then Tom said weakly, pointing to the ruts with his stick, 'I think that even if it was ten miles, I'd rather walk, thank you. I'm not partial to being bounced from here to kingdom come. It's as bad as being in a tank, let me tell you.'

Polly saw Verity snatch a look at her, a query in her eyes, and Sylvia double-checked, too. Polly smiled and shook her head. It was all right. Yes, her twin, Will, had died in a tank, but her joyous memories had steadily overridden her grief; and besides, she had Saul to fill the gaping void. As they walked she felt the ring, which she wore on a boot-lace around her neck. Soon she would have it sized and they could work out a wedding date.

Either side of clumps of spent snowdrops, daffo-dils were still in flower. Dog dashed in and out of the shrubs along the verge, and Sylvia murmured, 'I do make such a fool of myself.'

Verity whispered, 'We all have to learn. Some of us just take an interminable time.'

There was a silence. Sylvia gasped, then laughed as Polly reached past her and beat a giggling Verity with her oversized bobble. She then thrust it into Sylvia's hand. 'Go on, beat her.' Sylvia did, joining in the laughter. Verity winked at Polly over the girl's head. Crisis over.

They entered the rear garden of Spring Cottage via the ancient white picket gate, and walked down a crazy-paving path edged with lavender that had been cut down for the winter. White beehives were dotted about in a side-garden that was freely planted with bee-friendly plants. 'Ah,' said Sylvia. 'This is where our honey comes from.' She slipped free of Polly and Verity and spun on her heel. 'Thank you for all your honey. It makes such a difference.'

Polly picked up the amusement in Fran's voice. 'My pleasure, my dear. I think we should use what gifts nature provides, rationing or not.'

Ouch, thought Polly. What can Sylvia say now about Saul's poaching of pheasants? They were at the porch. Bet's voice carried from the gate, where she had slowed to keep Tom company, 'Boots off, then enter. Kitchen is on your right, Sylvia, if you are leading the charge. Towel in the porch for Dog's paws. She's allowed in, but not on the sofa.'

Sylvia clicked her heels and saluted. The others gaped, then roared with laughter. Fran called, 'You'll do.' Sylvia flushed and smiled.

Polly opened the door and entered. 'Bliss,' she sighed.

Sylvia squeezed her arm. 'It is rather, isn't it? This is another pause, Polly. You see, I'm trying to get it right.'

Polly hugged her. 'Just like the rest of us.' For a moment Sylvia allowed herself to be held, but only for a moment.

In the porch, Verity made Tom sit on the side-bench above the neatly parked boots. 'Let me help. I'll undo the laces of your boot and take the water-proof tarpaulin off the other, and you can get into the warmth and wiggle your toes in front of the range.'

He grinned at her, as she knelt before him. 'I like to see you on your knees before a higher being.' He leaned back out of swipe range. Sure enough she missed him.

She began to unlace his boot, saying, 'That's the last time I fiddle about replacing nursey's tarpaulin for anyone, especially a toe-rag like you. The least you could have done was allow yourself to be whacked.' She pulled off his boot, placing it next to its peers, with the tarpaulin sock at its side. She helped him to his feet, concerned because he looked so pale and drawn.

Tom grasped her hand, kissing it. 'I love you, Verity Clement, with all my heart, but I rather think I'd swap you for a coffee, if push came to shove.' He dodged her swipe again and followed her into the hall, tap-tapping on the flagstone floor and saying, when he reached the thick runner, 'So warm and cosy, and it makes me realise how tiny the cabins really are.'

Verity smiled grimly. 'Especially when there are three of us sleeping in one.' The door into the kitchen was open and shrieks of laughter were emanating from it, along with the smell of lamb roasting. 'Oh dear, lamb and pheasant,' she whispered to him. 'The guardian of our rationing – as well as every other conceivable moral – won't approve.'

At that moment there was a rap at the front door, but as Verity started to turn, Tom blocked her, held her close and this time it was he who was whispering, 'Be tolerant towards Sylvia. She was brought up in a Catholic orphanage and has no memory of her parents.'

Verity absorbed the words. Why had Sylvia told this man her life story, when they had known her for so much longer: what was she playing at? Jealousy flared and she snapped, 'Lucky her; that's a damned sight better than remembering far too well.' She stamped her way to the door, then opened it. 'Saul, you made it. Someone we know will be thrilled. And Granfer, you're here, too, not to mention Harry. Come in, but boots off first.'

Harry held his up. 'We done it already, cos Saul guessed, cos Polly told 'im what a ... did yer say "dragon", Saul?'

Fran's voice boomed down the hall. 'I was going to say, "Welcome to our humble abode", but perhaps I'd better just eat you all instead.'

Harry dropped his boots and stepped behind Saul. Polly ran into the hall and then to the front door. 'Come in, come in. We've made you tea, because you don't like coffee, but we've beer, too. Quick, shut the door behind you and keep the warmth in.' She flung herself into Saul's arms and he swung her round.

Harry dodged, and Fran laughed. Granfer whipped off his hat and said, 'When yer've finished, maybe the house'll still be standing, maybe not, but the dragon just has ter give a puff and that'll keep us all warm, as well as roast these pheasant. 'Ow about that?'

He passed by Saul and Polly, hooking Harry's collar and dragging him along as he did so. They stopped in front of the dragon.

"Ow do, Missus. This be 'Arry. He's our runabout for now.' Granfer handed her another couple of pheasants.

Fran crowed, 'Wonderful, we will live like kings for a while.' Saul had let Polly go, and as they approached, Fran started to say, 'Ah, Saul, I hear there are some more things to sort—'

Bet interrupted. 'Yes, Lettie's lonely, so it's good that you'll be popping into Buckby on your way to or from Birmingham more often. Come on, everyone.'

Verity saw Tom watching her from the kitchen doorway, and fingered the ring she wore around her neck. She didn't feel that the crochet wool was as safe as the bootlace Polly used, so she'd have to change it. Or perhaps he'd want it back, after she'd been so mean about Sylvia. She looked again, but he had disappeared with the others, who were being led by Fran into her 'dragon's den'.

Verity stayed in the hall. It was dark and was beginning to feel cold, very cold, and she could taste blood in the water, and hear the rushing in her ears;

and she pulled at the boots, pulled again and again, and she heard her mother calling, 'Don't be absurd, Verity. That is not the behaviour I would expect. Expect ... *Expect* ...'

'Verity, where are you?' It wasn't her mother, it was Fran. She opened her eyes and the water receded, as she knew it would, but why was her mother part of the panic? Fran beckoned from the kitchen doorway.

Verity waved. 'I dropped something in the porch. I'll be there in a moment.'

She opened the door, stepped out, eased it almost shut and stood, her arms folded, staring at the morning. There were still some cobwebs on the lavender stalks. How strange that she hadn't actually noticed that before. She breathed deeply and finally entered the cottage, almost bumping into Bet, who waited just inside and opened her arms.

'Come here, you.' Bet held Verity, listening as she whispered that she was mean, and that Tom would hate her. 'Don't be silly, he's in there waiting for you.'

Verity said, 'But it's not just that. I do so wish my family was like you and Fran at Spring Cottage. You're cosy, warm and you love us. You do, don't you?' She could hear the anxiety in her own voice.

Bet stroked her face, as Tom had the night he had held her, and at a distance she smelt again the scent of camellias, and felt a soft hand tucking her hair behind her ear, and heard someone saying ... what? And who?

'Of course we do, you're our lovely Idle Women – our Polly and Verity, who will be friends for the rest of their lives, and family for one another. Never forget that. Sylvia will be, too, if things go on as they are doing. I wasn't sure at first, but I do feel she has made progress, and that is because of you two.'

Verity stepped back, wiping her face and trying to smile.

Fran called, 'Coffee is made, and Tom will drink yours if you don't get a wriggle on. Don't forget, Bet, we have that letter for Verity.'

Verity looked puzzled. 'A letter, here?'

Bet pushed her ahead. 'Sandy knows that I live at Spring Cottage, in between trips. I expect she has something to say. Just one thing first.' She reached up and snapped the crocheted wool, catching the ring before it dropped. 'There, you said you'd dropped something. So make it this. Put the ring on your finger for now, and only take it off if he tells you to. When he does, I'll know that the sky has finally fallen in. Head up, now; you've had a hell of a time and he's leaving for war, so you're on edge, both of you. But remember the love that will remain. Let Polly find out her truth when it happens.'

At that, Verity turned, whispering, 'You do know something's up?'

Bet tutted. 'Lettie can't keep her mouth shut, and for a moment Fran forgot, so I decided to step in and do some fielding, before that particular ball dropped into a cowpat. It won't happen again.

245

Makes me feel a bit awkward, knowing Saul's trying, but I can see his reasoning. Best not to upset Polly before he has to, *if* he has to.'

Verity walked into the light of the kitchen, where most of them sat around the large pine table, chatting and drinking coffee or tea, while Fran busied herself at the Aga with Tom, his coffee in his hand and a spare mug in his other, his stick over his arm. 'Did you find it?' he called.

She held up her hand and the ring, and the wool. 'Amazing how far a ring can roll.'

Tom grinned. 'Come and get your coffee, or I swear I'll drink it. Is there any more in the pot, Fran? I'm a wounded hero and I'm sure I deserve another.'

Fran was bending bum upwards, basting the lamb in the oven. 'Pass me those sprigs of rosemary, then you and your lady love can go and pick some more, canoodling as you go, no doubt. And no, you broke your leg when some silly bugger on a motorbike hit your transport, so it's nothing that deserves a reward.'

From the table Harry could be heard saying, 'Yer know, that missus *is* fierce enough to be a bloody dragon, Saul.'

Polly corrected him. 'Fierce enough to be a dragon, you mean. No need for swearing.'

Fran didn't straighten, but just continued to baste and muttered, 'No lamb for clever bugger's monkeys, that's what I say, Polly Holmes.'

Tom downed his coffee, and Verity hers, before they foraged in the garden for rosemary. As he nipped the tips off, he said, holding it to her nose, 'I remember the gardener, old Matthews, doing this at Howard House when Mrs B was fiddling about with lamb. Funny how you remember scents, isn't it?'

She told him about the scent of camellias. 'I think it might be Nanny's scent, but she died.'

Tom put his arm around her as they walked around the flower beds towards the hives. 'As I said, you need to ask questions when you go home next. And you must go, if only to sort it out, especially if the camellias are a nice memory.'

Verity didn't want to think of home; didn't ever want to go back. Instead she led him to the hives. 'The bees'll be resting for the winter,' she told him. 'But when it warms up there'll be a frenzy of activity, because Fran and Bet have planted the garden to please them.'

She walked on a little, wondering about Saul, and worrying suddenly about Granfer. 'It'll be bad enough for Polly, but what about Granfer and the boats? And what was all that about Lettie being lonely?'

Tom said quietly, 'Fran whispered to me that if Saul goes, the boats will be returned to the company and Granfer will stay here with Lettie, so don't worry about him. You'll have two families to visit then. But remember, you must say nothing, just as everyone else has decided to do. It's so improbable it'll come to anything, after all.'

They wandered through an orchard in leaf with just a hint of blossom, so held back had it been by the cold spell. Every day it seemed there were more lies to bear, or perhaps secrets was a better word. The remains of last year's apples and plums lay on the ground. 'Fran likes to leave some for the wildlife,' Verity said. Then, while she looked up at the branches to the sky, she went on, 'I was mean about Sylvia. I was jealous. Why did she tell you what she hadn't told us? Aren't we kind enough? Is she after you? I just seem to be all over the place.'

'You *are* kind enough, but she doesn't know me well, and it's often easier to tell a stranger something, because they don't hang around. She knew I'd tell you, so she was making it easy for herself. Sylvia isn't interested in me; and if she was, I'm not interested in her. Never ever think I am attracted to anyone else. You are my girl. We will forge a life together. Do you understand me?' His grip on her shoulders was so hard it hurt. 'Tell me, because I leave once we get to Alperton, and I won't have any doubts plaguing you, is that clear?'

His kiss was hard, and his arms around her almost stopped her breath. 'Don't you have any worry that I will find anyone else?' Verity managed to say.

'Of course not, I am perfect.' He kissed her again. Then they walked back together. He said quietly, 'Yes, I worry, because you are so wonderful and I was a chauffeur, but I have to believe or I will be lost. And I can't be lost, if I am to come out of this

248

war in one piece. The one thing I ask is that if you ever stop loving me, you tell me. Just don't betray me.'

The shoulder of lamb was so tender it fell apart. Fran held back on where she had acquired it, and Sylvia forbore to ask, so all was peaceful. Saul and Polly talked and laughed; and Harry fell asleep with Dog on the sofa in front of the inglenook fireplace, when the eating was done. Fran said nothing, just slipped an old blanket under Dog, and a knitted one over Harry. She and Bet served brandy and coffee, refusing Saul and Granfer's request for tea. 'Certainly not, you can't have brandy in tea.' It was as though they had asked to eat something they had found under their shoe.

It was over coffee that Bet gave Verity the letter. She didn't recognise the postmark or the writing. She read:

My dear Lady Verity

I am writing to thank you most sincerely for your remarkable actions in saving my daughter Alexandra's life in that godforsaken lock; and your actions also saved her legs. She has told me so much about that day, now that it is clear enough for her to sort out in her own mind. She told me how you went into the very cold water to save her, and how your friend Tom called out instructions about tourniquets, and your friends Polly and Sylvia were on hand to help, one to telephone, the other to aid Bet.

We returned from the Argentine in 1942, where my husband was in the diplomatic service for His Majesty's Government. On arrival, one of my daughters wished to nurse to help the war effort, and Sandy, as we call her, decided upon work on the canals. We applaud her endeavour, her willingness to put aside her privilege and muck in. I doubt that she will be able to return to you, but she will do something else. That option is available to her, because of you.

I will be writing to your mama, now that my husband has managed to trace your family through things that our beloved Sandy has said. You and your friends – your team – have our undying gratitude. Please, I beg of you, tell them so. And my husband wishes me to forward his assurance to all of you that if, at any time, there is anything it is in his power to help you with, during or after this war, it will give him the utmost pleasure to do so.

With sincere thanks

Lady McDonald (Celia)

Verity handed the letter round.

Polly looked up. 'I know, let's ask for lamb every day.'

Sylvia shook her head. 'Oh no, brandy and coffee.'

Tom laughed, and handed the letter on to Bet. 'A corporal's stripe.'

Bet read the letter. 'That we all survive, and Harry grows up in freedom.'

Verity smiled, but wondered how on earth a letter from Lady McDonald would be received at Howard House; a letter intimating the news of Lady Verity Clement labouring on a canal boat, and what's more, that their ex-chauffeur was involved? But then she leaned against Tom. Perhaps it would actually soften her mother's attitude, to think that another titled girl had chosen the same life, with the approbation of her parents. Perhaps the Clements would even approve of her marriage. She half laughed, and stared out at the early-evening sky. Were pigs flying tonight?

She looked around the cottage sitting room. Saul and Polly sat on cushions on the floor, Polly leaning back in Saul's arms. Bet and Sylvia were in desultory conversation while they played 'Snap'. Harry still slept, his arm around Dog now. Fran and Granfer were in close dialogue, but what about? How hurt would Polly be that her best friend had known something about Saul's plans and said nothing? How betrayed would Polly feel that Tom had accepted Saul's choice and, when asked to help, had listened and expressed his ideas?

No, that wasn't for tonight. That was for whenever it happened. She looked again at Sylvia, who was one of them now, part of the trio, whether she liked it or not, and however much she fought against it.

Polly raised a toast: 'All for one, and one for all.'

Verity nodded at Sylvia. 'You see, you're part of us, in this pause.' No one else understood, as the girls smiled at one another.

Verity laughed slightly. She had drunk just enough beer but not too much, and then brandy, and this was the best day she thought she had ever had. She smiled, and as Tom put his arm around her shoulders and pulled her close, he whispered, 'I'll remember today, when things get busy out there. And we'll remember it together, when I'm finally home.'

Granfer left to call on his sister, and the others set out for the boats half an hour later feeling relaxed and at peace. Fran had signed Tom's plaster, along with all the others, to wish him good luck. Sylvia walked with Harry and called, 'This has been a good pause, a full one. One to remember.'

Chapter 15

Thursday 6 April – en route to Bull's Bridge

The day dawned fine, and the clock alarm sounded at five-thirty. In their butty cabin the girls rolled over and slept on, until Polly heard a violent knocking at their cabin door. She struggled awake. Sylvia checked the alarm clock, pulling out her earplugs and sitting bolt upright.

'It's seven o'clock,' Tom shouted from the butty counter. 'Saul went ages ago. In the words of Bet, chop-chop.'

Sylvia was already scrambling into her clothes. 'We're coming. Get the kettle on, let Dog onto the towpath.'

Verity pulled herself up on Polly, who hauled her out of bed. Polly was laughing, 'Come on, Verity, we're a disgrace.'

Verity was muttering as she scrambled into her trousers, 'It's Easter, we're entitled.'

'It's not Good Friday until tomorrow, so don't pull that one.'

It was only once they were dressed and washed that they realised they should have done all that in the motor cabin. Sylvia was brushing her hair, as she sat out of the way on the side-bed.

Polly folded up their blankets. 'I'm really sorry. Back to normal tonight, Sylvia, I promise.'

Sylvia just stuffed her hairbrush under the side-bed, in the box she kept for accessories. 'No, we'll do as we did this time. I can't have you trotting about in your pyjamas – it's silly. Leave your blankets folded at one end of the cross-bed. It's not for long.' She stopped, her hand to her mouth. 'I'm really sorry, Verity. I didn't mean to remind you.'

Polly smiled as she hurried up the steps, sliding back the hatch and shoving open the doors, because Sylvia had never said anything like that before. Tom stood on the counter. 'Tea.' He pointed to the roof. Toast was heaped on a plate, larded with honey. 'It'll help the headaches, of which I have the worst, I do believe. I'm off to see a man about a dog, and will leave you ladies to the bucket.' He limped back along the towpath, whistling to Dog, who bounded up to him and then away.

'What will we do without you, Tom?' Polly called, then met Verity's eyes as she emerged from the cabin, and it was her turn to apologise.

Verity grabbed her tea and called to Sylvia, 'Come on, loads of toast to cure our tiddly little hangovers.' She stroked Polly's arm. 'Don't be daft, Polly. We all know Tom's going, and he's one amongst thousands. We all have to do whatever we feel we should.' Her look was so intense that Polly was confused, but then Verity tore a slice of toast in half, folded it over and ate. Her cheeks bulged.

Polly stared. 'You look like a hamster, but their excuse is that they're storing food. I am appalled.' She handed a piece to Sylvia. 'Get that inside you, for goodness' sake, and let's potter on, shall we?'

'In a moment – ablution time.' Sylvia edged along the gunwale to the bucket. 'I'm coming back as a boy.'

By midday they had been through the Norton locks and welcomed the darkness of the Blisworth Tunnel, which eased their headaches; they wanted to reach Fenny Stratford if they could. They couldn't, because all the locks were against Polly, who was lock-wheeling and hating the bike, as it jerked and tossed her, and her hangover, in and out of potholes along the towpath. She did the afternoon shift as well, so that Verity could spend every second with Tom, and so that Sylvia could recover as she draped herself over the tiller, moaning that all she wanted was to lie in a darkened room.

In the afternoon Dog ran at Polly's side, and by three the sun was out, her headache was gone and she knew she'd be more than ready for the leftover lamb, which Fran had packaged up for them in greaseproof paper.

As dusk descended they moored up near Cosgrove and ate the meal, which Tom served with carrots and potatoes, with not a squeak from Sylvia, who merely mentioned that Bet had made the point that one mustn't look a gift horse – or, indeed, gift lamb

– in the mouth. It was such an unexpected joke that Verity choked on a potato, and caused general revulsion when bits of potato flew across the table and landed on Polly's sweater.

Polly swore, then said, 'A bonus for Dog.' She flicked the bits onto the floor, which Dog ate.

Tom muttered, 'That it should all come to this . . .'

On Good Friday they kept on going, stepping down through the locks to Leighton Buzzard and then to Marsworth Junction, where the Aylesbury Arm turned off. It was only six miles long, and led to Aylesbury town and a dead-end. Tom looked at the opening to the narrow canal and asked Polly, who'd come aboard for a cup of tea, 'Do you ever deliver cargo down there?'

'We have a couple of times; it's lovely, isn't it, Verity?'

Verity was sitting on the roof reading the newspaper, and was probably miles away, but she nodded and said, 'It was Saul's sister's favourite place on the canal, apparently. She used to dream about it. Something to do with the lack of villages; just nature and countryside, as though it was a path leading to a house, as though it was going home.' She looked thoughtful. 'I can see what she meant. On the Grand Union we just go on and on. At Aylesbury we go to a town, and there we are. To leave, we have to turn in the basin. It's as though we've taken time out of the endlessness of travel.'

Polly was standing on the gunwale, sipping her tea and checking for a sales table outside the allotment that edged the towpath. 'Yes, she was right. The main cut *is* an endless cycle, as though we're like some sort of hamster on a wheel. But yes, it's like a—'

'Pause,' Tom said. 'Everything these days comes back to pausing with you girls, doesn't it?'

Polly continued, trying to remember what else Granfer had said about the Arm. 'It was supposed to go on and link up the main Grand Union Canal with the Thames at Abingdon, but it never happened. As Granfer said, "It's them damned trains that did it. Took the cargoes, they did."'

They laid over for the night just outside Tring well behind Saul and Granfer and, to distract Verity from Tom's departure, Polly told Tom over their spam omelette that no one knew where Maudie was, or even if she was alive or dead. Leon still denied ever hitting her, or Joe.

Her ploy worked, and Verity chimed in, 'The POW told the police that Leon planned the firing of our butty cargo, and the club manager admitted he'd bought black-market goods off Leon, but of course they don't keep records of black-market deals, so it's one person's word against another's. The manager has sworn he'll give evidence, though, same as the POW. But we still don't know anything about Maudie's whereabouts.'

Sylvia took up the thread, and Tom was looking from one to the other as they interrupted, finished words and sentences and finally sat back, with Verity saying, 'And look at our lovely *Horizon*. You'd never think she'd been repaired. She's still a beauty.'

He cleared the dishes. Sylvia washed, Polly and Verity dried, Tom put away. Polly smiled. 'Do you know, young Tom, we might turn you into a decent trainee, if you stayed on.' Then yet again she could have bitten off her tongue.

But Verity just smiled. 'When he's here on leave, he can step straight back into the role – what do you think, girls?'

On they travelled the next morning, Easter Saturday, with Polly cycling ahead until she came to Farmer Elias's fields, and there, sure as eggs were eggs, was a bag hanging on the fence, halfway up the field where his sheep grazed. He left a bag every month or so, full of children's books for Jimmy and Joe, and anyone else who wanted them. He had done so since Joe, Saul's nephew, had seen one of his ewes in trouble and Polly had unhooked her from the fence. She tore up the field now, unhitching the bag from the post.

'Thank you, Farmer Elias,' she yelled, as she always did.

Sometimes he was around, sometimes not. He felt the children on the cut should be educated, to give them some choice, because he sensed the cargo-carrying cut was on its last legs as the railways and roads took over. He also felt happy for the boaters to poach pheasants, rabbits or whatever else was on offer, but not his livestock. That was in danger only from the rustlers.

The sheep in the field ignored Polly these days, and she ran back through them. Dog was on the towpath, knowing better than to enter the field. Polly clambered over the fence, then peeped in the bag. He had added vegetables, too. She yelled again, 'Thank you, Mr Elias.'

She slung the bag over her shoulder and cycled ahead to the locks to Kings Langley, opening and closing them for *Marigold* and *Horizon*. On they went, down alongside Cassiobury Park, and at last they unloaded the coal at a Watford factory.

'What does it make?' Tom asked.

The girls shrugged. 'Who knows. When it's wartime, who knows anything.'

On they went, grimy and tired, working the locks ever downwards; some of the locks were with them, others against. The closer they came to Bull's Bridge, the quieter Verity grew, standing close to Tom on the counter of *Marigold*. Polly was still the lock-wheeler and came on board in the longer pounds to grab a cup of tea. As they drew closer to Cowley, Sylvia took over the last of the locks and Polly steered the butty, suddenly exhausted.

Saul would be a good day's journey ahead, she reckoned, as Sylvia shoved at the beam of the last lock before Cowley. Soon it would be Bull's Bridge. And orders. Then Alperton. Poor Verity.

As they left the lock, Sylvia cycled alongside the butty, calling across, 'Cowley's with us, the keeper said. Polly, does the wind really help turn the boats in the wide winding areas of the cut, like he just said?'

Polly dragged her muffler around her neck, pulling it up to meet her woollen hat, and saw that Sylvia was doing the same, riding the bike 'no hands'. 'Show off,' Polly yelled. 'You'll hit a pothole and be bucked off.'

Sylvia laughed and tucked her muffler into the neck of her sweater, before gripping the handlebars. 'So, what do you think about "winding"?'

Polly yelled again, 'I don't know. Bet said that was why that term was used, but I think the whole of the cut is windy. And just feel the wind's edge today.'

Sylvia nodded. 'If you look to the left, you'll see a bluebell. Just one, but it's always cheering to see them.'

Polly followed Sylvia's finger and saw it between two large beech trees, battling the wind. 'There you go,' she shouted. 'What did I say? Never mind the bluebell, see that wind, eh?'

Sylvia's laugh reached her. Polly looked ahead again, as *Horizon* followed *Marigold*. They had cleaned the holds as best they could at Watford after the unloading, thinking what a way to spend the Easter Saturday, and had replenished the coal-store box from the gleanings. They would pick up more after they'd swabbed out the bilges at the lay-by when they finally arrived. Did it ever change? Any of it? Here they all were, lock-wheeling, cleaning, loading, unloading. Could she do this for the rest of her life? With Saul, yes.

Sylvia was roaring along now to the Cowley lock and yelling, 'It's with us, Polly. Look, you two love-birds, the lock is with us.'

Polly heard Verity's and Tom's laughter.

They were into the lock in what seemed just seconds, and the lock-keeper checked their docket, peering down to the motor. 'See yer've still got yer 'itch-'iker. Leaving yer at Alperton, I 'ear. You should all go up west and 'ave a drink or two to wish 'im well. Right on the Piccadilly Line, i'n't it?'

Once they set off again, almost at Bull's Bridge at last, with Sylvia back on board the butty, Polly thought that probably Verity wished they had been caught up in the worst queue in the world – anything to prolong her time with Tom. It's how she herself would feel, if it was Saul leaving.

Saul stood on the train back to Southall as it creaked, groaned and swayed on Easter Saturday, thinking that Polly would be reaching Bull's Bridge today and glad that she hadn't arrived before he left, or he'd actually have had to lie to her. As it was, he would see her soon. People were crowding around him, too close. He longed for the loneliness of the cut, but then stopped – perhaps soon he would no longer be there. He still didn't know, though.

Mr Burton's letter had been waiting for him at Bull's Bridge yard office yesterday, late Good Friday afternoon. Mrs Holmes had kept her promise to say nothing to Polly, too, or he'd have seen it in her eyes at Buckby. What *had* been in her eyes was relief that Tom was going, and not him. It made Saul feel sick in his stomach, and he wondered if he and Granfer were right to hide it; and to ask Tom too, as well. Granfer still said it was right, cos what was the use of pain if it was never goin' to happen?

Mr Burton's letter had given Saul a telephone number to phone as soon as he arrived at the depot, if he was serious. Mr Burton explained that he had been to school with an official who had agreed to see Saul. Alf in the Administration Office said he could use the office telephone, if he left fourpence on the counter.

He had been told by a lady with a proper posh voice to come first thing on Saturday. He had caught the train, after telling Granfer, and had found his way to Mayfair. It was war, and there were so many people in uniform, of different uniforms, that he hung his head, because he was young and not in one.

He saw a bloke called Mr P. O. Thompson, who sat behind his desk twiddling his thumbs as Saul stumbled through his thoughts. Mr Thompson's thumbs were clean, his nails too; and Saul put his hands down on his lap, covered by his cap. Could the bloke smell him? Well, his office could do with a window open, so stuffy it was, and Saul wanted to loosen his kerchief, but that'd show his hands, so he didn't.

Mr Thompson said, 'I'm an official concerned with War Transport, and it is I who set on the trainee girls – amongst other things. I am seeing you, even though it's the day before Easter Sunday, because Mr Burton has asked. And besides, there is a war on.'

Mr Thompson hadn't seemed ever to draw a breath as he talked.

Saul listened as the bloke kept going, saying that people were needed on the cut for the war, especially those who had failed the medical. Saul said what Granfer and he had worked out he should say: 'Granfer be old, and is set to live with Lettie, and Joe be living with a banker and goin' to school, and that only leaves me to run the boats. I be fit and 'ave been working me leg, and it be strong and better, and I 'ave a longin' to be serving; and if Granfer be gone, and Joe be gone too, I 'ave no one to help, and the boat must go back to the GUCCC.'

He realised he hadn't drawn breath, either. He didn't tell Mr Thompson that his leg still ached like the blazes, because that was nothing, in the scheme of things.

Mr Thompson had put his fingers together under his chin, like the steeples they spied far distant on the cut.

The train screeched to a halt now and people pushed past Saul to leave; one woman shook her head at him and held her scarf to her face. He knew he smelt, of course he did. More passengers got on; they were like sheep, all fretting at a gate. It was too hot, too crowded. Some read newspapers, and he could read and all, thanks to Polly. Darling Polly. He closed his eyes. She would be right hurt if he went, but it was something he had to do, or how could he live with himself, how could he be upright? It was pushing at him, this need was, cos he had to keep her safe.

Mr Thompson had put his hands down, flat on the table, as though he was trying to push it through the floor, but he couldn't push a boater out of the pub with those hands. They were soft, and his shirt cuffs were white, and Saul bet they could be seen in the dark. Mr Thompson then straightened the blotting paper on his desk, and at last he looked up.

'Of course we have need of many men for different types of jobs, at this stage of the war. And you are young, and you are right: you alone on a narrowboat is not a lot of use. Mr Burton spoke well of you. But you would need a medical. Fancy going off there now? You are, after all, under twenty-five, and the Discretionary Reserve is something I can overturn if I wish to release you.'

Saul kept an eye on the stations, cos he didn't want to miss Southall. Mr Thompson had said lots more about training, something called 'aptitude', and how necessary it was to obey orders and complete the basic training. He ended by saying that

Mr Burton had vouched for Saul, and it was therefore important not to let him down.

Mr Thompson had then stood and he was a straight-up bloke, cos he held out his hand, even though his own was clean. His handshake was firmer than the rest of him looked. His eyes were sharp and steady. Perhaps he was one of those who was not what he looked on the outside?

The doc was in the next office, creating paperwork – or was that clearing it? Saul couldn't rightly remember. But he'd had a good look at Saul's eyesight, his leg and his feet, which weren't flat. He'd listened to his breathing. He'd let Saul know in due course, the doc had said, or Mr Burton would, sending the decision to Bull's Bridge depot.

The train drew in to Southall. He forced his way through to the platform and then out of the station, where he laughed, because the smell from the sand-bags made him seem like a bunch of violets. He ran now, cos Polly might be moored up and he didn't want her to ask questions, when he had no answers, yet.

Saul headed down the road beneath gathering clouds, across the crossroads and on to the green. He walked on past the war memorial. All them names, and here he was, safe and sound. He passed the pub, where they went often enough. Then the Methodist chapel. He saw a notice saying it was Easter Sunday tomorrow. He'd forgotten, but the boaters would head off when they had their orders, whatever day it was. Then past houses, hedges and finally the cut, and he breathed a sigh of relief as he nodded at the depot guard, who grinned. 'Been shopping, 'ave yer, Saul?'

'I have an' all.' He felt for the chain in its box in his pocket. It was for the ring. Polly could get the size changed when she was ready. He wove between the men working extra shifts, hearing the tannoy calling steerers to the office with orders.

He walked along the lay-by. He wanted to see his Polly, of course he did, but he didn't want to lie, although with the chain in his pocket, it would only be half a lie. He passed Ma Mercy washing on the bank. The steam made her face drip as though it was sweat. She waved her tongs. 'Yer want to put something in my boiler, our Saul?'

He shook his head. 'No, thanks, Ma. Right kind, but got a heap to do anyway.'

She called after him, 'Your Polly ain't back yet. Locks against them, I 'spect.'

He smiled. 'Aye, I reckon so. We got through right quick, but 'ad a quick unload, as well as keeping going into the dark. Verity 'ad longer going slower, with 'er bloke.'

He strode past the boats with their sterns to the kerb, but she called after him. 'They'll be 'ere any minute, though, now the sun's going down. Steerer Porter were just in front, and 'ere he is comin' in.'

Sure enough, Jimmy's da was pat-pattering along, looking for space to squeeze in. Saul knew Polly had some books for Jimmy, and for Joe, and he slowed, deep in thought. He'd need to go and see Joe, if he got taken on. For a moment he faltered and nearly stopped, his mouth dry because there'd be so many people who'd fret at his news, and again he wasn't sure if it was a kind thing to do, but do it he must.

Chapter 16

Saturday 8 April – Bull's Bridge depot

Polly ran along the kerb of the lay-by to *Seagull* and Saul, but he didn't wait for her to reach him. Instead he tore towards her, dodging the steerers' wives, who were busy like Ma Mercy washing and gossiping, and picked her up, holding her tight, kissing her eyes and her mouth. She said, 'I'm covered in coal dust.'

He laughed, 'And I'm clean like driven snow?'

He set her down, because Jimmy Porter was pulling at Polly's sweater. 'We moored just ahead at you, so look at me words, Polly. Do look. Got 'em right, 'as I?' He waved his exercise book at her.

Polly and Saul just laughed. Saul ruffled the lad's hair.

'Come on, walk back with us,' Polly told the boy, taking his hand. 'I've books from Mr Elias for you, and we've looked at the work you've done.'

Jimmy walked between them. Polly carried his exercise book and they swung him high in the air, each holding a hand. He shrieked with laughter. 'More,' he called. More he got.

When they arrived back at *Marigold* and *Horizon*, Sylvia was waiting for her, a broom in her hand. 'Come on – bilge clearance, Polly. Then it'll be time for Saul.' She squatted in front of Jimmy. 'Shall I find a broom for you?'

Polly said, 'You see, Jimmy. She wears a pointed hat and uses a broom to ride on, when the moon is high.'

Tom and Verity laughed from *Marigold*'s counter. Too late, Polly remembered how strange Sylvia had been, when witches had been mentioned before. Sylvia stood now, looking down at Jimmy. No one moved or spoke, not even Jimmy, who sensed something was wrong. Finally Sylvia said, 'Ah, but I only take flight when it's not raining.'

Polly relaxed, took the broom from Sylvia and asked Verity to grab Jimmy's books from the shelf. They waited and Sylvia chatted about his homework, taking the exercise book from under Polly's arm and flicking through it. 'My word, how you've come on, but let's leave Polly or Verity to mark it. They're really good with a red pen and keeping people on the straight and narrow.'

She smiled gently at Polly, and clambered back on board the butty, which was riding high in the water. Polly watched Sylvia, disturbed by the sadness and conflict that had flickered across the girl's face.

Saul slipped his arm around Polly's shoulder. 'The lass has much in her 'ead. But it'll be spoken of, when she be ready. Or so Granfer said. Best that way, to speak when things is ready, don't yer think?'

Jimmy was reaching up to Verity, who had arrived at Polly's side, the books in a hessian bag. Polly said, 'Sorry, Saul, I wasn't listening. What did you say?'

Saul just shook his head. 'Just mithering.'

Polly smiled and turned back to Jimmy. 'Perhaps you'd like to write a note to Mr Elias to thank him, Jimmy. I know you did last time, but here are some more. He'd like to know which books you like, and something about your life. I know that Joe is still writing his storybook about the dog on the cut, and on each page he draws a picture too, so when it's finished we'll show Mr Elias that, as well.'

Jimmy took the bag. 'Thanks, Missus. I'll do that now, cos I 'ave more words and sees things better.' He turned to Polly. 'I's trying to help Timmy Stevens to read. I uses yer lessons. He 'as a book, so maybe you could mark his work. You, too, Missus Verity, but Ma said not to bother you none, as yer was busy with him.' Jimmy pointed to Tom.

Verity hid her smile and said, 'Bring it. I'm not that busy with him, except when he's really naughty.'

Saul walked back with Jimmy, and Polly watched them go, thinking that one day it would be their own child that Saul was walking with. Would they still be on the cut? If not, where?

Sylvia called, 'It's no good standing there with the broom. It's not going to fly into the hold and sort out the mess. It needs a handler. Come on. The sun is going down, we have work and are hungry. After checking with Alf in the office, Verity, what about sorting out spam? We could fry it with the onion that's left, and boiled potatoes. There's cabbage, too, but cook it in the motor, then it's Tom who has to put up with the smell.'

As she finished she took off along the gunwale of the motor, collecting a broom from the storeroom as she went. Verity and Polly watched her. Verity grinned. 'My word, she's getting just like us. What on earth did Bet say to her. Did you see them in deep conversation?'

Polly gave her the broom. 'Yes, but I have no idea, and no time to wonder. I'm off to the lavatory. You can get cracking.'

Verity pretended to sweep Polly along. 'I have never known anyone like you for dodging the ruddy bucket. But hurry up, then you can take over and I can go.' Polly nipped off towards the yard. There was no point in taking soap and the 'coal towel', because they'd need it even more once they'd finished their chores. Then they'd annoy the foreman, who ticked them off every time for mucking up the toilets. But he always bought them a drink at the pub, and was gracious in darts defeat, which was just as well, the girls told him, since he had yet to win.

Orders didn't reach them until Easter Monday, 10 April, so at least they could go into London with

Tom from Alperton, as planned. Verity and Tom had the motor to themselves and talked of things past, things present and things future, as she steered and he packed his grip in the cabin. They clung close on the counter, when all was ready. Tom knew that these past days had been the most precious of his life, and he was bloody well going to come out of this war alive, if it killed him.

He laughed softly and told Verity. She laughed, too, but her eyes didn't, any more than his own did.

They moored at Alperton at four o'clock, their first stop on the Regent's Canal. They were to pick up steel from Limehouse, and then deliver part of it, to Aylesbury, down the Arm, and the rest to Tyseley Wharf, as usual. Sylvia had said how extraordinary it was, having just talked about the Aylesbury Arm, and what a shame that Tom wouldn't see it. She had apologised almost the moment she said it, and busied herself polishing the butty's chimney brass.

Saul's delivery was straight to Birmingham, but he wouldn't rush, he whispered into Polly's hair when he too moored at Alperton, just a beat behind the *Marigold*, and came to see if they were going into London to see Tom off.

'Yes, Saul, and you must come, too.' Verity checked the motor cabin. There was nothing of Tom's left. 'All ready,' she said, her voice totally calm, though her fingernails dug into her palms. Tom picked up his grip from the side-bed. They had taken his uniform to a nearby laundry at Southall, and the moment they arrived at Alperton he had strip-washed in the cabin, while the girls kept the kettle boiling in the butty, so that he looked and smelt smart as a button – almost.

They wiped down his leg plaster, but worked their way around Bet's and Fran's rude messages, and those from *Marigold* and *Seagull* and the crosses of the boaters, plus Jimmy's signature, which he had written in capitals and had dug deep into the plaster.

Verity said, 'The plaster looks like a piebald pony. I had one, called Snowflake, but why on earth I named her that, heaven knows. It must have been dirty snow that year.' She was aware that she was talking, talking, as she stood on the counter – anything to stop thinking and feeling. Tom was beside her, laughing as he stepped onto the bank. He dropped his grip and held out his hand.

She joined him. He was warm and clean, much cleaner than any of them, but they'd done their best, sluicing themselves and wearing skirts and clean sweaters. The problem was that the smell of the cut seemed to sink into everything. Polly joined them, as Sylvia walked Dog towards Granfer, who was coming to say farewell to Tom.

Polly grumbled, 'I'd rather be in trousers. Your eyebrow pencil down the back of the legs isn't as warm as stockings. We need to meet some nice GIs who are lonely and have stockings to spare. Do you remember ... oh, what's his name? Ah yes, Al of

Idaho we met in Regent's Street on a night out when we'd just started on the scheme?'

Tom was shaking Granfer's hand and ruffling Harry's hair. He squatted and spoke earnestly to Dog, pulling her ears. Saul arrived, clean and dressed in his best trousers and jacket. They set off by four-thirty and saw that Sid had opened the pub door to shake out a cloth, but they wouldn't be visiting until their return this evening. By then Verity knew she'd need more than a few drinks; and yes, she did remember Al who had helped them across the blacked-out Regent's Street and then followed them into the London club where she had wanted to meet up with her impossibly arrogant friends. Friends she had soon realised were not her friends at all. She smiled at Polly, thought of Bet and Fran, then listened to Saul talking to Sylvia and Tom. These were her friends.

Granfer said he'd keep an eye on Dog, and that Harry would walk him. Granfer had even found an old cricket ball back at the depot for the lad to throw; it had almost lost its colour, but Dog was in heaven.

They took the Piccadilly Line to Piccadilly Circus, which was cluttered with men in uniform seeing the sights, just as they had been the last time she and Polly had been there.

Thoughts of Al of Idaho had helped Verity decide where they were to go, and she ordered a left turn down Regent Street. She nodded at Polly, who followed, an unspoken question in her every move.

Tom identified Polish, Canadian, Australian and American servicemen passing them or walking alongside. At every doorway sandbags were still piled high. Tape was pasted over the windows. Verity slipped her arm through Tom's as Saul carried Tom's grip and walked with Polly. Once they reached Jermyn Street, they turned into it.

Polly called, doubtfully, 'Is your club a good idea? Will it even be open at five-thirty?'

Verity said, 'It prides itself on never closing, so let's put it to the test, shall we?'

Polly caught up with her, pulling Verity back from the steps. 'Think, Verity. I repeat: is it a good idea? What if your friends are rude to Tom? Besides, they could report back to your parents?'

Tom's look was keen, but he squeezed Polly's arm. 'It's something she needs to do, and I'm happy with it, Polly. Perhaps it draws a line, a no-going-back line, for her.'

Verity smiled up at him and then at Polly. 'I don't need a no-going-back line, but I want everyone to see that I love Tom and we aren't hiding any more. If they're rude, we will leave. And as for reporting back, Lady McDonald is already blowing the gaff by writing to my parents. Have a word with Saul and Sylvia, though, would you? I don't want them to be uncomfortable, so if they say no, then no it is.'

Saul merely shrugged when Polly explained how posh it was, how snobbish, how rude, and that the night they had come there had been dancing, and a band, and women in cocktail dresses, and officers in uniform who had been less than kind. He said, 'We are who we is, and they is who they is, so we'll rub along. We could give them a tune, Sylvia, if there's a band.'

Tom roared with laughter. 'Oh, this I have to see and hear. For heaven's sake, get knocking, sweet Verity. This will be a memory I take into the fiercest battle, or when standing in front of the surliest sergeant.'

Verity skipped up the steps and knocked. The shutter opened. There was a brief pause before the doorman put a name to the face. 'Lady Verity, this is a pleasant surprise.'

'Hello, George, we're on a day's leave. All right to come in for a cocktail and bite of something?'

The door swung open. They entered. George, in his dicky suit, showed no emotion at their attire. The hat-girl was not the same one as before. She took Tom's grip without comment and the girls' mackintoshes. They climbed the stairs. Dance music oozed from the ballroom. They entered. There were only a few people sitting at the small round tables scattered about. Though it was early in the evening the men were in 'black tie' or officer's uniform, and the women in uniform or cocktail dresses.

Verity ordered beer for Saul and Tom, gin and tonics for the three women and whatever food was on offer, ignoring the raised eyebrows of the waiter at their jumpers and day-skirts. She put the refreshments on her account. Polly noticed the slight quiver of Verity's hand as she signed the chit. The waiter bore it off.

Verity grimaced at Polly. 'I've just thought: Daddy might have stopped my account so drink and eat up the minute it comes.' Smoked-salmon sandwiches and several rounds of beef ones arrived.

Sylvia whispered, 'Beef, I don't believe it.'

Polly muttered, 'I'll have yours, if you object on principle.'

'Shut up,' said Sylvia, eating quickly. 'Hurry, everyone, in case they take it back.'

They all dug in. The drinks arrived and more sandwiches, unordered. They began to relax and drank more, with Verity cavalierly signing chits while the others worked out the tip that would be required. Verity and Tom danced together. Saul shared himself between Polly and Sylvia, until an RAF officer asked Sylvia to dance. Would she or wouldn't she? For a moment Verity thought she wouldn't, but then Sylvia quick-stepped around the floor with the best of them.

Verity wore her engagement ring – too large for her finger though it was – and within an hour her friends of yesteryear began arriving. They did a double-take as their gaze swept the room, and locked on to Verity. For a moment it seemed as though each would pass the table without acknowledgement, but Verity greeted the first arrivals, just as Saul was beckoned over by one of the band. The saxophonist had spoken to him in the men's room, worrying because their singer had been called away. Saul sang for them, and gestured Sylvia over for 'Begin the Beguine'.

While they sang Verity introduced her fiancé to her passing acquaintances. 'You remember Tom – he drove us to Ascot one year.'

Each of them did. Several of the officers weren't sure what to do, since Tom should presumably have acknowledged their rank, but finally they shook hands. The women gave air kisses or smiled, wafting their cigarette holders and gliding on, whispering to one another.

The moments passed and Verity knew the time was coming to say farewell, because Tom had said he needed to catch the train for Catterick at 21.00 hours. They sat close together for the last hour, talking of nothing, but talking nonetheless, knowing that they had been offered the chance to redress their love, to come together and be given time, and to be enclosed by friends who cared. They had also been given the confidence to lay to rest their ghosts, here, amongst Verity's former circle. It was a declaration, and what these people did with it was their own affair.

As Saul and Sylvia sang their last song of the evening, a request was received from an Air Transport Delivery girl for 'The White Cliffs of Dover'. She was a friend of Verity's from the old days and looked exhausted, with streaks of grey in her hair. Verity, Tom and Polly pooled their cash for a tip to leave the waiter, while Saul and Sylvia sang. The tip would clean them out, but it had to be a large one, if Verity was to hold up her head.

The head waiter hovered behind the table, and for the first time that evening Verity felt flustered, but then she heard him say quietly, 'Please accept this evening as Blue Room's thanks to your guests for entertaining our members, and make sure they receive this.' He pressed an envelope into Verity's hand.

He stood straight, then turned to gesture Saul and Sylvia to the table, as a ripple of applause accompanied them on their walk from the bandstand. 'Our thanks. You are welcome as honorary members, should you ever visit us again – all of you. And, sir,' he turned to Tom, who waited at Verity's side, 'I wish you all good fortune. And you, Lady Verity, a happy and successful life, once Private Brown has returned. Please visit us again.'

He bowed them to the door. Several of Verity's friends looked the other way, but some waved. 'Come again, Ver,' one called. 'I've missed you.' It was the Air Transport Auxiliary girl.

Verity hurried across to her and gripped her hand. 'You keep safe, Gloria. I read in the obituaries about your husband, Clive, and I'm very sorry.'

Gloria smiled. 'War's war; things happen. Be happy while you can. God bless.'

She turned away, but not before they saw the tears spilling down her face.

*

Tom left them at the top of the steps leading down to Piccadilly station. 'Let me go on alone,' he insisted. 'Goodbye is too hard.'

He hugged Sylvia and Polly, then shook Saul's hand. Polly said, 'Don't forget your white handkerchief, or Mrs Green'll have your guts for garters, even if the Germans don't.'

Verity waited as her friends walked across to study the Criterion Hotel as though they had never seen it before. Tom turned her to him and held her, kissing her hair, her cheeks, her mouth. 'I'll write. I'll never stop loving you.'

He picked up his grip and ran down the steps without a backward glance. But then he stopped, turned. 'Go and see your parents. They will hear of this evening, as you intended. What's more, they will, as you know, have heard of us from Lady McDonald. It can't go on, can it? Get to the bottom of what seems so wrong between you and your mother, and try to kill the pain that's in you. It's not just about us, I'm sure. For your sake, my darlin' girl, just in case I ...' He left the rest unsaid, but ran down the remainder of the steps and out of sight.

He'd gone. Her Tom had gone, and though she loved him, Verity had no intention of seeing her parents. The others joined her and she couldn't bear to see their sorrow for her, so instead they all talked about the money Sylvia and Saul had found inside the envelope. 'A tenner,' Saul breathed. 'That's five trips.'

He re-counted the one-pound notes. He and Sylvia decided it should go into the darts kitty, for emergencies. Verity and Polly sat together, friends as always. At Alperton they walked down through Southall, and Verity dropped back as Sylvia and Polly sang 'Begin the Beguine' quietly. Walking alongside Saul, she muttered, 'How can you think of going to war when you don't have to, because that's what I think you are trying to do?'

She saw that Sylvia had dropped her purse and was groping for it, as they approached. Saul said, 'Something in me – something I can't control – says I must, and this feeling is bigger than me.'

Verity just shook her head and strode on. 'You men are such fools.'

Sylvia picked up her purse and ran after Polly, who hooked her arm through hers, and together they sang 'It Had to Be You', beckoning the other two to join in. Verity caught them up and, after a moment, Saul did, too. All four walked abreast to the pub, then filed into the fug and the chatter, and their own world. The table was reserved for them, as usual.

Chapter 17

Tuesday 25 April – nearing the completion of another trip

Marigold and *Horizon* pat-pattered south, passing the Aylesbury Arm where they'd offloaded a partial load on the way up. Saul was ahead of them, but Bet and her two new trainees, Cathleen and Beryl, followed a short way behind. Cathleen was a darts player and made up a four with Bet, Verity and Polly. Polly had made sure they played as often as they could, to keep Verity's mind off Tom and to fill the kitty, which had to be divided between the two crews.

Verity lock-wheeled past Berkhamsted and whistled as she cycled, and laughed with the lockkeepers. Sylvia and Polly on their counters watched her closely, as the pair dropped with the water in the last lock before Kings Langley, but finally Polly wondered aloud, 'I think she's happy, even though Tom's gone, because at last she trusts their love. She knows what could be in store, but she "believes".'

Sylvia didn't reply for a moment, but then muttered, 'How wonderful to have no doubts, to trust ...' She petered out and said abruptly, 'Tea, I think.' She disappeared into the cabin.

Polly looked after her. Doubts, Sylvia? Doubts about what? Was it about what to do with her life once the war was over? Who knew – it was all guesswork with Sylvia; but if you were an orphan, perhaps it made you solitary, and that was so sad. Polly realised, now more than ever, that her own parents were the foundation of her life. What's more, they encompassed others like Verity and Joe. She called after Sylvia, 'You have us, never forget that.' There was no answer.

They carried on descending towards Watford and then past it, and soon red buses were passing over the bridges, a train whistle blew, houses proliferated, some bombed and others not, factory windows were open and *Music While You Work* blared out of the wireless. They reached their favourite paper factory and pulled into the loading platform. Verity blew Bet's hunting horn.

Albert, the foreman, appeared and called back over his shoulder, 'Where's that blasted tea, Brian? Them baggages are here, dirty, tired and gagging for summat hot. Ain't that right, my girls? Leave us to take off the planks and tarpaulin, like the ruddy angels we are. But don't you be telling the other trainees, or the boaters, or there'll be 'ell to pay.'

They stepped wearily onto the wharf, taking the mugs from the tray that Brian brought over. Polly muttered, 'Thanks, Brian, and you, Albert, are such a dear. But we'll do it when we've had a slurp.' He'd been kind to them ever since they'd stood up to him when he was rude to them as trainees.

He put up his hand. 'Together, then.'

The men took down the top planks and between them all they untied the side-sheets, rolled them up on the gunwale, and then the top sheets and stowed them in the store on the forward counter. The girls kept up with the men now. But so we should, thought Polly, we do it so often. They tramped up from the factory wharf while the men began the unloading, and stood to one side, the factory towering over them, cutting out the sun. Polly watched as Albert directed his men. Saul had been ahead of them on the cut and he and Granfer had probably had their new orders by now and were gone, but at least they'd spent a couple of evenings together, with Granfer and Saul eating in the *Marigold*'s cabin, or they in *Seagull*'s.

She asked Verity, 'How are you doing?'

Verity tipped the dregs of her tea onto the yard. 'Surprisingly, all right. Perhaps because I have the certainty of love, even though nothing else in the whole benighted world can be called certain. Oh, I don't know, I can't quite explain it.'

Sylvia followed suit with her tea, dangling the empty mug from her little finger. 'Polly and I were talking about it and know what you mean; you believe in him, in yourself, in the decision you've both made.'

Verity slipped her arm around Sylvia's shoulders. 'You really do know.'

Sylvia said, 'Polly and I both know – we were talking about it, I just told you.' She slipped away from Verity.

That arm on the shoulder was a step too far, thought Polly. Albert came and stood by them, rolling a cigarette. Verity dug out her Woodbines and offered him one. He put his own makings away. 'Thank you kindly. I hears your bloke's gorn orf, Verity. But, 'e came in the end, that's the main thing. And it's all sorted, ain't it?'

Verity dug him in the ribs with her elbow. 'The cut is just an old women's knitting circle; it's gossip-gossip.'

Polly heard a barrage of shouting down by the *Marigold* and swung round.

Albert said, 'I 'ear Polly's Saul 'as—'

It was just a lorry backing too close to a billet, so Polly turned back. 'Has what?' she asked.

Albert was rubbing his ribs, shaking his head at Verity, who simply repeated Polly's question. 'Has what?'

'Been in touch with his Auntie Lettie.'

Verity smiled and patted his shoulder. 'Lettie knows she can write to him or Granfer, more likely, now the old boy can read the letter.'

The unloading was finished. Coal dust hung in the air and Polly was, as usual at this stage, sick of the sight and taste of it. She set off for the boats, then realised she was alone, and called back to Verity and Sylvia, 'Come on, stop nattering to Albert, we've places to go, people to see.'

Albert nodded. 'You take care now, you three.'

When Verity and Sylvia caught up with them, Verity looked so sad, Polly said, 'We could have coped somehow, if you had taken time away with Tom, Verity.'

Verity shook her head. 'He wanted to be on the boat, and you girls were the soul of tact and left us to it, and he says that now he can picture me about my business, rather than he and I sitting looking at one another, wondering what to say. But now I feel awfully tired, and was just thinking that I could take the leave we all have due, perhaps go and stay with Fran, if she'd have me. Anyway, there must be a place where the air is clear of coal dust and we're not swabbing out bilges.'

Sylvia was very quiet and simply headed for the butty. Verity leapt onto *Marigold*, went to the engine cabin and within five minutes got the engine firing. Polly pulled away, and hooted when Albert least expected it, as always. He jumped, as always, and shook his fist, then blew a kiss.

Polly said, 'I love that old wretch. Oh Lord, I forgot to ask about his daughters, was that what you were talking about?'

Verity eased herself onto the roof. 'No, just chatting. We'll catch up next time. I'm right, you know, we really should take a few days off, Polly. If I look as tired and old as you, then I'm in trouble.'

Polly burst out laughing and slapped Verity's leg as she steered to the centre of the cut, short-towing the butty. 'Bet was muttering in the pub about the three of us being more than due a break. I could go to Mum, and it's really tempting. Saul should be so far ahead I probably won't see him for several days anyway. Why don't you come? She'd be pleased to see you. I'll ask Sylvia, too, because we can all bunk up in my bedroom.'

They headed on towards Cowley Lock and then they passed the Bull's Bridge dry dock, before motoring alongside the yard frontage and the lay-by, looking for a space.

'There's a gap, let's squeeze in,' called Verity. They did so. 'Moor up, my hearties,' Polly yelled.

Sylvia tied up *Marigold*, as well as the butty, as Verity set off across the roof to the store cabin to pick up the brooms. Sylvia called out, 'You're right, Verity, we should take some leave. But I think I'll stay in London, although thanks for the offer, Polly. You see, I'd like to take in a show, then come back to the butty. It's just the thought of not having to answer to the cut for a couple of days that appeals. It's as bad as answering to the bells—' She stopped.

In the pause Polly said, 'The orphanage, I suppose.'

Sylvia nodded. 'I'm really tired.'

Verity agreed. 'So we'll try for a week's leave? We've done weeks and weeks without taking what we're owed.' She stood at the end of the roof, brandishing the brooms. 'But we're not doing anything until we've cleaned out the holds, then we'll march in a body to the office. However, I can share with you that Bet's already had a word.'

'Good old Bet,' breathed Polly. 'You coming, Verity?'

Instead of answering Polly, Verity said to Sylvia, 'You know, on second thoughts, can I come with you? I fancy a London show, and I know a nice little club near Marble Arch. Separate rooms, quiet, low price, and then I fancy a spell here at the lay-by, just to catch my breath.'

Polly smiled, but felt hurt because she hadn't been asked. 'Oh, well, tell you what: I'll come into London with you, and I can then go to see Mum while you two read here. How about that for a compromise?'

Verity just looked at her and then nodded. Polly reached across, feeling guilty at being so childish, when Tom was who-knew-where. 'Don't worry, Verity, he'll be safe, I can just feel it.'

Verity smiled. 'It's something some men feel they have to do. We *must* remember that. They think it's their duty, you do understand, don't you? Are you going to see if *Seagull* is here?'

Polly shook her head. 'There's no point, Saul'll have gone on. The cut is so busy at the moment.'

Verity just nodded.

Saul and Granfer had reached Bull's Bridge depot the day before when the office was closed, so first thing on 25 April Saul had headed there the moment it opened, hoping Mr Thompson had written. Bob, the old boy who stood in for anyone not on duty, had been leafing through files, a pencil stuck behind his ear. Saul waited, tapping the counter until Bob muttered, 'If you don't stop that tapping I won't give you the letter that came for you, Saul Hopkins.'

Saul felt as though he'd stopped breathing as Bob reached below the counter, holding up a buff envelope and studying it. 'Nope, that's not the one.'

He replaced it, then hooked out a bundle of letters and checked through them. 'Nope, not these, either.'

Saul could have seized the ruddy bloke across the counter by his overalls and shaken him, as he replaced the bundle and ferreted beneath the counter again. Finally Bob brought out another buff envelope. 'Aha, here we go.'

Saul snatched it from him and ripped it open.

Bob asked, 'Good or bad news?'

'I don't know.' He didn't because he'd never expected to be taken on, not really, not in his heart. Saul ran back through the yard, dodging the workers hurrying in their overalls from workshop to workshop. There were already clattering sounds from the cafeteria, as lunch began to be prepared, and shrieking from the machine shops. He leapt on board their butty, *Swansong*, brandishing the letter at Granfer through the cabin doors.

'Bring it on down, lad.'

Saul sat on the side-bed, with Granfer on the crossbed, knowing they wouldn't be interrupted because

Harry had gone trotting along the lay-by to see his da. Saul drew a deep breath. 'I'm to go, Granfer.' He handed across the letter with the instructions from Mr Thompson, and pointed with a grubby finger to the final comment:

Mr Burton has been your advocate. I know you won't let him down, and I feel that your experiences on the cut might be helpful to our needs in the near future.

Granfer nodded, placing his hands on his knees. 'I is pleased fer you, lad, but yer has to tell her now – and young Joe. Still intent on an holiday, are you, so yer can tell 'er, in peace? Bet's set it up, and Verity 'as made plans to take Sylvia orf, so our Polly 'as a free run at leave with yer. You was goin' to tell her, weren't yer, whether or not you'd 'eard? The secret's got a mite heavy fer us all, yer know.'

Saul nodded and gripped Granfer's hand. 'I'm going to hurt her – and Joe maybe. What about you, Granfer?'

'I'll worry, but you know I understands yer think yer's shirkin', and 'tis what I would feel.'

Saul waited until he saw Polly bringing the motor and butty to the lay-by that afternoon, and then he warned Granfer to stop washing all the pierced plates, prior to packing them up to take to Lettie's. 'Put 'em back on t'wall, if yer will, Granfer. Tom has booked a boarding house near Bridport, Dorset;

someone he knows who has two rooms, and I knows which train an' all. Yer sees, I want to give her peace, just for a moment, to sort of get her so she ain't so tired, and I'll tell her at t'end.'

Granfer nodded. 'I feels I coulda been wrong. P'raps we should a brought 'er in on it.'

Saul felt the hollowness in his stomach, because he didn't like pretending to his Polly, but neither could he have borne to bring her more pain than she had to feel; and as Tom had said to him, they needed good memories. 'It's too late to think that now, Granfer. I know my Polly – she'll know I did it out of caring. She's seen our Tom go, so she'll know that 'tis something men does.'

He helped Granfer hang up the plates again, though he knew he would never see 'em on these walls once he came back from Bridport, because Granfer would already be gone. The old man didn't do goodbyes.

Saul sat on the side-bed. 'Not sure how to feel on an 'oliday, Granfer. What does we do, d'yer reckon?'

'You'll find out, won't yer? Tek it easy, I reckon, but you'd best find yer lass and make sure she 'as some clothes for yer three days, and is willing.'

Chapter 18

Wednesday 26 April – Dorset

Saul had his good clothes on, and Polly hers. They travelled by train and bus, heading for Waterloo, and he thought his heart would wear itself out with all its beating, cos there were so many people, cars and buses going this way and that. So, too, there was the hooting of horns when there were no bridges to check – so why the hooting?

Sweat ran down his back as they walked between the traffic to get to the other side of the road and then onto the next bus, with a tired old conductor who put Saul in mind of Granfer, and who took the money and gave them a ticket and a tip of his cap to them. This holiday thing weren't to his liking, but Polly's dark eyes were shining like the sun and her whole body seemed to jig with excitement. She knew how to get to places too, because here they were, getting off the bus and into a great hall, which was Waterloo Station, full of people scurrying like the rabbits in Mr Elias's fields. They bought tickets that would bring them back, too.

Would she know by then? When would he tell her?

'Come on, Saul, if we run we'll make it.' Well, if there was one thing he could do, it was run, so side by side they wove in and out of people, as a tannoy like the one in the depot yard called out trains and times, and the people moved like the boats at Tyseley Wharf, jostling to get in, or out.

They showed their tickets to the bloke in the box at the rear of the platform. 'Get a move on,' he said. 'Guard's got his flag out.'

They ran onto a long lay-by with a train moored alongside, and smoke or steam gushing from its chimney. They tore past the guard, who was bringing up his green flag. 'Get yourselves in, for Pete's sake. There'll be more 'n enough stopping and starting on the line – so many troop transports it'll be bloody bedlam, so who knows what time you'll reach wherever you're going.'

Polly pulled at Saul's sleeve, pointing to some seats in a carriage. But a soldier was leaning out of the window of the door, holding hands with his missus, who was crying.

'Next one then,' Polly yelled and ran on.

They stopped at the next door. Saul twisted the handle. Steam and smoke were everywhere, smuts too, and the whistle was blowing. He opened the door and Polly flew into the corridor, dragging her grip. He followed and slammed the door shut just as, with a screech and a grind, the train jerked, juddered, then drew away.

Polly laughed into his face. 'We caught it. Oh, Saul, two whole days together before we have to come home.' She hugged him.

Along the corridor the soldier who'd been leaning out looked at Saul and shook his head in disgust. Sailors and soldiers lined the corridor. One jerked his head into a compartment. 'Seats in there for shirkers and women.'

Polly spun on her heel. 'He's got a damaged leg and is carrying canal cargo to keep you lot in guns, so you can just be quiet. It's a Reserved Occupation and he can't leave, so there.'

The soldier shrugged, and braced himself as the train jerked again. Another soldier said, 'Lucky bugger – good work, if yer can get it.'

Polly wrenched open the compartment door, but Saul shook his head. 'You sit, Polly. I'll stand, cos I keep tellin' yer, my leg is better. We'll be stopping, and others will need to be sittin'.'

Polly shrugged, the sunshine gone from her eyes, and the holiday excitement with it. Would it come back? He hoped so, but for himself he didn't know what it was about a holiday that caused all the fuss. It was just a mess: rush, noise, strangeness. They both stood, for the three hours it took to reach Dorchester, which is where the train finished, for some reason.

Out they all got, and Saul felt that eyes were boring holes in his back, though the soldiers had talked over shared cigarettes about the cut's cargoes, the life and their families, as though nothing had been said. But it had, and it was still there, and perhaps it would make Polly realise that he had a right to take up arms, now that his leg wasn't that bad any more. Yes, that was it; it was his right.

They now headed for the bus to take them to Burton Bradstock, a village near Bridport that Tom had said was pretty and within walking distance of the sea, and where they had rooms.

They arrived by the evening, and a coastal breeze was blowing. They had to walk up Shipton Lane to a house on the top of the hill, pressing themselves against the side of the hedgerows and banks as military jeeps, lorries and motorbikes roared past. The house was owned by someone Tom knew from his time as chauffeur to Lady Clement, and he had got a message to her. It was a Mrs Lamb and she had promised that they could have the two rooms that her young children used, saying that this once the kiddies could bunk on the cot beds in her bedroom.

They handed Mrs Lamb their ration cards, and were shown into two small rooms at the very top of the house. 'You're lucky,' the plump landlady in her well-washed apron said. 'There's troops every-where, but these rooms are still empty, although for 'ow long, who knows. We got commandos and GIs, and Lord knows what cluttering up the place and doing exercises.'

The rooms were in the roof and were tiny, no bigger than the *Seagull*'s cabin; and in Saul's there was an oil lamp too, and for the first time that day he felt calm and unthreatened as he sat on the narrow bed. It was quiet, it was small; it was what he knew. He clenched his hands around his knees. 'Get used to the world, Saul 'Opkins,' he whispered to himself. 'You'll be out in stranger places soon enough.' He swallowed, glad that he had brought Polly away; and glad for himself as well, because he wouldn't feel so peculiar when he finally left.

There was a knock on his door and it was her voice, his beautiful Polly's voice. 'Have you seen the sea? Can I come in?'

'Yes, o' course yer can.'

She opened the door and peered round. Some strands of her brown hair were wet where she had washed her face; the sunshine was back in her eyes, and the excitement. She gestured him over to the window, which sloped in line with the roof.

'Look,' she breathed, clutching his hand and kissing it. 'Look at the sea.'

In the distance was the sky and, beneath it, grey water, the colour of the clouds; and beneath that, and larger, were bloody big slopes down to the village, and smoke that rose from the chimneys of the cottages of Burton Bradstock. He stared over the straw-type roofs to the sea. He'd never seen so much water, and how odd it was that the far edge, where it met the sky, was curved. He said, 'It bends, look.'

'That's the horizon, and it shows us that the world is round.'

He stared. Yes, he could see that, and he realised how little he really knew, or had seen, and was scared for a moment of the people he'd meet, and the places he'd go to when ...

Polly said, 'Let's nip downstairs. I don't know if Mrs Lamb will feed us, but if not, perhaps the pub will.'

Mrs Lamb only did breakfast, so they walked down the hill, laughing together because they knew they'd have to walk back up. 'So best not to drink too much,' Polly said. She had brought her torch for later and Saul shook his head at her in wonder. 'Yer think of everything.'

'Only because I'm more used to it, but you know much more than me about the cut.'

He walked, holding her hand. Owls hooted as dusk fell, and the stars were as bright as they were on the cut, cos of course it was the same sky. He felt better with that thought in his mind. The breeze had fallen. There was a stillness. Yes, she was more used to it, and he would have to become so, too. They reached the bottom of the hill and walked through the village, which was full of strolling troops; some were larking about, while others were smoking in small groups.

They took the narrow lane by the church, heading south, following the noise. Troops spilled out onto the lane and stood around outside the pub. Saul braced himself as they threaded through the men to the bar. 'Two pints o' mild, if yer would be so kind,' he said.

The girl replied, 'Cider tonight, all right?'

Saul turned to Polly. She murmured, 'Made out of apples, and strong.'

He nodded. 'If yer would, please, and d'yer have food? We're on 'oliday.'

'Not leave, then?' she muttered. He shook his head, wanting to say: not yet. Instead he asked for the only thing on the menu that she pointed to, saying to Saul, 'Sausage and mash, but mostly mash.'

He nodded and paid. They pushed through to a table at the back of the bar and sat, waiting. Polly squeezed his hand. He heard strange accents around him. It was hot with the press of bodies. 'So much is different on an holiday that it fair makes yer tired.'

The girl brought the food. The noise bellowed. Some men played dominoes next to them, while others were playing darts, and someone was pounding out music on the piano. Some soldiers started to sing.

They ate and talked, and sipped their cider, and even that taste was strange. Polly rested her head on his shoulder. 'I love you. And the soldiers wouldn't have all their supplies without the boaters, and there aren't enough of us women to carry it all, so you are doing a necessary job.'

Ah, so she had noticed the looks coming their way in here, too. Saul's stomach had felt coiled since they entered, and his head was pounding. He wanted to return to his tiny room. He could tell her 'is plans now, cos she had talked of his job. He turned, but Polly said as the clock chimed ten o'clock, 'Can we go back now? I'm so tired. We can try and get closer to the sea tomorrow.'

They walked up the hill and still the motors passed them, their slit headlights keeping their speed down. The owls were in full voice. A fox screeched – had it grabbed a chook? That was better, the noises of nature. Yes, that was better. Saul walked with his arm around his Polly, trying to notice every moment, every movement, every breath she drew, because after this holiday he didn't know when, or if, he'd see her again.

The next day they walked down the hill and then up again, to the high cliffs overlooking the sea, but there was barbed wire and more troops, and overlooking Hive Beach was a gun emplacement. So they stepped back from the wire and looked across the sea, hearing the rattle and surge of the waves on the shingle, and the gulls, calling so loud. They walked along the roads, along the edge of fields with green shoots of wheat showing, and larks calling. They sat on a fallen oak and just held one another. Saul breathed in Polly's lingering scent of the cut and watched the birds, the clouds scudding, and knew at last what a holiday was, and it began to make sense to him. But how did you bring in words that would burst it all apart?

They ate at the pub in the evening and it was sausage and mash – mostly mash – again, and they laughed together. Saul itched to set his traps and bring the pub rabbit or pheasant, but this was a holiday and it was not his business.

The next day ran the same; and as the day drew towards night, their last night, he began at last to feel secure on the firm ground of the land, and at home in his tiny room in the roof. As midnight came and went, he leaned his head on the glass of the window, which was laced with anti-blast tape. He still hadn't told Polly, but tomorrow he must, before they went home. Home to the cut. Home. He should have told her by now, maybe, but good memories were important.

He stared up at the stars, wiping the glass, which was clouded from his breath. The stars seemed so close, now he was high up. Not a light showed, but of course not; it didn't even in London except for the searchlights. There were searchlights over Weymouth, dancing like the butterflies in the reeds of the cut. He ached to return. He missed the pat-patter, Granfer, Joe. Ah, Joe, he must see him, too. No, he'd telephone him. Saul felt fraught to his very marrow with it all. Yes, he'd telephone Joe and promise he'd be back, cos he couldn't say goodbye to his face.

He wiped the glass clear again. Tomorrow, on the train, he'd tell her, his Polly, and she must forgive him; she must.

*

They caught the bus, then the train the next day, and arrived in the shifting tides of London as wave upon wave of people crashed like the surf on the shingle and made his head dizzy. They caught the train and the bus and as they walked from the station, through Southall to the depot, Saul thought he could smell the cut. Yes, smell it. He almost ran. It should give him the courage to tell Polly, for he had found none yet, and the old shame was on him, cos he had failed her, and himself.

They entered the depot yard, waved to the guard and wove again, as they seemed to have done so often over these last days, though this time it was through the workers in their overalls. And still Saul couldn't find the words. They were at the frontage, and there it was: the cut, his cut, their cut. Steerer Ambrose pat-pattered past with his pair. "Ow do,' he called from the motor counter. Saul's soul ached.

Polly almost sang, 'How do, Steerer Ambrose, we've had a lovely, lovely holiday.'

'Whatever pleases yer,' he called as the butty came along now, with Mrs Ambrose knitting, the red, white and blue tiller under her elbow, her long skirt moving in the wind.

Was the breeze still blowing at the beach and in the valley? Were the men still exercising? Well, he'd be one of them soon. Saul's soul ached further.

He turned to tell Polly, at last, but she had dropped her grip and was running along the lay-by, holding the clinking hessian bag they'd lugged back, calling over her shoulder, 'I want to see if the girls are back, and give Granfer his present, though you said I shouldn't buy one for him. I hope he likes cider.' She stopped, turned and walked back. 'Oh, Saul, I've had such a lovely time, and I love you so much, and I don't care who hears me.' She faced forward and ran again.

'Wait, Polly, I must tell yer—'

She was moving too fast to listen.

Chapter 19

Saturday 29 April – late afternoon at Bull's Bridge lay-by

Polly tore along the lay-by, looking for *Marigold*, glad to be back and hoping that Verity was there, and Sylvia, too. Yes, they'd gone into London together, but whether they'd stayed there she didn't know. If not, she'd give Verity a bottle of cider, and Sylvia apples stored from the autumn; otherwise they'd keep. They were rather wrinkled, but still good, because she'd eaten one on the train.

She wondered what Granfer would think of the cider? Much the same as Saul perhaps, who had said, "Tis all right for holidays, but not for normal times.' She had laughed then, and laughed now as she passed Mrs Porter, who was heading for the town with her string bag. Polly wished she had brought back something for Jimmy, but never mind. She'd listen to his reading. She called after Mrs Porter, 'I'll come along later to hear Jimmy read, or he can come to us. Or perhaps he has homework to be marked? I had a lovely holiday, Mrs Porter, a simply lovely holiday.'

Mrs Porter waved and called, 'That be good news, Polly.' But she sounded a bit strange.

As Saul approached, Mrs Porter reached out and stopped him. Saul bent to listen and then shook his head. Mrs Porter patted his back and he walked on, kicking aside a stone. Polly shrugged. Oh well, perhaps everyone else was as tired as she'd been. She hurried on and saw washing fluttering on the line above *Marigold*'s hold. Well, someone was back. She started to run, but the clinking of the bottles would give the presents away, so she strolled, hoping Saul would catch her up.

She glanced over her shoulder, but Saul was talking to Steerer Brown now, who was shaking his hand. How strange. Further along, Ma Mercy on the butty *York* was calling something from her counter. Saul hurried to her. She handed him what looked like a scarf and gripped his hand, stroking it, before she disappeared along the top planks, while on *Lincoln*'s counter next to her Steerer Mercy tipped his hat.

She heard Saul call to Steerer Mercy, 'I'll cast yer off.' He slipped the strap from the mooring stud and threw it onto the counter, and watched as Steerer Mercy tucked the tiller beneath his elbow, stood in the hatches, slipped the gear and was off. She heard the pat-patter of the engine from here as *Lincoln* motored out into the cut, picking up the butty as his stern drew level with the butty's fore-end. It was all as it had been just three days ago, but it seemed the boaters thought she and Saul had been away forever, such was their attitude.

'Polly – oh, Polly, how are you?' It was Verity shouting from the roof of *Marigold*, along the lay-by, a bag of pegs dangling from her hand.

Polly called, 'We had such a lovely time. I thought you might be in London, but you're here.'

Verity looked confused, but then laughed. 'It would seem so, or am I a mirage? We only had a day in town, Sylvia and I, that is.'

Polly shouted over the noise of the tannoy, 'Did you have a good time? Every day was wonderful for us, and there were troops everywhere, British and GIs. Made me think of Al of Idaho, but I don't think I would have recognised him if he'd come up and said "Boo" and waved a pair of stockings. Burton Bradstock is so pretty, but there was barbed wire along the cliff. After the war we'll go, shall we, all of us? So write and tell Tom, thank you, for contacting Mrs Lamb.'

She quickened her pace as Verity slid from the cabin roof onto the counter, calling, 'Are you really all right? You sound so—'

Sylvia interrupted from the butty-cabin doorway, cutting across Verity. 'Verity, one of your sweaters is going to blow off – you've only pegged one side. Hello, Polly, fancy a cuppa?'

Sylvia jumped to the kerb, her blouse sleeves rolled up, and hurried to Polly, who had faltered, looking behind, because something wasn't quite right. But no, there was Saul walking along with Thomo, who had hurt his hip on his last trip; his limp was bad, or was it just that Saul's had improved to the point where it was non-existent? She side-stepped Sylvia, looking along the cut for *Seagull* and *Swansong*. There was Dog, sniffing. Ah, he must be with Granfer? But no, that was Thomo's boat. She shaded her eyes, checking the chimneys of the moored boats. Where was *Seagull*'s with its extra brass ring?

Sylvia called, 'Dog, look who's here.'

Dog turned, then roared along, leaping at Polly, licking and whining. Polly handed her bag to Sylvia, and it clinked. Dog was barking and chasing her tail, then leaping at her again. Polly laughed, 'Oh, Dog, oh darling Dog. *You're* just the same, while everyone's so ...' Dog wanted to play. Polly snatched an apple from the bag, and threw it. Dog roared after it.

Sylvia picked up the bag.

Polly said, 'It's cider from Dorset, and apples for you, Sylvia.'

Sylvia held on to the bag and slipped her arm through Polly's. 'Come on, tell us over a cuppa, and we'll tell you about Lupino Lane in *Meet Me Victoria*.' She raised her voice. 'Come on, for heaven's sake, Verity. You must have finished pegging up by now.'

Somewhere a motor sounded its horn. Elsewhere a child cried, a woman laughed. Polly stepped onto the butty, with Sylvia holding her arm, tightly. The bag clinked as Sylvia put it down on the counter. Verity ran along the motor-cabin roof, jumped down and over to the butty, slipping her arm around Polly's shoulders as Sylvia carried the bag into the cabin.

'I have broken biscuits for our cuppa; they were on offer in Southall,' Sylvia called.

Dog leapt onto the butty roof, and Verity and Polly sat there with her. Polly knew that things only felt different because she'd been away. She listened to the barrage of chatter as Sylvia brought out the tea and biscuits, and she could smell supper cooking in the butty range. She looked again for *Seagull* and *Swansong*, but could see no sight of the chimney, and no sight of Granfer.

As Verity and Sylvia talked of the songs they'd heard at the theatre, and Sylvia sang the first verse of 'You're a Nice Little Baggage', Verity shouted over her, telling Polly about Bill Fish, the cheeky, cheerful porter who hoped to marry Dot, but needed a promotion. 'And oh, we didn't know if he would get it, did we, Sylvia?'

Sylvia studied her tea, shaking her head. 'It was really good fun, wasn't it? I haven't been to a London show ever, but the singing ... It was as much fun as the pub.'

Silence fell for a moment, and Sylvia looked past Polly to Verity, as though asking a question.

Polly said, 'Did you feel it seemed strange to come back, too? And where's *Seagull*? Has Granfer gone on?'

Verity shook her arm, spilling Polly's tea. 'Oh, never mind that. It was just so lovely to see live theatre, and such excitement, even if it is just acting ...'

On and on the two girls chattered, and now Verity was down on the counter, acting out a scene. But here too was Saul, at last, standing on the bank in front of *Marigold*. He had her grip, which he put on the motor counter. Polly watched him, not listening to Verity, not drinking her tea or eating her biscuit, because she could see his face.

At last she understood and slipped from the cabin roof, dropping her mug. It smashed on the counter. Dog barked, startled. Polly kept her eyes on Saul, as Dog jumped from the roof onto the counter, whining beside her. Dog's hair was bristly, warm and solid as Polly gripped her collar, and nothing else seemed solid. Nothing.

'Shut up, Verity,' she yelled. 'Just shut up, all of you.'

Silence fell. Verity was beside her, reaching out. Polly brushed her away. For minutes Saul and Polly just looked at one another. He held out his hand, and somehow she was standing next to him on the lay-by, just the two of them; he taller than her, with his limp gone, with *Seagull* gone and *Swansong*, too.

'Granfer has gone to Lettie,' she said. It wasn't a question.

Behind her, on the butty, she heard Verity. 'Oh, Polly.'

It was all there, in those two words. The truth that she had known, deep inside. How could she not, because she wasn't a fool, but then again she was.

She looked at the girls, and then at Saul. 'You all knew.' She swept her arm along the moored boats. 'Everyone knew, and no one told me, no one made me see. You can't go, Saul. How dare you go. They don't want boaters; you're needed here. There aren't enough of us women.'

Saul was standing so close she felt his breath as he said, 'Mr Thompson said I can. My leg is well enough, and I is needed.'

Polly was confused. 'Mr Thompson, what's he got to do with it?'

Saul shook his head, 'I don't rightly know, but he's War Transport, and Mr Burton—'

Behind her she heard Verity groan, and Sylvia jumped down beside Polly. Her voice was fierce as she grabbed both Saul and Polly. 'You are to walk along this towpath, and you are to talk, not shout. Then you are to go, Saul, or you will miss your train.' She heaved them round, her pale face looking stern, her curls bouncing. She pointed. 'Walk to the end, away from the boats. Walk.'

Without knowing quite what she was doing, Polly put one foot in front of the other, as Saul clutched her hand. 'I didn't know how to tell yer, and when I tried something always interrupted us, and I didn't want to bring yer pain till I knew. I didn't know how to tell yer, because yer Will was dead, and how could I let you lose someone else? But I were driven, from inside. I asked Tom how I could try again with the officials. 'E said to try and get someone who knew someone ...'

Polly stopped. 'You lied,' she said.

'I never said nothing,' he answered.

'That's the same as a lie,' she muttered, a great and terrible rage sweeping over her. And she pushed past Ma Needson, who was smiling and saying "Ow do.' The netted bag fell from Ma Needson's hand, and potatoes rolled along the concrete. Saul stopped and picked them up, while Polly stormed on.

Ma Needson probably knew, too; everyone did. Well, bugger the lot of them; she didn't have to stay with people like this, who kept secrets, who supported the lie. She'd leave, go home, because Verity and Sylvia knew, too. And Bet? Yes, what about Bet?

She strode on, remembering Fran, who must have known at Easter about Granfer and Lettie, because someone had cut her off when she was about to say something. Yes, she'd go home, that's what she'd do, and leave this lot behind. They weren't her people, any more than Saul was. And what would her mother say, left with Joe because Saul was swanning off?

She swung round just as Saul straightened and handed the last of the potatoes back to Ma Needson, who patted his arm. Polly called, 'Don't pat him – he's a liar, that's what he is.'

She ran back now, heading for *Marigold*. She'd pack and go home, right now. But then she stopped. Saul had said Mr Burton had helped. Mr Burton? How did Saul know how to reach her old boss? And what about Joe? Had Saul told him?

Saul caught her up and just stood at her side, Dog at her other. Both seemed to be waiting, Dog's ears were down, her tail between her legs. And Saul, though his head was held high, looked unbearably sad. Polly's heart twisted, but a lie was a lie. She whispered, 'Joe? What's to happen to him?'

He held her gaze. 'Yer ma said she'd 'ave him.'

Polly's mouth went dry, and tears threatened.

Saul reached out, took her hand. She snatched it free. Somewhere a motor was heading out; she heard the wash, the hoot, the geese honking as they flew – where? A distant train screeched. He said, 'I made her promise not to say. I made 'er, you understand. It were me. I didn't want yer upset without cause, so I waited until I knew. But I had to try to go. Something's about to 'appen, yer can see that, and I have something in me that makes me need to help. If I can read about it, I can't not do something.'

She almost screamed, waving her hand at the cut, 'What's this, if you're not doing something? What the hell are we girls doing – nothing? And the boaters – nothing?'

He shook his head. 'Yer too good with words, my Polly. But all I can say is—'

'What about Leon? He might come back? Where will you be? Oh yes, I know, fannying about with a gun somewhere? What about Maudie, if she's found? You're just walking away, that's what you're doing.'

'There's Lettie and Granfer, if Maudie's found. Yer ma said she'd help and 'ave Joe. Leon's goin' to trial, so yer'll all be safe.'

Polly bit down the tears, let the rage surge. 'So, it's all tied up. Mum's made it easy for you. I expect she got Mr Burton to pull strings, and Dad would have known, too. Anything to split us up, eh? You know she doesn't want a boater's life for me, you know it. Saul, how could you do this?'

She was beating at his chest, shouting, hitting that precious face. He grasped her hands. 'Shh, shh,' he said.

She kicked him. 'Get away from me, I never want to see you again. You've taken everything, because I can't go home, can I? Not when I hate them, not when they've done what they always wanted, just like Verity's parents. You'll be killed, like Will.'

Suddenly there was nothing. No anger, no anything. She stopped hitting, she stopped speaking. Yes, it *would* be the same all over again. Just like Will, Saul'd be killed, and now they'd all lied to her, there was no one left. Saul let her arms go. She turned, looking along the bank, both ways. Dog sat by her side, leaning against her leg. Polly said to her, 'At least I have you.'

She heard Saul say, standing close, 'Yer have us all. We all love yer, I tells yer, Polly. I didn't think they'd really 'ave me, so I said to say nothing, cos I say again, I didn't want to cause yer pain if I didn't have ter. I'll be back, I promise I'll be back, cos I will never stop lovin' yer. So where would that love go, if I didn't come home, my Polly?'

He touched her shoulder. She shrugged him off. 'Get your train, and do what you like with your love.'

She turned away, heard Saul's sigh and then his footsteps diminishing. She waited until she could hear them no longer, and then she trudged towards the *Marigold* to pack all her clothes, not looking for a last sight of him. But Sylvia and Verity blocked the lay-by. She sidestepped, and they came with her. She sidestepped the other way. Again they blocked her.

Polly dug her hands in her pockets. 'I'm leaving the cut. You can run the ruddy boats yourselves. You knew and said nothing, and now Saul's gone, on a whim, because of your damned boyfriend, Verity. That's who he's copying, and you all helped him and never told me.'

Verity opened her mouth, but it was Sylvia who came up close, staring into Polly's face. 'You know perfectly well, Polly Holmes, that it has been tearing at him for a while – probably for months, if not years. Something is about to happen, we all sense that, and Saul did, too. Look at the activity we see on the bridges as the military pass over them; think of the loads we need to haul, the hours people are working at the factories. Your Saul was driven by something deep, something with which he agreed, and you can call it what you will, but for him it was duty.'

Polly tried to push past. It was Verity who held her back now. 'Listen, darling, to the oracle, because she's right. And do stop this unseemly tantrum; you are making a perfect fool of yourself, and of all of us women boaters. Tom's gone, too, and many others.' Verity raised her head as though to breathe, then looked her friend fully in the face. 'Polly, do grow up. You've had him for this long, now you have to let him go.'

Sylvia added, 'After this ridiculous display, you can see why he didn't want to tell you, because he knew how much it would hurt. And what if the powers-that-be had said no, or the doc had said his leg wasn't up to it? Nothing was certain, and you'd have hurt like this earlier and all for nothing. If you let him go like this, it's you who is absolutely in the wrong. You should admire Saul, and love him, for his protection of you. Yes, it might have been wrong, in retrospect, but it is how it is. We're sorry if it's made it worse, aren't we, Verity? But it was from the best of motives. As it was for everyone.'

Verity had pulled out her cigarettes and was frantically lighting two. She passed one to Sylvia, who miraculously took it and stuck it in her mouth, took one drag and choked. She handed it on to Polly. 'I wish I smoked just at this moment, but I don't, so perhaps you should have it, calm you down.'

Verity checked her watch. 'He's probably gone, but it's worth getting a wriggle on, to make amends. Chop-chop.'

Polly shook her head, dropping the cigarette and stubbing it out with her boot. 'I don't want anything of yours.' Even to her, it sounded ridiculous.

The other two girls now stood to one side, and Verity gestured Polly past. Sylvia said quite clearly, 'If you don't go, it will dog your life. Saul is so fortunate to agree with what he is being asked to do.'

Verity muttered, 'Enough of all that twaddle, Sylvia. Let me just say, Polly Holmes, you'll regret it, if you go away. But if you do, I'll pack your bloody clothes for you and chuck them – and you – in the cut. You can then drag yourself out, dripping and as wet as you already appear, and tantrum off to heaven-knows-where, with my boot up your arse.'

Polly stood her ground. 'Well, let me tell you that I won't be going to my parents, because they helped Saul in order to separate us.'

Verity slapped her now, right across the face. It knocked Polly back on her heels, and stung.

Sylvia gasped, 'Verity, that's uncalled for.'

'Well,' Verity said, 'it's what you do to hysterical idiots, isn't it? For pity's sake, idiot, get yourself after that fine young man, because you might never see him again – just like many, many thousands might never see their loved ones again. After doing so, you can then feel sorry for yourself. But I warn you, we have pheasant for supper and you're needed here, in this crew.' Her tone changed. 'We really do need you, darling; you've held us together, and up on our feet, so let us do the same for you. Besides, we're seasoned boaters with a reputation to uphold, you know that. And don't be absurd. Your parents accept you and Saul; why, they've even taken on Joe.'

Polly cried then, great gulping sobs. Yes, she did have somewhere to go; yes, the cut was here for her, and her memories, just as she had memories of Will; and yes, she was behaving like a complete and utter idiot. She ran then, still crying, along the lay-by and through the yard. The guard at the gate called, "E hung about for a bit, for yer, but he's gone on. Has a train to catch, ain't 'e?'

She tore through Southall until the breath was ragged in her chest. What had she done? But all the time her thoughts were saying that Saul might have felt he had to go, but her parents had done nothing to talk him out of it. She saw her mum's outraged face when she first realised that Polly and Saul were in love; heard her words of disapproval. Yes, she had taken in Joe; yes, she had asked Saul for lunch when Joe first arrived, but she had never spoken of any future for Saul and Polly. Her mum's words still resonated, clearer now than ever: 'Marry up – marry a solicitor, someone like Mr Burton, but younger.'

She pounded along the pavement. What if he'd gone? But then she spotted his back view, his grip in his hand, his head hanging down. 'Saul, Saul.'

He swung round, dropping the grip, unsure, smiling and then not. She saw him brace himself for more wounding words, but instead she flung herself into his arms.

'I love you. Come back when it is over, do you hear me?'

His kiss was gentle. 'I will. Yer know I will.'

She knew nothing of the sort, but nodded.

'I'll write to yer, cos I can do that, thanks to yer and Verity. She's yer friend, and Sylvia, yer remember that; and don't leave the cut, we need the cargoes.' He picked up his grip. 'I have to go.' He was backing away from her. 'Love yer parents, Polly, like they love yer. I wouldn't let 'em tell you, I made 'em promise, but I'll thank yer ma for the rest of our lives, because she 'elped me do it, cos she knew I must.'

Polly listened, watched and loved him, but her fury hadn't really died, and as Saul disappeared into the station, past the stinking sandbags, she made for the telephone box, the pain tearing her into pieces.

She asked for the number and pressed Button A. 'Mum?'

'You know, don't you, about Saul?' her mum asked. 'I'm sorry, but he needed to go and didn't want you hurt unnecessarily, so requested secrecy.'

The pain was worse now. 'You could have said Mr Burton wouldn't help. But oh no, Saul's gone and you have a replacement son, Joe; and I have a space for someone to fill – someone more suitable. I hate you. I will never see you again, or Dad.'

'Polly.' It was a shriek, full of pain.

Good, because it couldn't begin to match her own feelings. She slammed down the receiver, resting her head on the glass of the telephone box. Her mouth tasted sour, her mind ran in circles. She was tired, and the holiday seemed a sham, and she walked out of the telephone box and back to the depot, and work.

Chapter 20

Sunday 30 April – a trip to Howard House, Sherborne

Verity woke in *Marigold*, dressed and crept from the cabin. It was dawn and she'd hoped she'd sleep in, but the habit of early rising was ingrained, damn it. She stood on the counter and stretched; they were still on leave, but what on earth were they to do with their time? She didn't dare to go off to London again and leave Polly, who was doing her best to be the Sulky Sue of the universe. Even the pheasant casserole that Sylvia had produced yesterday evening, plus the cider, which went with it so well, hadn't perked the wretched girl up.

She levered herself onto the cabin roof, sitting and thinking for a moment, and then rolled a cigarette, wondering why she tried to alternate between Woodbines and roll-ups. Yet another habit, she supposed, but they were trying to cut down anyway, and roll-ups took longer. She lit up, picking a shred of tobacco from her tongue. A mist hung over the cut, and smoke curled from the chimneys of the moored boats.

She sighed. Well, they could *all* go into London and try another show? She and Sylvia had used the darts-kitty money for their tickets last time, and had also put a pound into the collection box at the station, for those who had been bombed out in the Blitz. There was still plenty of money left and so, to be fair, Polly should use some, if there was anything she wanted to do.

Bombs, eh? Been a long time since one was dropped, but the transport of the troops they were witnessing all the time brought the war into sharper relief. Did all the activity really mean the invasion of Europe? Would that lead to more bombing of British cities? But how, when the Luftwaffe would be kept busy trying to stop the advance? She shut off her mind. It didn't do to trespass into the world of 'what if?' which led to 'would he be safe?', 'would he return?'

The smoke from the cigarette rose straight into the air. No wind, then. The trouble was – and it was what Sylvia and she had talked about, after Polly had gone to bed – Polly knew the harsh reality of war only too well, and platitudes wouldn't help. Poor Will. Verity wished she had known him, but by knowing Polly, she realised she probably had.

The cabin door of the butty squeaked open. Sylvia stepped onto the counter and beckoned Verity across. They huddled together, Sylvia waving Verity's cigarette smoke away. 'I'm simmering the kettle.'

Dog pushed open the motor-cabin doors and jumped onto their butty counter. 'Let's go to the lavatory and then walk Dog, shall we?'

Sylvia nodded her agreement. 'Come on, Dog.'

Dog ran along in front of them to the yard and waited patiently for them outside the lavs. As Verity washed her hands and face, her fingers brushed the chain that held her ring. Well, she could get the ring made smaller at the very least, and Polly her ring too, even though Saul had bought her a chain. She stared in the mirror. Had Saul asked Polly's parents for her hand? He was going to once he knew, and he'd be phoning Joe from Catterick, if that's where he was destined. But there were too many questions with no answers. She tucked the ring away again.

She met Sylvia in the yard, but was deep in thought about Mrs Holmes, who was nothing like her own mother. Mrs Holmes was kind – look how she'd taken on Joe – so surely she wouldn't hope to split up Polly and Saul? On the other hand, Mrs Holmes had been disappointed that Polly hadn't made her relationship with Reggie, the RAF bomber pilot, work; the one who had a good future in the engineering industry, if he survived. Verity shook her head; life was ridiculously complicated.

Sylvia and she walked back with Dog, who was dancing about the place, joining in with the children who were running wild, before their 'imprisonment' on their parents' boats. Verity found herself studying them, and the mothers who were watching with eagle eyes in case the children strayed too near the water. What *was* it that had happened between herself and her own mother? Was there really something 'other'? Was it her mother who had been cross and unkind? It must have been, because surely it was her nanny who had been kind, and she must have been the one who smelt of camellias; her mother wore Worth perfume.

Dog brought back a stick and dropped it at Sylvia's feet. How interesting, Verity thought. Dog has suddenly decided Sylvia's one of the pack. Well, perhaps they all had. Sylvia threw the stick. 'We could all see *White Horse Inn* – if we can get tickets, that is,' Verity suggested.

They were drawing close to *Marigold*. Sylvia said, 'Well, we could ask Polly, I suppose. We can't just do nothing or she'll sink even further.'

It was then that they saw Polly on the counter, her arms crossed as she watched them approach. She snapped, 'Why don't you just ask me if I want to see *White Horse Inn*? You forgot to whisper, you realise. And I've helped myself to tea, and yours is here.' She pointed to the cabin roof. 'Drink it up quickly, because I don't want to go to the theatre. We have another few days' holiday. Verity, Tom wanted you to find out about your family, so while we're facing up to home truths, we'll go down and sort it out – all of us – and see just how brave you are? I don't want to stay here. I want to achieve something, then we can get back to work. Think about it.'

She stepped off the motor, called Dog and walked along the lay-by towards the lavatories, where else.

Verity watched her dearest friend, who had been stony-faced, her eyes almost bruised from crying, and whose words were not suggestions, but barked orders.

Sylvia said, 'She's accepted it, and she will come to terms with whatever her mother's real motive was, but in her own time. Personally, I believe her mother is a good, kind woman, but Polly has to be cross with someone. And she also feels she's made an awful fuss, which she has, and doesn't quite know how to climb back from it.'

Verity kept her eyes on Polly, who was storming off, and hid a smile. Ah, Sylvia was on the case, too, and there was comfort in that.

Sylvia said, 'Don't worry about Polly. It'll get sorted in time. Let everyone settle down and say nothing more, until they know what to say.'

Polly had reached the yard, and was walking at a lesser pace. Perhaps she had walked off some of her angst. Verity looked carefully at Sylvia. 'Your orphanage was run by nuns, wasn't it? Did you learn how to advise people from them? I always think nuns look wise.'

'We all learn from the people we live with, don't we? But perhaps the Sisters don't always know what's best for people, any more than anyone else does.' Sylvia finished her tea, took Verity's mug and stepped up onto the counter of the butty. 'I'm going to sort out the cabin.'

Verity thought that sometimes life was like a conker shell: prickly. She sighed. Well, she would write and tell Tom that she was following things through with her parents, and then perhaps they would stop off at Woking, and Polly could talk things through with her mother. She sighed again.

The train to Dorset was full of troops, and slow, because they pulled in at sidings to let other trains pass, loaded with military vehicles covered in camouflage. Verity heard one soldier say, 'They usually move the buggers at night, so what the—'

'Harry, shut it,' he was warned. 'Yer don't know who the 'ell's listening.'

At last the train drew into Sherborne and they hurried out of the station to the bus stop, after Polly barked, 'There're no soldiers heading to London to give us a lift, like last time, Verity.' She added, her voice softer as they trundled along the highways and byways, 'I wonder if the GIs who gave us a lift had a good time in London town?'

Verity laughed. 'Who knows, but they were delighted to be free of us and our Waterway Girls smell. Do you remember how they opened the windows the moment they dropped us off at the gates?'

Polly did.

The bus left them at the top of a T-junction. They plodded along as Sylvia muttered, 'I suppose it would have been polite to polish our boots, as we're visiting a rather grand house with upper-class people in it.'

Verity and Polly laughed, and it was the first time Polly had done so since Saul left. Verity flung her arm around Sylvia's shoulders. 'By the time we've hacked up the drive and our boots have been scratched to bits by the gravel, all the dirt will have been shaken off. Anyway, if we polished them, it would only show up the rest of our clothes.'

It was two o'clock, and they were all hungry and hadn't thought to make some spam sandwiches before they left, because they'd been too busy finding a dog-sitter. Eventually they had pinned down Mary who worked in the canteen kitchen and lived near the depot. What's more, she loved Dog. Their last sight had been of Dog lying in a cardboard box on a blanket, by the cooker in the canteen, looking like the cat who'd got the cream. All quite against the rules, but who was going to tell on Mary? She'd have their guts for garters.

They reached the high, imposing wrought-iron gates of Howard House, which were slightly open. They entered, Sylvia whispering, 'What will they say when they see there are three of us?'

Verity shrugged. 'I have no idea, because I haven't told them *I'm* coming, let alone you two.'

Polly and Sylvia grimaced. They walked on. Polly asked, 'I know the drive is a quarter of a mile long, but how much land have you?' She waved to the parkland on either side of the drive.

'Oh, several hundred acres, I'm not really sure. Tell you what, we'll take this path to the left and slip round to the back, and grab some lunch from Mrs B. *She'll* be pleased to see us, anyway.' Verity heard her own nervousness. She almost marched up the path that skirted alongside the silver birches her grandfather had planted, though she doubted he had actually dug anything. He probably just gave his orders.

She and Tom had used this path when they returned from the pub. It led to the side and the rear of the house. Did he actually know what lay behind her mother's behaviour? Or did he just know *something*? Or perhaps he didn't know anything, but simply sensed it. Come to think of it, that's what he had said really. Well, she was here to find out more, but already her courage was waning. Just then she felt Polly's hand on hers, and she loosened fingers which had tightened into a fist.

Hand-in-hand they walked along, and now she saw that Polly had grabbed Sylvia's hand, and soon they were all half marching, swinging their arms, singing quietly that they were the Three Musketeers. 'All for one, and one for all.'

Then they laughed, startling the birds, which flew from the trees. Verity hushed them. They continued without speaking until Polly stopped, pulling them both to a halt. 'I'm sorry I've been stupid, rude and embarrassing. I feel a total fool.'

Verity said, hurrying them on, 'Well, darling idiot, you were, but we've all done it. Strange to say, Miss Polly Holmes, no one is perfect, not even you.'

They were laughing again as they approached the side of the house through a walled garden that contained weed-covered vegetable beds enclosed by overgrown box hedges, and neglected fruit trees that had been trained along the walls. Verity hushed them when they saw a doorway, through which they could see a yard, and she whispered, 'Your dad would soon sort this lot out, Polly. Simon, the new young gardener, went off to war of course. The flower beds at the back will be as bad, though I'm sure Mother will have done her best.'

A small cottage lay to the right of the path that led through the yard to the rear of the house. 'The old gardener's cottage,' Verity said. 'I liked to go in, because old Matthews was a nice bloke and used to hang herbs over the range. Mrs B would give him hell, because the range dried them too much, and would then stuff him with cakes to show him she didn't mean it. Mother had a soft spot for him too.'

Suddenly, as they passed more shrubs in the walled garden, Verity thought again of the scent of camellias and remembered that old Matthews had nurtured a scented camellia somewhere around here. Is that what she remembered – not perfume at all, but the flowers? She shook her head, sure it was perfume, because she had smelt it on a person.

At the end of the walled garden, Verity put up her hand and peered about to check that the yard was clear, but before they moved forward, Sylvia said, 'You do still love your mother, you know. It was in your voice just then, wasn't it, Verity? She is your mother, after all. I mean, perhaps it was just a tantrum, or a concern, that made her trick you and Tom?'

Verity ran the words through her head, then muttered, 'It's more than that. I'm not sure she's ever liked me. I can remember being bathed by someone who was cross. I thought it was the nanny pulling me about, but Mother has often been cross, just like that. Oh, everything is so blurry. All I know is that there was someone else who was kind, someone who smelled of camellias. She was gentle, and sang to me. Now what was it she sang? Oh, I can't remember. I was just a toddler. Mother and Father never talk about my life – about their lives – back then. But parents don't, do they?'

They crossed the yard, and just before they reached the steps down into the kitchen, Verity stopped, feeling a rushing, a darkening; but no, she was not going to panic, was not going to let fear and the memory of Sandy, the water, the blood, the uncertainty of what was to come, drag her down. No, that was in the past. No. She breathed deeply, and again.

Polly said, 'Verity?'

She made herself turn and smile, feeling her heart beating wildly. She said, 'Across the yard you can see the garages. The old Rolls is not there, so at least Father is absent, and Mother might have gone with him.' She was gabbling, panting. Sylvia gripped her arm. Then it was over, all gone, like a wave, and now there were just the echoes as she spoke again, strongly and slowly. 'We can talk to Rogers and Mrs B, which will be better. Above the garages is where Tom lived. He loved the smell of oil, grease and petrol.'

Polly murmured, 'Sylvia's right, you know. You did sound as though you love your mum. And I love mine, but sometimes you just can't forgive.'

Sylvia turned to stand in front of them. 'Forgive whom? Yourselves or them, Polly? You might not forget, but you must forgive. You too, Verity. Life is much too short to do anything else.'

Verity pushed past and headed off down the stairs, because there was no *must* about it. Polly stamped down the steps behind her, clearly thinking much the same.

The boot hall was dark, but of course it was – where did the light come from in a basement? The kitchen door off the hall was half open, and the lights were on. Verity entered. Mrs B was chopping carrots on the centre table, her back to them; a large range oozed heat. Gleaming copper pans hung from the ceiling, and at one end of the table sat Rogers, doing what looked like accounts. Verity felt love for these two people, but as for ...? She didn't know at all.

Rogers looked up, his face breaking into a smile. 'Why, Lady Verity? This is a surprise.'

Mrs B put down her knife and held out her arms. Verity almost fell into them. Mrs B whispered, 'No, it's not a surprise, silly old devil. Tom has written to us, so we knew you'd come sometime, and also why. We are so glad that your plans with him are clearer, my love. First, though, have you eaten lunch?'

She ushered Verity to a high stool beside her, and the other two girls to those on the opposite side.

'Sandwiches, and perhaps leek-and-potato soup. Rogers and I had some for our lunch, but there is plenty, isn't there?'

They ate. Rogers provided cups of tea, and in the warmth and familiarity Verity found courage. Lord and Lady Clements were due to arrive home at four, apparently. They had been invited for luncheon with a neighbour, so it was to be a light supper, Rogers told them, nodding towards the clock. It was now ten past three. Once they had eaten, Rogers busied himself above stairs, while Polly and Sylvia asked to look round the walled garden. On their way out Polly turned and smiled, mouthing, 'Find out what you can.' Aloud she said, 'We'll be back by four, in case you need us.'

Verity nodded, so pleased to have the real Polly returning to them. They clattered up the steps to the yard. It was a noise that was so familiar from childhood that she could almost feel the peas that she had shelled with Mrs B, and the carrots that she had cut into long, slim slices, though her mother had not approved because it stained her fingers. As she had worked, the staff and tradesmen had come and gone, and the chatter had been cheerful. Now, as she washed the dishes with Mrs B in the scullery, no staff entered, because there were no more than just the two of them. She and Mrs B didn't speak, beyond mentioning the canal boats and the weather.

At last they sat at the table, the copper pans glinting in the electric light. Mrs B leaned forward, her plump arms on the table. Verity gripped Mrs B's hand. 'So, you know why I've come?'

Mrs B nodded. 'Tom explained, and I have to tell you, it will be a shock for you to learn more – and it is your parents who should tell you.' At that moment they heard a car in the yard, and Mrs B snatched her hands away and said, 'You must go upstairs. It won't do to be tittle-tattling in here, it's not fair on your mother.'

Both turned to the back door as Verity's mother, standing in a cream silk outfit, said, 'What isn't fair, Mrs B? And, Verity – such a nice surprise. I noticed your friend, Polly, and one other wandering around the flower garden as we drove into the yard. I am delighted to see you all, of course, but I do wish you'd telephoned; we could have made sure we were here. We've missed you, haven't we, Mrs B?'

Mrs B smiled. 'Indeed we have, even though she's such a little monkey.'

Lady Pamela was pulling her gloves off. 'Mrs B, perhaps tea in the drawing room in twenty minutes, for five of us, if that doesn't interfere with your plans?'

She waited, smiling at Mrs B, who said, 'Of course. I think I have some scones.'

Lady Pamela smiled at Verity, though she seemed strained and nervous. She turned on her high heels and left, mounting the stairs to the yard again.

Verity sat, feeling as though all the breath had left her body, a reaction her mother had so often created. If only the woman would kiss her, or reach out to her in some way. Mrs B was bustling into the pantry and came out with some scones and honey, arranging them on a plate, just as Rogers rushed in. 'You know they have returned?'

Verity nodded. 'Don't worry. Mother overheard Mrs B insisting that I talk to them, not to you.'

Rogers shook his head. 'We're not worried about that, are we, dearest? We have been with them so long, and there is a reason we stay. Your mother – not your father, my dear, whatever you might think – is the heart and mainstay of this family, and whatever you hear, you must remember that. You need to leave time and space to follow through on all that you learn. The person they will talk about, and your father in particular, is ... Well, we have an address, should you need it.'

One of the bells above the door rang. It was the drawing room.

Rogers smiled tiredly. 'I believe that is for you, not for us.'

Polly and Sylvia could be heard pounding down the steps from the yard. 'I'm sorry – they saw us,' Polly said.

'And now we need to present ourselves in the drawing room.' Verity rose.

The girls walked across the majestic hallway, skirting the silk carpets. Even Verity found herself walking on tiptoe beneath the portraits of her ancestors. The drawing-room door was open.

Her mother called, 'Do come in, please, because Mrs B is quite right, this discussion is long overdue.' There was a mettle in her voice that there hadn't been in the kitchen. Out of her natural surroundings down there, Verity thought. Perhaps the silk rugs gave her mother a sense of importance, superiority. She felt anger stirring, as it always did, and resentment.

The three of them entered the room. Her father was standing by the fireplace, his walking sticks over his left arm. For a moment Verity thought of Tom. Had he cast both his aside yet? The fire was laid, but not lit. Her mother sat on her usual sofa to the right of the fireplace. Her father smiled. 'Darling Verity, here you are at last. I feared, after your last visit, we wouldn't see you again, but I'm relieved you haven't given up on us. And so good to see you, too ...' He hesitated, looking at Polly. 'Polly, isn't it, if I remember correctly?'

Verity walked to the sofa that was placed opposite her mother's. She stood behind it, with the girls beside her. They looked ridiculous, Verity feared, like three starlings on a telephone wire. She breathed in deeply. No, like the Three Musketeers.

Her mother said, 'We had hoped to see you sooner. We do miss you, dearest Verity.' Though she sat ramrod-straight, she looked fragile, though she had lost weight. Her father, though, looked as he always did. Well, únlined, though when he moved, as she did now, he was clearly in pain.

Verity said to her mother, holding Polly's hand for courage, 'You could have come to Bull's Bridge. Or written.'

Her mother looked surprised. 'But I did write, to the address you left here.'

Verity shook her head slightly. Always an answer – never at fault. She murmured, 'Oh dear, and I suppose the postman didn't deliver it? How convenient.'

Her mother looked at her hands, then at her husband. '*Them*. Them, Verity, my dear. I wrote several letters and left them for posting in the hall. Your father takes them ...' She stopped, thought, then looked at him as he stared into the far distance, as though he had nothing to do with the things being said.

Verity shrugged, knowing that her father wasn't about to be disloyal to her mother and expose her lie. After a moment her mother said, 'I had things I needed to say, amongst which was to congratulate you on helping Lady McDonald's daughter, Alexandra. That took great courage.'

Verity squeezed Polly's hand. 'And if it had been the postman's daughter?'

Her mother sighed. Polly nudged her and frowned.

Verity knew she was being churlish, but she didn't care. She said, 'So, you know from Lady Celia that Tom and I have found one another again. He travelled with us to Birmingham and back on the *Marigold* and has now returned to the war.'

Her mother sank back against the cushions. 'I wrote to you trying to explain why I took the actions I did, to prevent such a liaison. Basically it was out of love, Verity, and experience.'

Verity looked at her father, then back at her mother. 'I'm not sure you know about love, Mother. But I am to marry Tom.' She dragged the ring on its chain out from beneath her sweater. 'I love him, he loves me, and nothing – not even lies – will stop us.'

Her mother put her hand to her mouth. Verity's father said, 'Pamela, be very careful. I will take over now.' He looked at the girls. 'I do wish you'd all sit down, it's like some strange seance or similar.'

None of the girls said a word, but just waited.

Verity's father muttered, 'Very well.' He picked up a gold cigarette case from the mantelpiece, using it to reflect the light, then replaced it before turning to face them, taking both his sticks and leaning on them. 'We love you very much, dearest Verity. Your mother spoke the truth. We utterly do.' He stopped, staring at the floor as he struggled to find words, but to say what?

Lady Pamela spoke into the silence, face pale beneath her make-up, her hands clasped in her lap. 'Your father is quite right, we both love you, and perhaps I acted out of turn with Brown.' She stopped, shook her head. 'No, let me start again, with Tom. But it was out of fear, you see ...' Now it was she who petered out.

Verity leaned forward. 'But, Mother, it wasn't just that you acted out of turn. You've spoken to me, dealt with me for as long as I can remember, as though there is no love in you for me. As though you have a barrier between us, one you've built to keep me at a distance.'

Tears were streaming down Lady Pamela's impassive face, but she had not issued a sound.

Verity felt something twist, but her father said, 'Collect yourself immediately, Pamela. Verity, what we should have told you years ago is that you are my child – the beloved issue of a relationship between me and another woman, in the early days of my marriage to your, shall we say, stepmother. Your real mother was a rather beautiful woman, one of our staff, and I was mesmerised. You were conceived and your ... Well, Lady Pamela insisted that the right thing was for you to be brought up here, by your real mother.'

Verity clutched at Polly's hand as the water threatened to engulf her, and the darkness, and the ... No, not now. Now she must listen. She breathed slowly, pushing away the rushing and surging as she listened to her father.

'Most sadly, your real mother died when you were two, so you were a gift, if you like. You are our daughter, and I believe that your ... perhaps we should call ...' He wafted his hand towards his wife. 'Lady Pamela, your stepmother, feared that with Brown – no, so sorry, Tom – heartache might ensue. I mean that perhaps he was not quite what he seemed.' His voice broke. He pressed his lips together and couldn't go on.

As he was speaking Verity had realised so many things. She looked like him, and not her ... 'My mother was my nanny, wasn't she?'

There was a long silence. Lady Pamela's silent tears had stopped, but she was diminished somehow, almost a shell, though still she sat upright and immobile. Her hands were clasped together so tightly that her knuckles were white.

'She was my lady's maid, before you were born.' She spoke, but her voice was thin and defeated.

Verity's father had slung his sticks back over his arm and had opened his cigarette case, but clicked it shut now and tossed it back onto the mantelpiece. 'It was a mess. I behaved without honour. It was difficult for us all.'

'Why did she die?'

Lady Pamela whispered, 'Pneumonia. Your father brought in the best physicians, but nothing could be done. She was taken to hospital, where she died.'

'Where is she buried?'

Her father had picked up the cigarette case again. It had his initials in the corner and the family crest, and Verity wished he'd leave the damned thing alone and look at her. 'Her family insisted that she return to them. We, of course, paid all expenses.'

Verity felt her legs trembling. 'Where are they – my family?'

He shook his head, and Lady Pamela pleaded, 'Henry, you must ...'

'They were in the East End, that's all we know,' he admitted.

'What did she look like?' It was all Verity could think of to say, above the hammering of her heart, and she held Polly's hand so tightly that it hurt her, so it must be just as bad for Polly. She loosened her grip.

Her mother rose and began to leave the room. 'Your father has a photograph. I will fetch it for you.'

Verity rushed around the sofa. 'Stay here, you two. I'll be back.'

She ran after Lady Pamela, who was hurrying up the stairs, her trembling hand clutching the bannister. Verity stayed two steps behind, trying to absorb the information and fit the new knowledge into her memories of her kind real mother, and the scent of camellias. And then, as they reached the landing, she thought of herself, and of Tom, and how she would feel if he loved another, under her own roof. How could she bear it? How? Again something inside her twisted, but as they walked towards her father's bedroom, she realised that it must take a heart of stone to endure such a thing.

She thought of the crossness and the slapping she had endured as a defenceless young child; of the distance that she felt as she grew up. It wasn't *her* fault. It was theirs. Her mother – no, her stepmother – should have been able to keep her husband's love; her father should have resisted temptation, and her real mother should have walked away before anything happened. Had she no loyalty towards Her Ladyship, and how could she stay here, with a child? Her father – how could he, how dare he?

Lady Pamela swept into her father's room. There was an adjoining door between this room and her mother's – no, her stepmother's. Was it ever opened? The room could only have been a man's: dull colours, bare, matter-of-fact. On the dresser were three photographs. One of her grandparents; one of herself on Star, before her mother – no, her stepmother – had ridden and killed the mare; and one of ... well, her real mother, laughing, with blue eyes and blonde hair.

Verity had always thought she took after her father, because he was blond and blue-eyed, while the woman she had thought of as her mother was dark-haired, dark-eyed and those eyes were now swollen from crying and looked as bruised with hurt as Polly's had. Something twisted again. Lady Clement held the photograph out to her; her hand still trembled and was stick-thin. 'This is your mother, dear Verity. You see, she's beautiful, like you. You are a mixture of both your parents.'

Verity held it and traced the outline of her mother, who wasn't in a nanny's uniform, but a long skirt, with the sun on her hair. She returned it. 'It must have been so hard for you. What do I call you? Stepmother? Lady Pamela?'

Her mother did as her father had done and pressed her lips together, but only for a brief moment. She then stood quite straight and looked into Verity's eyes. 'Only you can decide that, but I did love you, and I do still, though I have made mistakes, and for that I am more sorry than you can imagine.' She looked out of the window, as though a great stillness had fallen on her. 'I just wanted to keep you from harm, especially with Tom. You see, things aren't always—'

Her father's voice from the doorway cut through his wife's words. 'I think we've been over it enough, my dear. I have apologised, as have you.' His voice was like ice, but underneath it trembled, as though in fear. 'All we can do is assure you of our dearest love, Verity. And you had your mother's love, too; your mother was a fine woman.'

Lady Clement moved to the window. 'You must always remember, Verity, that we are who we strive to be. You are beautiful, as she was, and are such a wonderful young woman in your own right. As I said, I have made mistakes and I ask forgiveness, though I know that for you to forget is too hard. But I welcome Tom, if he is good and kind to you, I sincerely do.'

Verity looked from one to the other, the words of forgiveness and forgetting so similar to Sylvia's that they resonated more than they might have. She moved to the window, too, looking out over the lawns, feeling that she knew neither of these people – one who stood next to her, one behind her. Perhaps it was no surprise to feel this about her mother, but how could her father betray his young wife and then stand by, while she was unkind to a child? How could he keep the woman who was her real mother in the house, along with his wife? How cruel was that? How utterly awful. And how could Lady Clement stay? Verity wouldn't have; she'd have swept away, taking the family silver as she went.

She shook her head. 'I've got go. We have work to do, cargo to deliver.'

She rushed from the room and down the stairs, into the hall where Polly and Sylvia were waiting. She dragged them to the green baize door, then down and into the kitchen, where Rogers was standing, about to deliver tea on a huge silver tray.

'I know,' Verity shouted. 'At last I know.'

Mrs B thrust a piece of paper into her hand. 'Not everything. Trust me, not everything, for your father would not reveal the complete picture. This is where your mother's family lived. Perhaps they still do.

Go and learn the reality. Go and recover your family – this family, I mean.' She pointed above stairs.

Verity nodded, then shook her head. This family, here? No, her family was at this address. She read it; it was close to Poplar, in the East End. Her head was spinning. 'I don't even know her name.'

Rogers said, 'Jenny Rivers.'

Verity shoved the address into her trouser pocket, kissed them both and stepped back. 'I don't think my father has any idea what he put that poor Lady Clement through. But how she could be so cruel to a young child, and how she could go on being so cold? And, lastly, how she could stay? Has she no pride? I don't know, I just don't know any more.' She spilled out the sorry saga to her friends, standing there in the kitchen of her family home, which now seemed a stranger's.

After a long silence, when only the ticking of the clock could be heard, Sylvia put her arm around her. Polly stood in front of her. 'We're going home, to *Marigold*, *Horizon* and Dog, do you understand, Verity? We're going home, and we'll come with you, if you want to try and find your other family. But you have Tom, you are safe. And let's face it, you have parents who absorbed you into the family, when perhaps others wouldn't.'

Sylvia said, 'But it *is* a bloody mess.'

This got through to Verity like nothing else. She stared at Sylvia and said, 'Language, if you please.'

342

Their laughter was high-pitched and strained, but it was at least laughter.

The train journey seemed interminable, but Polly sat on one side of Verity, and Sylvia on the other. No one spoke. Perhaps, Polly thought, they were all trying to assimilate what they had heard. The Clements had kept the child, brought her up, when Jenny Rivers could have been sent away, disappeared, gone home to the East End in disgrace. Without a doubt, Lord Clement should have known better. How dare he? His poor wife. It was all so odd, and in some ways so gallant of Lady Clement, but why be so unkind to a child and then so detached? Why not just leave? It was too much and they all gave up and sat back, moving with the train.

They arrived at Waterloo at ten o'clock at night and were hurrying to the Underground when they heard a shout. 'Sylvia, Sylvia.'

They turned as one, to see a nun in a black habit, waving and hurrying across the concourse. Sylvia whispered, 'Oh no, it's Sister Augustine. Wait for me, you two, please. I won't be long.' She hurried over.

Verity said to Polly, 'There's time to telephone your parents.'

Polly shook her head. 'Not after today. Who knows what people are really like.'

They stood while travellers hurried around them. Beneath the clock Sylvia was shaking her head, then standing with it bowed, as Sister Augustine talked and talked. Then she pressed Sylvia's hand and blessed her.

Sylvia returned, looking confused. 'Come on, please.'

She hurried ahead and the two of them followed. Verity called out, 'Is everything all right?'

Sylvia just said, 'Some people never give up. Polly, you should be pleased that your Saul accepts whatever is pushing at him. Some of us have a voice guiding us, but it's not necessarily where we damn well want to go.'

Chapter 21

Monday 1 May – Confidences and worries – shared on the cut

Dog was back with the girls, but made it her duty to visit the canteen, before and after lunch the next day, and returned licking her lips. The girls knew that Mary was wooing her to stay, but Polly said, 'Let's see what happens.'

They had cleaned the boat and butty already, but did so again, mostly to keep busy and try to make sense of yesterday, though it didn't seem to help. Verity insisted that she didn't want to go to her newly discovered family yet. One revelation a week was enough. What if she didn't like them? What if they didn't want to see her?

They were still on leave, so they lounged about the next day instead, because Polly wasn't prepared to travel to Woking to have a set-to with her parents, either. They read the war news and their books. Polly brought back a letter from her parents, sent as usual c/o the Administration Office, which she stuck in a book on the shelf and ignored. There was another from Saul, which she devoured. He'd had his hair cut and was being taught to march, though what good that would be, he wasn't sure. His corporal had said it taught him to walk into the face of the guns when he was bloody well told.

They avoided the pub in the evening, unable to feel jolly. What's more, Polly had no idea how she would be received, after yelling and shouting at Saul. All three slept as though they had climbed a range of mountains, so exhausted did they feel. The next day they heard on the tannoy, 'Steerer Holmes to the Administration Office, immediately.'

Polly couldn't face the boaters if she crept along the lay-by on her own, so the other two went with her. Everyone on the lay-by tipped their hats and said, "Ow do', and the women smiled as they busied themselves with their washing, or cast off the mooring strap and headed off to Limehouse. Polly wondered if she'd been called to the office because her mother, or Verity's, was in reception. But no, for old Bob said, 'We're so busy, we know you've another day of leave, but we need you lasses – we need everyone.' It was what they wanted, to take them away from all the strangeness, the questions in their heads, the doubts, the anger, the happenings. 'Nip across then and get yer orders, there's good girls. 'Eard from Saul, 'ave yer, Polly? Got used to fighting an enemy before he went, I heard. Worse than a sergeant-major yer was, I gather, but good practice for him.'

Polly felt the heat of her embarrassment, but simply said, 'So you'd best do as you're told, or I'll start on you next.'

They queued in the Orders Office, where Ted looked over his new glasses. 'Sorry, lasses, it's steel again, from Limehouse. I know yer'd like Brentford, cos it's quicker, but beggars can't be choosers.'

Verity said, 'Just be good to get back into it.'

Ted laughed. 'That's the first time I've heard that.'

Polly leaned on the counter. 'Oh no, it's not. We all want money after all.'

Ted winked. 'I know, but I 'spect yer girls want to put some space between you and the panto on the lay-by the other day.'

All three of them groaned. 'That's yesterday's news.'

They set off almost immediately, heading towards Limehouse Basin, the wind in their hair, the tillers under their elbows. They pulled in overnight at Alperton and sighed as they set off for the pub. It was Polly who went first, bracing herself, pushing open the door into the lobby and then into the cigarette smoke, the rumble of talk, the laughter, the smell of beer. She stood and the room fell silent, as the boaters turned. Steerer Brown lifted his beer. 'Wondered where you lasses had got to. Leave, was it? We was 'opin' you hadn't done a runner, our Polly. Table's ready by the fire, and the darts are free for the taking.'

Sylvia nudged her and said quietly, 'We're home – you're forgiven. But while you two are beating your breasts, I will explain why I resent Sister Augustine. I shared with her that I fear God's will is that I am to be a nun, but though He might want it, I think I do not. Sister Augustine explained that I need to work out if it is His voice, or just my imagination working overtime because I miss my community. Or perhaps I should say "missed", because when we came back from Dorset, I felt that I was coming home, to the cut, to our community.' She went to the bar, calling back, 'I'll buy them.'

Verity and Polly watched her for a moment, stunned. Verity whispered, 'It makes our problems seem almost mundane. And how strange to tell us now, just like that, in a crowded bar.'

Polly shook her head as they reached their table. 'No, it's like running into the sea to get it over with, rather than dithering in the surf. She has opened up when we're busy with many things in our own lives, so we're not likely to go on about it. Or that's what I think, anyway.' She sat, looking into the fire. 'It must be really hard to struggle against what you feel you must do, when it's not what you want. Sylvia must be glad in a way that there are bigger problems, like the war. It delays the need for a decision, because our problems are tiny in comparison to what's going on.'

Verity muttered, 'Well, with the Germans occupying Hungary, the British sealing off Eire in case the Germans get at us that way and, oh yes, Monte Cassino still being an armpit, you have a point.'

They were both edgy as Sylvia arrived at the table with the drinks. 'I thought you might be on your way to help me carry these, Polly, but clearly not.

Please don't refer again to what I have just told you. I felt you should know, and now you do. It is between me and … Well, it is my decision.'

She lowered the three half-pints of mild, which had slopped over the tray. Verity reached for hers. 'You can't trust our Polly to be helpful; she's just a dilly, you know that.'

Sylvia picked up her half-pint, shaking her beer-splashed hand over Polly, who said, 'Sit down, stop being useless and drink up. And what's happened to the sweet sherry?'

Sylvia pulled a face, and Verity lifted her glass. 'Cheers.'

The door opened and Bet came in, with the new trainees Cathleen and Beryl. Bet called out, 'Ah, the reprobates are here, what a surprise. Calmed down, have you, Polly? Got it out of your system?'

Polly lifted her glass. 'Nice to see you, too, Bet. No, you may not sit with us.'

Bet came over, laughing, taking the spare seat and calling to her trainees at the bar, 'Same as usual, please, girls.' She leaned towards Polly, digging in her pocket. 'A note from Granfer for you.'

Polly's heart sank. 'Oh, a ticking-off?'

'I haven't a clue. Would I read someone else's letter?' She looked the picture of innocence as she held out the folded paper. 'Go on, take it.'

Polly read it while Thomo called over, 'Darts in ten minutes, girls? I've a team ready to take yer on.'

Bet replied, 'Make it twenty minutes and you're on. I need something to perk me up first.'

Polly read Granfer's note, written in pencil and capitals:

HELLO OUR POLLY. I HEARD ABOUT YER SORROW AND CROSSNESS AND I UNDER-STANDS BUT WE THOUGHT IT BEST IN CASE HE WEREN'T TAKEN. THEN THERE'D BE NO SORROW LIKE YER FEELS NOW.

YER MUST NOT BE HARD ON YER MA SHE WANTED TO TELL YER AND FELT BAD NOT TELLING YER BUT I THOUGHT IT BEST. AND SO IT IS THAT SAUL THOUGHT THAT WAY SO DON'T BE HARD ON HER OR HIM. SHE HAS BEEN A GOOD WOMAN FOR US AND IN YOUR HEART YER KNOW THAT.

She passed it to Bet, who barely read it, which meant that of course she had already done so, because this woman would not have passed on anything that would upset her. Polly stared into the fire. That's it: her mum was protecting her. Everyone was protecting her. Verity snatched the note, and then Sylvia. They scanned it, and Sylvia handed it back to Polly, tapping her arm. 'You know he's right.'

Polly looked around the pub, at the boaters and then at her friends. Cathleen and Beryl were heading towards their table with half-pints of mild. Polly patted Verity's leg. 'Drink up, we have a darts match to win. And, Sylvia, you can come on the team, and with Bet that's four. Thomo can bring in one of the other steerers to bulk up his lot.' Sylvia grimaced. Polly laughed. 'No, don't pull that face. It's the only way to learn, and enough of this soul-searching; we need to put everything aside for a while, because we don't know what the hell any of us are going to do about our lives.'

As she walked to the dartboard, she felt more at ease, because of course there was a measure of protection involved. But she still didn't trust her mum, and again the rage surged and she preferred it to the pain of missing him. Saul should have been here, safe.

The month of May merged into loading and unloading cargoes, and visits to soothing public baths and comfortable beds at Mrs Green's, and the hauling of the butty through the Brum Bum. Not to mention the winning and losing of darts matches, and Sylvia developing a good throwing arm.

They chewed on coal dust, cleared out bilges and missed Saul's pheasants and rabbits, until Thomo started to leave them on their roof whenever they coincided. They saw an endless trail of military vehicles and troops crossing bridges. They read newspapers and studied headlines that shrieked war news; Cassino had finally fallen, the Allies were approaching Rome, and progress was being made in the Far East.

They listened to rumours that Allied bomber pilots were fair game for lynching by German civilians if they were captured, and they feared for Reggie, Polly's bomber-crew friend. There were rumours of an imminent Allied invasion. Was it true? Was Tom with them? Would he live? And what about Saul?

Tom's letters stopped as the end of May drew near. No one had heard from their sons, husbands and friends, either, the girls were told as they travelled the cut. Suddenly there were no more troops to be seen, marching or being transported. What was happening? They all felt they were holding their breath: both those on the cut and those on the bank. Was this the beginning of the end of the war?

Saul's letter finally came through on 30 May and it was clear that he was still training. May became June, the days ticked past, and the boaters worked into the long summer evenings, working, working to play their part. It was the thought of what lay ahead for Britain that drummed through the girls' heads, not the need to sort out their own lives. And so the letters that all three received from parents and nuns were ignored. Their minds were not ready, their decisions not made.

Chapter 22

Tuesday 6 June – D-Day

Tom felt even more nauseous than he had done in the ship that had transported them over the Channel, as the landing craft bucked and corkscrewed in the surging seas, circling in convoy towards the beaches of Normandy. He muttered, 'The Channel has been rough enough; couldn't we have a break, you bastard weather.'

His pack felt too heavy, his gut was churning too much and, to make it ruddy worse, he hated the waterproof waders they had to wear, which were like a ghillie's massive fishing trousers. Were they so big because they had to fit all shapes and sizes? Whatever their size, rumour had it they were to protect against gas. Forget about gas, he thought, what about the bloody waves?

He knew he was rambling as he stood next to Paul and Don, who were lurching all ways, just as he was. In the lull in the shelling and gunfire coming from the land there was the sound of someone vomiting. Tom was in the front rank, behind Sergeant Humphries, and yelled, 'Brings back Dunkirk, does it, Sarge?'

'Too bloody right, it does – only we're heading the opposite way, and about bloody time. Now, you lot, no stopping to brew a cuppa once you get on land; and you'd be surprised at how many will. Get yourself off that bloody beach. Keep going, whatever happens, or you won't make it. If your mate goes down, leave 'im. You 'ear me?'

'Yes, Sarge,' they yelled above the chaos of sound. Someone else, or the same person, was vomiting near Tom.

When the landing craft were within striking distance of the beach, they broke from the convoy and tore towards the shore, first one craft and then another, ramming their prows into the beach. The one before them was hit by a shell and exploded. Tom staggered as his craft shuddered to a halt on the shingle. Don grabbed him to steady himself, his helmet slipping over his eyes. 'Bloody thing.'

A sailor lowered the ramp and there they were, exposed, with the beach in full sight, the chaos and the screams louder, the bullets zipping over them, in front and to the side, and into them. Don fell. The sergeant swung round. Tom checked his mate. 'He's gone, Sarge.'

They lugged him to the side. The sergeant and corporal were outdoing one another as they shouted orders. 'Out you get, into the surf. Have a paddle, why don't you?'

'Listen to the sarge, keep yer 'eads down and don't bloody stop.'

Down the ramp Tom went, the craft slipped back, he stepped off into deep water. 'Bugger.' It was Corporal Jones. 'Sarge, it's four foot if it's a bloody day.'

The noise was growing, with explosions behind, in front and to the sides. And screams.

'Got to get 'em off, as the guide leader said to the scout leader.'

Those were the last words Tom heard as he fell beneath the waves. The sea filled his waders, and he was being dragged this way and that as he scraped along the bottom. He fought to the surface, his pack weighing a bloody ton. Someone knocked him aside, and down he went again. He found his footing and barged his way clear of the squad, struggling on as bullets flew over and into the water.

He was on shingle, on his hands and knees, being rolled over and then back, his waders so full that they pinioned him. He saw someone upright to his left and started to haul himself up on them. It was the corporal, who heaved him to his feet, then left Tom to help someone else. Others were struggling forward alongside, in front and behind. The bullets still flew. A man surged past, holding a collapsible cycle high.

Tom followed, the water churning and buffeting him. He forced himself on, cursing his waders. A helmet nudged him. Step by step, he thought, just like the bastard Brum Bum. Step by bloody step. He slipped backwards on the rising shingle slope, but rammed his boots into it, taking another step and then another, holding his soaking rifle above his head. He fell again in shallow water, dropped his rifle, feeling for it, finding it and crawling out of the surf, coughing. Someone fell over him. It was Paul.

Behind him the sergeant called, 'I said no time for a bloody brew, Brown. Get up and stop muckin' about.' Paul heaved him up. Together they struggled forward. Somewhere bagpipes were playing, or that's what Tom thought. Was he going mad?

Paul yelled, 'The bloody Scots are here. God bless the daft buggers.'

Tom laughed like an idiot. Paul and he tore at their waterlogged waders, ripping them off, heedless of what the sarge might say. He said nothing. They struggled up the beach, with the beach master and his men waving them on, ever on; over and around bodies. Yes, bodies. He felt sick again, and it was nothing to do with the sea. Tin hats lay all around, their owners splayed out near them. A shell landed, and the smell of cordite filled the air. Paul staggered.

Tom pulled at his arm. 'Come on, we need to get off the beach.' But Paul was on his knees, staring at the shingle. 'I can't,' he whispered. 'I can't go on.'

But it wasn't a whisper, it was a shout that Tom could barely hear. Another shell landed and there was a blinding flash; the spraying shingle stung and cut, the smell of cordite drenched them. He dragged Paul to his feet. 'Come on, come on. If we stay here, we die. We have a chance off the beach. Keep going.'

On they trudged, heads down, bullets chattering, zipping. 'Keep going,' he said to himself with every footfall. 'Keep going like the girls, day in and day out, lock after lock. Keep going.'

Paul pulled him round. 'Listen.'

They heard a voice above the mayhem, to their left, nearby. It was a lieutenant. 'Lads, I need a hand.' He was trying to drag the cover off a Bren-gun carrier. They crunched over, yanking at the tarpaulin, releasing where it had caught, like the girls on the boats. They stared at the destroyed carrier beneath. They struggled on. Tom swung round to see how far they had come, and then forward, and could have wept. There was so much further to go. There was a sound, a sort of squeak. It was Paul, prostrate. Tom turned him over. It was his shoulder. 'Get up.'

Paul screamed. Tom scrabbled for his morphine ampules and the attached needle, and shoved one in his mate's arm. 'Get off the beach, mate,' Paul muttered.

Tom stared around. Casualties were collecting nearer the waterline, over to the left, where the medics tended them. Oh God, all the way back? He heaved Paul up, kept his arm around him and dragged him, almost slipping down the shingle. It's what Verity would do, it's what she did – what they all did. One for all. He kept going, seeing Verity, and suddenly it seemed all right. He could see her, hear her and if he drew his last breath, it would be with her here, in his mind and heart.

He slid and fell, and Paul with him. A medic came over. 'I've got him, lad, you go on. Do your job.'

Tom nodded, turned and struggled back up, footfall by footfall. As he reached the dunes he saw that some infantry had started to dig in, and were brewing. Not here, not now, he wanted to yell, but he had no breath and kept walking. And now he realised the dunes were protecting them from the wind, a wind that he hadn't realised was blowing. Behind him someone yelled, 'Get your arses off the beach, you bloody tea-drinking idiots.'

He could hear the mortar fire, rapid but flying in an arc over them. He found others from his company. He was not alone. But he hadn't been, for he had been with her; her courage, her endurance, the endurance of them all. They all passed into the last of the dunes, and the sergeant came after them. 'All right lads. Take five.' They fell on the sand. Ahead was a signpost that had seen better days: *Achtung Minen*; it was old, weathered, decrepit – like bloody Germany, Tom hoped.

The sergeant was looking at his compass. Tom sat and rested his arms on his knees, his head on his arms. It seemed mere seconds before the sergeant was saying, 'We'll skirt round this little lot.'

They marched on, out of step. 'Get yourselves sorted,' bellowed the sergeant. They did, reaching tarmac: a road, pitted, potholed and blasted, but a bloody road, and houses, a shop. But it was sniper alley, so they ducked off it, but still the snipers found them. They hugged the few motorised transports that had been hit, and a blasted German military jeep, zigzagging between whatever they could find, even a lamp post. How bloody silly; who was skinny enough for that to make a difference?

Mortars were still falling, whistling above them, crashing, flashing, smelling. Somehow they lived, somehow they continued until a rest was called, in a ditch, with the clouds scudding above them and a gull wheeling. How could it still be flying? All the time Tom had pictured the girls hauling their butty through the filth of the Brum Bum, enduring; so he could, too.

He grappled for his water bottle. It was empty. There was a bullet hole in it. 'Bugger,' he said, his mouth so dry it was a mere whisper. The sergeant threw him his own. 'Take a gulp, son. And I would have stopped for a mate, too. Perhaps he'll be all right. Perhaps he's on his way home, or will be soon. For us, it's just begun.'

Tom muttered, 'The beginning of the end. Better bloody be, I've got things to do, and someone to do it with.'

Bill, a Geordie with a lance corporal's stripe, lifted his head from his knees. 'Aye, lad, reckon we all have. About time this bloody lot learned to mind their manners and stop being so bloody greedy.'

Chapter 23

Sunday 18 June – at Bull's Bridge on the lookout for doodlebugs

All the way down from Birmingham's Tyseley Wharf the three girls had listened and looked, even down the Aylesbury Arm. 'I was thinking, not so long ago, that the bombing was over and done with, and then the buggers start sending these damned doodlebugs over,' Polly shouted.

Verity steered *Marigold* back towards the main cut and shouted, 'They're not bombs, they're Hitler's bloody rockets, and the correct term is a V-1, ignoramus.'

Polly, on the other side of the tiller, elbowed her. 'Stop showing off, for heaven's sake. Whatever the buggers are, they scare the wotnot out of me. Doesn't ruddy Hitler know he's beaten?'

Verity shook her head. 'Clearly not, darling. Maniacs never do.'

They headed on for Cowley lock, where Steerer Ambrose shouted as he passed, heading north, 'Yer 'ear t'engine buzzin', then it cuts out and seems to fall backwards, but fall 'em do, makin' a right mess.

I 'spect it's bad over east like it were in the Blitz, so keeps yer 'eads down. Someone should shoot that bugger 'Itler.'

Verity felt almost hysterical as she shouted, 'You've got it in one, Steerer Ambrose.'

Tom was heading Hitler's way, like so many others, all combining to stop the maniac and his bloody stupid army. She knew that, because otherwise he would have telephoned to let her know he hadn't gone with the invasion force, just as Saul had, leaving a message at Tyseley for Polly to say he was still in England, training.

They reversed into the lay-by at Bull's Bridge just before lunchtime, watching the sky and listening hard for the buzzing, over the engine's pat-patter. Sylvia grabbed *Marigold*'s mooring strap, once she'd tied up the butty. 'I'll say it again: try not to worry about Tom,' she called.

Verity nodded. 'And I'll reply, again, darling: that is like trying to stop a bull charging.' She jumped onto the kerb.

Polly was running over the cabin top carrying the brooms. 'Come on, let's clean the holds, then we can find a pub. We need it, we've barely stopped.'

'Lavatory first, thank you very much,' Verity snapped. Polly was all right; her bloke was safe, not like Tom. She stormed off, stalking past the wash boilers on the kerb.

''Ow do,' Ma Mercy called, as did the others. Mrs Brown approached, her string shopping bag bulging with vegetables, calling out, 'I miss our Saul's rabbits, that I do, and the pheasant. Didn't know rightly how much 'e catched for oos, I didn't. Makes yer wonder when the lad slept. Not 'eard from yer Tom then? But I got a good feelin' in me waters, I have, about the lad.'

Verity stopped dead. 'Have you really?' she asked, reaching out a hand.

Mrs Brown's gnarled fingers gripped hers. 'It says it in the tea leaves. The lad'll be home. That Saul, too.'

Verity stared at her. 'Saul's gone?'

'So's I feel, and I's usually right.'

Verity walked on into the yard. She used the lavatory and then called into the Administration Office. Bob looked up, tired and with bags under his eyes.

'How's it been?' she asked.

Bob grimaced. 'First the Blitz, now this. You be careful; but yer might be lucky and 'ave a pick-up from Brentford, and you can get back out and away quicker, which is what I 'ope for yer. London's copping it, no rhyme or reason, they're just falling all over the place. Barrage balloons are helping to snarl 'em and bring 'em down, and our lads take up their planes to try and whack 'em. Ack-ack is busy too.'

He was groping under the counter.

'I got a message fer yer mate, young Polly – on the QT, I reckon. A telephone call: Saul said he's off. Yer tell her, would yer? I'm sick of giving these bloody messages and seeing the faces. 'E said something about a fruit or summat.' He leaned forward, beckoning her closer. 'I 'eard from a bloke in the pub that some of 'em 'ave been building a floatin' harbour for landing supplies. Top secret, it were then, but I reckon now it's getting in place over there, it ain't a secret no more. Called summat like a Gooseberry, so it could be a Mulberry instead. Got something to do with War Transport. Makes sense for a boater, don't it?'

Verity was about to snap about some people being bloody lucky, then stopped. What the hell was she thinking? Perhaps he saw, because he said, 'Yer lasses are lucky; yer got one another to prop up against.'

She nodded. 'I don't know what I'd do without the other two – we're family, you know.'

He handed over the letters for *Marigold* and the message from Saul, which he'd written on a scrap of paper. She shoved them in her pocket and hurried off to the Orders Office to hand over their dockets. 'Any orders, Ted?'

He shook his head. 'Yer could get off for the afternoon, but take care, them's aren't seagulls up there.'

'Has there been much damage?'

'Over London, south especially and the east, so don't yer be 'anging about.'

On her return to the boats she waved the letters. Polly and Sylvia called in unison from the hold, 'File them.'

Verity stuck them on the bookshelf. One was from her mother, one from Polly's mother and another was for Sylvia. She took her place in the hold, cleaning out the coal dust and filling the hessian sack with the usual lumps for the coal bucket. She handed Polly Bob's scribble, saying, 'The Mulberry could come under War Transport, so maybe Mr Burton used that to swing it.'

'My mum swung it, don't you mean?' Polly's tone was like acid; corrosive and damaged.

Verity lugged her sack of coal into the store and stared at it; at the tools, and the bucket. Were they both being prima donnas, sitting in judgement on their families and knowing nothing, really? Bet's words, when they were training, came to her, loud and clear. 'It's like running a kindergarten.'

She leaned back against the wall. They were too tired to think straight, and worried almost out of their wits, but the men were fighting and dying while they were being cross, bitter and hugging slights and wounds that were in the past. It really was time they not only shut up, but grew up – she and Polly at least. Sylvia was different, very different, and her problems were nothing to do with growing up.

Polly's voice reached her from roof. 'The hold's all done. I'm nipping off to help Sylvia to finish the butty. What about orders?'

Verity edged out onto the gunwale. 'None for the rest of the day. And what's more, Pol, I'm going to stop sinking into self-pity, or fury, or whatever you like to call it. We've been stoking one another and it's time for the truth. I'm off to find my real family, and then I'll know who and what I am. London's taking a pounding, yet again, and if I don't do it now, who knows if they'll be around to ask later on? Who knows if they're even alive, anyway? All this hating is making me feel sick. And what about you? How'd you feel if your mum was killed by a doodlebug while you're flouncing about?'

Polly was stepping onto the butty and didn't acknowledge the question. Had she even heard? Verity moved across to the butty hold, and all three swept and shovelled, and carried up the hessian sacks into the butty store, after which Polly stormed into *Marigold*'s cabin, saying, 'I'm going to have a stand-up wash and come with you. You're right, you need to sort this out.'

Verity followed her into the cabin. 'I repeat, idiot, that *we* need to.'

Polly wiped her face and slammed out of the cabin. Sylvia poked her head round the door. 'That's your answer, for now. I think she knows you're right. Perhaps calling her an idiot didn't help.' She disappeared and then called, 'I'll be in the butty, having a wash, and then I'm coming with you, too. But we need to get a move on, in case we're called.'

Verity yelled, 'We're laid off until the morning, don't forget.

She was stripping off when Polly returned and elbowed Verity away from the bowl, muttering, 'I need a proper wash, so shove over, idiot. And by the way, I've dug myself into a hole and I'm not sure how to get out of it. I know Mum is wonderful, and Dad, but although I know it, I've hurt them, blamed them, and part of me still thinks they've betrayed me. Give me a bit more time, and then I'll sort it.'

They didn't reach Poplar until three in the afternoon, and as they rushed along, several doodlebugs roared over, their tails flaring, their engines buzzing. A couple cut out, exploding a little further on. The ground shuddered, the windows shook and previously damaged houses lost more dust, more bricks – even a fireplace hanging off a deserted building crashed into the ruins. It made them think of the one hanging off the wall near the public baths in Birmingham. A chimney smashed into the ground ahead of them.

Their nerves jangled, but all around them everyone just kept on doing what they were doing, including a telegram boy who cycled head down, as though all this was normal. Watching him winding his way around bricks and debris, they tried not to hunch over, but to walk upright, as though they were out for a stroll in the park. They failed.

Polly said, 'It's a horrid damp day.'

'That's the most idiotic remark anyone could come up with, when it's raining doodlebugs,' Sylvia muttered.

Verity held both their arms. 'We're British, so we talk about the weather when the world is going crazy.'

Another doodlebug buzzed high overhead in the cloud layer, but kept on going. They tried to ignore the awful screeching and growling of its engine, and the air raid sirens. They passed a damaged terrace on their right. An ARP warden blew his whistle. 'Get in a shelter, for Gawd's sake, the lot of you; it's not ruddy Blackpool pier and a stroll in the sun.'

They did, sitting there for an hour, and then the all-clear went. They continued on their way, smelling cordite. Trees lining the street near a church had gone, felled by the blasts; the leaves were crushed and that smell was stronger for a moment than the dust and explosives. They crunched over broken glass and slates, listening, always listening.

Sylvia stopped, her head up. The other two paused, but no, they were hearing things. 'It's June, the sun will come out soon,' she said, coughing in the dust.

Polly muttered, 'Bugger that. I want the rockets to stop, that's what I want. I thought all this was over. I thought now that we had invaded, that was it.'

Verity whispered, because she was so busy trying to listen for buzzing over the sirens that were starting up and the ack-ack guns, 'Stop going on. They'll never stop until we are at the gates of Berlin and knocking on Hitler's door with a noose. And don't talk to me about forgiveness, Sylvia.'

More RAF fighters were heading out to bring down the rockets. The barrage balloons looked as though they were sagging. In the distance they could hear ack-ack.

'We could always find a shelter, or you could, while I go on,' Verity said. 'You're only here because of me.'

The ARP warden shouted, 'Get to a shelter.'

The other two yelled back to the warden, one after another, 'We haven't time.' 'Things to do.'

They walked on, but no more doodlebugs came over and they straightened up, still walking arm-in-arm, trying to chat and even laugh, as others were doing around them as they emerged from shelters, or had ignored them in the first place. The clouds seemed lower, the breeze cooler, though it carried the smell of burning. The tenements took what light there was, and loomed, dark, and childless, because the evacuation programme had begun, again.

'Left and then right,' Verity said, folding up the map. 'Let's see if the Rivers family – my family – still live here.'

None of them spoke as they followed her directions and headed for number twelve. The house on the corner of the terrace had been hit, but rosebay willowherb was growing in the ruins, so it was an old Blitz wound. The rest of the terrace was untouched. A pack of dogs were snarling at one another, then disappeared down an alley. A barefooted child in pants and vest was running along with some older children. 'They should have been evacuated,' muttered Sylvia.

A chair stood to the left of the doorway of number twelve. Verity moved to stand just in front of her friends and knocked on the door, barely able to breathe as they waited.

A man of about sixty opened the door. He was wearing a dirty vest and had tattoos on his arms. His trousers were filthy, held up by braces. His two top fly-buttons were undone. A roll-up hung from his bottom lip. 'Whaddya want?' he said.

'Mr Rivers?'

'Who's asking?'

'I'm Jenny's daughter, Verity Cl—' She stopped. Who was she? 'Jenny's daughter,' she repeated.

He peered at her, several days' stubble on his chin. 'Better come in then.' His cigarette wobbled. He turned and walked down the hall. They followed. It smelled of … dirt, but not the boaters' dirt, just years of grease and grime.

He stood in the kitchen, leaning back against the sink in which dirty dishes were piled, dishes that also spilled onto the draining board. On the Formica table several cigarettes had been stubbed out on a dinner plate, smeared with the echo of fried egg, or something. They stood. He crossed his arms. 'Jenny's kid, eh? That makes me yer granddaddy. Well, well. Yer goin' to see us right, are yer?'

'See you right?' Verity queried, searching this man's face for a resemblance to the woman in the photograph. It wasn't there. He was her grandfather, and he was awful.

'Too bloody right,' he grunted, his cigarette moving as he talked, the ash growing longer, just as Gladys's did, although she was nice. He went on, 'Jenny said she 'ad a plan, was gonna to marry His Nibs by 'aving a nipper. He was buggered if he were going ter play ball, but she sticks in and does alrighty, then the silly bitch ups and dies. So, as I says, yer going to see us right?'

'Plan?' Verity said, moving nearer.

He laughed, belched and the smell of stale beer was overpowering. She stepped back, into Polly, who gripped her waist. He said, ''Ow else do the likes of us get on in the world? Full of suchlike plans, she were, silly cow. But as I said, she upped and died before she could swing it. Got something for us, have you – your old granddaddy an' all – cos we're family? And yer done all right fer yerself, with them daft buggers.' He held out his hand.

Polly pushed Verity to one side and stepped forward. 'What have *you* got for *us*?'

He stared. 'Whaddya mean?'

'What have you got left of your daughter's?'

Sylvia took a step forward, too. 'Then we'll see what we have got for you. And shame on your soul, for selling your daughter's memory.'

The man's mouth dropped open, his cigarette falling onto the worn and torn lino. He ground it in with his boot. 'Never sure she were mine. The missus put herself about a bit, and she's long gone.'

A deal was something he seemed to understand, though, and he stared at them as if calculating some sort of sum. Verity recognised the look; it was in any darts team's eyes as they worked out the best throw.

Finally he nodded. 'We'll talk about it when you 'ave a look at what I got.' He rooted about under the sink and pulled out an old rusted OXO tin. He levered off the lid. Inside was a pencil, a pen and a small notebook. 'Reckon a tenner'll do it.'

Verity started to dig in her pockets, but Sylvia took a step closer to the man and gripped the OXO tin. 'You'll take a fiver, and that's it.' She yanked the OXO tin from his hand, leaving him with the lid. She passed the tin to Polly, with a jerk of her head. Polly nodded, turned and left.

Verity was appalled, and confused. 'Money,' insisted Sylvia. Verity dug into her pocket and Sylvia stepped back, then checked her own pockets, as Mr Rivers looked from Sylvia to the lid.

'Oh dear,' said Sylvia. 'We only seem to have three pounds between us. Well, that'll just have to do.' She passed over the notes and said quietly – pressing so close, too close, to the man, Verity thought, frightened for her, for them both – 'You can leave now, Verity. I am right behind you.'

Verity backed to the kitchen door, then waited. 'I'm not going without you. And I have to ask something important. Mr Rivers, did your daughter, my mother, wear camellia perfume?'

He looked from Sylvia to Verity. 'Yer what? If she wore anything, it were lavender water, like her ma. Smart girl, Jenny were. Knew what she wanted. Yer look a bit like her, I reckon. Yer could do well, an' all, if yer got out o' them clothes and tarted yerself up. Or yer could do well when the men get back, any'ow.'

Sylvia put up her hand and laid it on the man's chest. 'You will not move from here, you will not follow us.'

He lifted his arm, his hand fisted.

Sylvia kicked him hard, her boot connecting with his shin. 'I warned you,' she said as he yelled, dropping the money. 'You'd better pick that up,' she instructed as she backed from him, then walked swiftly in Verity's wake.

Verity thought she'd been trembling before, but now she was shaking all over, and her legs were jelly as she rushed through the hall to stand in the street, looking at Polly, who was as shocked as she was. Sylvia stepped from the house onto the street, slamming the door, and shouted, 'What are you doing, standing about? Get a move on, let's get out of here.'

They ran, crunching over glass, plaster, bricks, faster and faster, with Polly clutching the tin. On the street corner a woman stopped them. 'You need to keep clear of that Rivers beggar. He's not like the rest of us. On the take, he is. Well, the world is, but not like 'im. Nasty lot, though there's only 'im left now.'

They tore on, running over and around the debris, heedless of the sirens and the ack-ack until the ARP warden blew his whistle and yelled, 'Head for a shelter.'

Sylvia shouted, 'We are, we'll get down the Underground.' At last they reached the Underground station and tore down the steps. It was four in the afternoon, and some inhabitants were already bagging their pitch on the platform, clearly sleeping there overnight, as they had in the Blitz. The girls stood close together, panting, looking at the train lines. Just looking and then turning to check behind. Had he followed?

At last they heard a rumble, felt the movement of air and a crowded train arrived. They pushed their way on. As the train started and they stood, squashed together, the trembling and shaking really took over and Verity braced herself for the darkness, water, blood. But none came. She breathed deeply and stared at Sylvia, pressing hard into her. The man behind was almost asleep on his feet. Verity said, 'Thank you. How on earth ... ?'

'I was brought up in an orphanage, but did you think, because it was run by nuns, that we sat drinking tea with our little fingers stuck out? We learned to survive, probably just like you two.'

Verity snatched a look at Polly, who looked as ashamed as she felt. 'No, not like us; we've been spoiled, privileged, safe.'

*

That evening, safely home and sitting in the *Marigold* having eaten spam fritters, the other two suggested that they leave Verity in peace to read the notebook.

'I'd rather you stayed,' she said. She scanned her mother's childish handwriting and read out the bits that mattered. 'She talks of my father – a fool, she says, and I'm paraphrasing this. Apparently Jenny taught herself to read and write, so that she could move on up, but decided instead to do that the easy way. Her mother said she was sitting on a fortune, so Jenny should use what she needed to use. She says that my father had so much, and she "had got nothing and he were soft and easy. He liked it when I said nice things. Men are fools, and that woman can't see what's under her nose."' Verity looked at her friends, shaking her head.

Polly said, 'Don't go on. It'll upset you.'

Sylvia shook her head. 'She should. It will show her the truth.'

Verity read on silently for a moment, then she read aloud again:

'Like mum said, when his bloody lordship weren't going to chuck the missus out: get yourself up the duff and kick up a fuss, saying you'll make it known he's the father. He'll pay yer off or turf Lady Muck out, then you can have a tidy pile either way. Ma wanted to share the money, to get away from the old man. But his

374

bleeding lordship wouldn't turf her bloody
ladyship out, and he wouldn't pay me off. She,
that bloody missus, said NO. She said I wouldn't
take care of the brat. Wouldn't bring it up nice.
She said she was frightened for it. She said
they'd pay me to stay here, with the baby. All
I had to do was to look after it and everyone
would be kind to me, no matter what had gone
on. Like some sort of bloody saint, she were.
Couldn't 'ave none of her own, I reckon. She
said she could, but wouldn't, cos the brat must
have her full attention.'

Verity looked up, leafed through the notebook and
read on. It was like a novel, but it was written by
her mother – *her* mother. She stared at the badly
formed letters and thought of the house that Jenny
Rivers had known; of the father she had lived with.
Why wouldn't she think this way? And she was
right: Lord Henry Clement was a bloody fool. She
read on:

'I had the little house by the stables. All smart-
ened it were. Bloody boring, cos I had no duties,
I was a sort of Lady Muck too. I walked the
nipper in a pram they bought. I left her outside,
cos who wants to hear a brat crying? How were
I to know it would rain again. She'd been left
before, and the wet didn't hurt her none. Should
have heard the bloody fuss. That Rogers hates

me, so do the cook. They said I weren't looking after her. That Lady Muck showed me how to bath her, but I don't want to know how; so she does it if I let her, but she nods and says I have the right to say if she can. That's what she says: you have to say I can, she says, because you are her mother – all posh like, trying to be kind. He don't even look at me, but he likes the kid.'

Verity had come to blank pages. She looked up. The other two were staring at her, shocked. Verity said, 'She stopped there.'

Sylvia took the book and flicked through. 'No, look, there's this scribble. She's put a date: 1926. You're twenty now, so you must have been two. Have you read enough? Shall we put it away?'

Polly said, 'It's awful, and sad; and oh, again, just awful. What on earth was she thinking? What were any of them thinking?'

Sylvia handed the book back. 'The only one thinking with their heart was poor, poor Lady Clement. Her concern was for you, Verity, and to some extent Jenny, and even your father. For the family, I suppose. Perhaps for what people would think, but I don't think so. I think she cared.'

Verity put up her hand. 'Let me read this:

So I'm goin, when they're not here. I'm taking the silver and what I can find, and I'm going. But Mum says I have to get rid of this chest first, cos I'll need me energy to get set up again, even with what I can take. But I want a man of me own, and I don't want a kid, not now, so they can 'ave her and good luck with it. I had a plan, but it's all gone wrong.'

*

They went the next day to tell Ted the orders would have to wait, just for one day, then caught the train to Sherborne. They took a taxi from the station this time and arrived with a rattle of gravel at the front door, at the time Verity had insisted upon in the telegram she had sent. The emergency kitty paid, and it tipped the taxi driver, too. Verity mounted the steps beneath the portico, with the girls some paces behind.

Her confusion was still there, still chaotic, still exhausting. She ran through the hall, over the silk carpet – what did she care about that? She burst into the sitting room, where her father stood at the fireplace and her mother sat on the sofa, as always. 'Come in,' Verity called to the girls.

They refused. 'No, this is between you and your parents.'

Verity barely heard them, but left the door open and sat on the sofa opposite the woman she had thought of as her mother. She didn't look at either of them, but said, 'I have been to Jenny Rivers's home. I have spoken to her father, I have read her diary. It's like some appalling, sad mess of a story.' She looked at her mother, and then at her father, to whom she said, 'How dare you do that to your wife? How could you be such a fool? Jenny was also a fool, with idiotic plans, but you …' She shook with rage. 'You were older, her employer, in a position of privilege. Yes, Jenny plotted, but oh, how easily you joined in.' She handed him the notebook. 'Stop looking so puzzled – read this.'

He did so, flicking over the pages, his colour rising. He read to the end and slapped the notebook shut.

Staring at it and nothing else, Verity ordered, 'Now pass it to your wife.'

Lady Clement took the notebook. She began to read, looked up at Verity, her gaze so sad, and then she read on.

Verity said to her father. 'Were you insane, or just cruel?'

He said nothing, just turned his cigarette case over and over on the mantelpiece. Then he muttered, 'Yes, I was – insane, I think. No excuse, except the war. It was so dark, so bad, so many dead and injured. I seemed lost. I kept feeling strange, as though I was back there. It was as though Jenny was another place. Away from everything – a sort of pause in the hell. She was kind.'

Verity thought of the freezing cut, and the feelings that had come over her, the darkness. But he had a wife, one to whom he should have turned. 'And your wife wasn't kind?'

Her father looked at Verity, and then at his wife. 'She was – and is – strong, and my equal, and very,

very kind. But ...' It was as though he was thinking aloud, struggling for words, even fighting for thoughts. 'I was a fool, you're right; insane, and cruel. And I fear I have been so frightened of facing it that I have continued to be so. It is I who held on to the letters your mother wrote to you, fearing that at last she would tell the truth. She has long felt you deserved to know and that, if we told you, perhaps we could stand between you and the pain of the knowledge.'

'Oh, Henry dear,' her mother said, with such a measure of compassion that Verity was astonished.

She turned to the woman she had known as her mother. 'How could you let him do this to you? What about me?' she wailed. 'Where was your compassion for me? If you forgave him, stayed with him, loved him, why were you always so angry with me? It wasn't my fault that Jenny was my mother. You hurt me in the bath, you slapped me. Why couldn't you see ...?' Verity pressed her lips together. No, she would not cry. She saw the shock on Lady Clement's face quickly replaced by an even deeper sadness.

There was silence as Verity, at last, saw the truth that had been written in the notebook, but which had not registered. Why had it taken so long? What the hell was the matter with her? She leaned forward. 'Did you once wear camellia-scented perfume?'

Lady Clement rose, her face impassive, but not her eyes. 'Follow me, if you would.' Her voice was like tattered thread. She looked at her husband. 'You, too, if you would be so kind, Henry.'

She walked out into the hall and up the stairs. Sylvia and Polly stayed sitting on the upright chairs, looking stressed and pale beneath their boaters' weather-beaten tan. Verity and her father followed Lady Clement into her bedroom, adjoining his. She led them to the dressing table, on which were several perfume bottles. None were of camellia scent. She opened a drawer and pointed. There lay a perfume bottle, on a baby's cardigan. Verity reached in and took both, holding them close to her face, smelling camellia, just like the shrub that old Matthews had grown.

She gripped them so tightly it hurt. She looked in the mirror. Lady Clement stood behind her, her father next to her, not meeting his daughter's eyes. Verity said, 'It wasn't you who slapped me, was it? You were the kind lady. It was my mother who wasn't.'

Lady Clement nodded. 'I loved you then, I love you now. I kept these together because I wore camellia-scented perfume at that time and, once Jenny died, wearing it made me feel sad for her. Somehow, though, I couldn't just throw it away. It seemed like throwing away her existence. I kept the cardigan because Jenny liked it; she thought you looked sweet in it. Oh, Verity, believe me when I tell you that your mother did care. She even chose your name, but she was young and life had been hard, and she had learned the wrong lessons.' She shut the drawer.

Verity opened it and replaced the perfume and the cardigan. 'They should stay here,' she whispered.

Her father moved to stand by the window, as Lady Clement talked to Verity's reflection. 'Your father made a mistake, and we couldn't find a way out. I chose not to have children, for I never wanted you to feel you were not like them. You were a child in need of protection. Therefore when your mother died, we hid the secret. But it just grew bigger, and so too did my fear that every time you were rebellious you were turning into Jenny and, if so, would I be able to protect you against yourself? Then came Tom Brown, and I feared that he was like Jenny had been, and I couldn't bear either the hurt for you or a resurrection of the hurt that I endured. I behaved badly. And yes, I was cruel. You must know by now that Tom would not take a penny. But I was out of control, fearful, angry, worried ...'

Her father came to stand beside his wife now. 'Verity, it was all my fault. I acted like a fool, took advantage of Jenny, when I already had true love. I began to see the truth, but it was too late, because Jenny was pregnant. Your mother – my wife, I mean – insisted that we consider the baby, and only the baby. All hurts and slights had to be reduced to nothing, in the face of you.'

He reached out to his wife, who took his hand.

He continued, 'We both felt that was an absolute priority, and wanted your happiness above all else. I was – am – your father, so I couldn't let your mother take you back to that family. Was I wrong? Sometimes Jenny would look after you, but more often she would not. Your mother is right: Jenny was as she was because of circumstance.' He shook his head. 'We haven't done a very good job, have we?'

Verity looked from one to the other. 'I think my mother,' and she reached out to Lady Clement, 'has done a remarkable job. And you, Father, are a very lucky man.'

The day wore into evening and the girls left to catch the train before dinner, as they had to take the boats to Limehouse Basin the next day. They knew the cargo would be steel. 'There's a war on,' Verity told her parents – because that's what they were.

As she left, her mother pressed the camellia perfume into her hand. 'Perhaps it will remind you of my love.' Lady Pamela Clement stood on the step, and Verity's father brought round the car to drive the girls to the station. Verity reached for her mother's hand, but instead Lady Pamela kissed her cheek. 'I love you so much, and am so proud of you. You have the best of your mother in you: her spunk, her energy. Who knows what she would have been, had she had a different life. Never forget that.'

Verity hugged her, whispering, 'I don't know how you have coped, all these years. You'd make a boater, you know, Mother, but Father needs a good kick up the arse.'

Her mother gasped and then laughed. 'What man doesn't? Even your Tom will. We will try and find out his whereabouts – perhaps Sandy's father can help – and will keep you informed.'

Chapter 24

Friday 23 June – Mulberry B invasion harbour, Arromanches, and back to the cut

Saul Hopkins felt the shifting and creaking of the flexible floating steel roadway beneath his boots. The storm had finally blown itself out, and the supply ships were once again queuing to moor at Mulberry B harbour. The lorries were stacked up, ready to load, whilst at the same time the storm damage was being repaired by sappers, using material from the Americans' Mulberry A, which had not withstood the storm nearly as well as the British Mulberry B. Saul beckoned to one of the military lorries, guiding it as it backed up. He refused to vomit again, but before he could count to ten he was hanging over the side, heaving.

He was not alone. A seaman was alongside, wiping his mouth with the back of his hand. 'God dammit, this is worse – much worse – than being on board ship.'

Saul stared past the scuttled ships and the caissons, the watertight structures that had been towed across and then sunk to create a breakwater. It was supposed to ease the nausea to fix your eyes on the horizon. It didn't. The sergeant shouted, 'When you're quite finished, 'Opkins, passing the time of day with your belly and the sea, get back here.'

He did, supervising the loading of supplies, and longed to be going with them along the six miles of roadway to the shore, and then on, joining the advance.

Sergeant Williams stomped up and gave him a sweet. 'Suck it, lad, try and keep it down. It should help, or even if it doesn't, it'll get some energy into your system. Bloody nightmare, eh?'

'You look no better'n me, Sarge.'

The next lorry came up, the driver shouting, 'Hurry it up – can't stand this. Chucked up already, I have.'

Soon the Allies would free up the ports. Antwerp would be best, and they could bring in supplies that way. They worked on, he and the other lads, some of them off waterways, others off farms, some regular soldiers and others conscripts who'd been at Dunkirk. All sorts. Good sorts.

At the end of the day Saul tipped himself into his billet on land, thank the Lord, thinking of her, only her: his beloved girl, his Polly. He remembered her slaps, her fury, her hurt; but she'd realise, he knew she would, cos she wasn't a daft girl. He felt his eyes closing, and he half laughed at the thoughts he'd once had that he'd never be glad to be off the water. But the sea was different. It turned his stomach, but it made him feel better that it did the same to the sailors, when they were on the Mulberry.

As he drifted off, he thought of his sister Maudie, as he always did. Where was she? He thought of Leon. His case must come up soon, and how long would the beggar get? What about Joe? Did he ever think of his da and, if so, had he got over his fear, now that Leon was locked away? As he was falling asleep Saul heard a crash, and woke with a start. It was Alex, the corporal, coming in late, falling over someone's helmet and cursing. But why not, for his mum had been killed by a doodlebug in Wandsworth, poor beggar. Saul was wide awake again.

He felt the shiver of fear that came over him when he allowed himself to think of the doodlebugs and Limehouse Basin, and the Regent's Canal, and *Marigold* and *Horizon*. 'Keep yer heads down, all of yer,' he whispered. 'Just keep yer heads down.' He forced his mind away from that. It was better to wonder where Tom was; but no, not that, because what if he was hurt or worse? Instead Saul thought of the men they'd offload tomorrow, and the supplies, and the gulls that flew over.

He thought of the men who had dreamed up the harbour. How clever was that, to have such ideas, and have people build 'em? He thought of Granfer at Auntie Lettie's and imagined how, if he was here, Granfer would be standing on the Mulberry pontoon, scratching his head and saying, 'Large brains, some 'ave, don't they, lad? And they use 'em, not like some.'

It made him smile, and Polly made him smile, and at last he slept.

The three girls reached Tyseley Wharf on 28 June and toiled out of Birmingham the next day, consumed with the war, and the Rivers family; and each evening, no matter how tired the day had made them, they talked of both, and of Lord and Lady Clement. Each evening, just before she and Polly turned off the oil lamp, Verity remembered some fragment that broadened out, to wipe away the misremembered past. As they pulled up along the Brum Bum she talked of the sense of protection, confidence and warmth she now recalled. As they carried their coal cargo from Coventry through the flight of locks leading to Blisworth village, past the old mill, she remembered the sense of leaning on others, being part of them, unaware that she was a separate being. Yes, she remembered belonging.

As they worked their way along the lock flight to Marsworth Junction, Polly finally allowed herself to remember her childhood, too, and although she had always thought it was her twin, Will, who had sheltered her, and on whom she had leaned, she admitted that it was in fact her mum and dad. Parents who would not lie, if asked directly, but would protect her if they thought it best.

They turned down the Aylesbury Arm to unload the coal from the butty in the Aylesbury basin, passing reeds, scabious and wild marjoram alongside the towpath; it was the tranquillity of uninhabited countryside. They let Dog run alongside them as they pat-pattered the six miles, smiling as she dipped into the hedgerows, ferreting out the pheasants that flew chaotically into the air. The days were long, the nights short, but both were scorched by thoughts of doodlebugs; and, for Polly, by her harsh and stupid words. When she reached Bull's Bridge a telephone call must be made, and apologies given, but would that be enough?

Nearing London, with their senses alert to the sound and sight of streaking doodlebugs, they blew Bet's hunting horn as they approached the paper factory, and again Albert summoned tea for them as the men shovelled the coal ashore. They breathed in the coal dust and ground it between their teeth.

Sylvia asked, as she handed back her mug to Albert, 'How are your girls, Bert?'

He shook his head. 'Shirl, the youngest, copped it when one o' them bastards came down as she were seein' her auntie over east. The wife and t'other is picking their selves up. Leaning on one another, we are. 'Tis all we can do.' He nodded to the East End.

Polly stared into the dregs of her tea, unable just for a moment to bear to look on the old man's stoic grief. Finally it was Sylvia who laid her head on his shoulder. 'Dear Albert, dear, dear Albert.' It was enough, for his arm came around her, and together the young and old stood as Polly took the mugs that dangled from their hands and walked to the canteen. Yes, she must make that telephone call.

A worker came out of the canteen. 'You all right, pet?'

He reached out for the mugs, then looked past her to Albert and nodded. 'Ah, yes. Yer dry yer eyes and take your boats on, and we'll see you again, God willing.'

Cowley lock was with them, and Polly took in the *Marigold*, while Sylvia swung *Horizon* in beside her. Verity wound the paddles, the sluices opened and the level dropped, the walls as slimy as always. Verity opened the gates, shoving at the beams, and out they pat-pattered as Polly nudged the tiller and steered for the centre, finally reading her mother's letters, which dealt firmly with her nonsense.

It made her smile, made her regret her anger. After the first letter the subject had been ignored, as her mother wrote of Joe's progress at school, his talent for art; and with one letter was enclosed his pencil drawing of Saul. She smoothed it out on the roof of the cabin and called Verity. 'Come on out, look at our boy. He's got the likeness absolutely.'

Verity thought so, too. Polly refolded it and placed it in the back pocket of her trousers. Verity grinned, 'Close to your heart then?'

'Shut up,' Polly laughed.

Bull's Bridge was in sight now, and Verity picked up the hunting horn and hooted. Over to the east they saw a doodlebug streaking, but could not hear it, for it was too far away. They passed the dry dock, the frontage to the yard, the moored boats, looking for a spot, and finding one. They moored the boats, tying up next to *Cambridge*.

Mrs Porter came out onto the counter. "Ow do?'

"Ow do, Mrs Porter, how's our Jimmy? Has he homework to show us?' Verity called.

Mrs Porter said, 'When yer done.'

'We'll never be done,' Verity laughed. They were home once more and, as always, the tiredness seemed to drench them for just a few moments, but then they rallied. They grabbed brooms and swept out each of the holds, shovelling up the sludge from the bilges, because this was their life and they were bloody lucky to still have one.

'Race you to the lavs,' Polly cried, after she'd snatched three of the shabby towels from beneath the side-bed, brandishing them on the kerb. The other two leapt after her as they raced along to the yard, dodging the wash boilers, the shoppers, the children, with Dog at their heels, barking. Polly reached the door first, panting, and turned, her arms outstretched, barring the way.

'Me first, so very there.' They were all three laughing too much to talk. She turned, opened the door and the other two barged through in front of her. 'Hey, that's not fair,' she yelled after them.

'Ah, but what is?' Verity called back. 'Come and share the sink, idiot.'

Sylvia added, 'Hot water, for once, can you believe it? Quick, Polly.'

All three of them crammed around the sink, washing everywhere that showed, even their hair, and leaving with towels tied around their heads. They nipped into the Orders Office, but Ted said there'd be nothing before tomorrow and to come back without the headgear, if they didn't very much mind. They laughed and marched through the yard, in step, singing, 'You must have been a beautiful baby ...'

They heard a baritone joining in behind, and Polly felt someone take her arm. It was the blacksmith, in step with them, singing. Behind was a welder and he was joined by his mate. They sang and marched to the frontage, with other workers in overalls weaving around *them*, just this once. The men laughed and peeled off, and the girls went on singing as they ran now, back to the pair, with Sylvia yelling, 'We're in time for a canteen lunch. Come on, let's try and sort out our hair and get there. We've got thirty minutes.'

But at the *Marigold* they skidded to a halt. Polly's towel came undone and slipped from her head as she stared at her mum and dad, with Mr Burton, all crammed onto the counter. 'Saul?' she cried.

'Don't be dramatic, Polly,' her mother said firmly, her lightweight hat perched on the back of her head, her ancient summer skirt and twinset fluttering in the breeze. 'Any notification would come to you – surely you realise you are down as Saul's next of kin? It is not quite factual, of course, but it is how he thinks of you.'

Her mum was stepping down onto the kerb, and the other two followed, much as goslings will follow a determined goose. Dog leapt off the roof of the cabin and clung to Mrs Holmes's side.

Polly had never loved her mum more and, as Mrs Holmes held her arms open, she rushed into them. 'Oh, Mum, I'm so—'

'Hush, I knew you'd see sense and understand we'd done only what we thought was best. No point in distressing you unnecessarily, was there? But on to more serious matters than your tantrums.'

Verity was hugging Mr Holmes and then Mr Burton, who almost managed to evade capture. Sylvia was swept into Mrs Holmes's arms, and then it was Verity's turn. 'Tea?' Polly asked.

'Mr Burton will explain,' Mrs Holmes ordered, as her husband, Thomas, and Mr Burton, Polly's former boss, winked at the girls. She gestured to Mr Burton to step forward, which he did, rescuing his briefcase from the ground beside him. He placed it there again, warning Dog with a look not to go near it.

He said, 'You will remember that when Leon had the temerity to burn *Horizon*'s cargo of wood – an action for which he is awaiting trial – the police were called, and Joe was removed to a young offenders' place of correction.'

Polly clutched Sylvia's hand and squeezed it, because Sylvia had wrongly implicated Joe in the arson.

Mr Burton continued, 'We explained the fact that Joe's mother Maud, Saul's sister, was missing, and his father was Leon Arnson, who had organised the crime. It resulted in your mother being allowed to retain Joe, if I, as a solicitor, guaranteed the behaviour of the boy. Even though Saul and Granfer are relatives, the authorities thought, as is their wont, that this domestic arrangement would lead to a more stable environment. This arrangement was, of course, agreed to by Granfer and Saul.'

Mrs Holmes was tapping her foot, and Polly felt Verity press against her, knowing that soon Mrs Holmes would snatch the reins from this man and take over. Within seconds it happened.

'Come along, Mr Burton, this is all old hat, and you know the girls need lunch in the canteen, and we might as well enjoy it too, so do get on.'

Mr Burton tipped his hat and continued. 'I pressed the police to maintain some level of search for, or at least distribute information about, Mrs Arnson as a missing person.'

Polly's father wrenched at his collar and looked too hot on this balmy day. He muttered, 'The long and short of it is: they think they've found her. And now I need me dinner, and less chat. I could eat an ox, me fist or, hopefully, liver and bacon, if my memory serves me right from last time. We can pick up on this later.'

'It was overcooked liver, Thomas, but warm, I grant you.' Mrs Holmes sniffed, jerking her head towards the boats. 'Go and sort out your hair, girls, and we'll tell you more, but it requires your participation. Hurry now.'

Polly shook her head. 'No, Mum. Tell us now. Has Maud been found, alive?' She knew the other two were waiting to hear, too. Could it be? After all this time? Where the hell had she been? How could she have left Joe?

Her mum nodded. 'Yes, alive, but not quite well. The details can be relayed after lunch, because we need the help of all three of you to bring about a satisfactory outcome.'

Polly could have screamed, but from the set of her mum's face she knew that nothing else would be forthcoming until they'd all eaten. She muttered, 'You are a cruel and wicked woman.'

Her mum laughed. 'Perhaps, but we have to feed the ravening beasts or we will get little co-operation. And I don't mean from you girls, but these two men. Rest assured, I have thought of a way to bring our Maud back into the world, and to her son.'

'Into the world?' Polly felt the joy at the news of Maud's survival replaced by confusion. 'Oh, Mum, it sounds serious?'

'All will be well.' Her mother's chin was up, and Polly knew that look well. Yes, Maud was found, and was not dead; and she would be all right, but not yet. Polly couldn't stop smiling and then frowning. But how would her mum manage without Joe?

Verity clutched Mr Holmes's arm, saying, 'It's unbelievable, Joe will be overjoyed. We must tell him.'

Mrs Holmes swung round. 'No, we must not, yet. There is work to be done.'

Verity, Sylvia and Polly exchanged a look, knowing they were to be the foot soldiers, and glad of it, but wanting to know more. They walked into the canteen, their hair sorted, Polly alongside her mum. They didn't need to talk; it was enough that they were together, and her mum was in charge, and Maud was found, and although the war was awful and people were dying, sometimes miracles happened.

The muggy warmth enveloped them, the clatter of dishes and the roar of men's voices burying all possibility of conversation, but not of thought: was Maud in prison? Disabled? What?

It was indeed liver and bacon on the menu. Her mother tapped her husband on the shoulder. 'You're to avoid any and all onions, because we'll be squashed together in Mr Burton's car and I'm not putting up with it, do you hear me, Thomas?'

Thomas clearly had, because he raised his eyebrows at Polly and pulled a face, before turning back. Mrs Holmes wasn't done with him, though, because she tapped him on the shoulder again as he held out his plate to Enid, one of the servers, saying,

'I saw that, Thomas Holmes, and if the wind changes, you'll stay like it.'

Polly, Verity and Sylvia were shaking with laughter, and it stopped all the second-guessing. Her mum turned and winked at them, whispering, 'They have to be kept in order or they'd run amok.'

The thought of either her dad or Mr Burton daring to run amok was an image too far, and the girls' roar of laughter made the men at the nearby tables swing round. Polly's mum appeared satisfied and said, 'We have to laugh, or we'd cry. What a world.'

She carried on along the line, asking for less mash but more carrots, if that wouldn't be too much trouble, and fanning herself against the heat. Verity pointed out a table with free spaces on the bench, next to one of the carpenters. 'Why not find a place and sit yourself down, Mrs Holmes? Over there – look, next to Arnold.'

Mrs Holmes set a cracking pace, sweeping around other tables and arriving at Arnold's bench. Mr Burton followed, clutching his briefcase to his chest as though it contained the Crown Jewels, while Sylvia trotted in his wake, carrying his plate. Dog had accompanied them across the yard, but would now be in position by the range, where she'd get the scraps.

Enid, who was serving, looked at Polly. 'Oh, the family's visiting? I'll save some Spotted Dick for you all, with custard.'

They ate, while Polly was on tenterhooks, hardly able to believe it, and the questions were tearing at her. How was Maud? Where was she? Where had she been? Was she well?

Her mother ate daintily. 'A very substantial meal. I'd be happy if you could eat like this every day, girls. You've all lost some weight, I think, but I dare say you think about your men, and worry. We have said prayers in church for them, and I hold them in my heart.'

Arnold patted Mrs Holmes on the back. The feather on her hat wobbled. 'You go on doing that, Missus. It can't do any 'arm, and who knows, it might do some good.'

Mr Burton wiped his mouth with his starched folded white handkerchief. 'Indeed, that's what my wife and I say about our son.'

Polly stared at him. He had never spoken of his family as she took down his letters in shorthand, and she'd had no idea he had a son, let alone one who was serving.

Arnold asked, wiping up the gravy with bread, 'Infantry?'

Mr Burton replaced his handkerchief in his suit pocket. 'Submarines.'

Into the thoughtful silence Verity said, 'Pudding, I think. You take the dirty dishes to the trolley, Polly, while Sylvia and I fetch the Spotted Dick.'

The Spotted Dick was ambrosia, although it had very few spots, because currants were in short supply, but the custard was good; perhaps it was sweetened with honey? And the sponge, too. Polly thought of Fran and her beehives, and of Granfer. Perhaps he had been told? Not now – later, she chastised herself, impatience dragging at her, as it had all through the meal.

At last they were out into the fresh air, and it was Sylvia who stopped dead just a few paces from the canteen, dragging Mrs Holmes to one side. 'You need to tell us or I am going to scream. What is all this about Maudie?'

They learned the story as they hurried back to the boats, finally crowding into *Marigold*'s cabin. Mr Burton placed his briefcase on his knee on the side-bed, while Mr and Mrs Holmes settled on either side. Mr Burton withdrew a file and read from the stapled papers. The three girls sat on the cross-bed, giving him their full attention. 'Apparently Maudie was found some months ago, wandering up and down the towpath of the Aylesbury Arm of the Grand Union Canal. She was thin, frozen and had a broken arm, and head injuries, and had to be sedated before she would leave the canal. She was black and blue, and had no knowledge of who she was.'

Polly remembered how Saul had said it was a favourite stretch of the canal for Maudie; a tranquil and beautiful place.

Mr Burton continued, his voice calm and devoid of emotion, 'Maudie received hospital treatment and was released into the care of a small wartime psychiatric home near London, well, near Aylesbury, for those with mental problems. This was done not only because had she lost her memory, but because her behaviour was disturbed. She rocked, she moaned, she picked at her clothes and was unreachable. She remembered nothing of who she was, or where she'd been, or how she'd been hurt.'

Polly asked, 'So how did they know who she was?'

'Ah well, as luck would have it – though not for those hurt, of course,' Mr Burton looked around at them, apologetically, 'the hospital was damaged by a gas explosion just ten days ago. The blast demolished part of an annexe in which Maud was kept. I use that term advisedly, because containment was deemed necessary. She was found, along with other patients, wandering the canal. When the patients were returned to what remained of the home, which has since been made safe, she said quite clearly, "I am Maudie. I need the water, I need a butty, for it is quiet." They didn't understand what a butty was.

'The authorities contacted the police because they finally had a name, though only a Christian name. The police checked their records, and contacted me. I collected Granfer for an identification and brought him to the home. It is indeed Maudie, but she wouldn't approach either of us. She is scared of men, but looks out of the window, seeking the canal. It is only the thought of it that brings her peace. So, we have come for you girls.'

Ah, so Granfer knew. Polly and the other two girls exchanged a look. But what about Saul? Mr Burton was wiping his forehead with his handkerchief. 'I found it distressing, to be perfectly frank, because she so loves water and cries to be on it. The question is – and this is a question that will be asked of you by Granfer, for no one will send a message to Saul until we have the answer ...' He smiled a little. 'Yes, this is clearly emotional blackmail, but I doubt it is needed, although they say it's best to train all the guns one has, to bring about the appropriate result.'

Mrs Holmes tutted, 'Oh, come along now, you've held the stage for quite some while, Mr Burton, and it's time to wriggle on.'

He chuckled, but then grew deadly serious. 'The question is: will you take Maudie on *Marigold* or even better, the butty? If it causes ructions, she will naturally be returned to the home until somehow she recovers, or does not. Naturally, if Saul was still here ... But he is not. You, Polly, are part of his family in all but name and, having discussed this with the doctors, they deem it suitable. I doubt Maudie would be allowed to leave in these circumstances, were it not wartime. But the thought of the canal seems to be the only thing, thus far, to bring her a vestige of peace.'

Mrs Holmes said, 'Thank you, Mr Burton – at last. Now perhaps you'd like to go onto the counter while I talk to the girls. You may go too, Thomas.'

The men obeyed, but before Mr Burton shut the doors behind them, he came back down and said, 'It would be at the doctor's discretion, and under my auspices as a legal representative. Therefore I agreed with the doctor when he suggested that a bit of a trial run take place, within reach of help. A short trip, perhaps to Cowley lock – from which, if all goes wrong, Maudie can be collected.' He left again, winking at Mrs Holmes and saying, 'My last word, I promise.' He shut the cabin doors behind him, as the girls and Mrs Holmes laughed.

Mrs Holmes looked round at the girls. 'That man has a heart of gold, but he does go on and on, because he likes to cross the t's and dot the i's, but at least it means we know exactly where we are. So I suggest that we all go to visit Maudie and try to assess her reaction to us, and the medical team will be assessing you. We will then present a plan to that team. I have to tell you that at no time has Maudie been a danger to others, or herself, beyond walking out after the explosion. And she returned placidly, as though her heart was breaking. As I say, this is only a suggestion.'

She stopped and settled her summer hat more firmly on her head while the three girls grinned at one another, because it was not a suggestion; it was an order, and they nodded at one another.

Seeing this, Mrs Holmes was off at a gallop again. 'You are aware that although we do this for Maudie's sake, it is primarily for Joe. He deserves a mother, one who is his protector, and not vice versa. Now, what I gather is that you girls pick up your cargo at either Limehouse Basin or Brentford. Having done so, you must pass this depot once more, on your way north. Have you any thoughts about how you could collect Maudie as you pass the depot?'

Polly watched her mum closely. 'The thing I want to know is how will you feel if, and when, Joe goes back to his mother?'

Mrs Holmes shook her head slightly. 'Dear Polly, that day was always a possibility, and it will be better for him. How I will feel is distressed, but happy for him.' Her clenched hands refuted that thought. 'Now, back to the matter in hand. What thoughts have you?'

This redoubtable woman clearly had a very good idea what should happen, but it had to come from them. Polly looked at her friends. Yes, it had to come from them.

Verity murmured, 'We need to try Maudie on the butty for a short while, which would constitute a trial, as Mr Burton said.'

Sylvia leaned back on the cross-bed. 'Yes, without an engine the butty is quiet, and I would be happy to share the cabin.'

Polly and Verity stared at her, amazed, but then not so amazed, because Sylvia was changing. Polly said, 'To cross and dot the t's and i's, we could pick up Maudie from the lay-by, once we have loaded at

Limehouse. We could then take her as far as Cowley lock as per Mr Burton's suggestion, which is just around the corner. If it suits her, we could go on to Buckby. Perhaps she could visit Granfer? If she would like to remain with him, then fine. If not, then she stays with us. What does everyone think?'

Verity was nodding, but it was Sylvia who would bear the brunt.

Polly warned her, 'We don't know how she will be, Sylvia. Maudie could be untidy, and perhaps frightening.'

Sylvia just grinned. 'And you two are not? More to the point, what would the Grand Union Canal Company think?'

Verity had been looking impatient and now said, 'Oh, never mind the Company, why should they know? It's Dog that is worrying me; we can't get rid of our lovely girl, even for Maudie. Neither should we take Maudie into the pubs; the noise, and everything else, could upset her.'

Sylvia said, 'We could keep Dog on the motor, and take it in turns to stay in with Maudie if we decide to go out?'

They planned for the next ten minutes, working out that Mrs Holmes must be at Cowley lock to take Maudie back to the home by taxi after the short trial, if it was unsuccessful.

Mr Burton opened the cabin doors and put his foot down for once, so they knew it was serious. 'If we don't go to see Maudie now, we won't go at all, because the traffic will build and I'm not driving home on slit headlights.'

Polly said, as they gathered their belongings, 'Animals sense pain. Dog will be fine.'

Mrs Holmes picked up her handbag and asked, 'What about the boaters? It's all very well for you to say the Company won't know, but someone could tell them.'

They stepped onto the counter. Polly took Dog to Mrs Porter, who was happy to have her, then ran after the others in time to hear Verity explaining that the boaters looked after their own, and although they might recognise Maudie, nothing would be said.

Chapter 25

Tuesday 4 July – the *Marigold* and *Horizon*
approach Bull's Bridge, after loading at
Limehouse

The girls fell silent as they travelled from Alperton
with the boats abreast. They had moored in front of
Sid's pub briefly this morning, for Verity to run and
post another letter. It was to thank her mother for
unblocking Uncle Freddie's trust without Verity even
asking; not that she had anything she wanted to buy,
but it was a gesture of reconciliation and belief.

Verity elbowed the tiller slightly and the pair kept
to the centre, and the pat-patter of the engine was
so normal, the sun on her straw hat and shoulders
comforting. She had told her parents that Maud
might be joining them at Bull's Bridge. She had
added all the background to Maud's story. It was
news she felt able to share with them now.

Sylvia joined them on *Marigold*, so they could run
over their plan again. Verity steered, while the other
two girls and Dog sat on the cabin roof in the blazing
sun, feeling satisfied it all sounded tickety-boo. Polly
brandished her Woodbines. Sylvia refused as usual,

but Verity dragged out her matches from her trouser pockets, lit both and inhaled. Sylvia smoothed down her bouncing curls and said, 'I'm glad we bumped into Bet at Limehouse.'

Polly elbowed her so hard that she fell back.

Sylvia corrected herself. 'Sorry, I couldn't resist, but it wasn't a massive bang, Verity, and Bet didn't mind too much. *Sky* was only slightly scratched.'

'She should have had her tender sorted,' Verity growled.

They were ten minutes from the lay-by. Verity blew smoke over Sylvia, who fanned it away and continued, 'Anyway, I'm glad we saw her – is that better?'

The other two nodded. 'She agreed that we were doing the right thing with Maudie, but just to stay alert in case she wandered off. She thinks the cut will work its magic.'

They had said this to themselves twice already on the trip, but Polly and Sylvia both looked as nervous as Verity felt, and Dog was quiet as though she had picked up the tension. Ahead Verity saw a pair pull away from the lay-by and squinted. 'Ah, Steerer Ambrose's coming our way to pick up a load.' She blew the hunting horn. As she did so, the sirens went in the distance, and the ack-ack, but the doodlebugs were over central London, from the look of their flaring tails.

Steerer Ambrose was hooting his horn as he approached, and he slowed, yelling, ''Ow do. Yer

406

visitor 'as arrived with yer ma, Polly. Nice to see 'er again, and yer ma.' He passed, and his butty on short tow approached. Ma Ambrose shouted, 'We 'ad a whip-round. Ma Mercy's given yer ma a long skirt, wide belt and blouse for our Maudie. Never fear, she'll get better quick, now she's back. She don't like blokes, though, and who can blame her? That beggar Leon ...' They were past.

Verity was shaking her head. She said, 'I would really, really love to know how word gets around so quickly.'

She didn't expect any answer. Sylvia said, 'It is the mystery of our age, quite frankly, but it doesn't matter. The thing is, we won't be alone – the rest of the boaters will be on hand.'

They were smiling as they reversed into Ambrose's space between Thomo's *Venus* and the Mercys' *Lincoln*. Ma Mercy was on the butty, *York*, and called across, "Ow do.' That was all, but the jerk of her head said more. They waited. 'I 'as the clothes, I'll chook 'em on yer butty counter.'

Verity said, 'You're all saints, you know. Thank you.'

Ma Mercy threw the package as Verity moored up and looked along the kerb. Mrs Holmes was walking slowly with Maudie. Dog leapt down next to Verity. 'Quiet,' Verity hissed. Dog seemed to know and just sat, though her tail was thwacking against the concrete. Mrs Holmes was carrying a string bag full of vegetables. 'From the allotment,' she called.

The pair drew nearer. Maudie was walking strangely sideways, as she had done at the home the day they visited; her head was down, too, as though she was looking for cracks through which she might fall, so tentative were her steps. She wore a headscarf that hid her long hair. Was this to disguise her? Verity wondered, as she waited. But hadn't anyone told her that Leon was in custody? Ah, Maudie probably didn't understand.

At last the pair reached them. Polly slipped down onto the kerb and stood beside Verity, before approaching her mother from the side, unwilling to scare Maudie, who stood, still looking at the ground. She was hunched, her hands clenched together in front of her, her feet pigeon-toed, as though every part of her was turned inwards. It was just as she had been in the relatives' room at the home. It was a large comfortable room furnished with sofas, tables and newspapers.

The only thing Maudie had said, when she was asked if she'd like to go on the water in a narrow-boat, was, 'Yes.'

'With these women?' the doctor had asked.

Maudie had sat, looking at them through her hair, which she had pulled across one side of her face, like a curtain. The girls had wondered then if they should have worn skirts, as Maud didn't like men. Maud had risen, walked across almost crabwise and picked up Verity's hands. She had turned them palm upwards and run her fingers over the callouses. She had pushed aside the collar of her blouse and seen the healed blisters and callouses from hauling the boats on the Brum Bum. She checked the others, too.

She had then walked in that same crabwise way back to the sofa and sat down. She had looked at no one as she said, 'Yes.'

The doctor had said, as they left, 'She has the same blisters, scars and callouses. She recognises you as ... Well, what?' It was a genuine question.

It was Mrs Holmes who had said, 'The boaters they are.' She had tears in her eyes, and stood with them and whispered, 'I didn't know how hard you have worked, you see. I really didn't know.'

Now Sylvia slipped past Polly and led Maudie to the butty, not touching her, but pointing the way, walking slowly at Maud's pace. Mrs Holmes would travel by taxi to the Cowley lock and wait, in case Maudie preferred to leave the canal there.

Polly said quietly, 'Thank you, Mum, for helping Saul's family.'

Her mum hugged her, tighter than she had ever done. 'You stay safe, and why wouldn't we help – we're all family after all. So, all of you, do your best for Maud if she wants to go on after Cowley lock. I'm banking on you, and so is the Hopkins family.'

Verity smiled, as she too was hugged. The two girls watched as Mrs Holmes turned on her sensible court shoes and walked away, the feather in her summer hat bobbing. Polly ran after her mother, spinning round in front of her. 'I'll do my best, Mum, just like you've done for me, all my life. I do know that, and I want you to know that I know.'

Her mum reached out her hand and touched her face. 'You're a good girl, Polly Holmes, a very good girl; you all are.'

On the counter of the *Marigold* Verity was about to unhitch the mooring strap, but catching sight of the bundle of clothes collected by the women boaters, she called to Polly, who had reached the motor and was on her way to the engine cabin, 'Be back in a minute.' She dashed down into the cabin, took money from the darts kitty and then climbed onto the butty counter and called, "Ow do, Ma Mercy.'

Ma emerged from her motor cabin now, her arms covered in soapsuds. "Ow do, lass.'

'I've had a thought. Did Maudie knit, or do crochet?'

Ma Mercy shook off the suds and wiped her arms on her apron. 'Crochet, I reckon, or as I remembers, anyhow.'

Verity reached out. 'Have you a hook to spare, and wool?' She had two shillings in her palm.

Ma looked at the money. 'Aye, I 'ave, but 'tis a gift, lass. Yer put that away.' She disappeared into the cabin and emerged again with a hook and wool. She stood there, casting on. 'There, might trigger 'ow to do it. Seems to me minds get tired when life becomes over-full with nastiness, if yer get me meaning.'

Verity leapt onto Ma Mercy's counter, as more doodlebugs scorched across the London sky and the ack-ack roared, and hugged the boater, who flapped at her as though she was an irritating bee. 'Off yer go, get out o' London, and be safe.'

Sylvia popped her head out of *Horizon*'s cabin. 'Are we off? I think Maudie's getting restless.'

Verity thrust the crochet at Sylvia. 'Try her with this.'

Sylvia grinned. 'Clever idea.' She picked up the bundle of clothing, and disappeared back into the cabin.

They pat-pattered away from Bull's Bridge, with the butty on a short tow rather than abreast, to give Maudie and Sylvia some quiet time away from the engine noise, and headed to Cowley lock, praying that no doodlebugs buzzed and roared near them. In no time at all *Marigold* was slowing for the lock and passing through the wide stretch. Beech trees lined the cut, as always, and the rich green leaves shimmered, as birdsong drifted on the wind.

Would Maudie come onto the counter to see and hear? Verity waved to Sylvia, who was steering the butty beneath the branches. Sylvia waved back, alone on the counter. Was Maudie hiding in horror, or sitting at peace? Sylvia gave a thumbs up. Ah, good. Polly was lock-wheeling and would be brought up to date when they were in the lock. As they entered the open lock, she looked behind as the butty fragmented the beech reflections. Was this how Maudie's brain felt?

Marigold's prow nudged the sill. Verity unhitched the short tow-rope as *Horizon* glided in alongside. As *Horizon*'s stern counter came parallel, she dared to snatch a look. Sylvia was on the tiller, but Maudie was standing on the top step, crocheting, her head back. She appeared to be almost smelling the slimy walls, as Polly closed the gates and opened the paddles.

The pair rose and suddenly Dog jumped from *Marigold*'s counter onto *Horizon*'s. Verity bit back her shout, fearing it would alarm Maudie more than Dog herself. Dog lay down on the butty roof. Sylvia looked from Verity to Maudie, her hands open in a question. Verity mouthed, 'I don't know.'

They waited as the boats rose. Polly was looking down, concerned, while her mother, who had arrived by taxi, stood with the lock-keeper. It seemed as though everyone was frozen, waiting. Slowly Maudie reached forward and touched Dog, who lay quite still. 'Please don't move, Dog,' whispered Verity, feeling as though she was holding her breath. 'Please, please stay calm, Dog.'

She snatched a look at Polly, and then at Sylvia, who stood near Maudie, ready to contain her if she leapt back. But instead the touch turned into a stroke. Then she presented her hand to Dog, who licked her. They heard Maudie say, 'Good girl. Good, good girl.'

She resumed her crochet as the pair of boats continued rising until they were level with the upper cut. As Polly and the lock-keeper opened the top gates, Verity asked Sylvia, quietly, 'Are you happy to keep going along with Maudie?'

'Absolutely.'

Polly was waiting to set off on her bike to the next lock, and Verity gave her the thumbs up. Mrs Holmes, on the kerb by the lock-keeper's office, waved, turned away and headed for the taxi that would take her to Waterloo and home, while *Marigold* and *Horizon* travelled on.

As the hours passed, slowly, very slowly Maudie's shoulders lifted; her head, too, and the headscarf was removed and her hair blew in the breeze. They intended to eat in the *Marigold*'s cabin when they moored up near Leighton Buzzard, well out of range of the doodlebugs, but Maudie wouldn't leave the butty. So instead Sylvia carried two plates of pheasant stew to *Horizon*'s cabin and ate with Maudie. Thomo would be pleased to learn of the clean plates that Sylvia returned, because he had taken the place of Saul as poacher of the cut.

Sylvia sat for a moment with the girls on *Marigold*'s counter, though Dog wouldn't leave the butty-cabin roof. Verity rolled a cigarette for Polly, while Sylvia made her report, as Polly called it. 'Maudie's still very quiet, but as you saw, she stands on the counter, she accepts Dog, she crochets. She barely speaks, but she lifts her head and only shrinks occasionally. She has the cross-bed, while I have taken the side-bed. Perhaps we should call in at Aylesbury Arm on our return, whether we are to discharge a load there or not? After all, Saul says it gives Maudie peace. Have you written to him, by the way?'

'Yes, I'll post it when I can, but I'm not sure about Aylesbury.' Polly lit the cigarettes. They all fell silent, thinking. She went on, 'Might it set her off, because that's where she was found?'

Verity said, 'If we're calling in at Buckby to take her to Granfer's, why don't we drop in on Fran? She'll know, or if Bet catches up with us, we'll ask her.'

They finished their cigarettes, sitting on the roof, and then settled down for the night, without Dog, who insisted on lying on the butty-cabin roof. 'Keeping guard on the weakest of the pack,' Polly murmured.

The two girls talked a little about Sylvia and her quiet compassion, and her strength, and realised that today neither of them had worried about their men. And finally they slept.

The next day took them towards Fenny Stratford, heading through the locks and on to Wolverton, Cosgrove and Stoke Bruerne, where Polly posted her letter to Saul and another to her mum. All the way they checked the bridges for children who would gob or shout, or hurl manure, which could upset Maudie and take her backwards. But all was well. The next day Blisworth Tunnel loomed, with its mile of darkness. Verity chewed her finger and

Polly fretted. The only one who didn't was Sylvia, who called across, 'We must trust.'

'In what?' Verity called.

'In whom,' Sylvia corrected her.

Polly and Verity stood either side of the tiller as they entered the gloom, with the butty on tow. 'Whom, eh?' Verity said.

Polly replied, 'Ah, yes, but one swallow does not a summer make. Sylvia never said she'd stopped believing in God, just that she didn't know how far to take it, or I think that's what she meant.'

They laid up after Blisworth, and again Dog slept on the roof; and again Sylvia took two plates of supper to her butty. In the morning the report was that Maudie had slept better and had prepared a cup of tea for them both, seeming to know where things should be kept. She had also taken it upon herself to light the oil lamp yesterday evening.

They climbed through the locks leading to Norton Junction, and instead of heading through the Braunston Tunnel and ultimately to Tyseley Wharf, they moored at the Buckby frontage. By now it was evening, and the glorious day had turned into a gloriously long evening. They explained to Maud that they had to give Dog a walk and would like her to come.

They set off, all five of them heading past Spring Cottage, where Fran was working near the hives. They called to her that they were walking Dog and might knock on the door later. She had obviously heard the news and waved her trowel. 'It's a nice walk, if you keep straight on. There's a lovely vegetable garden that edges the road. You might find some people working it.'

They carried on, presuming this meant that Granfer and Auntie Lettie would be visible in their side-garden, and they blessed the speed of messages along the cut.

They passed cottages with their windows wide open, and children playing in the lanes. Maudie stopped to watch them, a puzzled look on her face. One boy in short trousers playing cricket called to a woman digging up potatoes in her front garden, 'Can I have another half hour, Ma? I'll get up for school, I promise.'

Maudie looked from the boy to his mother. Was she remembering Joe? The three girls stood with her. Maudie walked on with Dog at her side, her face blank. They saw Granfer in the distance, with Auntie Lettie. Dog rushed up, barking and wagging her tail. She rested her front paws on the rickety white picket fence, while Granfer and Lettie petted her.

Granfer called to the girls as they headed towards them, 'Nice to see yer. Out fer a stroll, are yer? *Marigold* running nice, is she?' He continued to pat the dog. Maudie took no notice of him and did not change her pace.

Sylvia answered as they drew closer, 'Yes, she's running well. We have Maudie to help. Did *Seagull* used to run well, Granfer, and *Swansong*, for you and Saul?'

Maudie kept walking until she was past Granfer and Lettie. Sylvia stopped, stroking Dog, while they all watched Maudie, disappointment in the air. Sylvia called to her, 'Come and say hello to Lettie, if you want to. Then it's time we returned to the boat, Maudie.'

Maudie turned and walked back, and everyone started talking about the garden. She stopped by Sylvia and looked at Granfer intently, and then at Lettie, then down at Dog and waited. Verity sighed and patted Granfer, as Maudie nodded and walked on, with Sylvia hurrying to catch her up, Dog at her heels.

Granfer said, 'She didn't flinch, and she looked, and I is a man. At t'home when I went to identify 'er she'd not look, just shrank and scuttled away. There be a reason; it be that darned Leon, and he ain't comin' back, so in time, lasses, in time ...' He petered to a stop and Lettie slipped her arm through his.

'There now, young Artie.'

Verity and Polly looked at one another. It was so strange to hear that Granfer had a first name.

He said, 'She'll get better, our Maudie will, and I tells yer why. Cos she's already better than she were. She walks upright, not like that damn crab thing she did. She's unfolding into the light. I thanks yer from the bottom of me 'eart, yer lasses.'

Polly asked, 'Should we take her down the Aylesbury Arm on our way back, because it was her favourite?'

'Do what yer waters say, that's the thing,' Lettie said.

As they followed Sylvia, Polly slipped her arm through Verity's. 'Let's get Maudie straight back. Fran won't mind, and we don't want to overload Maud; and as for the Arm, we'll do as Lettie says.'

Verity smiled. 'Ah, see what our water says, when we reach it on our return trip, eh?'

'That's the one.'

Chapter 26

Monday 10 July – Maud revisits her past

The first big change happened at Tyseley Wharf when Maudie helped untie the side-sheets and roll them. They then explained to her that one of the boaters would care for Dog while they had a bath, and then they would sleep at a house owned by a banker, and it would be good if she came.

Maudie merely nodded and joined them as they walked to the tram, as though she had her orders. Polly carried the clothes that the boaters had given Maudie, and which she had so far refused to wear.

As they waited for the tram, Maudie said, 'I doesn't know if I ever been on a tram, but I 'ave had a bath.'

There it was. There: the past. There: words.

They caught the tram, sitting as others stood swaying and hanging on the straps. They stopped and walked to the public baths. They entered. Maudie faltered, staring at the white tiles and the woman in the white coat. Verity froze and whispered, 'The coats. She might run. The doctors wore them.'

The reverse happened. It was as though it was a home from home. Mrs Green waited outside Maudie's cubicle, because Verity and the girls explained what had happened. There was no sound beyond splashing. Polly had left Maudie's boater clothes on the chair, just in case. When their time was up, they knocked on Maudie's door. It opened. Maudie was wearing her boater clothes. She had left her others on the chair. 'I needs 'em no longer,' she said. 'I belong in a different place ter that.'

They didn't all go into the pub, just Polly, who ordered portions of chips to be wrapped in newspaper. She carried them outside and handed the parcels round. 'No ash, I hope.'

They walked to Mrs Green's and sat, squashed on a bench in her back yard, eating in the subdued heat of the late evening, and the chips were indeed ash-free. They disposed of the newspaper in the bin, and found their way to their bedrooms. Sylvia was to share with Maudie, because she felt too worried to leave her alone.

The next big change happened when they were hauling the butty along the Brum Bum to load up with coal. While Polly motored *Marigold* ahead through the locks, Maudie stood on the butty counter steering, looking up at the factories, cringing at the darkness and the smell, the tyres in the water, the dead dog that caught around the tiller and which she shafted free.

She called to Sylvia, who was hauling with Verity on the bank, 'I been 'ere with an unkind man, but I with yer now, and yer are kind. All of yer are kind, but I 'as a missing feeling, I 'as a big 'ole.'

Sylvia said, 'Holes fill up, but sometimes it takes quite a while.'

As they passed through the next lock, Maudie took over one of the haul ropes. 'I belongs here,' she said. 'See.' She showed Verity the callouses on her hands and shoulders.

Verity said, 'It's a small part of where you belong. Each day you might find another part, or it might take longer. But just so long as you know you are safe.'

As they approached the next lock Maudie called, 'I is safe because that man is not 'ere.'

'He won't ever be again,' Verity called. 'But he is the only one who is unkind. All our other friends are kind – the men, too.'

As they loaded with coal and returned through the Braunston Tunnel, Verity, Polly and Sylvia wondered whether to visit Granfer again, but thought it best to take it one step at a time. They travelled south, and after two days reached Marsworth Junction and decided, after listening to their waters, that they would go down the Aylesbury Arm. They turned off down the Arm and travelled on a short tow past wild flowers, and butterflies darting, with Sylvia and Maudie on the butty, and Dog on the cabin roof.

They 'winded' at the basin, and pat-pattered back. There had been no horn sounded from the butty, which was to be the signal from Sylvia that all was not well. And so it continued, until they were at Bull's Bridge at the end of the day, reversing into a space. Maudie was brewing tea in the butty cabin as they moored. She brought it to them, once the holds had been swept. 'I will sweep next time, and I will boil my clothes to become clean again.'

Sylvia asked, 'You remember?'

'I 'ave seen all the women at their boilers, and I knows 'ow to set up the fire, 'ow to boil, 'ow to throw away the water and 'ang the clothes. So if I knows, then I must 'ave done it. Perhaps that is remembering? I knew the cut we went along, the reeds, the butterflies, the bees, the quiet. I knows the ducks and geese that does fly over.' She looked around. 'I knows so much of this, but I can't see myself 'ere.'

Sylvia said, 'You will, I promise.'

Verity and Polly called into the office and picked up their mail. One each from their parents. They read them immediately, smiling at the day-to-day news, savouring the loving sentiments as their mothers signed off. Halfway along the lay-by Dog met them, tail wagging, and they walked back as the women passed them on their way to the shops, or washed their clothes and hung them behind the cabins. ''Ow do,' they called, but none asked how things were.

Polly murmured. 'They have eyes, that'll be enough for them.' She nodded towards *Marigold* and

422

Horizon, where they could see Maudie hanging out clothes behind the cabin.

Polly looked on past their pair, still half expecting to see *Seagull* and *Swansong*, and Saul. Where was he? Was he safe? What about Tom, how was he? What would he think of Maudie's return? She must write again, telling of Maudie's awakening, which is how the girls thought of it.

The tannoy crackled. 'Steerer Clement to the office.'

'Already?' Sylvia called from the butty.

Within an hour they were off to Brentford, scanning the skies, seeing the scorching tails of the doodlebugs and hearing the screeching, the silence, the explosions; and Maudie was unmoved, it was as though noise didn't affect her now, just like a boater.

'Well, it's what she is,' Polly muttered to Verity as they left Brentford Wharf.

Verity nodded and then said, 'Wonder if the Rivers bloke survived?'

'Would you mind if he was hurt?'

'I never think of him. It's best not, because I feel sorry for Jenny in a way, but not for her father. They're nothing to do with me, not really.'

'I can't say I understand how you must feel, but I can imagine.'

The ack-ack was firing, the sirens howling.

Verity said, 'It seems unreal anyway, and unimportant, with all that's going on. Evacuation seems as urgent as during the Blitz, the Allies are approaching Caen. Is Tom with them, and Saul, or is he still on the Mulberry? Then there's Maudie – improving, but will she ever really be better? And what about Sylvia's decision? Polly, really, truly there are so many things of much greater importance than my past.' She meant it. She knew who her family was now. It was these girls, and the Clements, and Holmeses.

They pat-pattered on up the Grand Union Canal, their world unchanged. After all, their hands were still blistered, the rain still soaked them, the wind still tore through them, though it was summer. The windlass still rubbed their hands raw, and the beams wore out the seats of their trousers.

What was different was that they didn't stop at the pubs, and it was Thomo who brought them pheasant, not Saul. There he was at Berkhamsted, where they moored up for the first night, standing on the towpath, as Dog leapt from the counter and sniffed around his heels as she had done with Saul. Thomo laughed, holding a brace out of her reach and calling to Verity and Polly as they sat on *Marigold*'s roof.

'A couple of tiddlers for yer, though I wish I were with Saul. I tried again just now, but they wouldn't let me – too bloody old at thirty, too valuable 'ere, so they says. Daft buggers. Timmo and Peter are out finding the rabbits. Take these and I'll 'ang t'others on the hook at back of yer cabin as an' when.' He turned on his heel, saying as he walked away,

424

'Reckon Granfer's lass is taking steps. Boaters need the cut, it's where they belongs. Healing, it be.'

Verity looked at her hands, and at the callouses that had rubbed raw again, and laughed softly. 'Healing?' But they both nodded, knowing Thomo was right.

Then his voice rang out. 'We's makin' a packet on the darts, so best not come back into the game.'

Verity felt the laughter surging, as the clouds scudded over the moon. 'Oh, Thomo, Thomo,' she yelled, 'dangerous words. We'll take you to the cleaners very soon now. Mark my words, your days are numbered.'

His laugh rang out as he trotted down the towpath to his motor.

They reached Tyseley Wharf on the fourth day, but there was no time to visit the baths, or Mrs Green. Instead they were given orders for Coventry, and coal again. Exhausted, Polly said, 'Let's toss to see who takes the motor through Brum Bum's delightful locks and short pounds, ladies.'

Sylvia tossed the penny, but it was Polly who won, and when the time came she motored ahead, with Verity and Sylvia shaking their fists in mock fury as they'd tied the haul ropes around their shoulders and waists. They stopped only when they saw Maudie's face as she stood at the tiller, cringing in fear. Sylvia held up her hand. 'Maudie, it's only play. No one will be harmed.'

Maudie watched them as they smiled and opened their arms. She said, 'I know 'arm. I know it. I've felt it.' She touched her face and the side of her head, her arm. 'But I can't remember it.'

'You steer, Maudie, because we have to take the butty to Coventry to load it with coal.' They had decided the best thing was for her to resort to work, to ease the 'knowing' and not let it overwhelm her.

They reached Coventry at last and were loaded, and then they travelled on and within three days they were back at Bull's Bridge. *Venus* and *Shortwood* were already moored, and they must thank Thomo, Timmo and Peter for the rabbits that they had hung on the rear of the butty, when *Marigold* and *Horizon* had been moored up one night after Coventry.

First, though, the four girls boiled water in the cabins and took turns for a stand-up all-over wash, then boiled their clothes on the kerb. As they finished, Timmo came over from *Venus*'s counter onto the lay-by and walked towards them. Dog ran to meet him, and Timmo hunkered down, hugging Dog, who stood quite still suddenly, her tail down, her head pressed against Timmo's. Verity called, as she and Polly wrung out the final pair of rinsed trousers. 'Thanks for the rabbits. Tell Thomo and Peter we're grateful, will you?'

Timmo stood up and, with Dog by his side, walked the rest of the way towards them, his head down.

Polly yelled, 'Oh dear, frightened we'll be back with our darts, are you? Don't fret, you tell Thomo it'll be a while yet.'

Timmo stopped, squatted, stroked Dog's head again, then stood, sending her back onto *Marigold*'s counter. 'Go on then, Dog. Yer stay with yer owners, eh?' He looked up and his face was gaunt, his eyes red. 'Can't tell our Thomo, Missus. He took the train further east, picking up summat for Granfer. One o' them damned doodlebugs must 'ave cut out above him and come on down. Missed him, but the blast got him – killed outright, so them say. I got the tool Granfer wanted. I'll leave it on yer counter. A spanner, it were, and it weren't 'urt, not one bit.'

Verity dropped the trousers onto the kerb, as Polly rocked back on her heels. Sylvia jumped down from *Horizon*'s counter and ran to the girls. They clung together, as Timmo tipped his hat and walked back to his motor, and only when he was back on board did they weep, soundlessly, because Maudie must not be disturbed.

Later he brought them the spanner to leave with Granfer at Buckby. ''Tis more'n we can bear to take it, fer the time bein',' he said.

Marigold and *Horizon* motored on to Limehouse Basin, and the girls refused to look up into the sky, or listen, because what could they do if a doodle-bug's motor stopped and it dropped? They were loaded as quickly as possible at the wharf, because the dockers were frightened, too. Everyone was, because bloody Hitler was killing as many as he could, before he gave up.

They travelled up the cut, with their quietness and their tears, which they tried to hide; but they failed and, magically, they were comforted by Maudie, who brought them tea and whispered, as they climbed the Tring locks, 'I knows your tears. I knows them, and they come after the fists when yer 'eart does 'urt, too. I knows the face of the man with the fists, but I don't know who 'e is ter me.'

At Norton Junction they turned right for Buckby: they had a spanner to deliver. They moored and, accompanied by Dog, they all walked into Buckby. There was no one in Lettie's garden. They opened the picket gate and walked along the crazy-paving path, where camomile grew. It oozed its scent beneath their feet. They knocked on the door. It opened. It was Granfer. Sylvia held out the spanner.

Granfer said, 'I knows about Thomo.' His face was as sad as theirs.

Maudie reached out and touched his cheek. 'I knows you, too. I knows yer sadness, but not who yer is. But I knows there is kindness 'ere, not like 'im, the man with the fists.'

Granfer let her trace his features. Then he said, 'I know yer too. Yer belongs to us, like yer belongs to the cut.'

Auntie Lettie came from the side-garden. 'I have laid out tea in the garden. Come.'

She led Maudie to the table set in the warmth of the sun, and Maudie turned and gripped Granfer's hand. 'I knows I belongs, but I can't remember. I just knows, but there is another ...' She stared round the garden, as though searching, and then allowed herself to be pressed onto a chair by Lettie.

Polly pulled from her pocket the picture of Saul that Joe had drawn. She kept it with her always. 'Is this who you know?' She laid it down on the table, then stepped back.

Verity gripped Polly's hand, hardly daring to breathe. Sylvia walked quietly to sit beside Maudie, and Granfer sat on the other side. Runner beans wound around bamboos, but as yet it was too early for a crop; lettuce flourished in neat rows, and tomatoes would soon glisten with red fruit.

'Yes,' breathed Maudie. 'I knows 'im, too, but there is yet another ... I can't see 'im, not in me head. I can't feel him, I can't smell him, but he is kind, too, but he knows the fists ...' She was crying, and although Sylvia sat on the seat next to her, Maudie turned to Granfer and sobbed into his shoulder.

'*Granfer's* shoulder,' Polly breathed. 'She has chosen him.'

Granfer whispered, 'Yer is safe from them fists. They will never come near yer no more.'

Verity and Polly moved closer. Was Sylvia all right with this transfer of attention? Sylvia smiled at Granfer over Maudie's head. The girls relaxed, thinking of the sharp-tongued, competitive young woman Sylvia had been, and the compassionate person she now allowed them to see.

The three of them made their way quietly to the gate, led by Lettie, who shut it behind them, waving and calling softly, 'We will get a message to yer if yer needed. We will, too, get a message ter Timmo and Peter at Bull's Bridge. God speed, keep yerself safe, our dear beloved girls.'

Chapter 27

Thursday 27 July – *Marigold* and *Horizon* return to Bull's Bridge

The cargo haulage trips were relentless and merged one into the other, but while the doodlebugs flew, crashed and killed, what did exhaustion matter? They were alive, and the army must be supplied, and so must the country. *Marigold* and *Horizon* reversed into the lay-by, next to *Venus* and *Shortwood*, which were now crewed by Timmo, Peter and their uncle, Trev.

The girls cleared out the bilges, which were deep in coal sludge. Polly shook it from her hands. 'I'm just about sick, sore and tired of the feel, smell and even the taste of this muck.'

Verity shrieked with laughter. 'Stop eating it then, idiot.'

Polly laughed. 'It's not that I'm eating it, but it gets in your teeth – surely you find the same thing.' She felt so tired that her head was throbbing. And no, she grinned to herself, it was nothing to do with the darts match, and supping too long afterwards on their winnings.

The tannoy sounded. 'Steerer Holmes to the Administration Office, chop-chop.'

Polly raised her eyes at Verity. 'That Bob is getting too big for his boots now he's been taken on full time. Bet's been talking to him, I bet. Chop-chop, indeed.'

The tannoy crackled again. 'Steerer Holmes, a Mr Burton is here for you.'

Polly was up and out of the hold, tossing the broom into the store cabin and running off down the lay-by, followed by Verity and Sylvia. They sped past the shoppers, the washers, the children, but Dog easily outran them, thinking it was a game, although it wasn't. Mr Burton? Polly's mind was churning: Mum, Dad, Joe?

Verity drew alongside Polly as they sped into the yard and over to the Administration Office, yanking the door open, letting it slam against the wall and bursting in. Sylvia was a beat behind. Mr Burton sat on the bench, his briefcase on his knees. He was immobile.

Bob called out, 'Blimey, you got on a turn of speed, you three.'

Mr Burton looked up and lifted his hat momentarily. 'Ah, the Three Musketeers. Excellent. Perhaps we could take a little walk.' It wasn't a question.

He clipped out of the door, immaculate as always. Polly heard her own panting replicated by the others as they followed him. Dog jumped up at Mr Burton, but one word from the solicitor was more than enough to have her walking quietly to heel. Mr

Burton gestured towards the frontage. 'Down there.' Again it was not a question.

Good heavens, thought Polly, he's been taking lessons from Mum. He was never like this when I worked for him.

He stopped at the kerb, and the cut lapped as a passing pair caused a wash and Steerer Porter called, "Ow do?'

'Lord,' whispered Sylvia, 'the whole cut will know.'

'But know what?' Verity whispered back.

Mr Burton snatched a look at his watch. 'I have bad news.'

Verity groaned, 'Mrs Holmes ... the doodlebugs?' She was holding Polly.

Mr Burton snatched at his hat, as the wind tried to remove it. His grey hair was cut in a short back and sides. The sound of normality was all around: the blacksmith's banging, the carpenters' sawing, while somewhere a welder was hammering; but for Polly it seemed far away. Mum, Dad, Joe, she thought again.

Mr Holmes was shaking his head. 'Forgive me for alarming you. It's nothing like that. But prior to the Leon Arnson case, which was to be heard any minute, the German prisoner of war has withdrawn his statement, and now says that Arnson had nothing to do with sabotaging your butty. He insists that he acted on his own initiative for the – and I quote – "Glory of the Fatherland".'

Polly shouted, 'What?'

Mr Burton stared at the two boats passing abreast, but wasn't seeing them. '"What?" indeed. Police Inspector Hodges thinks the doodlebugs have rekindled the prisoner's belief in the ultimate victory of the Fatherland, so he is prepared to be imprisoned as the great Nazis' saboteur, until the even greater victory, and his subsequent release. I fear he hankers for an Iron Cross and is as deluded as the rest of the Germans.' He sighed. 'All too tiresome, and this is by no means all. I have to inform you that, most unfortunately, a V-1 rocket saw off the nightclub owner, when it hit his bungalow in Kent. He had agreed to give evidence in return for his own immunity, and was on bail.'

Polly was following Mr Burton's words, seeing the fury in the working of his jaw muscles. She said, 'So that leaves Leon.'

'The police have had no alternative but to release him.'

There it was: Leon was out. Leon who had beaten his wife and son. Leon who had fired their butty and threatened them, who had hurt Dog. Leon was free.

Sylvia clutched at them. 'He'll come after us.'

Mr Burton patted her arm. The police have said they will be keeping an eye on him, and have warned Leon against making approaches to you. He doesn't know where Joe is, or indeed that his wife, Maud, has been found. He will assume that Mr Hopkins the Elder is still on the canal. I implore you to be alert from now on, in the unlikely event that Leon will reappear. I suspect that, after his incarceration, our Mr Arnson will not wish to return to the confines of a cell. And since he has been refused work with the Grand Union Canal Carrying Company, he is no longer in the locality. Indeed, he has been given work on a farm in Yorkshire – the police have their ways, especially in wartime.'

Mr Burton left almost immediately, patting Polly's shoulder.

'I have things to do, dear Polly, as indeed have you. Perhaps a letter to Granfer, as you call him, to update him with the latest news? I gather our Maud is with Mr Hopkins.'

'Yes, yes, she is. But what about Mum and Dad?' said Polly.

'They know, but I repeat that Arnson has no idea of Joe's whereabouts and has been warned against making enquiries. Joe does not know, and the police will be keeping a weather eye out in the area.'

He shook hands all round and hurried off. Bob let them telephone Fran with the news. Fran said, 'You are not alone, remember that. The boaters will look after you, and the villagers will keep an eye on Granfer and Aunt Lettie, who I will of course inform. They will not tell Maudie, that's my guess.'

That evening the girls went to the pub in Southall and drank a glass of mild, and played darts against Timmo, Peter and Trev, but it wasn't the same.

Nothing was. That night they locked their cabin doors, and Dog slept on the floor in Sylvia's butty since security took priority over perceived lack of hygiene. Verity tossed and turned, and Polly lay awake, worrying about Joe and her parents. But Mr Burton was right; Leon had no idea where Joe was.

What's more, there was no one in Woking, or at the school, who knew Joe's true identity. He was a relative of the Holmes's, that was the fiction, which had not been questioned. And his surname had been given as Hopkins, not Arnson.

Chapter 28

Early November – with Mrs Holmes in Woking

It was early November, and a dim-out, rather than blackout had been in operation for a short while, which allowed lighting if it was no greater than moonlight. But it was a relief, no matter how limited, and stopped Joyce Holmes worrying so much when Thomas cycled home of an evening. She rubbed her arms against the chill, which was so harsh it seemed to soak through her coat and into her bones, as she set off to meet Joe at the school gates.

The new V-2 rockets had been pulverising London and the south-east since September; she had thought the V-1 doodlebugs were bad enough, but the V-2s were silent killers. They made no noise and just dived and exploded with no warning, causing many deaths. Would this war never end, would that maniacal country ever surrender?

She looked both ways, and again, as she arrived at the main road: all clear. She hurried over, relaxing a little because there was still no sight or sound of Leon, and she dared to think that he too had been killed. She shook her head and tutted;

how dreadful to wish for the death of someone, but it was the thought of Leon finding Joe and taking him from them – to what? It was something she had not prepared herself for. She had been too busy bracing herself for Joe's return to Maudie, which was only right and proper, however painful it would be. But for Leon to take him ... No, that was insupportable.

There were very few mothers waiting at the school gates these days. Mrs Holmes prepared to cross the final street, looking right, left and right again, and behind. Checking, always checking, because she suspected that someone like Leon had ways of finding things out. Perhaps they should have used Holmes as Joe's surname, not Hopkins, but he hadn't wanted that, and why should he? The bell sounded, the school doors opened and those children who hadn't yet been evacuated spilled from the building and set off across the playground. Weeds were growing through the asphalt.

Mrs Andrews, whose son Philip often played with Joe, murmured, 'We're evacuating, Mrs Holmes, and staying with my family in Shropshire. So many are dying from the V-2s, I can't take the risk, not any more.'

Mrs Holmes nodded. Bernard, Joe's friend, had already gone to Somerset after a doodlebug landed just outside Woking, and she had been thinking and talking and trying to decide, but where would they go? It had to be 'they', because Joe mustn't go alone, unprotected; and she didn't like the idea of her Thomas being left here, without her to take care of him. But he'd never leave the allotment, or his job. 'Some must stay,' he'd said last night.

Joe was kicking stones across to Philip, who returned the favour as they approached. Mrs Holmes smiled and waved.

'See you when you come back, Philip,' Joe said.

'Good luck,' Mrs Holmes said to Mrs Andrews.

Joe came through the wrought-iron gate. 'Hello, Auntie Joyce.' They set off for home, Joe walking beside her, his socks down around his ankles, his knees grubby.

'Did you play marbles in your lunch break?' Mrs Holmes asked.

He nodded. 'I won.'

Mrs Holmes laughed. 'Don't tell our girls or they'll scoop you up for their darts team.'

Joe wouldn't hold her hand these days because he was too old, he'd said a few weeks ago. She remembered Will saying just the same. They reached the main road and looked both ways, and then again, and she felt his hand slipping into hers. She looked down at him in surprise.

'I saw Dad today at playtime,' he said. 'He was waiting at the gate, but he'd gone by the end of school.'

Mrs Holmes kept walking, her heart like stone, but by some miracle her voice sounded unsurprised and calm. 'Perhaps you were mistaken?'

439

'No, I'm not. He waved to me. I didn't wave back, because I didn't want to see him, or know him.' His grip was tight. Joe snatched a look behind, and Mrs Holmes longed to as well and so, as they reached another road, she looked right, left and right again, with a quick look behind them. She thought she saw Leon. But only thought.

She wouldn't hurry; no, that man wouldn't see that she was frightened. But when they arrived home she bolted the front door, and checked that the back door was locked and all the windows closed. Joe removed his shoes, put on his slippers and took his satchel to his bedroom, while she used the telephone in the hall, giving the operator her husband's work number in a low voice, knowing that she should only do this in an emergency.

'Come on, Thomas,' she whispered, tapping her foot. The number was engaged. She replaced the receiver. How foolish; of course it wasn't an emergency – nothing had happened, and perhaps it wasn't Leon, because he should be in Yorkshire. But what if he wasn't? Should she telephone the police? But there was a war on; they were busy with these V rockets and heaven knows what.

Joe tore down the stairs and into the sitting room, sprawling on the sofa. Mrs Holmes slipped to the bow window, standing behind the sofa, staring out and then to the left. It was a cul-de-sac, so Leon would have to come from the left. No one. The clouds hung dark and heavy as they so often did in

November, and so although it was only four o'clock, it was surely dark enough to draw the curtains without looking alarmist.

'Against the chill,' she told Joe, who was bent over, writing in his book. It was the one in which he wrote his stories about Lettie, the sheepdog who lived on the cut. He had worried about the name, because he didn't want Auntie Lettie or Granfer to be upset. Mrs Holmes had said Auntie Lettie would be pleased; after all, sheepdogs were lovely. Joe had written and asked Auntie Lettie in the end, promising to send the story to them in Buckby when it was finished. Granfer and Auntie Lettie had been pleased.

Mrs Holmes made tea and poured a glass of milk for Joe. While he was drinking it, she shut the sitting-room door behind her and telephoned again. This time Thomas answered. 'Wilkins Stores, how can I help?' She told him, and Thomas said he'd leave work right that minute, and she was to telephone the police only if she saw Leon, because there was a war on and they were busy.

'That's what I thought,' she said.

She kept an eye out for Thomas through the opening between the curtains, seeing him cycling down the avenue fifteen minutes later, his lamp with its larger slit bobbing up and down in the mist that had fallen. He turned into the drive, leaning his bike against the laurel hedge. He bent down to remove his cycle clips, and it was then that Leon stepped out of the side-passage of the house.

Mrs Holmes wished she'd telephoned the police straight away, but she couldn't believe what she was seeing. How could that dreadful man grab Thomas and punch him so many times, and so quickly, kicking him as he lay on the grass, and cursing and swearing? Joe came over to her. She telephoned the police and the ambulance, of course she did – and bother the explosions and the rockets; this was her Thomas.

'Sit down this minute, on the sofa,' she shouted to Joe, because he'd rushed to the front door. He did so. She in turn rushed to the kitchen for the frying pan, then down the hall again, telling Joe not to come out of the sitting room, because this was between adults. She slammed the front door behind her as she tore into the garden and hit Leon, hit him and hit him, feeling the judder up her arm. And she was shouting, 'No, no, no, you don't, you horrid, horrid man.'

Leon turned from Thomas, holding up his arm and trying to kick at her, his face ugly, spitting fury, but he stopped when Mrs Holmes whacked his nose. The frying pan rang out. Leon's nose burst with blood. She hit him again – whack – on the side of his head. He staggered, then they all heard the police siren.

Leon ran off, shouting that he'd be back for the boy. 'His ma's dead, so he's mine,' he said, as Mr Sinclair came rushing from next door, waving his walking stick and calling out, 'What the hell's happening? Where are you, Thomas? Who's that bloody thug?'

Thomas lay on the grass, his head in the rose bed. He shouted to Mr Sinclair, 'I think it's my Joyce who's the bloody thug, Sandy.' He was laughing, but then he groaned and fell quiet as the police turned their car in order to chase Leon, while the ambulance came up. Joyce fell on her knees beside Thomas, and so did Mr Sinclair, wheezing that he could get down, but God knew if he could ever get up again.

Polly received the tannoy summons to the office in the early evening, then together the three girls took the train from Waterloo to Woking, leaving Dog with Steerer Ambrose, and ran through the streets to Woking hospital. They sat for hours on hard benches with Polly's mum and Joe, while ack-ack and sirens sounded outside. All the time Polly gripped her mum's hand tightly, while Sylvia and Verity sat on either side of Joe, pale and shaken, but talking to him of his story about Lettie. They chatted about Dog, and how Dog had looked after M— But then they stopped, because Joe mustn't know about his mother until she remembered him, they'd all decided.

The police came, and Mr Burton, and one of the police constables talked to a doctor, scribbling in a notebook. The policeman then joined them, while Mr Burton walked Joe along the corridor, chatting about this, that and the other as the policeman drew the women nearer the top end of the corridor, out of the boy's hearing. 'We'll go and interview your neighbour, Mr Sinclair, and get a witness statement. And this time, when we get Mr Arnson, he'll be easy enough to snaffle, looking as battered as he sounds, and with an eyewitness.'

'*If* you get him, you mean,' said Polly.

The policeman, who was elderly, said, 'No, *when*. This has got to stop. The good thing is that Mr Sinclair said he heard Mr Arnson shouting that the lad's ma's dead. That means he doesn't know Mrs Arnson is alive, and so she's safe. Not just that, but why did he think she was dead? We will pursue this, with commitment – war or not.'

By the morning Polly's dad was out of surgery. His boss had arrived and was talking to Mr Burton. The doctors had thought they might have to remove Thomas's spleen, but that had proved not to be the case. The surgeon said, 'He's a lucky man, Mrs Holmes. He has a broken arm, cuts, bruises and, of course, concussion.'

Mrs Holmes, the girls and Joe waited outside the recovery room, eager to visit him once he was awake. The nursing sister said, 'Only two at a time.'

Joe and Mrs Holmes went in first, and then the three girls, because as Polly said to the nursing sister, 'If I leave one outside, the other will sulk or, worse, have a tantrum, and we don't want that, do we?'

Sister Newsome assured her they did not.

444

Polly sat by her father's bedside and stroked his hand, while the other two girls sat on the other side. 'You were so brave,' she said.

Her father shook his head. 'No, I wasn't. Leon was on me before I had me bike clips off. I just tried to defend myself, and I didn't do a good job. It was your mum with her frying pan who saved the day, but she's cross because she dented it and the handle rivets have sheered.' The girls laughed and laughed, and then all three found they were crying, until her dad said, 'Oh, do brace up. I'm really quite well, but I will have to take time off work. And what about me allotment, that's what I want to know?'

Two days later a V-2 landed on the allotments, and that was one problem solved, said her mother, when Polly telephoned from Alperton on their way to Limehouse Basin. She also told her that Mr Burton had said she really should think of evacuation for the three of them, until Leon was apprehended, because then the wretched oaf would have no way of knowing where they were.

'But where?' asked Mrs Holmes.

Two weeks later Mr Holmes and Lord Henry Clement were both limping around the walled vegetable garden at Howard House – Lord Henry on his two sticks, and Mr Holmes with his arm plastered, his stitches removed and his bruises healing. They stood together, staring out at the neglected plot.

'D'you really think we can do something with it, between the two of us?' muttered Lord Henry.

'We'd better,' growled Mr Holmes, 'or our Joyce will be after us with the frying pan. As she said, "You've got your legs, Thomas, and Lord Clement has his arms so it's not beyond the bounds of imagination for you to sort it out between you," so we'd better manage something. The girls will expect it.'

'Ah yes, the young and old girls,' Lord Henry sighed, heading for the bench set up against the wall. 'Thomas – if I may be informal – rest your bones for a moment.'

'Of course, Henry – that's if I may?' said Thomas, sitting beside him.

The two men laughed.

Henry drew out his cigarette case. Thomas took one of his host's Players and offered a light from his match. The two of them sat smoking, as Thomas scanned the garden. There was some produce that could be picked: cabbages, leeks, and who knew what else amongst the chaos. The espaliered trees growing flat against the walls could be pruned to produce apples and pears the following year, and the box hedges that enclosed the herbs could be clipped.

Henry said, 'Are you settling into the gardener's cottage?'

Thomas smiled. 'Thank you kindly, it suits us down to the ground.'

Henry stared at the top of his cigarette. 'You were more than welcome to stay with us in the house. Joyce and my wife, Pamela, seem to have hit it off; and of course Joe is just wonderful. To have some young blood about the place again brings it alive. I hope he'll be happy at school, when the new term starts. There's a bus stop quite close by.'

Thomas nodded. 'It's kind of you to have us, but just until the V-2s have finished their spree.'

Henry shrugged. 'Oh, I think we must leave the date of departure to our daughters, don't you, or they'll be after us all with *their* frying pans. They and Sylvia are a monstrous regiment, are they not?'

Thomas laughed, nodding. 'That they are.'

Henry shook his head slightly and tightened the scarf around his neck. 'Wouldn't change a thing, though, would we?'

The two men looked at one another and smiled.

On the *Marigold*, three days later, they moored at Fenny Stratford and the girls ate the pheasant that Timmo had caught for them. They had stewed it, of course, with a bit of bacon and lots of carrots. Sylvia put her knife and fork together. 'To think I was once so soppy and thought we shouldn't add to our ration. Have you heard from your mothers?'

Verity waved her letter from Dorset. 'Indeed we have. They are a mafia, and have manoeuvred the two men into taking charge of the vegetable garden while they amuse Joe. They're even taking on a

447

farmer's pony, as there is plenty of grazing at Howard House and it'll be nice to have Star's stable used again.' There, she'd said it, with no residual anger at Star's death. Accidents happened after all, Verity could see that now. 'It was an excellent idea of mine, I do think, to bring the two families together,' she added.

Polly looked at Sylvia and groaned. 'We're never going to hear the end of this "good idea", are we?'

Dog sat up and yelped. The girls tensed, but then they heard an owl. Sylvia reached down and stroked her head. 'Good girl, you'll look after us until the police catch Leon, won't you?'

Verity grinned. 'Oh, come on, Sylvia, we'll look after ourselves, won't we? If your mum can wield a frying pan, Polly, then so can we.'

They remembered then that they weren't afraid of Leon any more. There were three of them and they were that 'monstrous regiment', as her father had written to tell Verity they were called now. They just needed to bear in mind that they might have to fight a bit of a battle should the wretch appear, but no more or less than everyone else, as the Allies pushed through France and the British home front endured for a while longer.

Want to know what happens next?

Look out for the next book in the series

Hope on the Waterways

Milly Adams

20 September 2018

Pre-order your copy in paperback or ebook today

Hear more from

Milly Adams